NURSERY RHYME COMICS

:01
First Second
New York & London

See page 118 for further copyright information.
Published by First Second
First Second is an imprint of Roaring Brook Press,
a division of Holtzbrinck Publishing Holdings Limited Partnership
175 Fifth Avenue, New York, New York 10010

Edited by Chris Duffy
Book design by Colleen AF Venable

Distributed in the United Kingdom by Macmillan Children's Books, a division of Pan Macmillan.

Cataloging-in-Publication Data is on file at the Library of Congress

First Second books are available for special promotions and premiums.
For details, contact: Director of Special Markets, Holtzbrinck Publishers.

FIRST
EDITION

First edition 2011
Printed in May 2011 in China by South China Printing Co., Ltd.,
Dongguan City, Guangdong Province

1 3 5 7 9 10 8 6 4 2

BY ART
WE LIVE

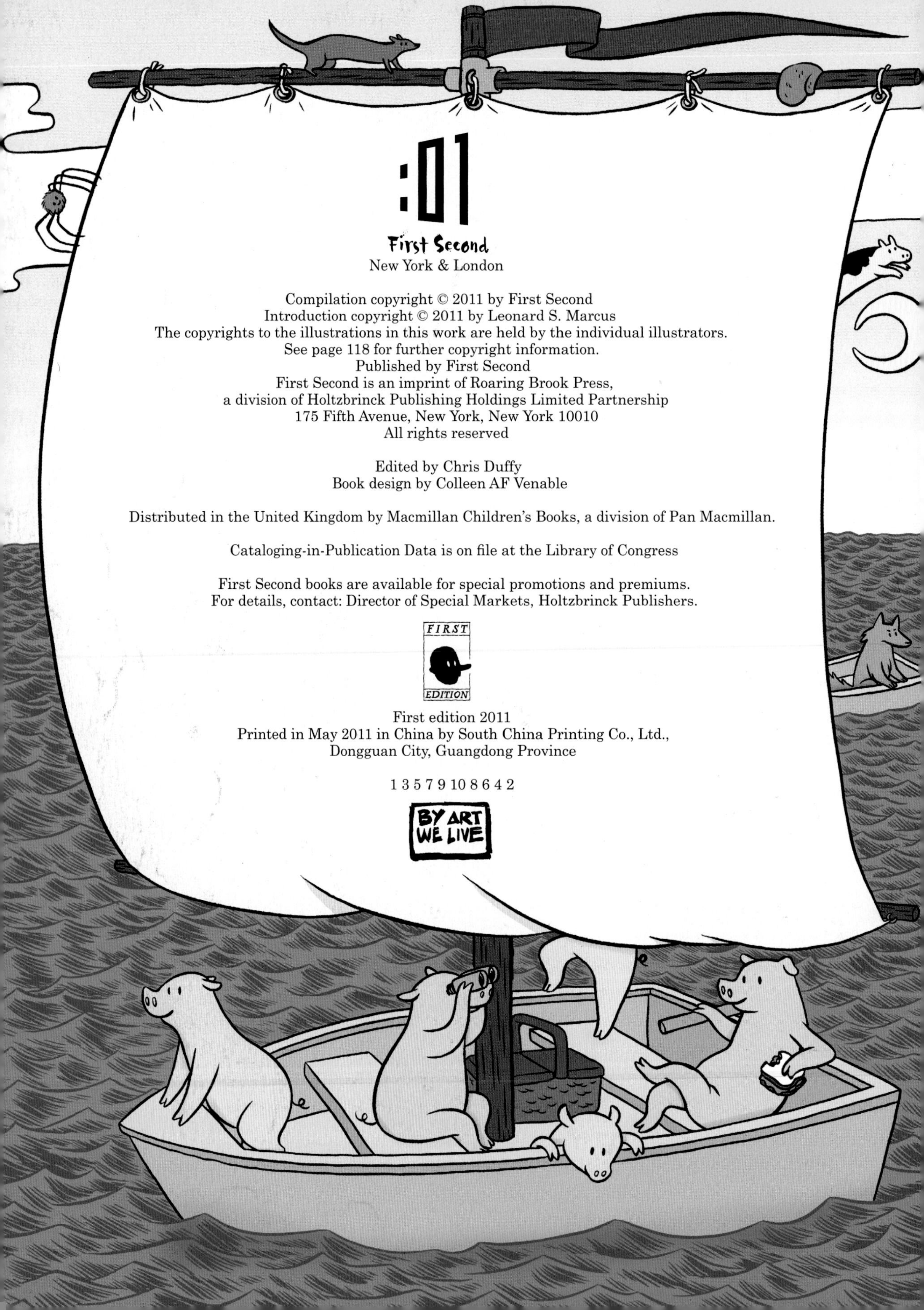

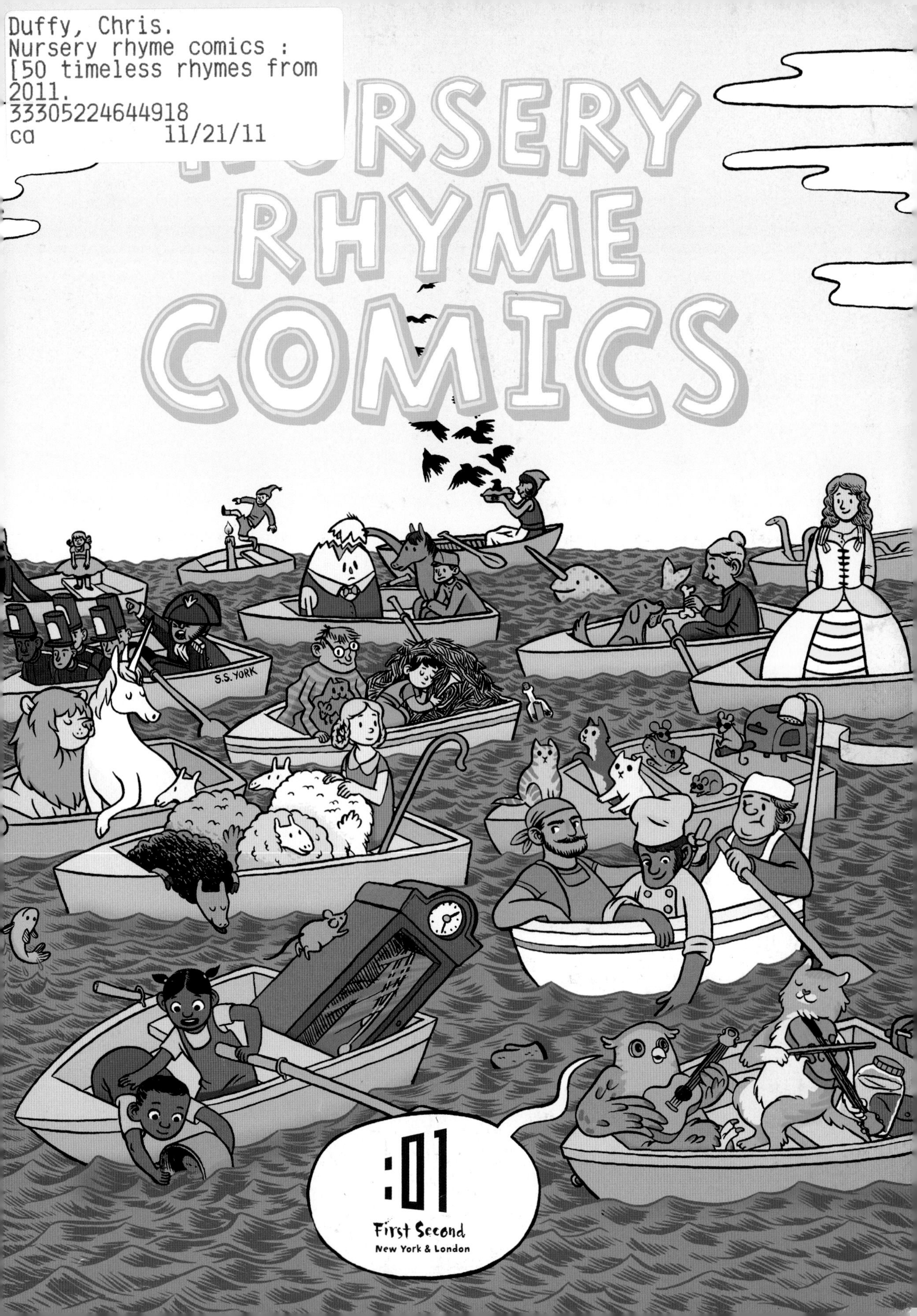
NURSERY RHYME COMICS
S.S. YORK
:01
First Second
New York & London

CONTENTS

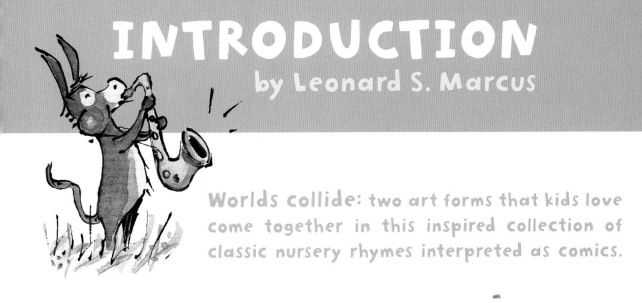

INTRODUCTION
by Leonard S. Marcus

Worlds collide: two art forms that kids love come together in this inspired collection of classic nursery rhymes interpreted as comics.

Spry, melodic rhymes like "Row, Row, Row Your Boat" and "One, Two, Buckle My Shoe" have entertained generations of children while also demonstrating that words have the power to *delight*—not just to convey more pedestrian messages like "See Spot run" and "Put away your toys." It's no accident that so many of these (mostly anonymous) rhymes have lasted for centuries, passed down by word of mouth and a forest of illustrated books, though none illustrated quite like the book you have before you.

Everything about the rhymes lines up to make them memorable: their pulsing, beat-the-drum rhythms, close-knit rhyme schemes, and nutshell narratives featuring quirky, vivid characters with quirky, vivid names: Hector Protector! Georgie Porgie! Little Bo Peep! Before long, kids know their favorites by heart, whether they are drawn to nonsense chants like "Hey, Diddle Diddle," which seem to exist solely to put more fun into the world, or to the many rhymes that make pert, knowing comments about human folly in all its glorious, over-the-top ridiculousness.

It's no wonder that nursery rhymes make fertile ground for comics artists. The comics we discover in these pages are new-made fantasies spun from the whole cloth of fantasies we thought we knew, the old-chestnut rhymes that beguile in part by *sounding* so emphatically clear about themselves while in fact leaving almost everything to our imagination:

> *Hickory, dickory, dock.*
> *The mouse ran up the clock.*
> *The clock struck one,*
> *The mouse ran down,*
> *Hickory, dickory, dock.*

1

The clock

♪ BONG ♪ (((( ))))

struck ONE,

What exactly *is* going on in this strange little poem? As a child, I decided the mouse must be a hapless bystander who'd gotten the fright of his life simply by being in the wrong place at the wrong time. But Stephanie Yue thinks otherwise! *Her* mouse is an endearing slapstick superhero: the scampering bell ringer who arrives at his post at the appointed hour to wield a clown-sized mallet that a creature twice his size would have a hard time lifting.

Each of the fifty artists showcased here has done a similarly persuasive, and unpredictable, job of back-story elaboration. Gene Luen Yang sets "Pat-a-Cake" in of all places an alien spacecraft and teases out an elegant (not to say comically off-the-wall) subplot from the mundane-sounding baking instruction "Mark it with a B." The oddball gent of "There Was a Crooked Man"—exclaiming, "This is THE LIFE!" in a word balloon—looks at last to have found his true element in Roz Chast's squiggly universe of frazzled, over-caffeinated worrywarts. Nick Bruel ventures a guess as to how the Three Little Kittens may have lost their mittens and gotten them back in time for dessert. Gahan Wilson takes the measure of the Itsy Bitsy Spider and discovers a lumbering, vain creature weighed down for the trek up the waterspout by oodles of luggage. For the rhyme that begins, "Donkey, donkey, old and gray," Patrick McDonnell pictures his subject first as a droopy-eared creature grazing in a meadow, then (what a difference a frame makes) as a very changed donkey indeed, tootling wildly on a tenor sax to "wake the world this sleepy morn." And on and on! While many of the contributing artists have made their mark primarily as comics creators, others hail from the neighboring latitudes of editorial illustration, magazine and strip cartooning, and the children's picture book. Lucky us to be living in a time of such free-flowing cross-pollination in the graphic and narrative arts.

There are many ways to use and enjoy this collection. An adult can read it aloud, of course, to a toddler first making the acquaintance both of the rhymes and the vast toy chest of visual treats that illustrated books hold in store. Slightly older children—those just learning to read—will recognize in the comics format, with its characteristically small word clusters, abundance of visual cues, and funhouse ambiance, precisely the kinds of support that are most helpful for honing and testing their fledgling skills. *Their* older brothers and sisters, if they have developed any interest at all in comics for more sophisticated readers (graphic novels, manga, and the like), will in turn be pulled, fascinated, into the rich, loam-like mix of the book's assembled company of artists, some perhaps well known to them and others ripe for discovering.

Exposed as we all are to a mind-bending barrage of images aimed at momentarily engulfing our attention, it is refreshing indeed to come across a book that encourages readers to linger over each and every one of its pages: the impish riff on short- and far-sightedness, good and bad fortune that is Cyril Pedrosa's "This Little Piggy" no less than the noir-ishly operatic high drama about strange but true love that Craig Thompson unfurls around Edward Lear's enigmatic "The Owl and the Pussycat." From each of the artists' efforts gathered in this collection we come away not so much knowing what to think about this or that rhyme as realizing that there is no end to where our own thoughts might take us, given only the chance. We are all, it seems, in the same boat after all—the one which, as the old rhyme says, is ours for the taking, "gently down the stream" of our own wildest dreams.

the Donkey

Patrick McDonnell

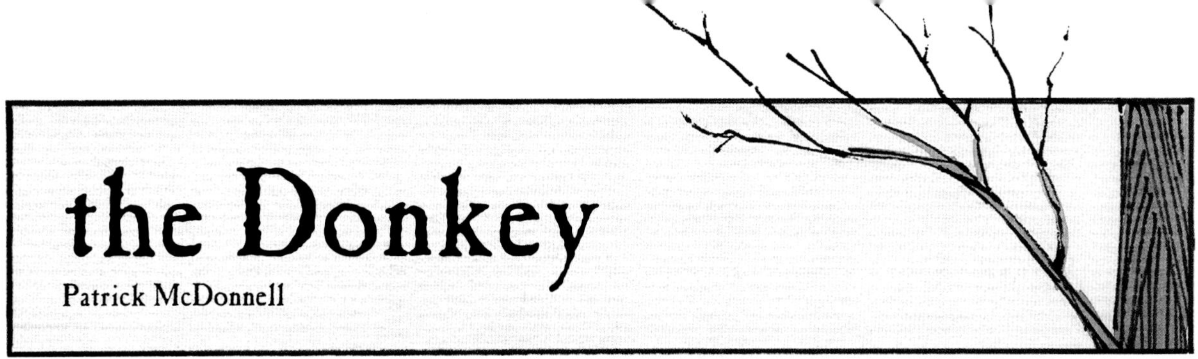

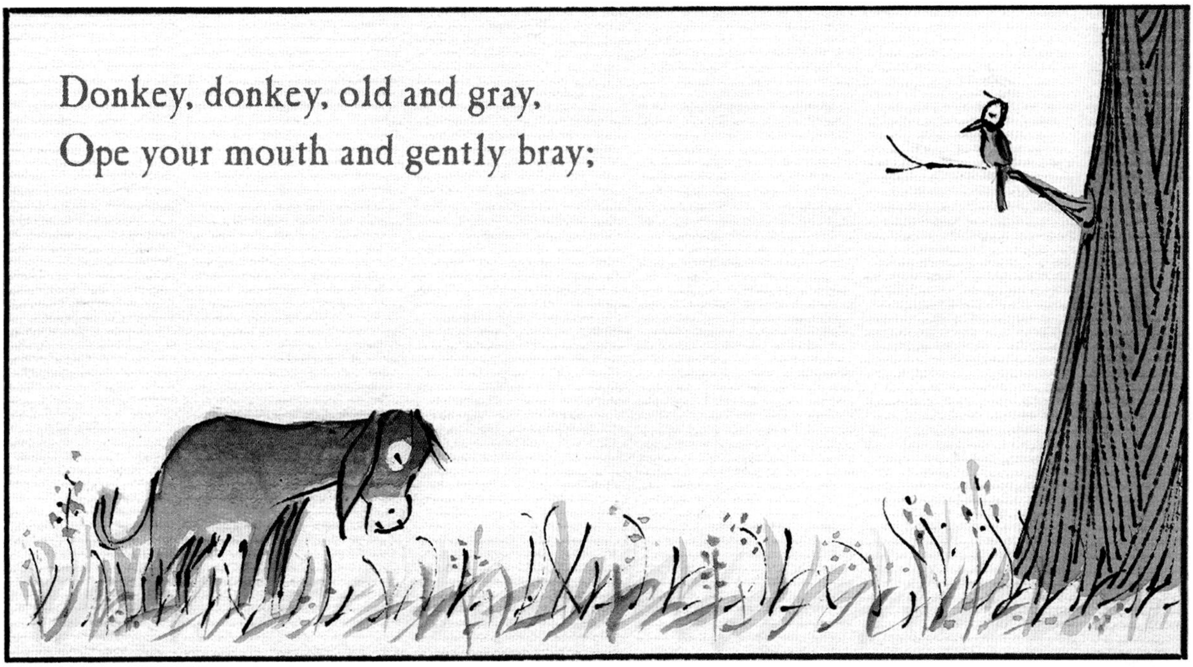
Donkey, donkey, old and gray,
Ope your mouth and gently bray;

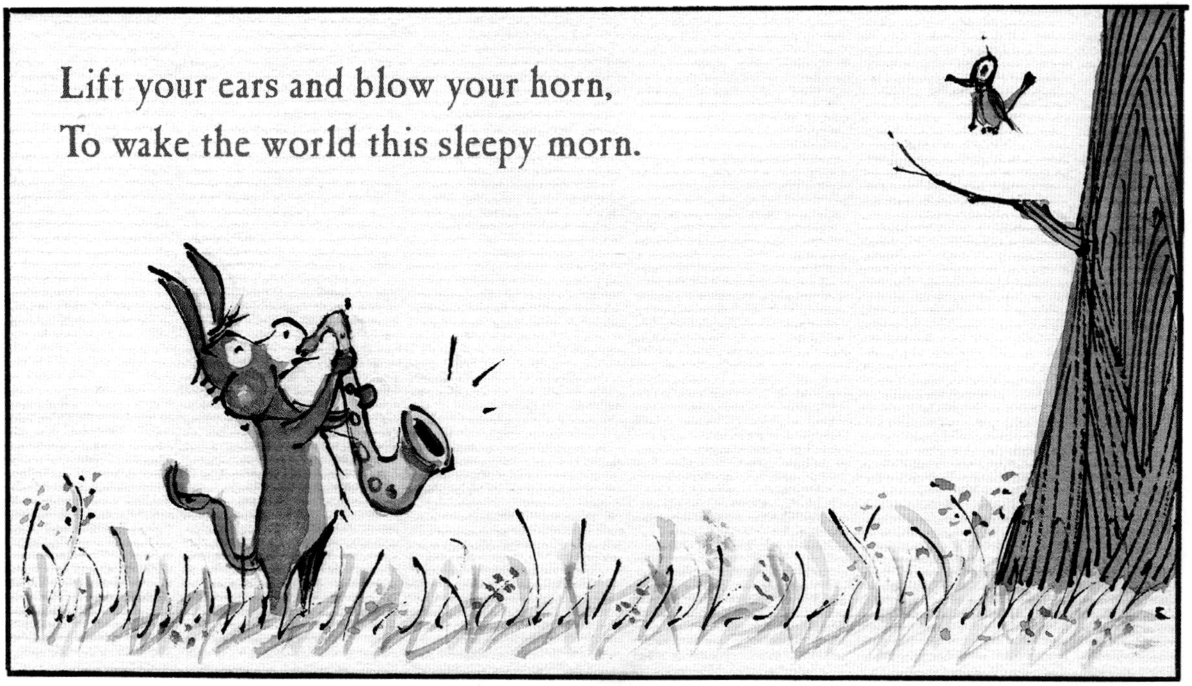
Lift your ears and blow your horn,
To wake the world this sleepy morn.

Three Little Kittens

by **Nick Bruel**

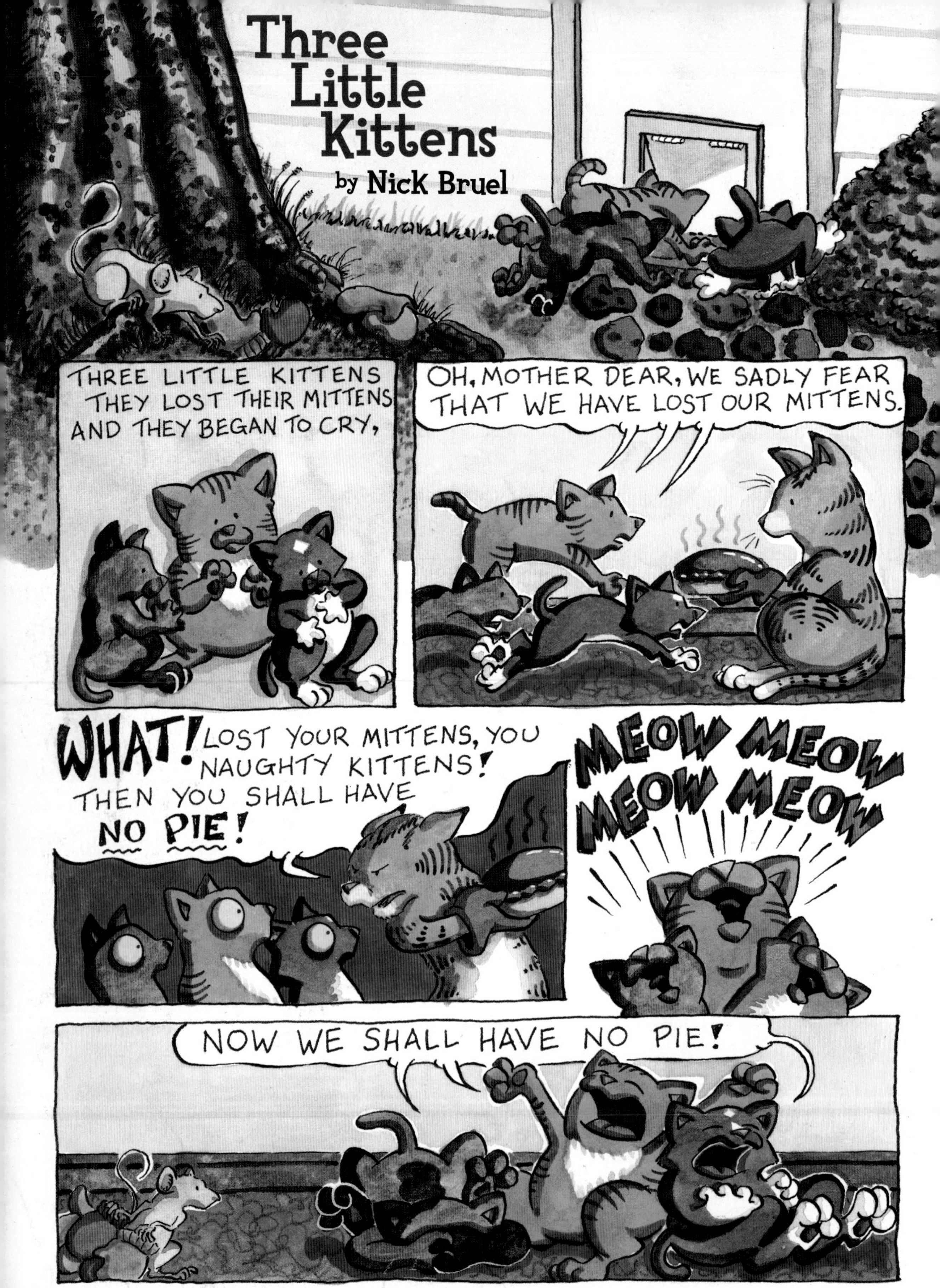
THREE LITTLE KITTENS THEY LOST THEIR MITTENS AND THEY BEGAN TO CRY,
OH, MOTHER DEAR, WE SADLY FEAR THAT WE HAVE LOST OUR MITTENS.
WHAT! LOST YOUR MITTENS, YOU NAUGHTY KITTENS! THEN YOU SHALL HAVE NO PIE!
MEOW MEOW MEOW MEOW
NOW WE SHALL HAVE NO PIE!

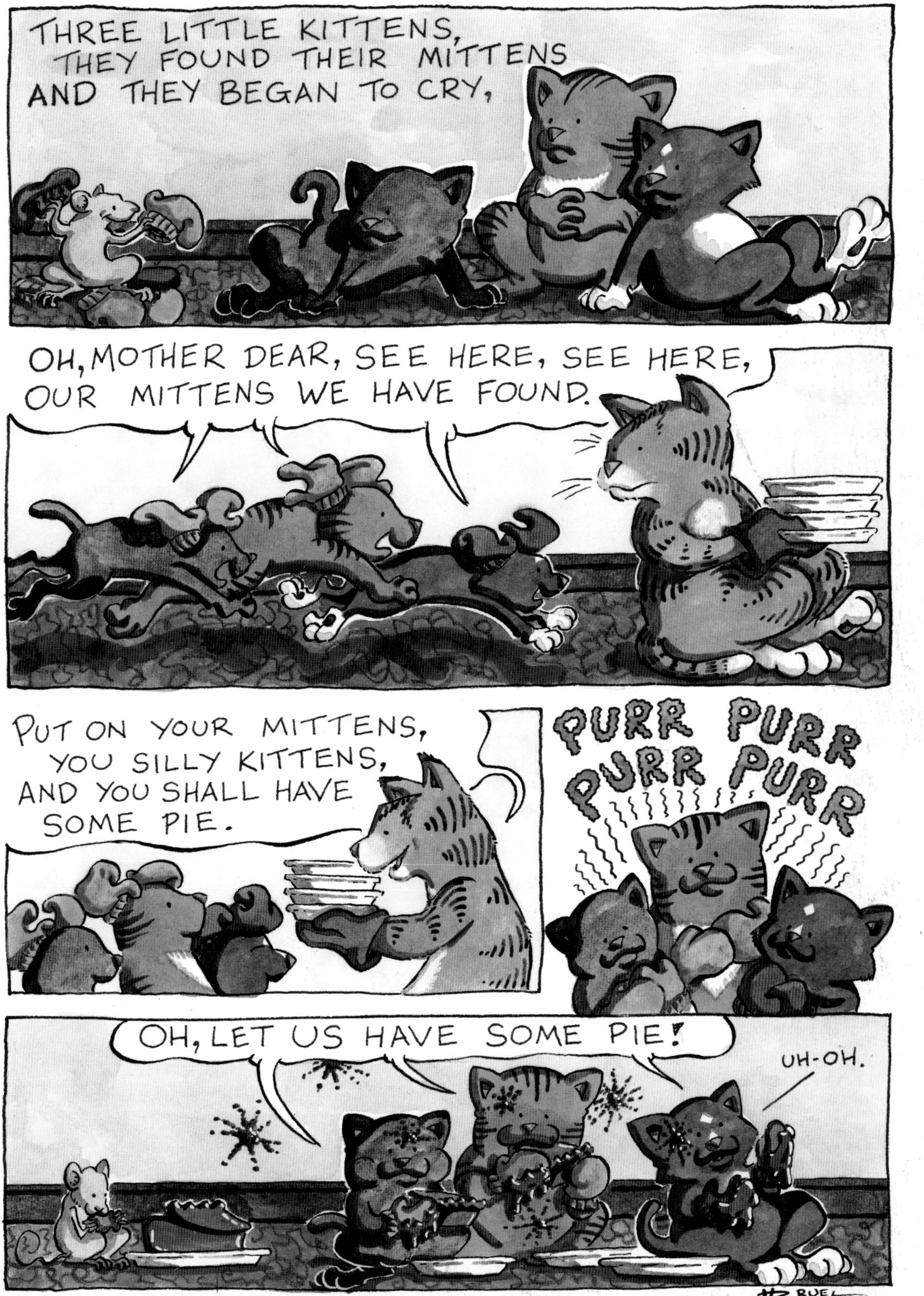
THREE LITTLE KITTENS, THEY FOUND THEIR MITTENS AND THEY BEGAN TO CRY,
OH, MOTHER DEAR, SEE HERE, SEE HERE, OUR MITTENS WE HAVE FOUND.
PUT ON YOUR MITTENS, YOU SILLY KITTENS, AND YOU SHALL HAVE SOME PIE.
PURR PURR PURR PURR
OH, LET US HAVE SOME PIE!
UH-OH.
BRUEL '010

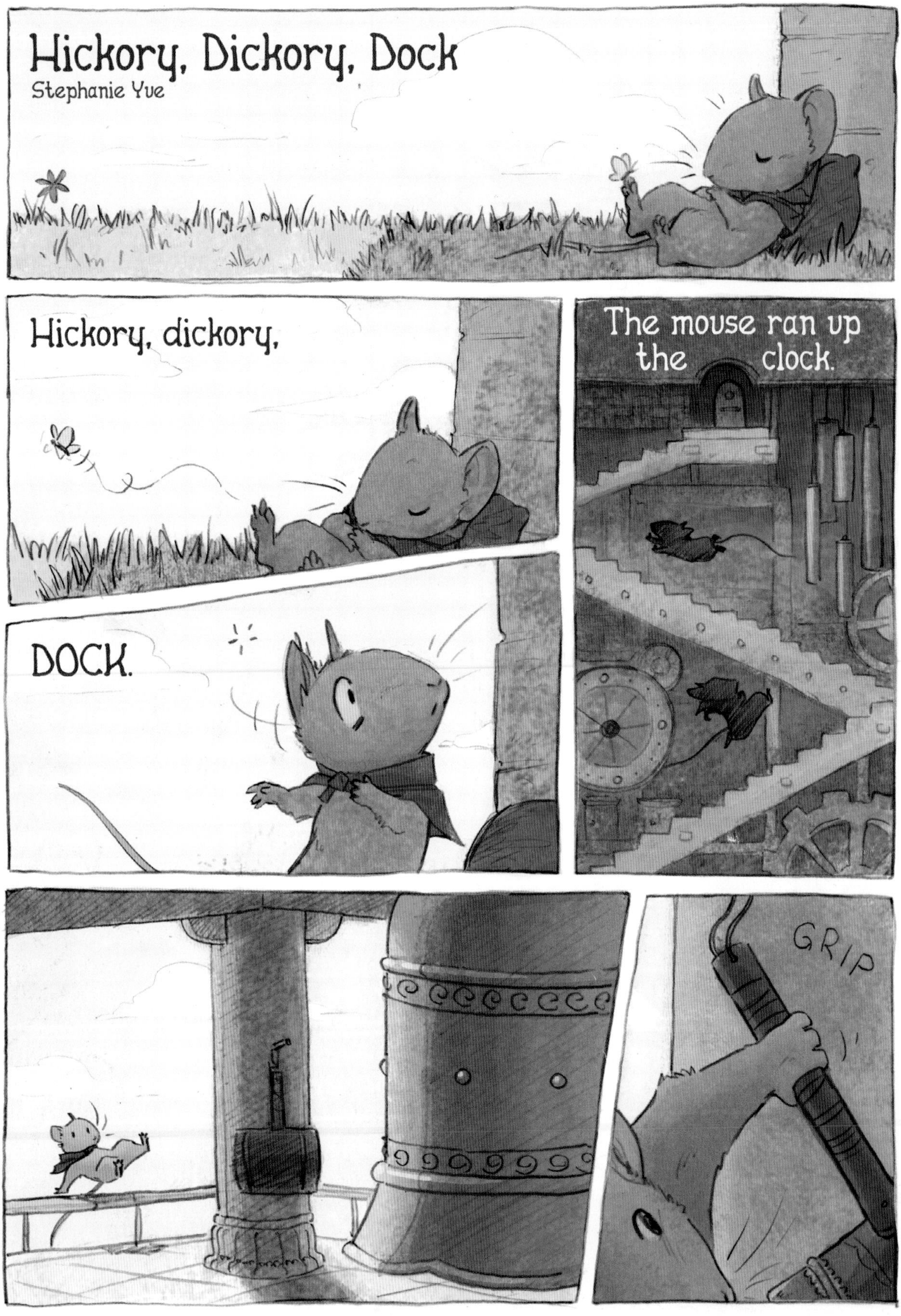
Hickory, Dickory, Dock
Stephanie Yue
Hickory, dickory,
The mouse ran up the clock.
DOCK.
GRIP

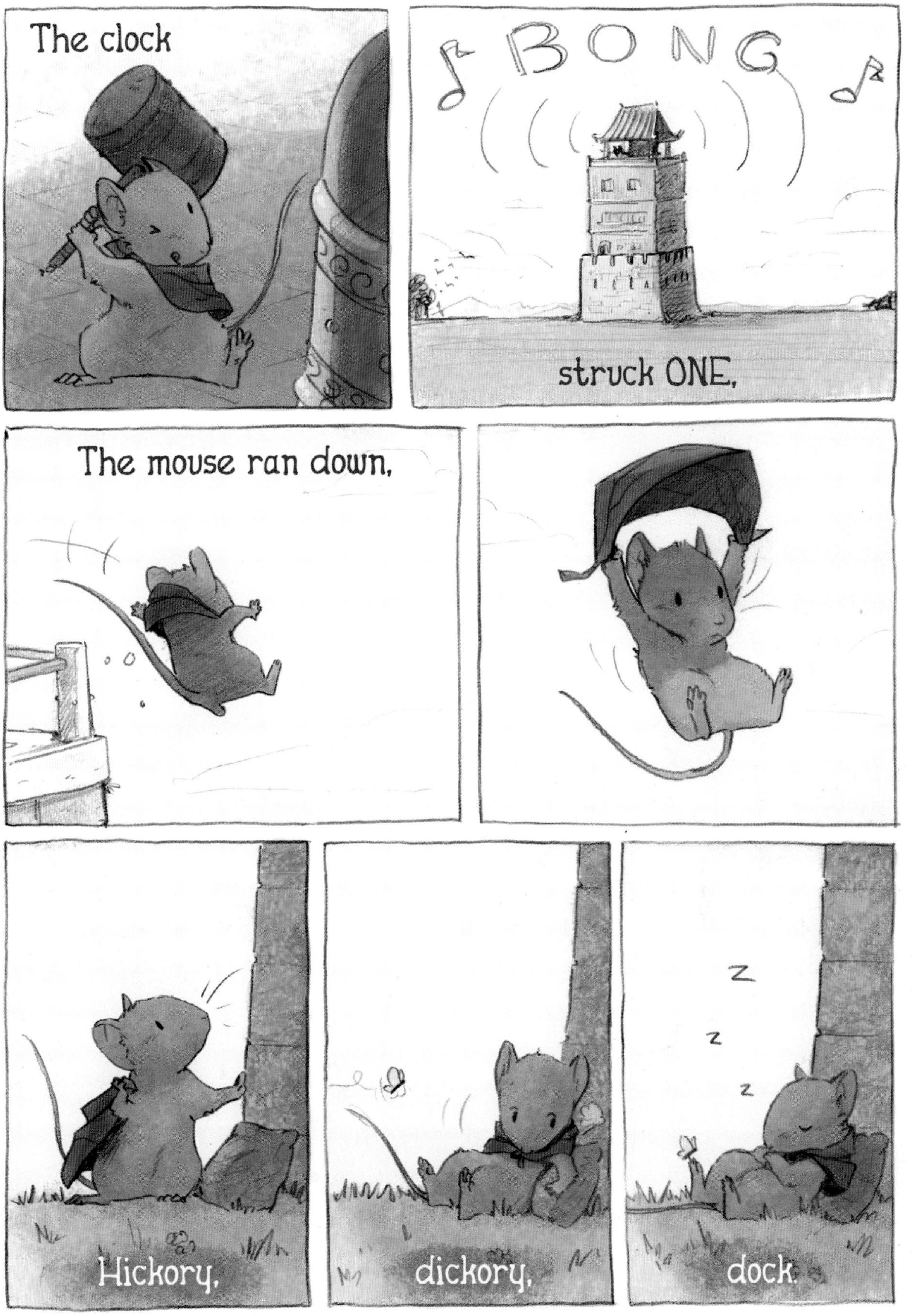
The clock
BONG
struck ONE,
The mouse ran down,
Hickory,
dickory,
dock.

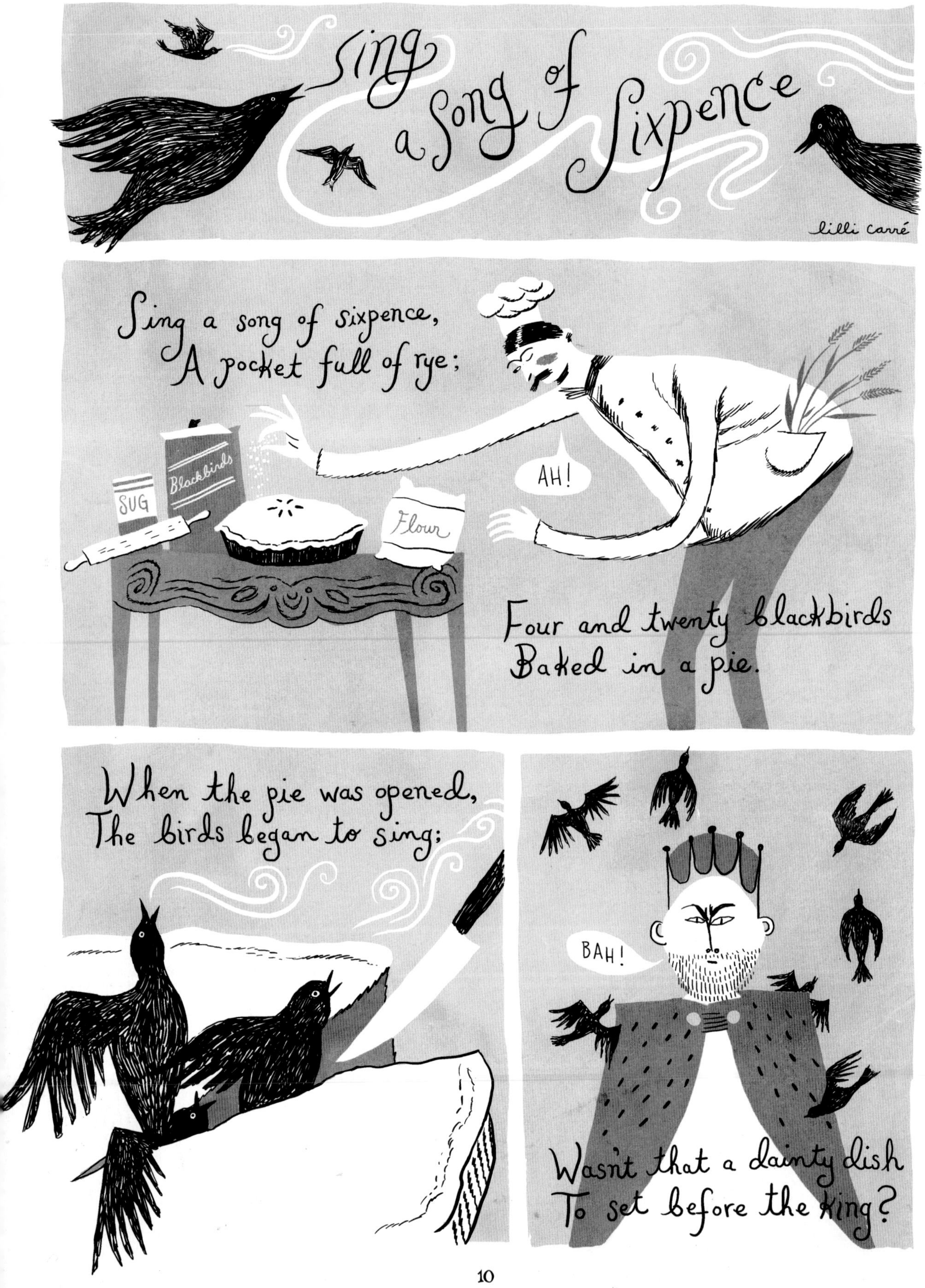
Sing a Song of Sixpence
lilli carré
Sing a song of sixpence,
A pocket full of rye;
Blackbirds
SUG
Flour
AH!
Four and twenty blackbirds
Baked in a pie.
When the pie was opened,
The birds began to sing;
BAH!
Wasn't that a dainty dish
To set before the king?

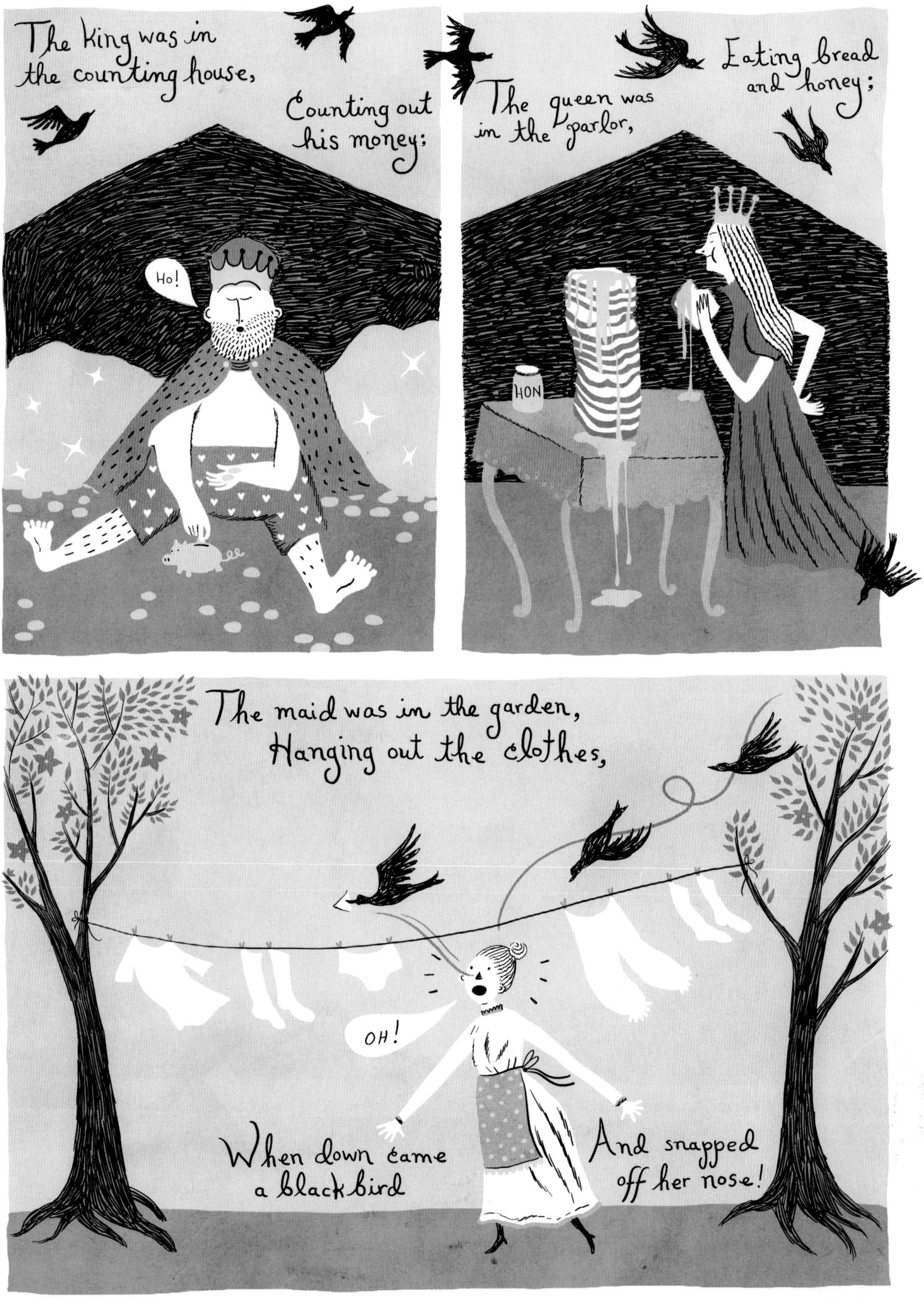

The king was in the counting house,
Ho!
Counting out his money;
The queen was in the parlor,
Eating bread and honey;
HON
The maid was in the garden,
Hanging out the clothes,
OH!
When down came a blackbird
And snapped off her nose!

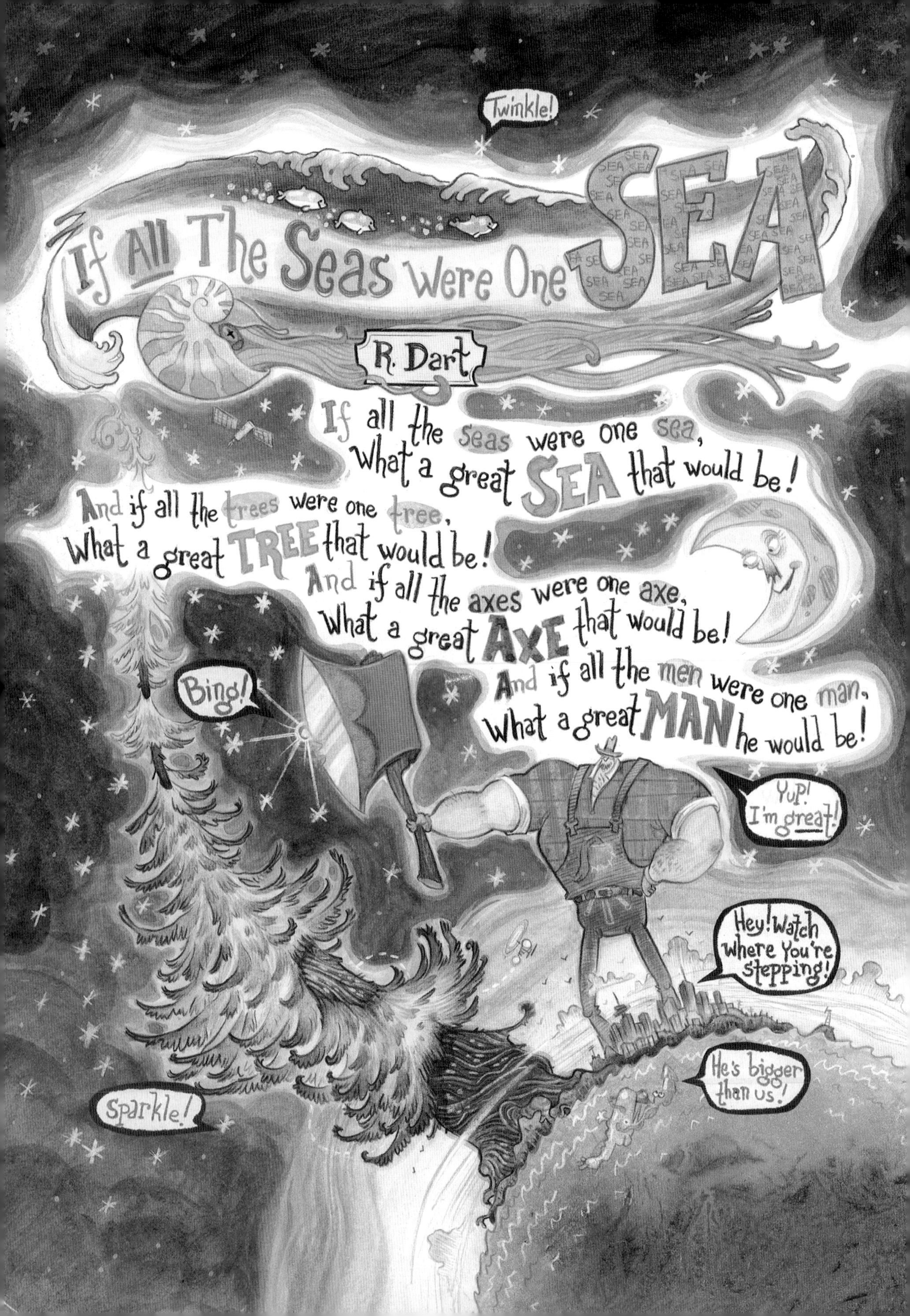
Twinkle!
If All The Seas Were One SEA
R. Dart
If all the seas were one sea,
What a great SEA that would be!
And if all the trees were one tree,
What a great TREE that would be!
And if all the axes were one axe,
What a great AXE that would be!
And if all the men were one man,
What a great MAN he would be!
Bing!
Yup! I'm great!
Hey! Watch where you're stepping!
He's bigger than us!
Sparkle!

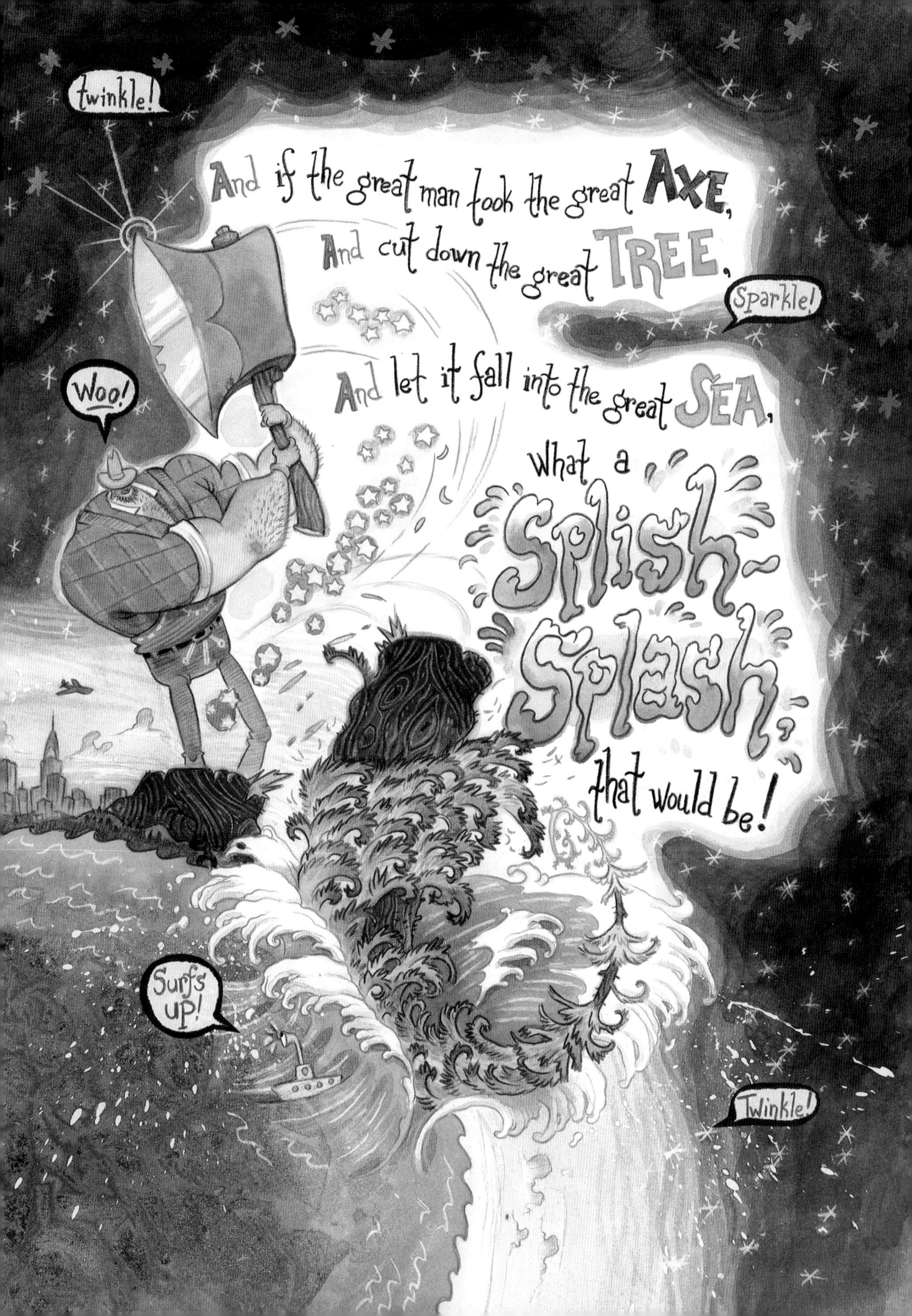
twinkle!
And if the great man took the great AXE,
And cut down the great TREE,
Sparkle!
And let it fall into the great SEA,
What a Splish-Splash that would be!
Woo!
Surf's up!
Twinkle!

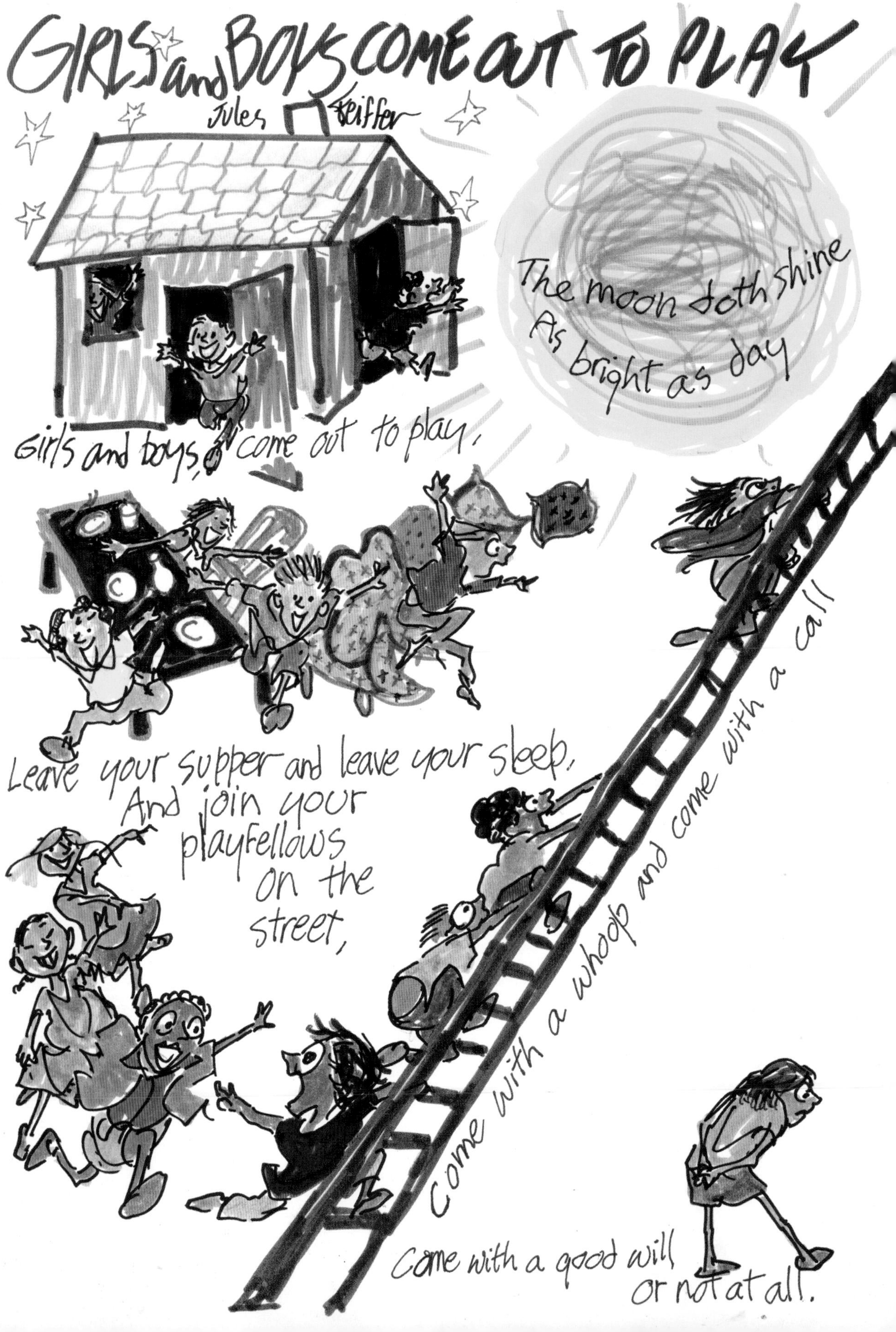
GIRLS and BOYS COME OUT TO PLAY
Jules Feiffer
The moon doth shine
As bright as day
Girls and boys, come out to play.
Leave your supper and leave your sleep,
And join your
playfellows
on the
street,
Come with a whoop and come with a call
Come with a good will
or not at all.

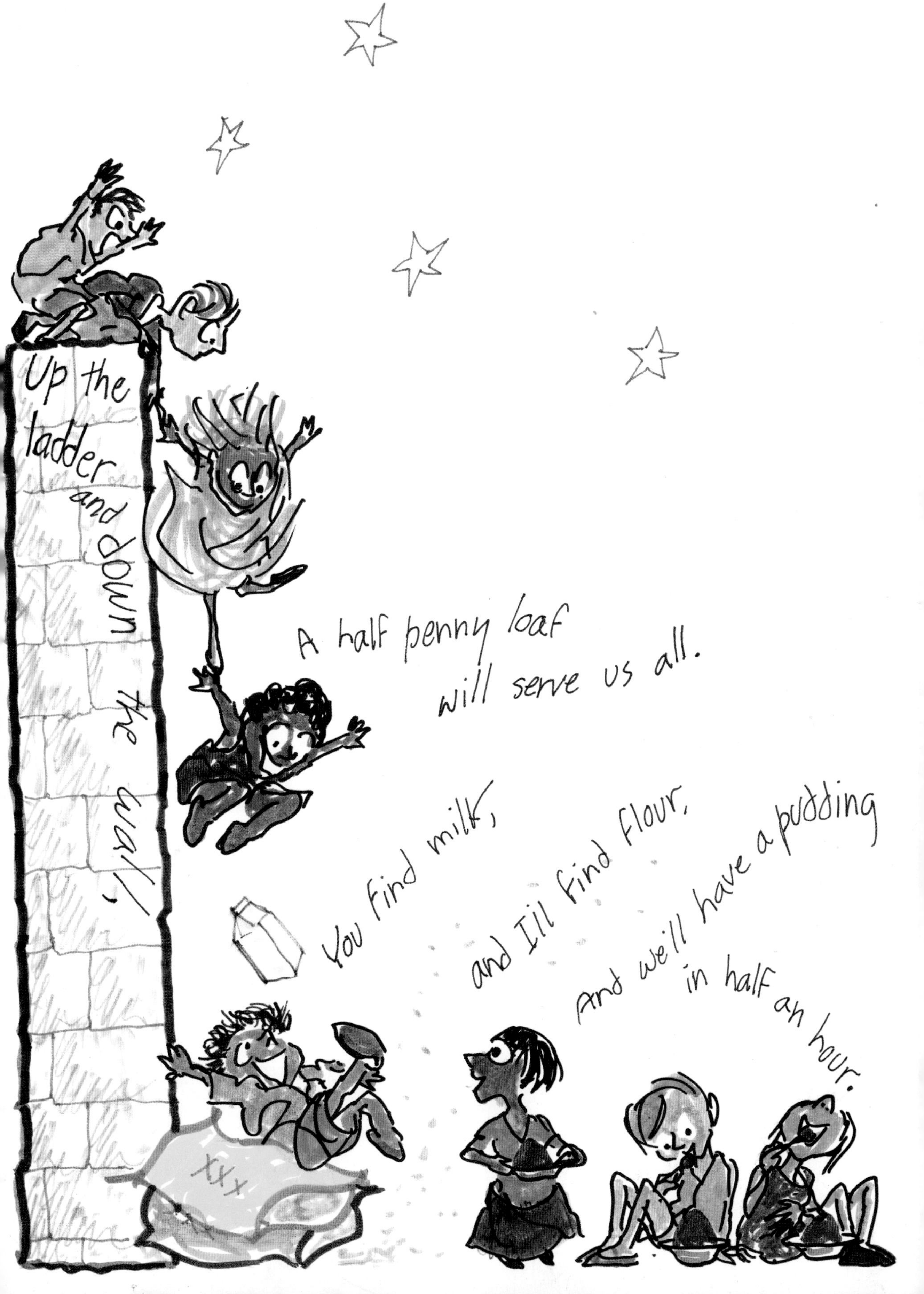
Up the ladder and down the wall,
A half penny loaf will serve us all.
You find milk,
and I'll find flour,
And we'll have a pudding in half an hour.

THERE WAS AN OLD

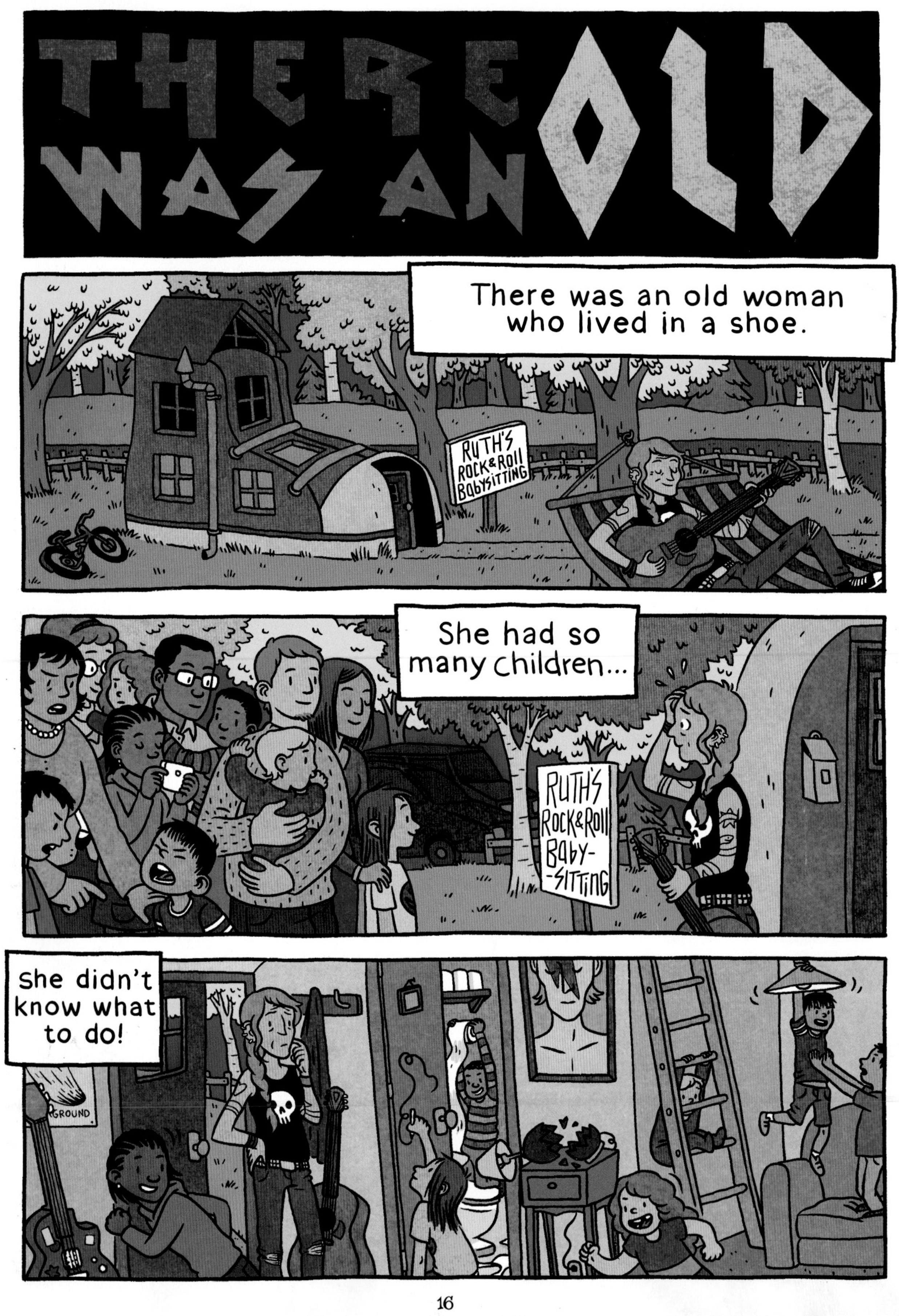
There was an old woman who lived in a shoe.
RUTH'S ROCK&ROLL BABYSITTING
She had so many children...
RUTH'S ROCK&ROLL BABY-SITTING
She didn't know what to do!

WOMAN WHO LIVED IN A SHOE

Lucy Knisley

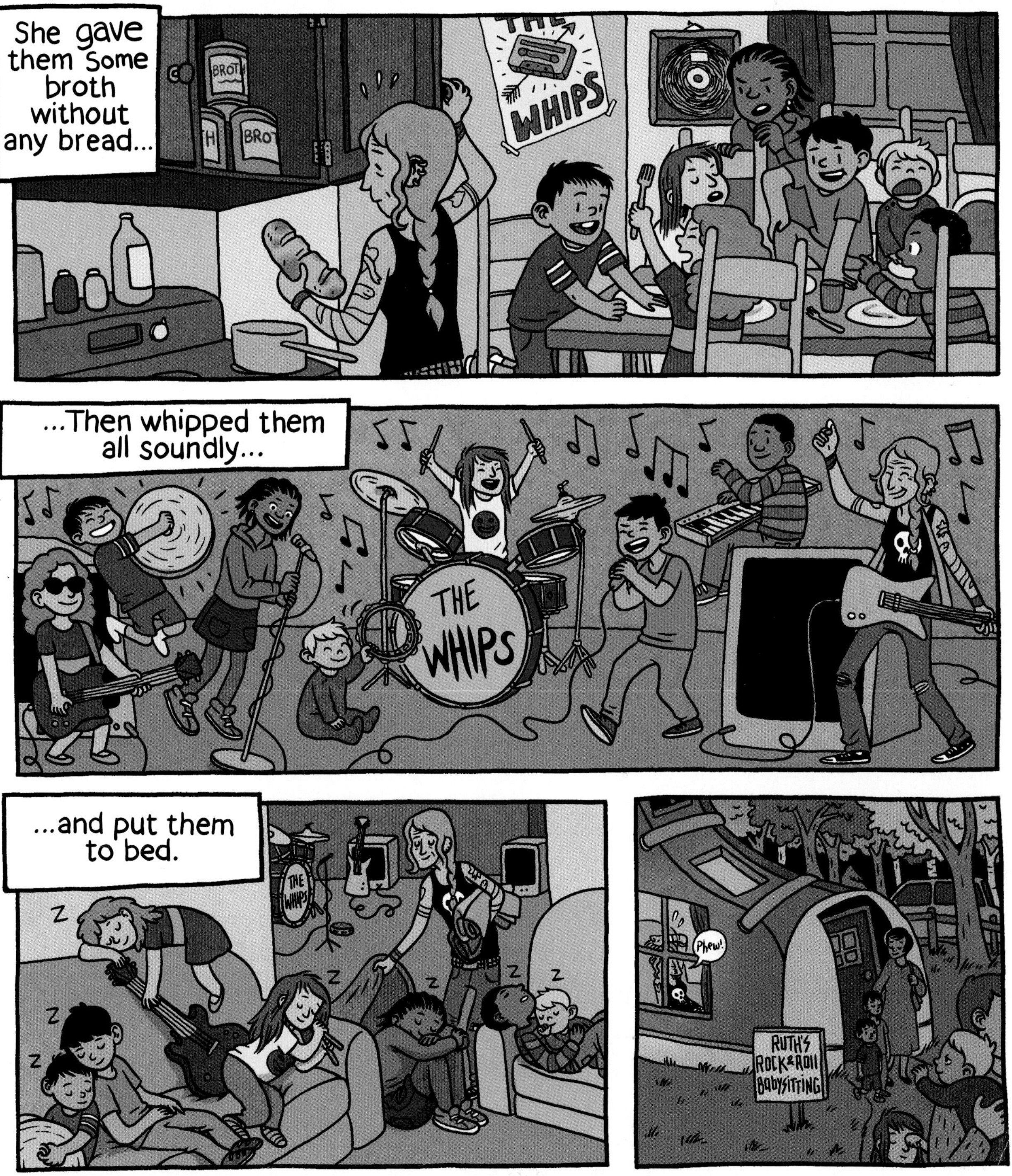
She gave them some broth without any bread...
BROTH
TH
BROT
THE WHIPS
...Then whipped them all soundly...
THE WHIPS
...and put them to bed.
THE WHIPS
Phew!
RUTH'S ROCK & ROLL BABYSITTING

CINDERELLER

Vanessa Davis

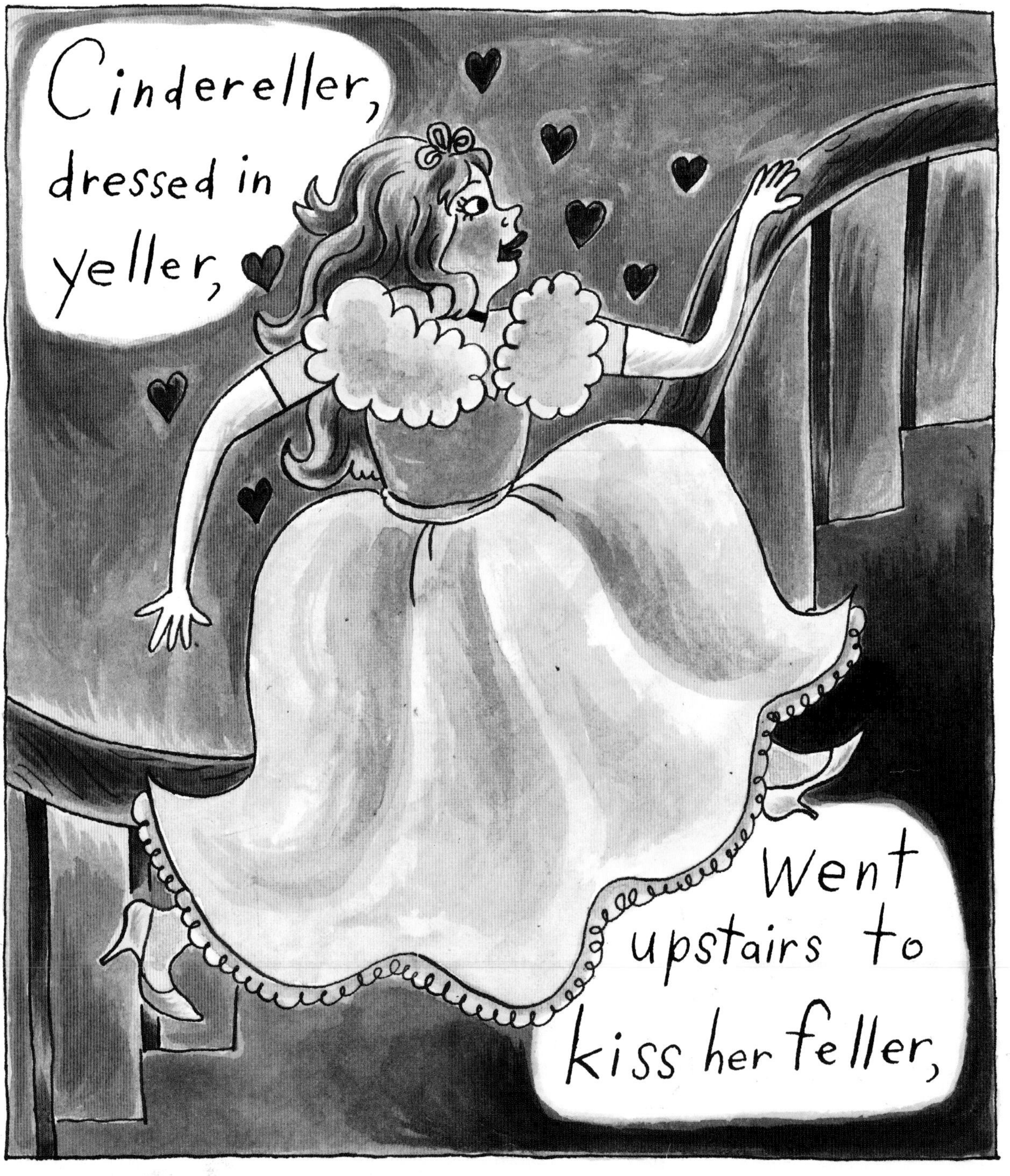
Cindereller, dressed in yeller,
Went upstairs to kiss her feller,

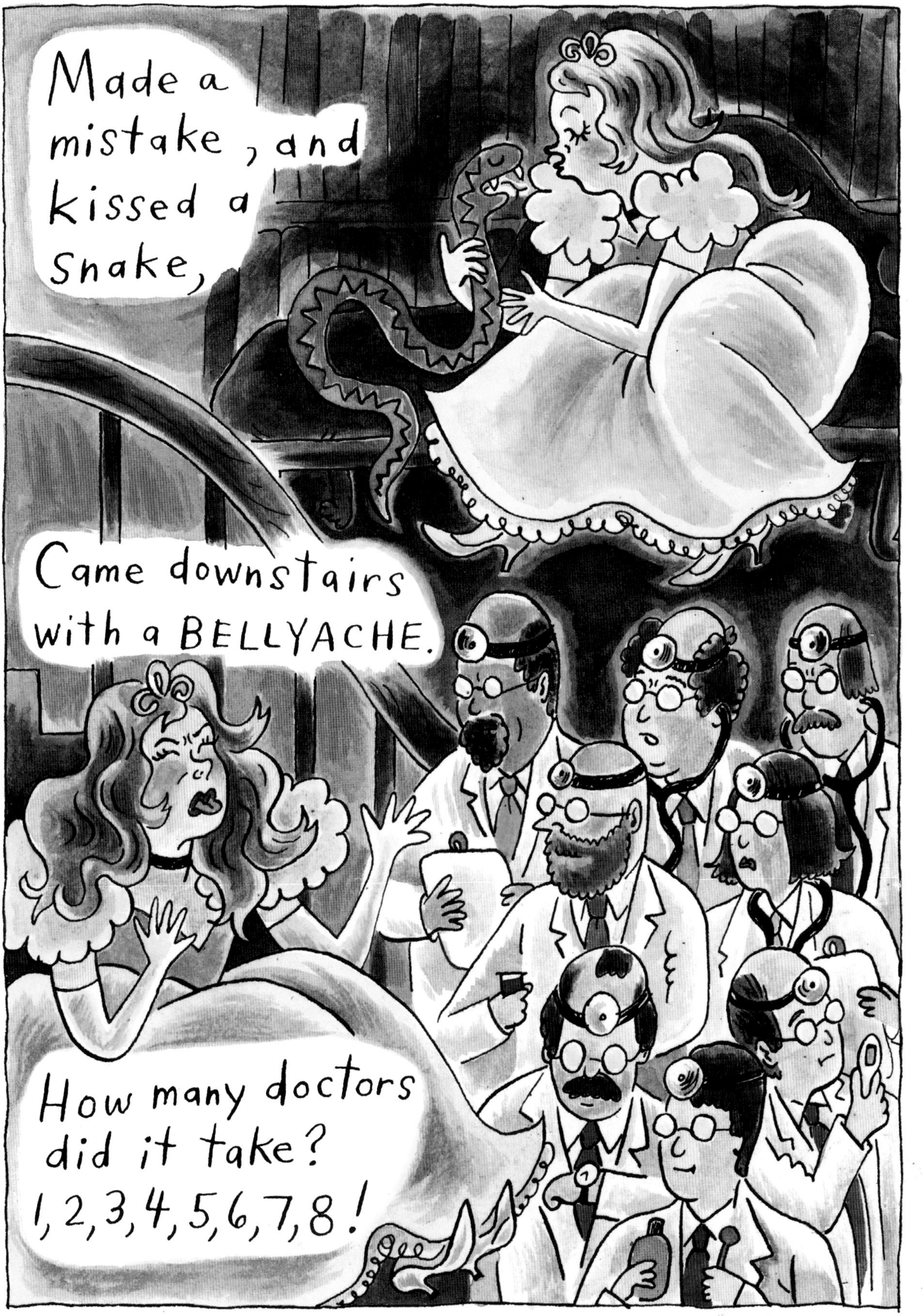
Made a mistake, and kissed a snake,
Came downstairs with a BELLYACHE.
How many doctors did it take? 1,2,3,4,5,6,7,8!

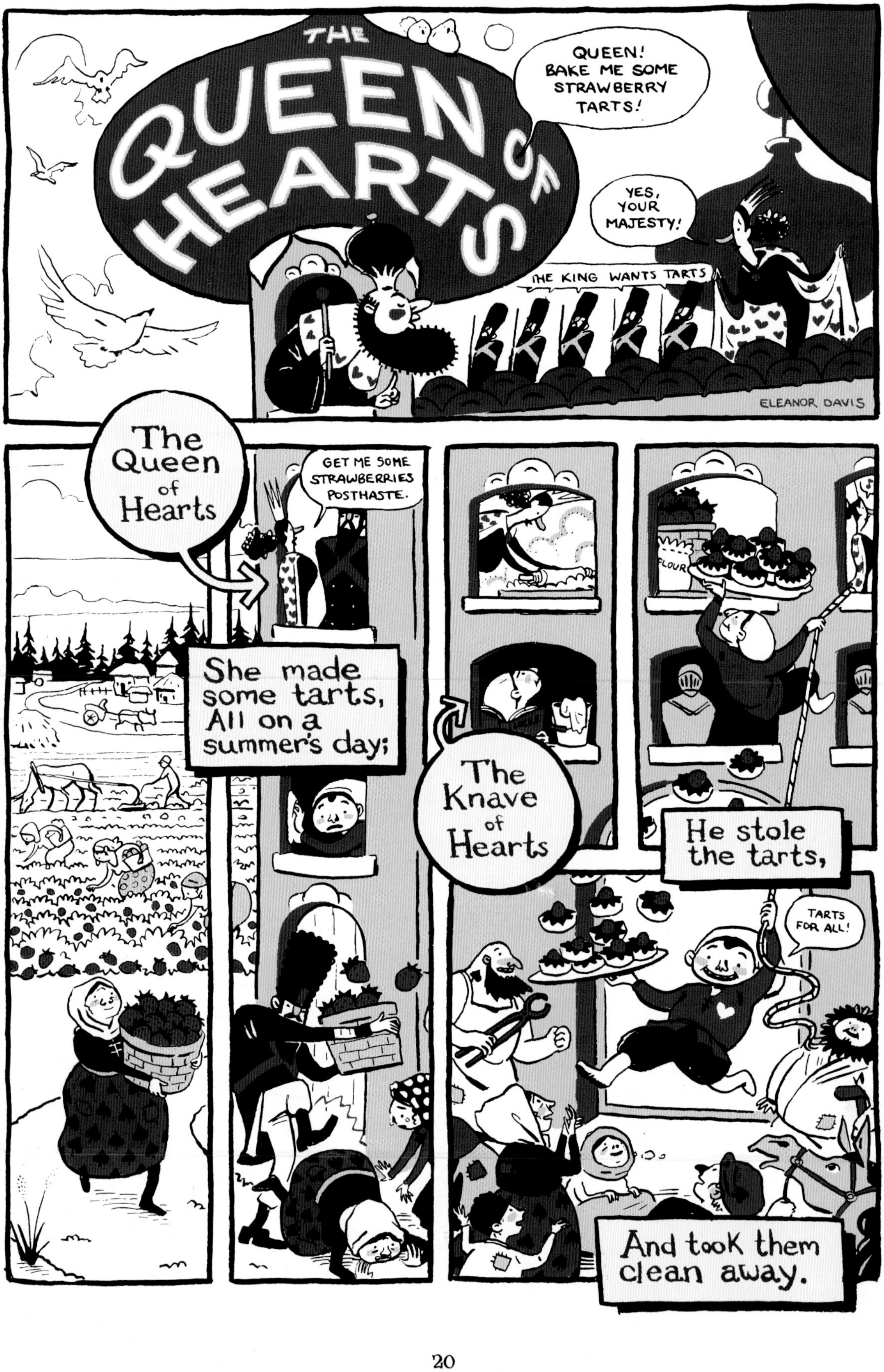
THE QUEEN OF HEARTS
QUEEN! BAKE ME SOME STRAWBERRY TARTS!
YES, YOUR MAJESTY!
THE KING WANTS TARTS
ELEANOR DAVIS
The Queen of Hearts
GET ME SOME STRAWBERRIES POSTHASTE.
She made some tarts, All on a summer's day;
FLOUR
The Knave of Hearts
He stole the tarts,
TARTS FOR ALL!
And took them clean away.

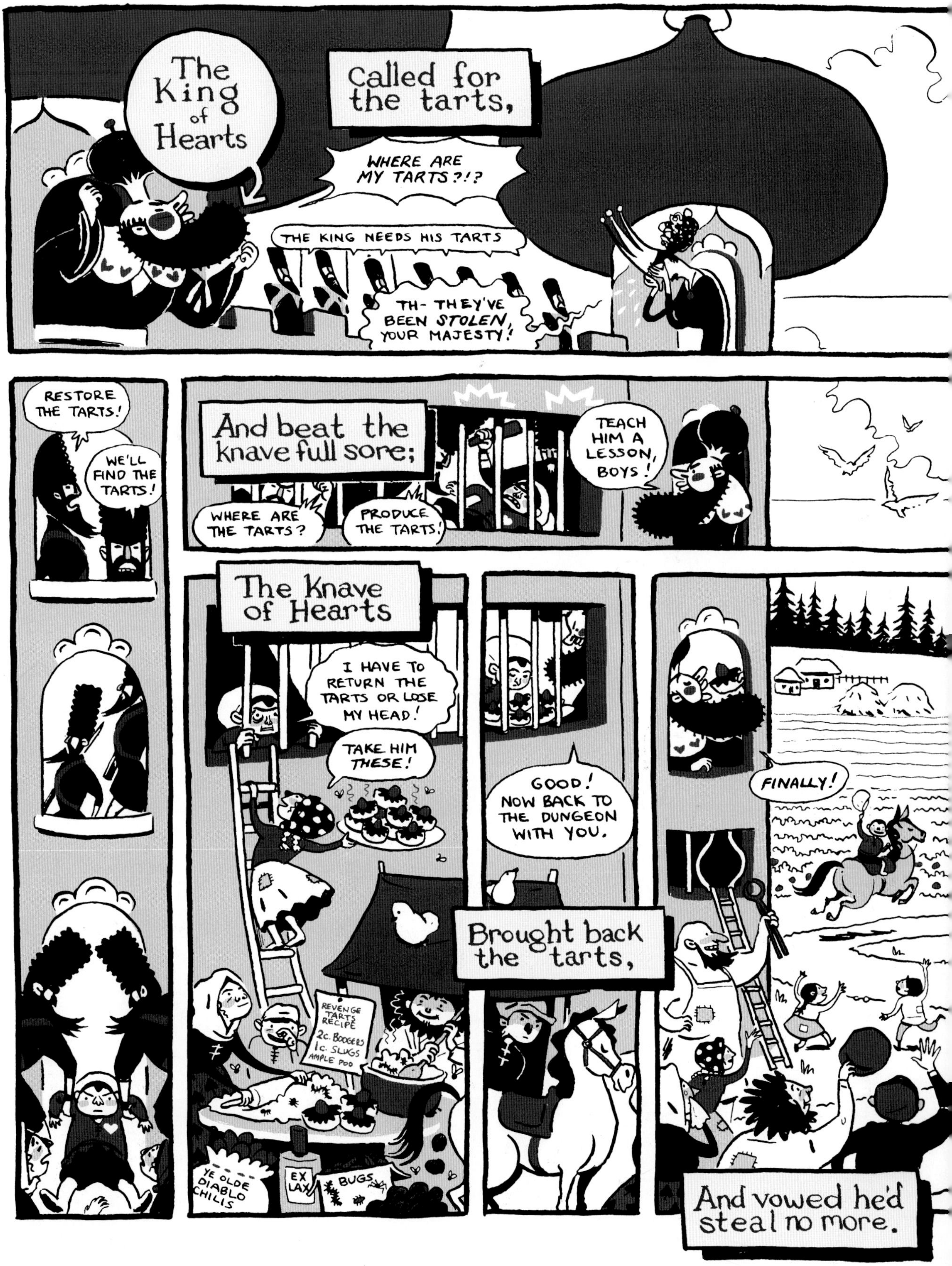

The King of Hearts
Called for the tarts,
WHERE ARE MY TARTS?!?
THE KING NEEDS HIS TARTS
TH- THEY'VE BEEN STOLEN, YOUR MAJESTY!
RESTORE THE TARTS!
WE'LL FIND THE TARTS!
And beat the knave full sore;
WHERE ARE THE TARTS?
PRODUCE THE TARTS!
TEACH HIM A LESSON, BOYS!
The Knave of Hearts
I HAVE TO RETURN THE TARTS OR LOSE MY HEAD!
TAKE HIM THESE!
REVENGE TARTS RECIPE
2c. BOOGERS
1c. SLUGS
AMPLE POO
YE OLDE DIABLO CHILIS
EX LAX
BUGS
GOOD! NOW BACK TO THE DUNGEON WITH YOU.
Brought back the tarts,
FINALLY!
And vowed he'd steal no more.

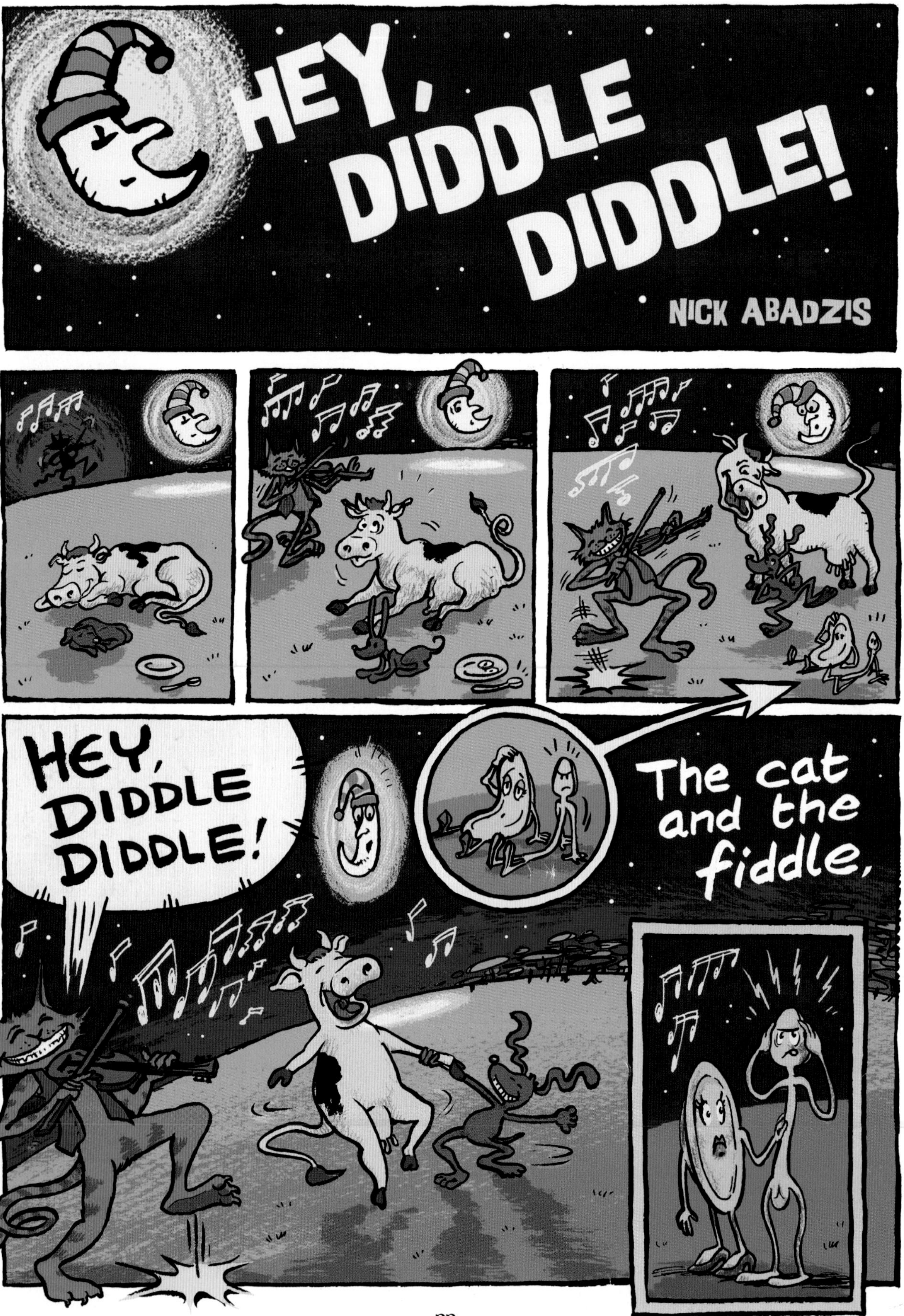
HEY, DIDDLE DIDDLE!
NICK ABADZIS
HEY, DIDDLE DIDDLE!
The cat and the fiddle,

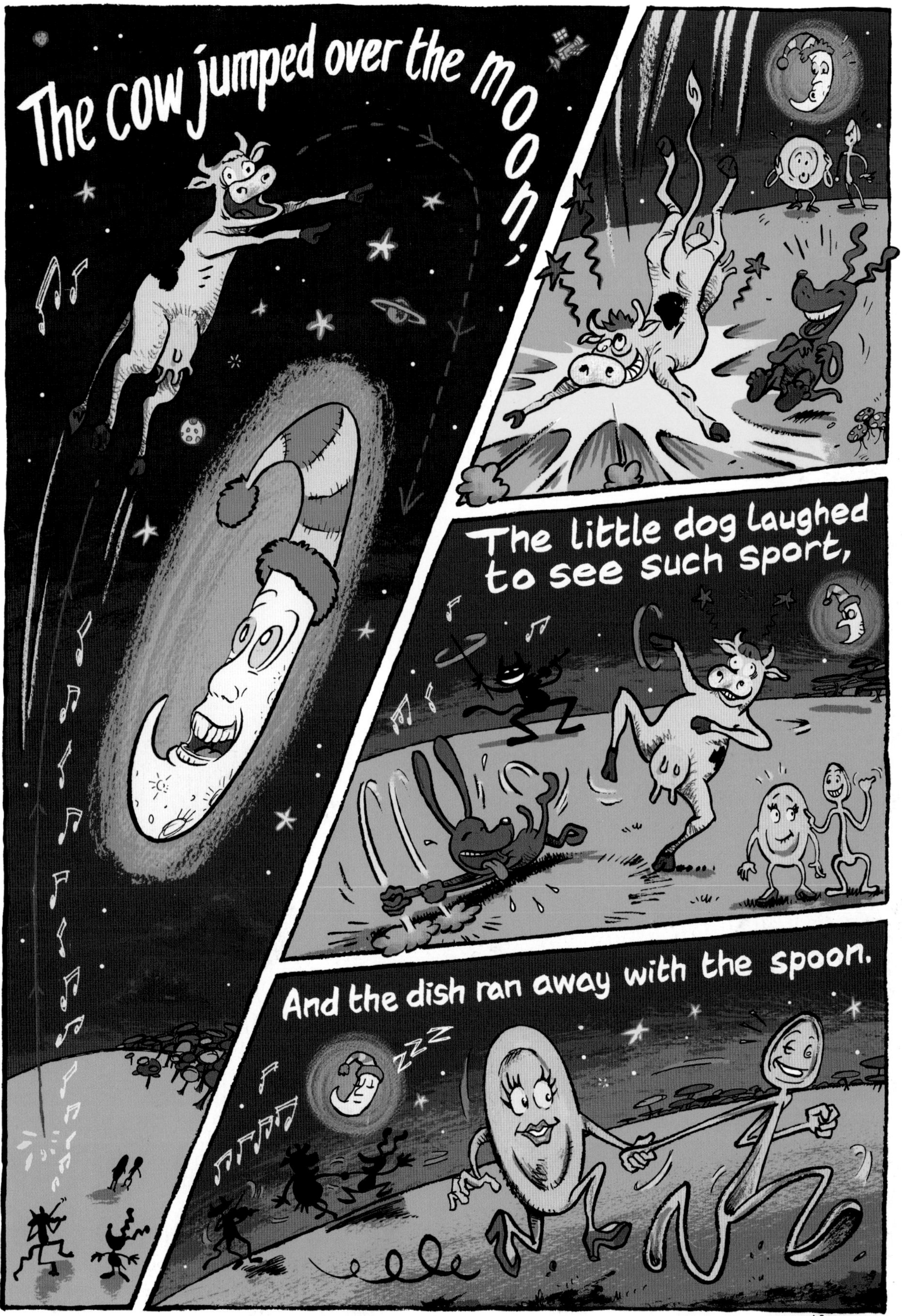
The cow jumped over the moon;
The little dog laughed to see such sport,
And the dish ran away with the spoon.
ZZZ

There Was an Old Woman Tossed Up in a Basket

Richard Thompson

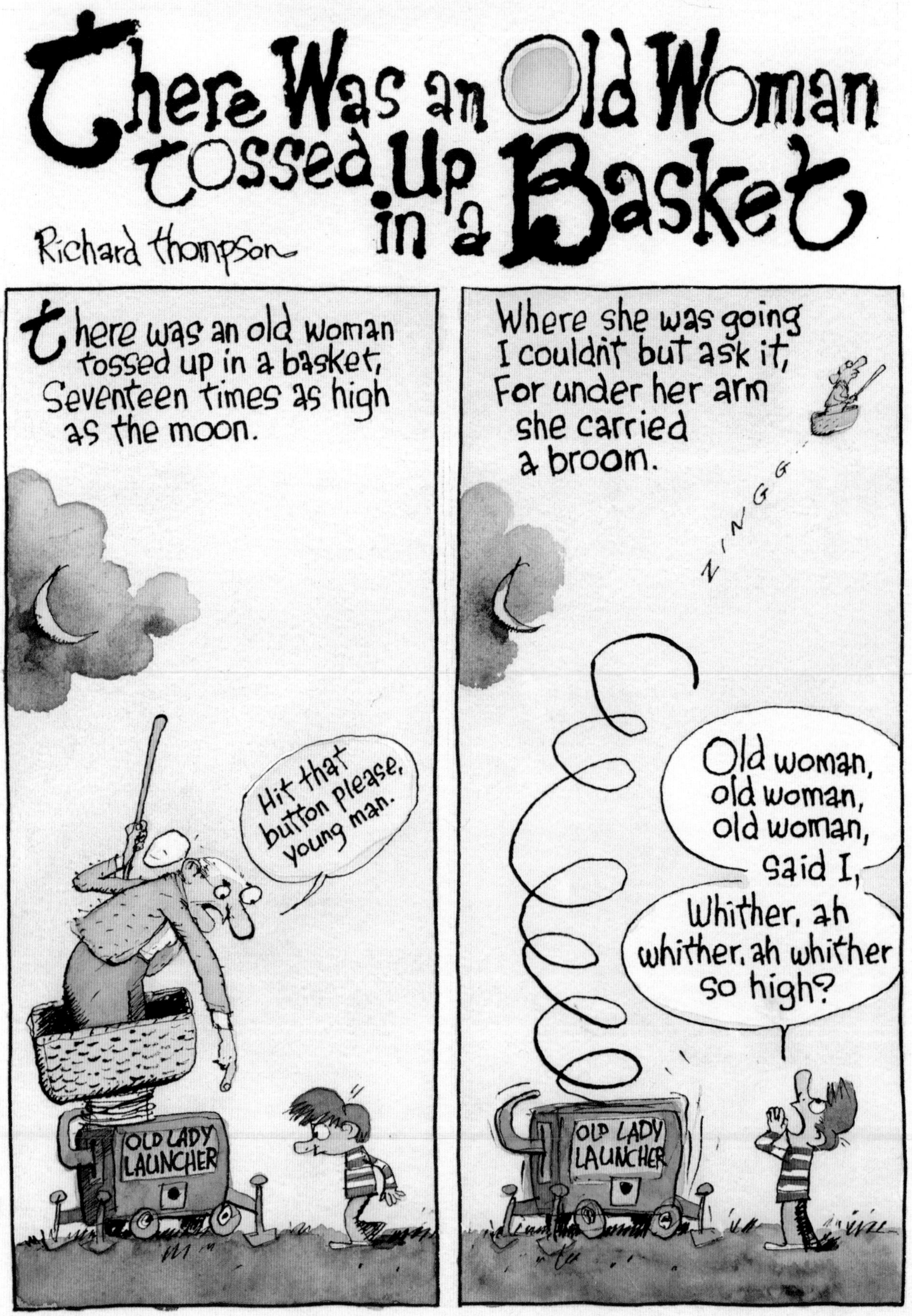
There was an old woman tossed up in a basket, Seventeen times as high as the moon.
Hit that button please, young man.
OLD LADY LAUNCHER
Where she was going I couldn't but ask it, For under her arm she carried a broom.
ZINGG...
Old woman, old woman, old woman, said I,
Whither, ah whither, ah whither so high?
OLD LADY LAUNCHER

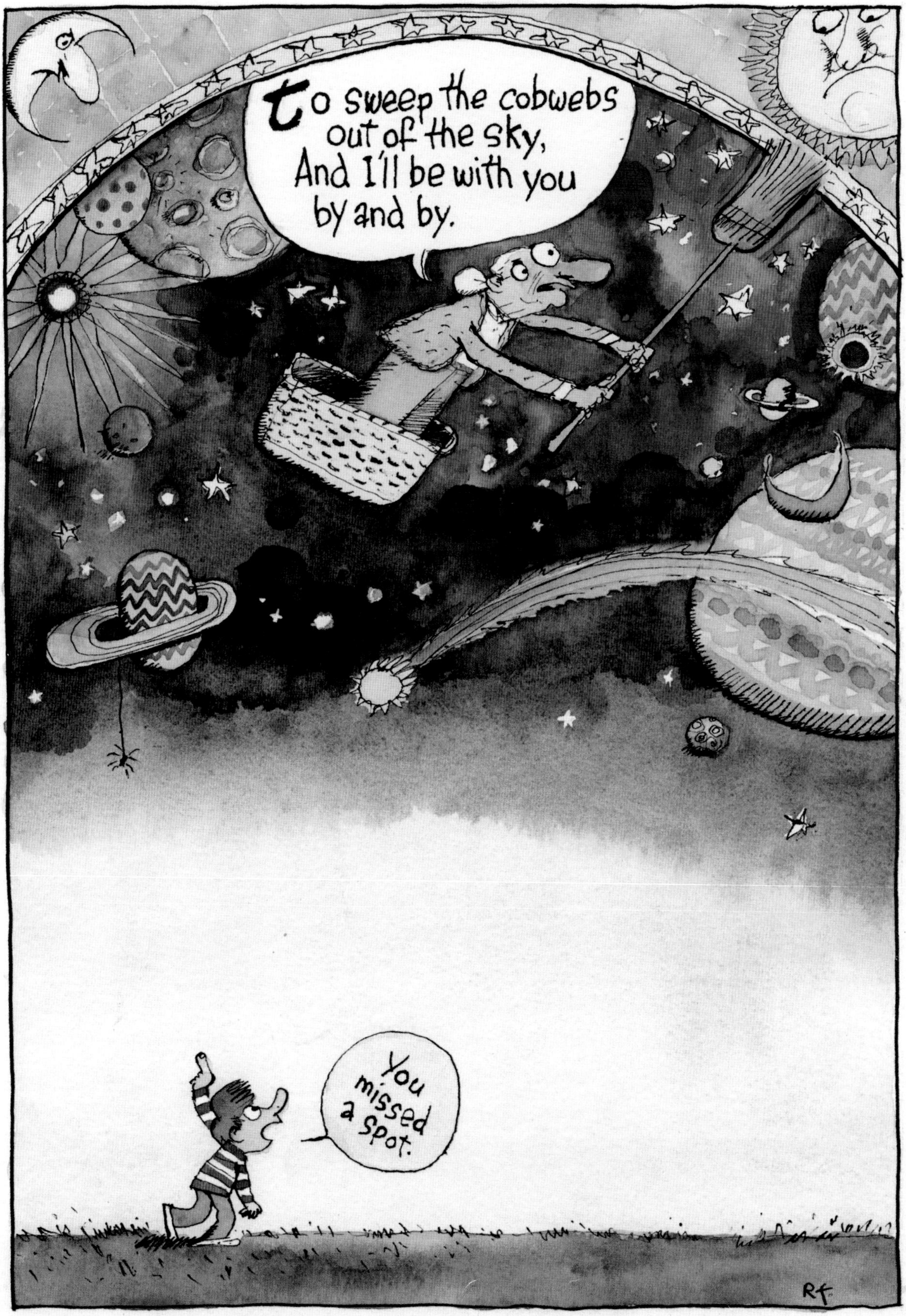
To sweep the cobwebs out of the sky, And I'll be with you by and by.
You missed a spot.
RF

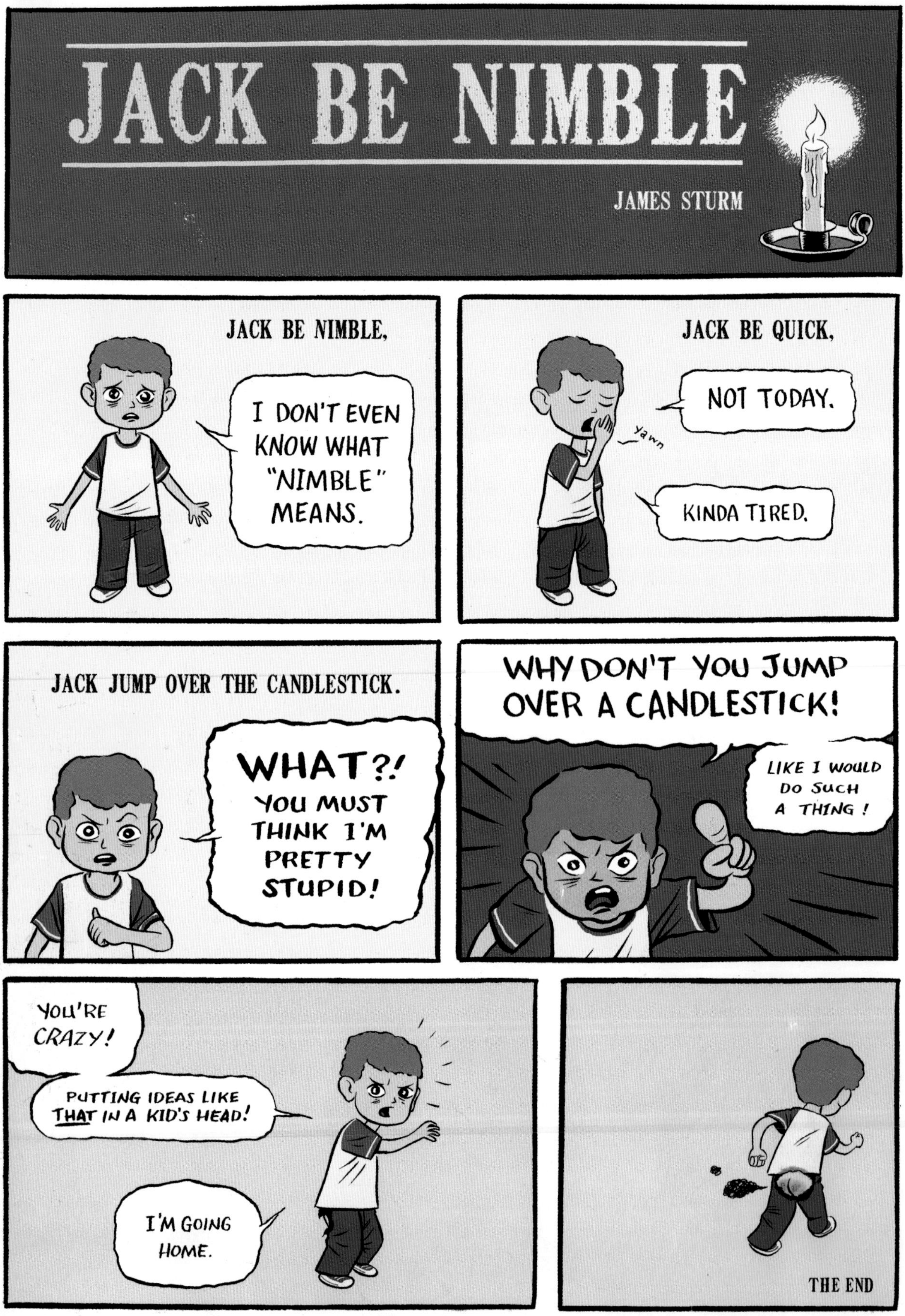
JACK BE NIMBLE
JAMES STURM
JACK BE NIMBLE,
I DON'T EVEN KNOW WHAT "NIMBLE" MEANS.
JACK BE QUICK,
yawn
NOT TODAY.
KINDA TIRED.
JACK JUMP OVER THE CANDLESTICK.
WHAT?! YOU MUST THINK I'M PRETTY STUPID!
WHY DON'T YOU JUMP OVER A CANDLESTICK!
LIKE I WOULD DO SUCH A THING!
YOU'RE CRAZY!
PUTTING IDEAS LIKE THAT IN A KID'S HEAD!
I'M GOING HOME.
THE END

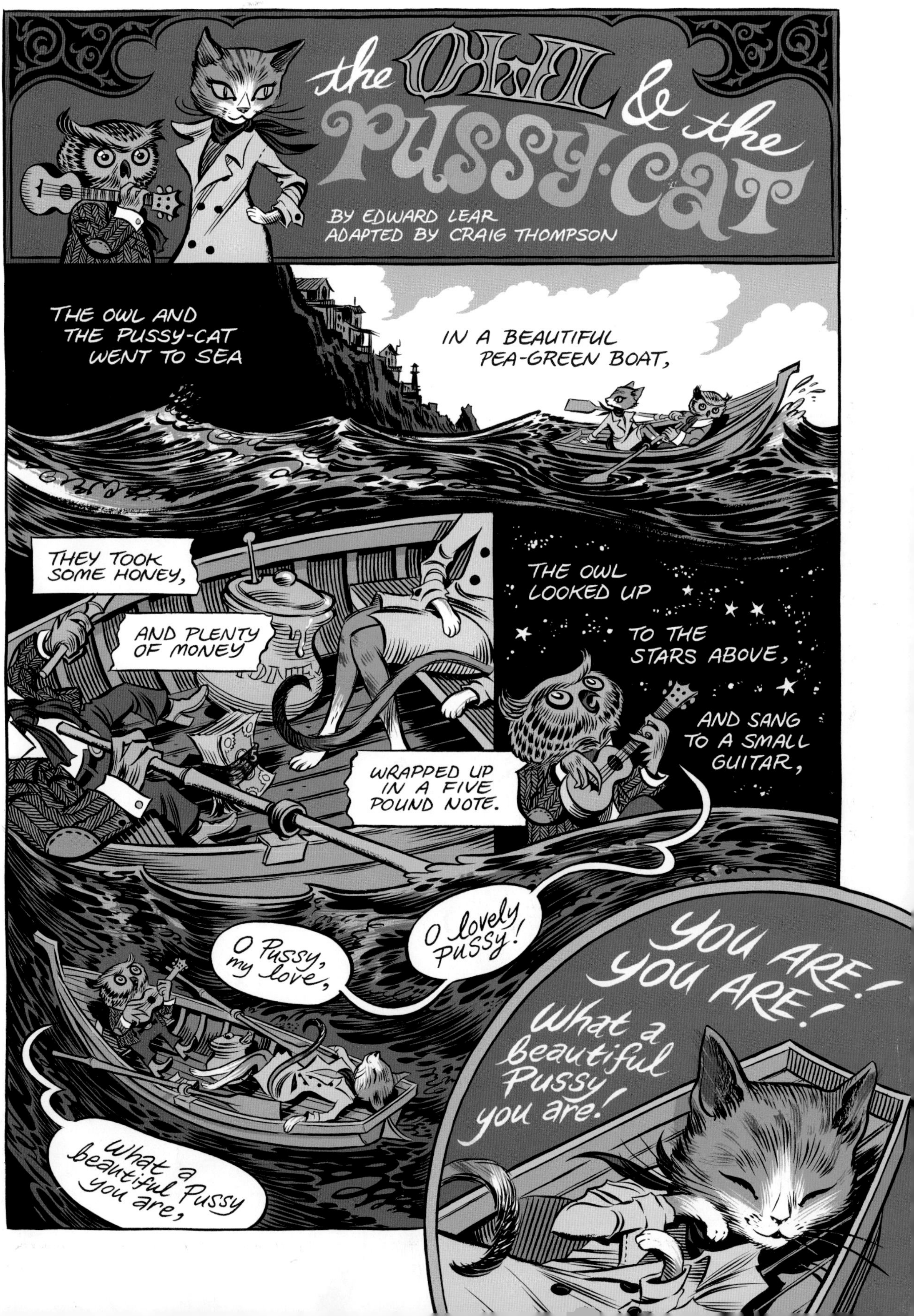

the OWL & the PUSSY-CAT
BY EDWARD LEAR
ADAPTED BY CRAIG THOMPSON
THE OWL AND THE PUSSY-CAT WENT TO SEA
IN A BEAUTIFUL PEA-GREEN BOAT,
THEY TOOK SOME HONEY,
AND PLENTY OF MONEY
WRAPPED UP IN A FIVE POUND NOTE.
THE OWL LOOKED UP
TO THE STARS ABOVE,
AND SANG TO A SMALL GUITAR,
O Pussy, my love,
O lovely Pussy!
YOU ARE! YOU ARE!
What a beautiful Pussy you are!
What a beautiful Pussy you are,

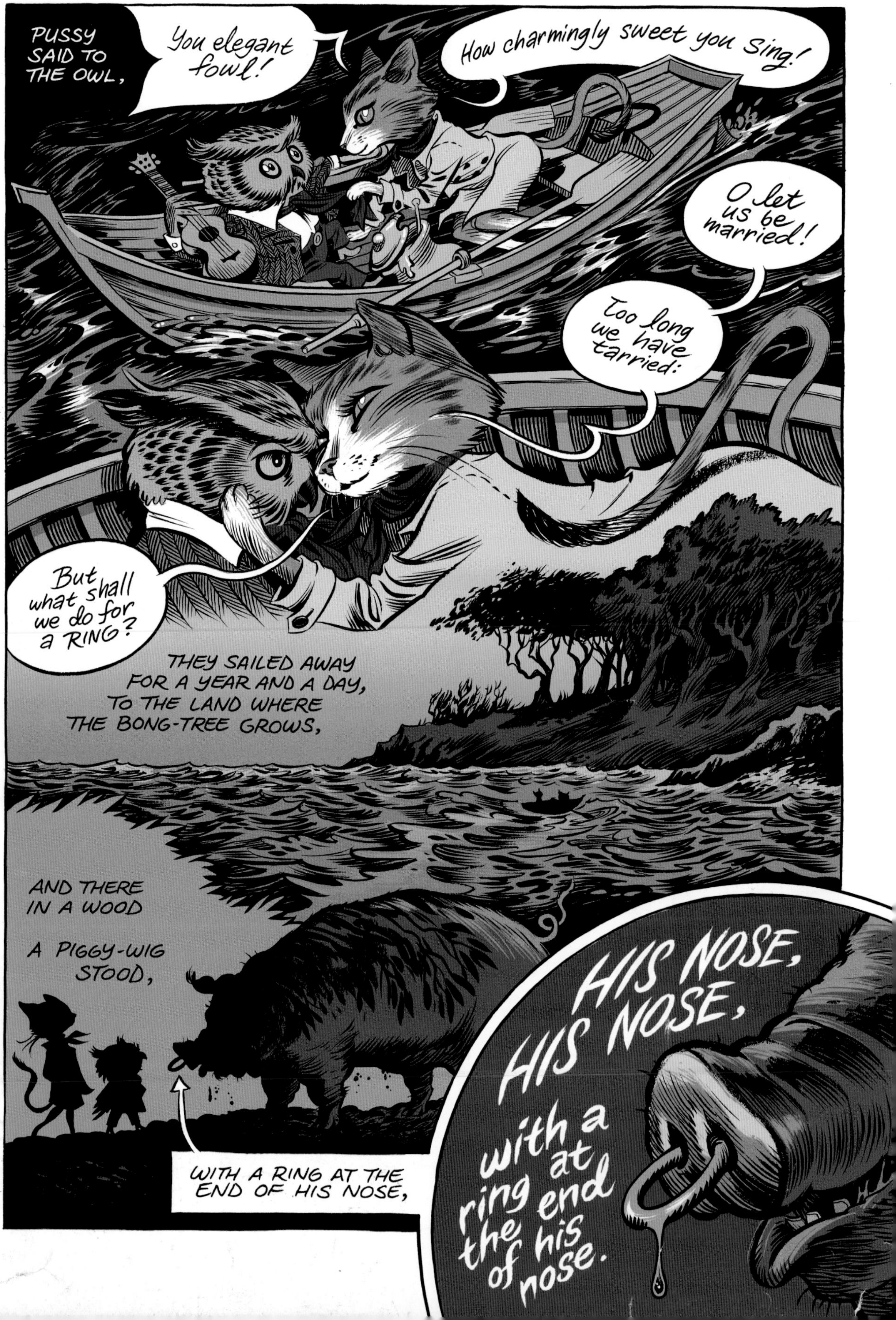
PUSSY SAID TO THE OWL,
You elegant fowl!
How charmingly sweet you Sing!
O let us be married!
Too long we have tarried:
But what shall we do for a RING?
THEY SAILED AWAY FOR A YEAR AND A DAY, TO THE LAND WHERE THE BONG-TREE GROWS,
AND THERE IN A WOOD
A PIGGY-WIG STOOD,
WITH A RING AT THE END OF HIS NOSE,
HIS NOSE, HIS NOSE,
with a ring at the end of his nose.

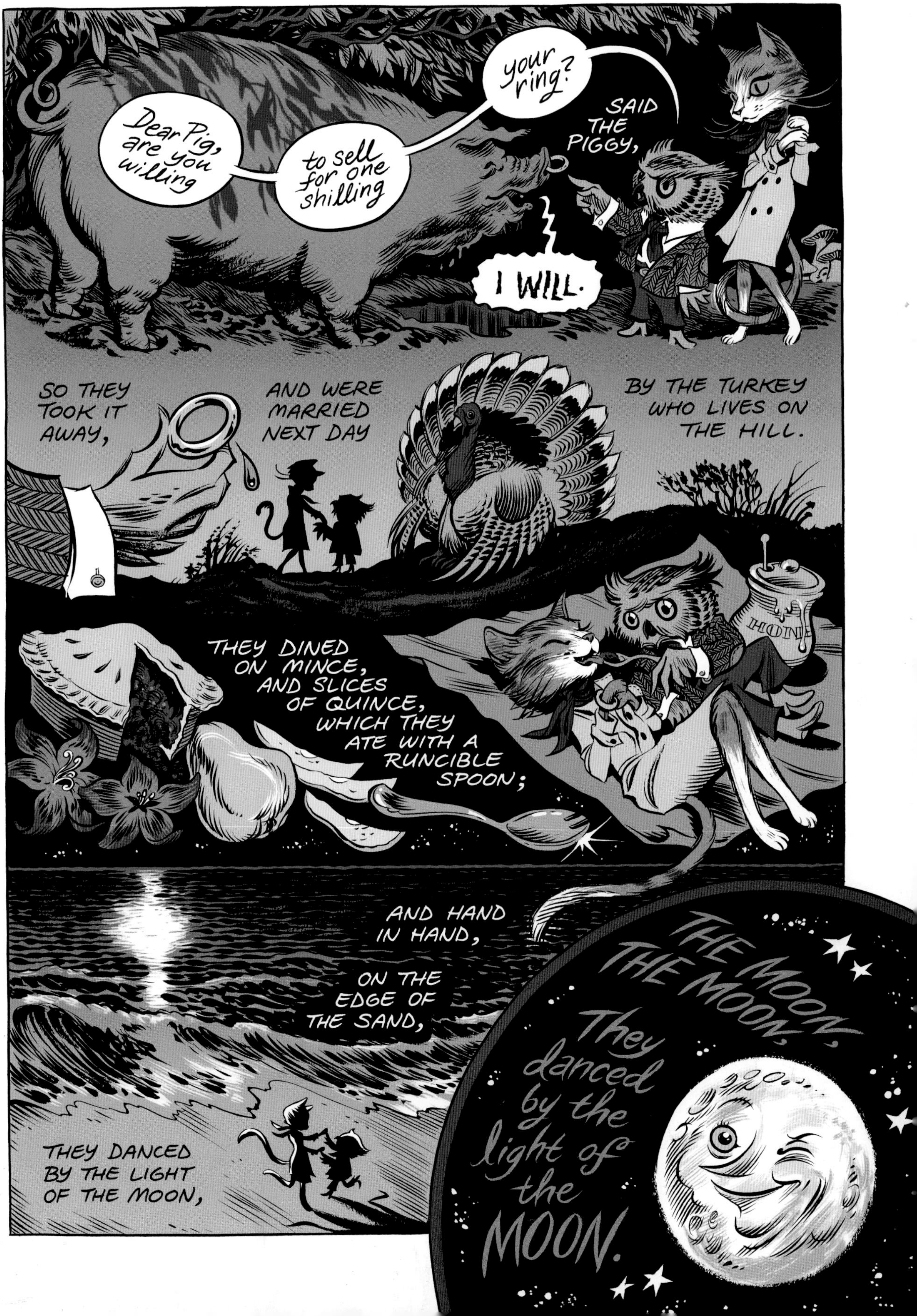
Dear Pig, are you willing
to sell for one shilling
your ring?
SAID THE PIGGY,
I WILL.
SO THEY TOOK IT AWAY,
AND WERE MARRIED NEXT DAY
BY THE TURKEY WHO LIVES ON THE HILL.
THEY DINED ON MINCE, AND SLICES OF QUINCE, WHICH THEY ATE WITH A RUNCIBLE SPOON;
AND HAND IN HAND,
ON THE EDGE OF THE SAND,
THEY DANCED BY THE LIGHT OF THE MOON,
THE MOON, THE MOON,
They danced by the light of the MOON.

THE ITSY BITSY SPIDER

GAHAN WILSON

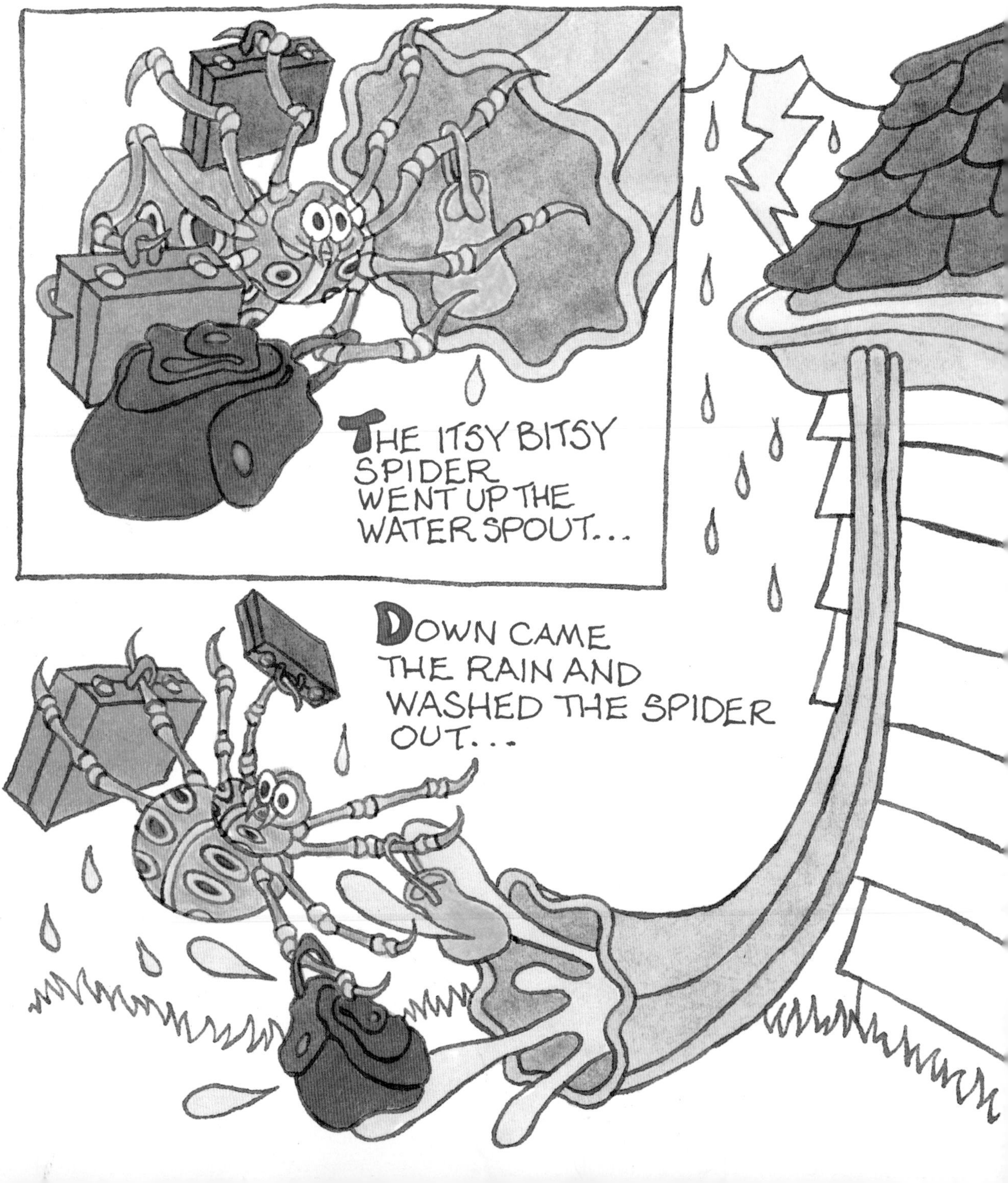
THE ITSY BITSY SPIDER WENT UP THE WATER SPOUT...
DOWN CAME THE RAIN AND WASHED THE SPIDER OUT...

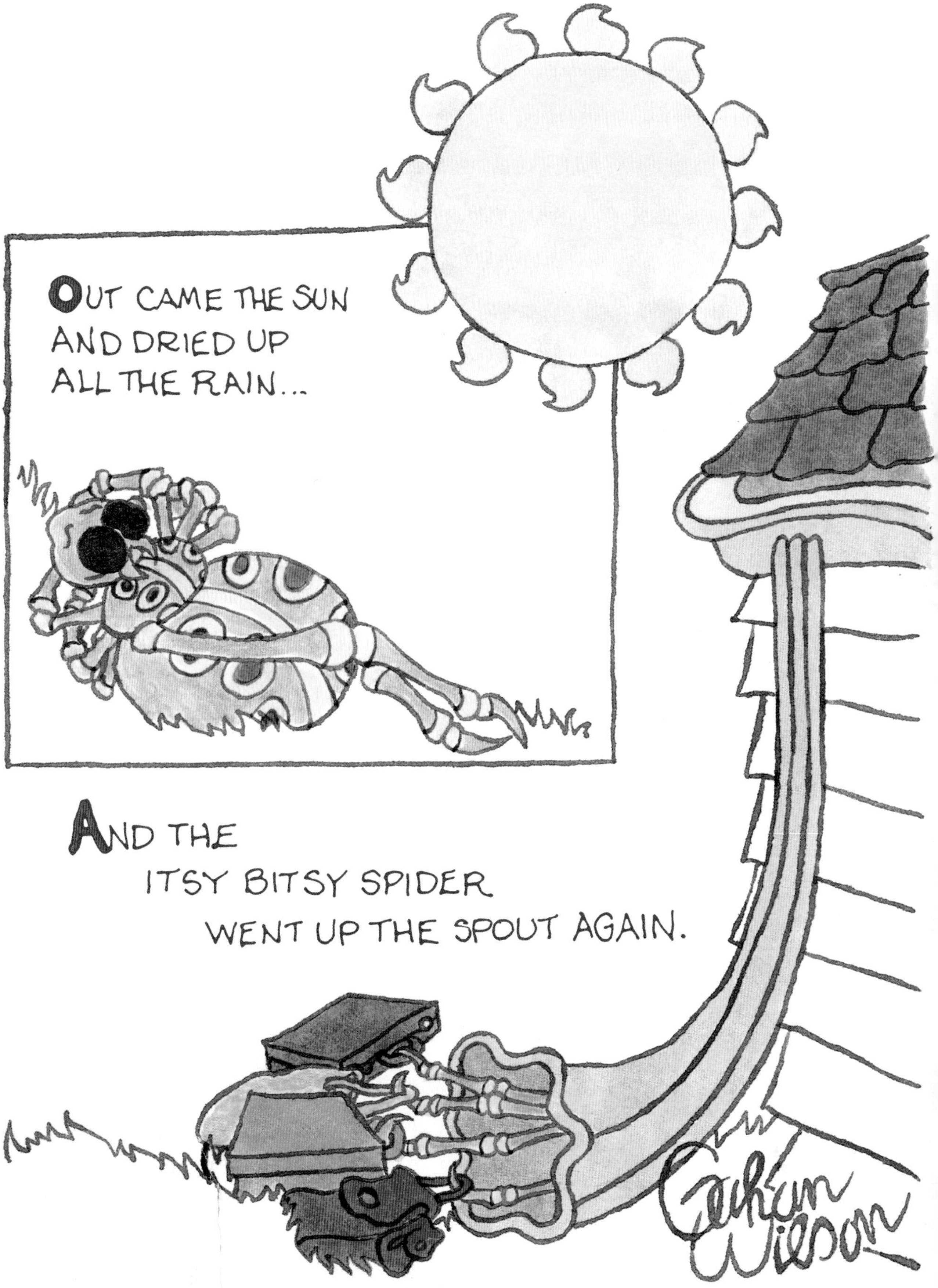
OUT CAME THE SUN
AND DRIED UP
ALL THE RAIN...
AND THE
ITSY BITSY SPIDER
WENT UP THE SPOUT AGAIN.
Gahan Wilson

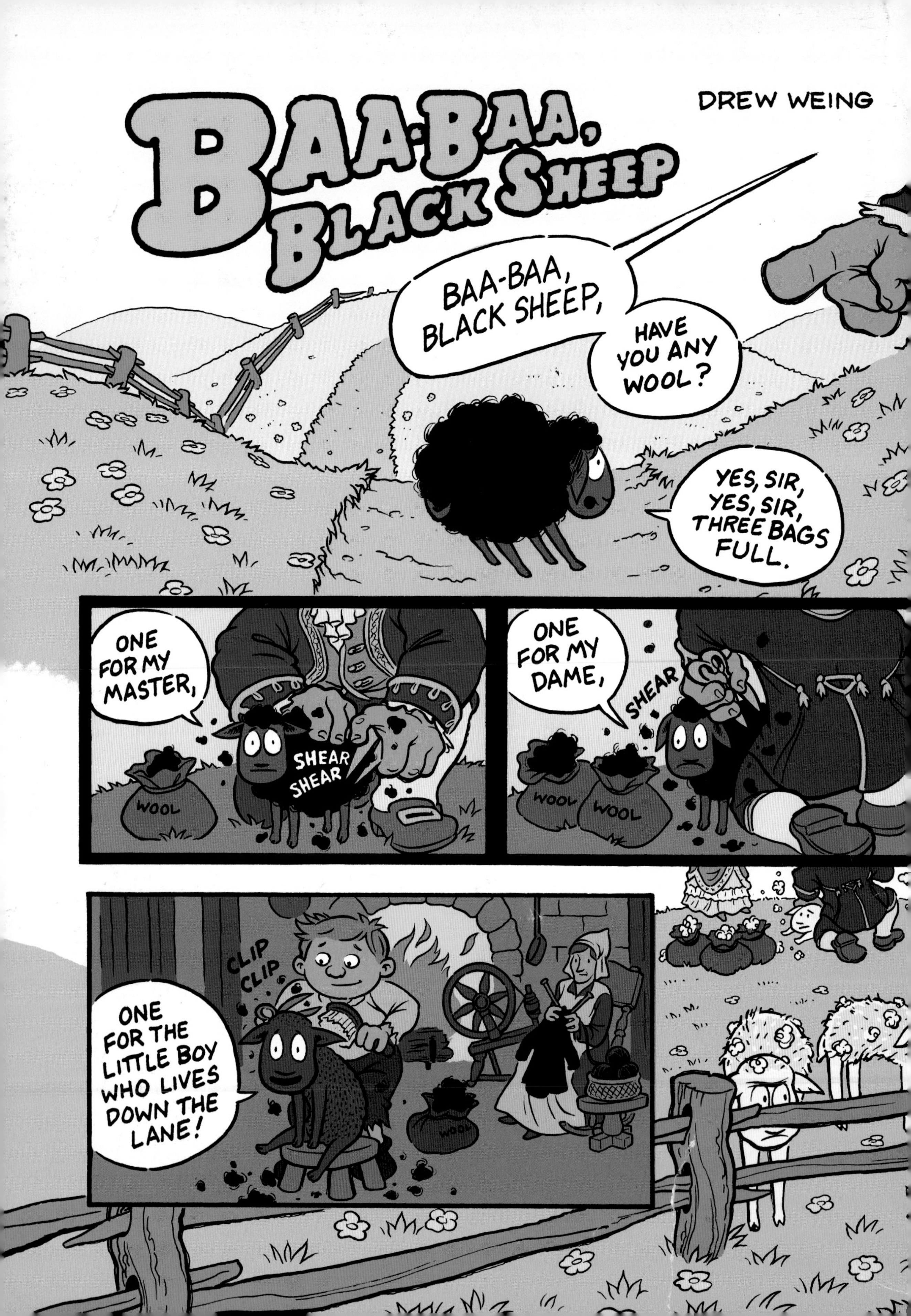
BAA-BAA, BLACK SHEEP
DREW WEING
BAA-BAA, BLACK SHEEP,
HAVE YOU ANY WOOL?
YES, SIR, YES, SIR, THREE BAGS FULL.
ONE FOR MY MASTER,
SHEAR SHEAR
WOOL
ONE FOR MY DAME,
SHEAR
WOOL WOOL
CLIP CLIP
ONE FOR THE LITTLE BOY WHO LIVES DOWN THE LANE!
WOOL

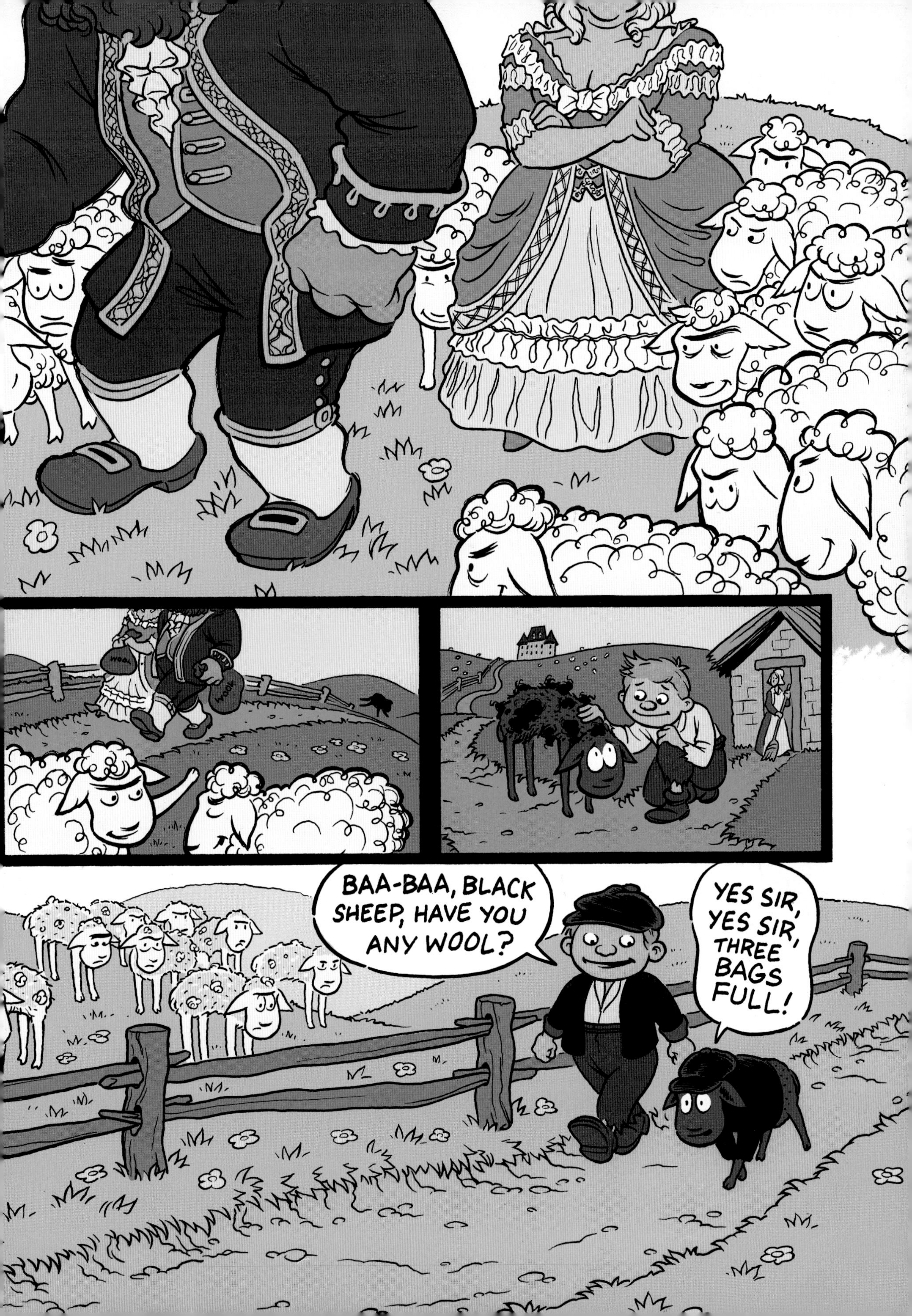
WOOL
WOOL
BAA-BAA, BLACK SHEEP, HAVE YOU ANY WOOL?
YES SIR, YES SIR, THREE BAGS FULL!

HECTOR PROTECTOR

STAN SAKAI and TOM LUTH

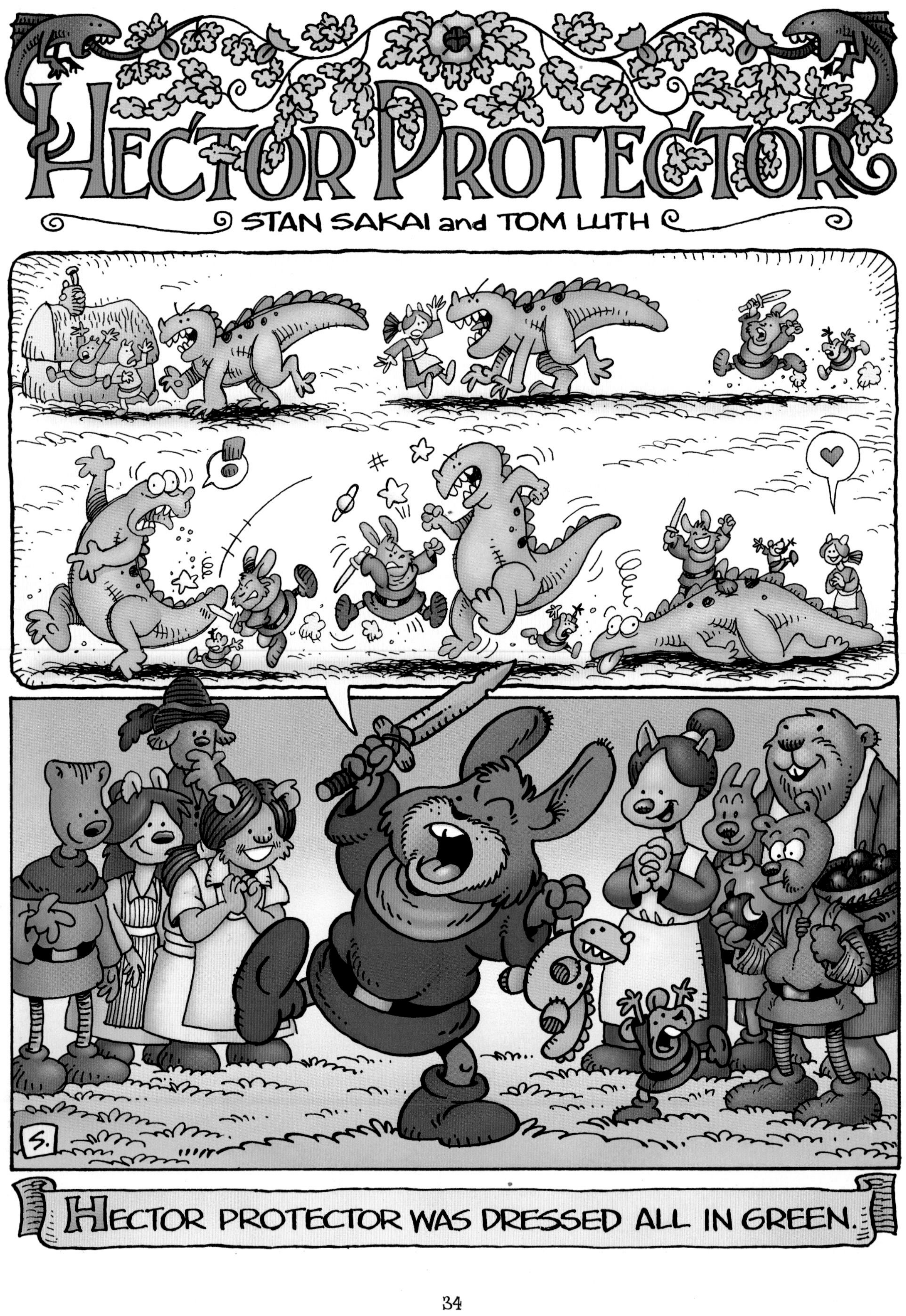
!
HECTOR PROTECTOR WAS DRESSED ALL IN GREEN.

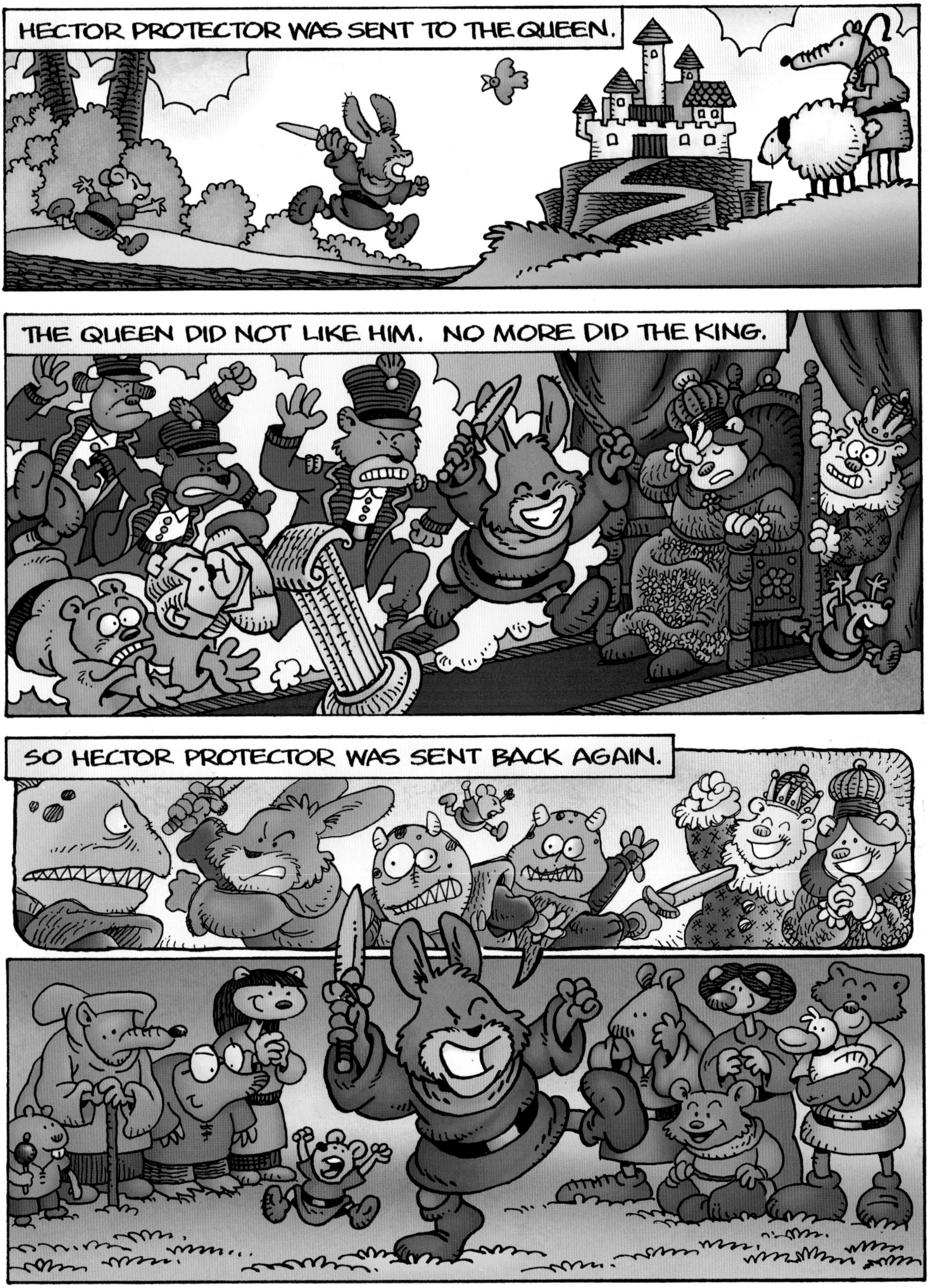
HECTOR PROTECTOR WAS SENT TO THE QUEEN.
THE QUEEN DID NOT LIKE HIM. NO MORE DID THE KING.
SO HECTOR PROTECTOR WAS SENT BACK AGAIN.

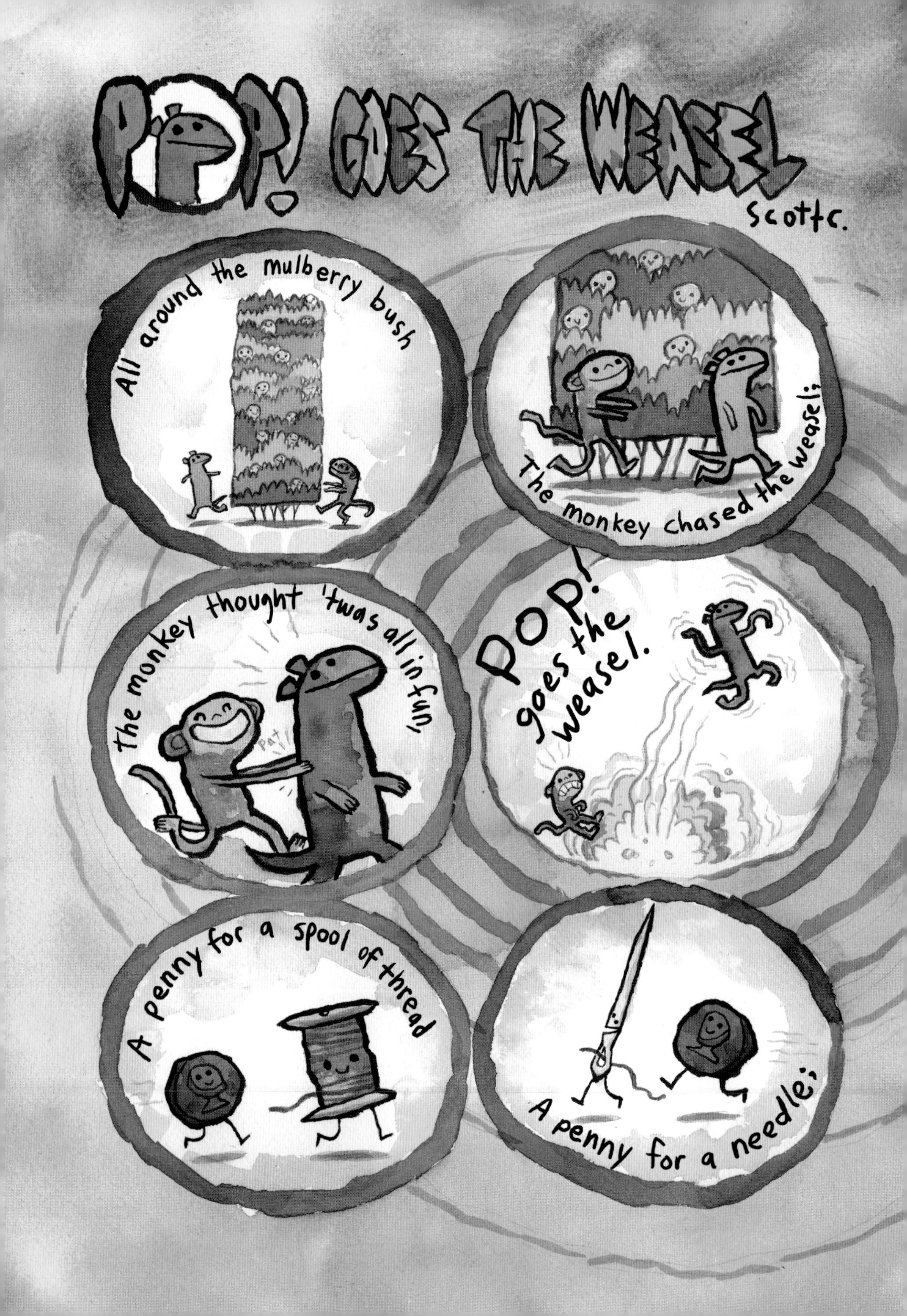
POP! GOES THE WEASEL
scott c.
All around the mulberry bush
The monkey chased the weasel;
The monkey thought 'twas all in fun,
Pat
POP! goes the weasel.
A penny for a spool of thread
A penny for a needle;

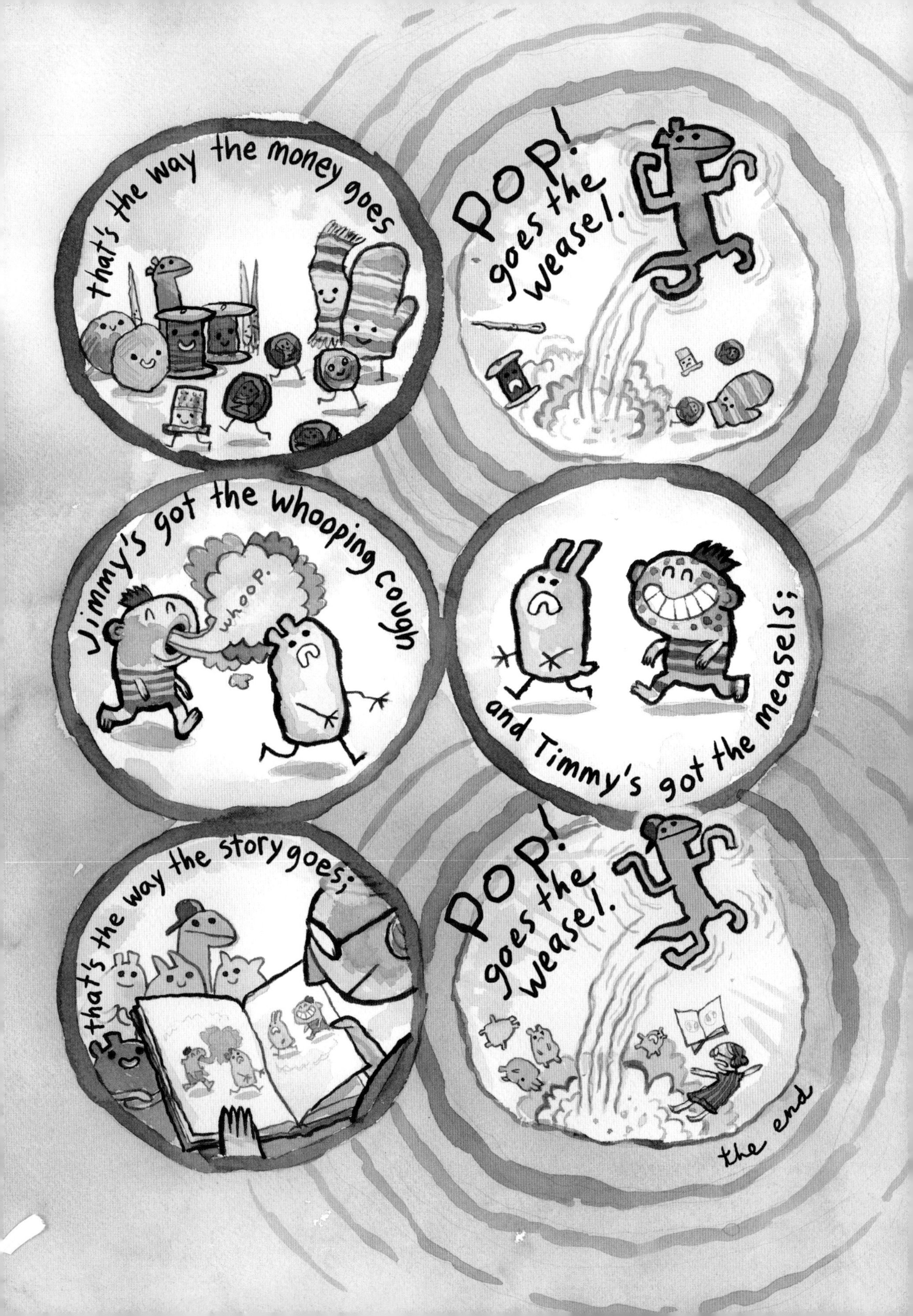
that's the way the money goes
POP! goes the weasel.
Jimmy's got the whooping cough
whoop.
and Timmy's got the measels;
that's the way the story goes;
POP! goes the weasel.
the end

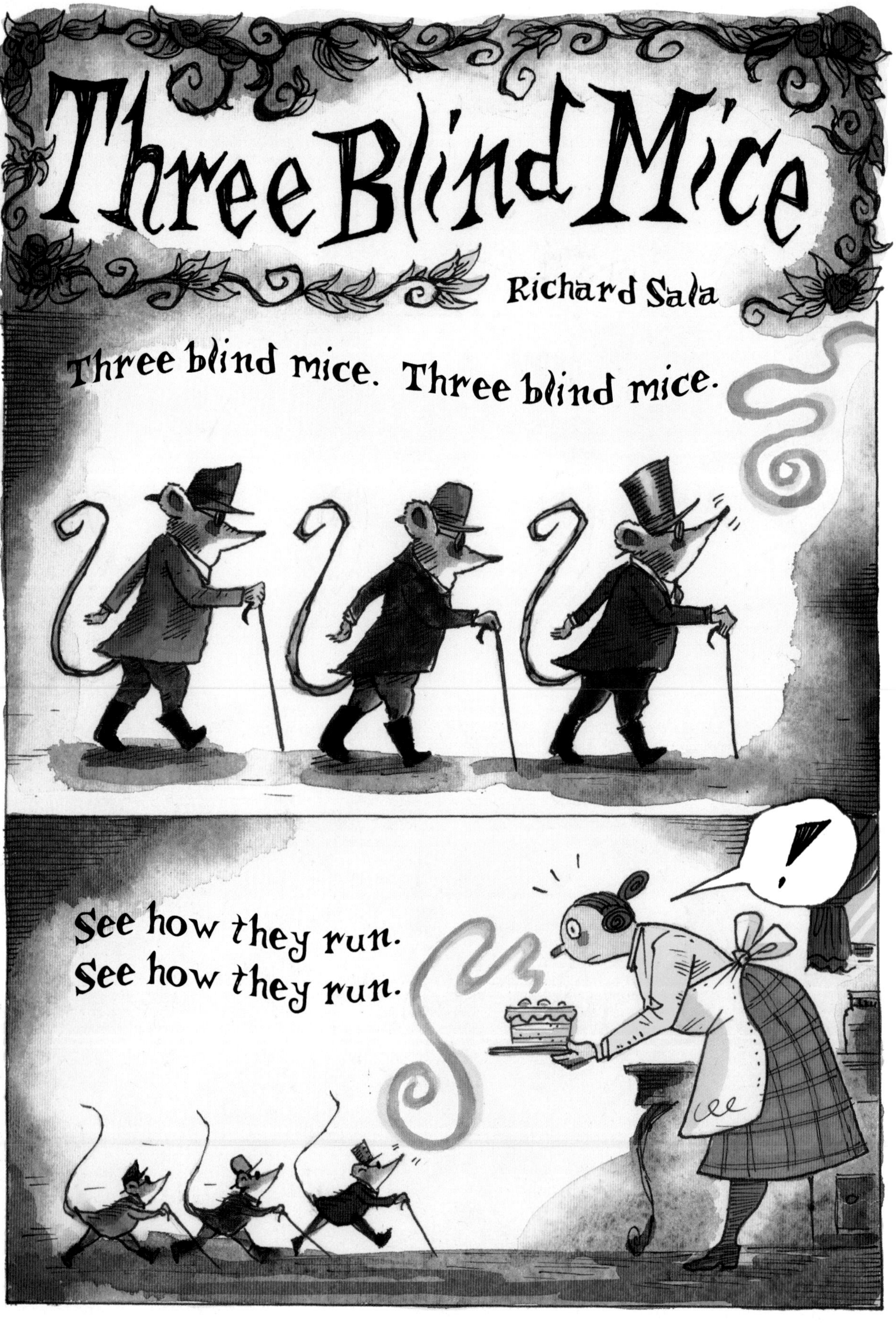
Three Blind Mice
Richard Sala
Three blind mice. Three blind mice.
See how they run.
See how they run.
!

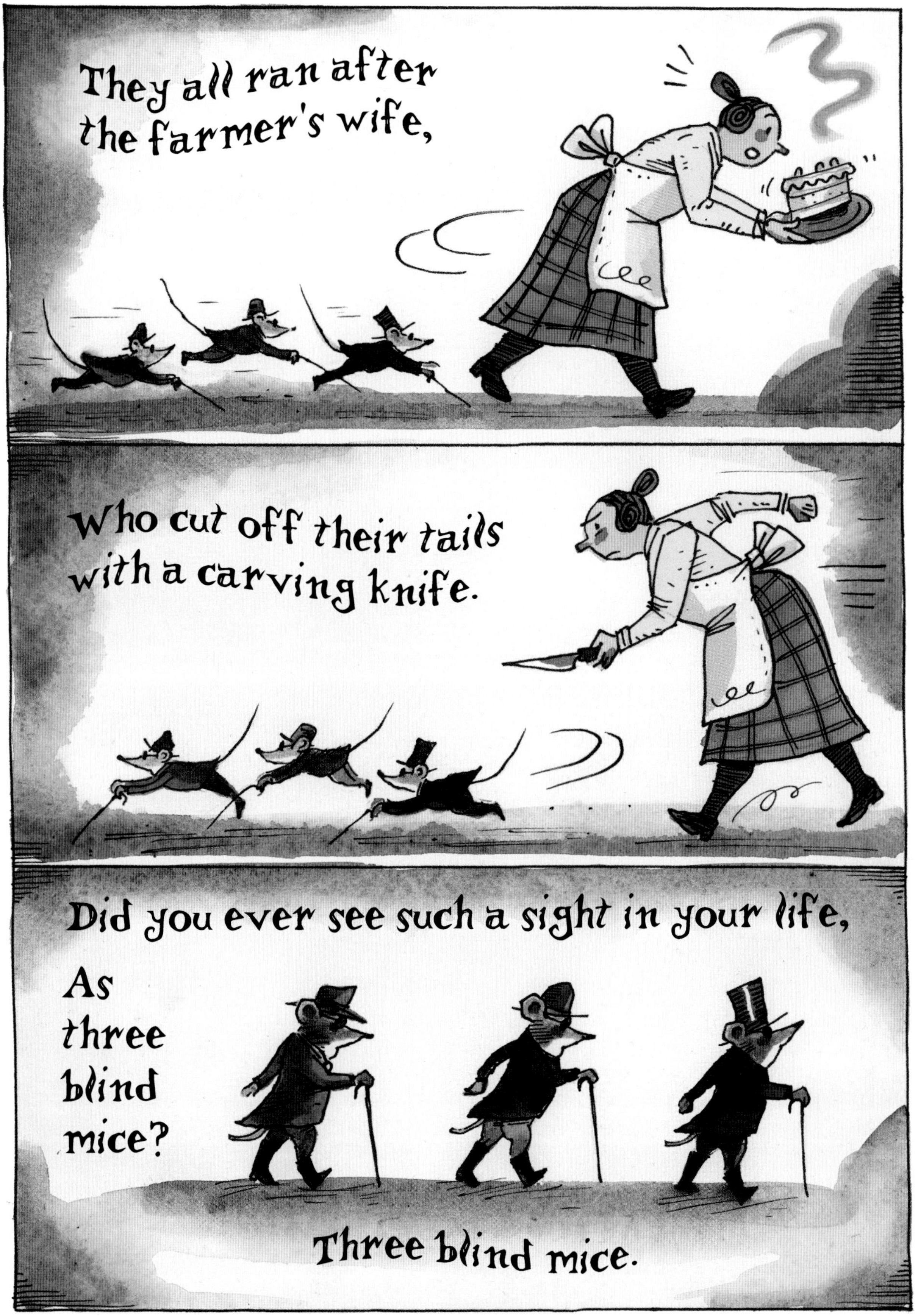
They all ran after
the farmer's wife,
Who cut off their tails
with a carving knife.
Did you ever see such a sight in your life,
As
three
blind
mice?
Three blind mice.

THERE WAS A

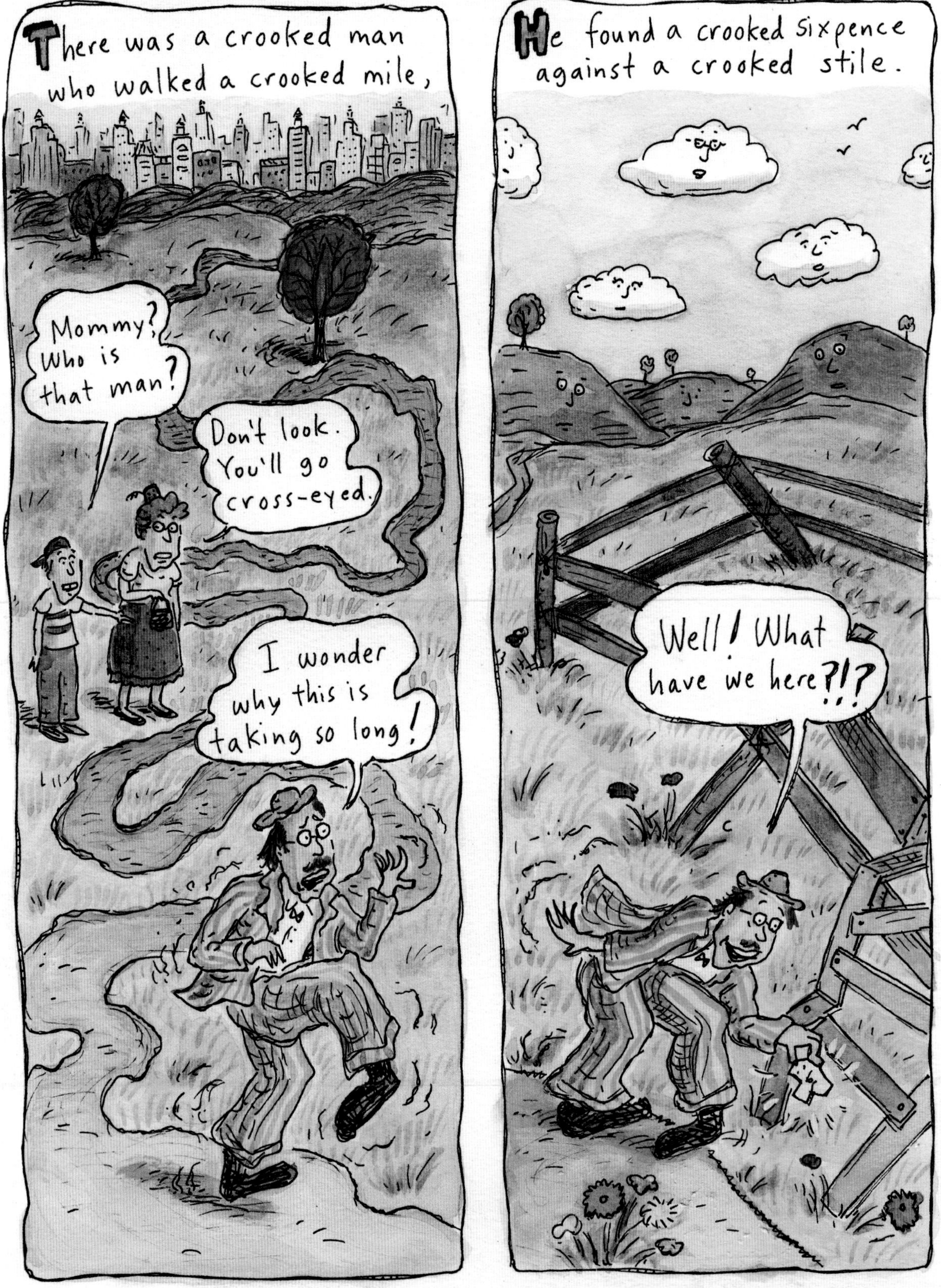
There was a crooked man who walked a crooked mile,
Mommy? Who is that man?
Don't look. You'll go cross-eyed.
I wonder why this is taking so long!
He found a crooked sixpence against a crooked stile.
Well! What have we here?!?

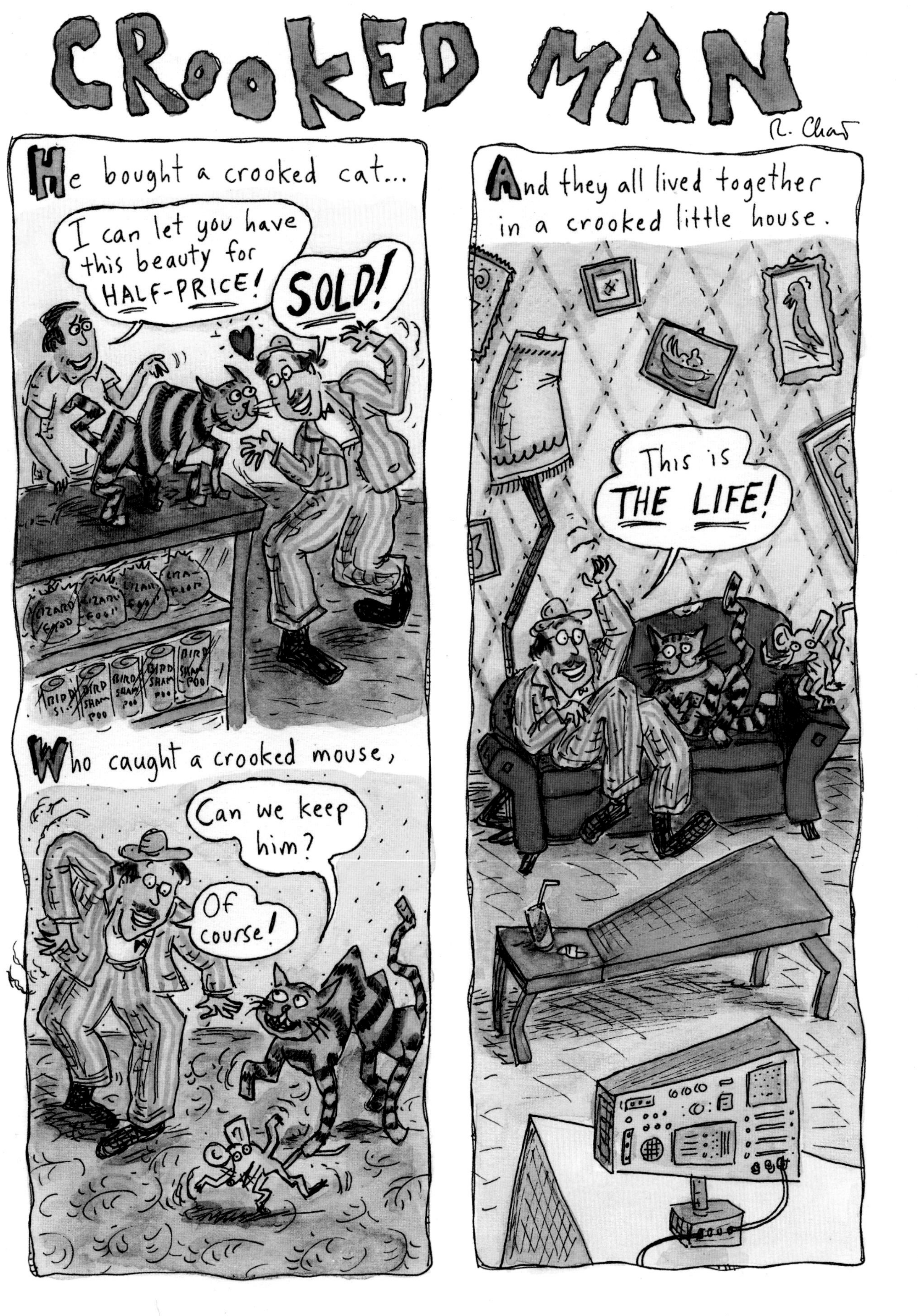
CROOKED MAN
R. Chast
He bought a crooked cat...
I can let you have this beauty for HALF-PRICE!
SOLD!
Who caught a crooked mouse,
Can we keep him?
Of course!
And they all lived together in a crooked little house.
This is THE LIFE!

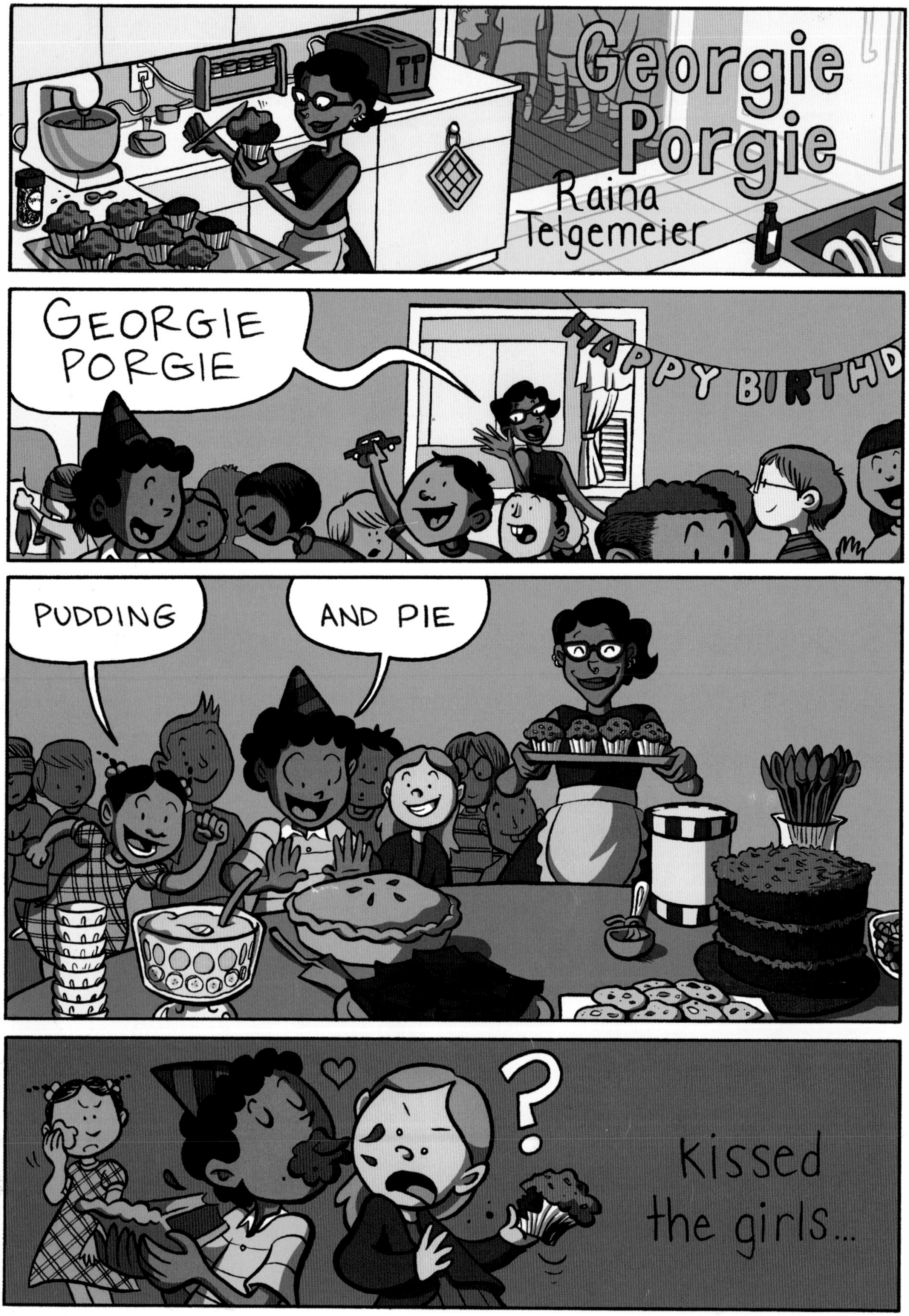
Georgie Porgie
Raina Telgemeier
HAPPY BIRTHD
GEORGIE PORGIE
PUDDING
AND PIE
?
kissed the girls...

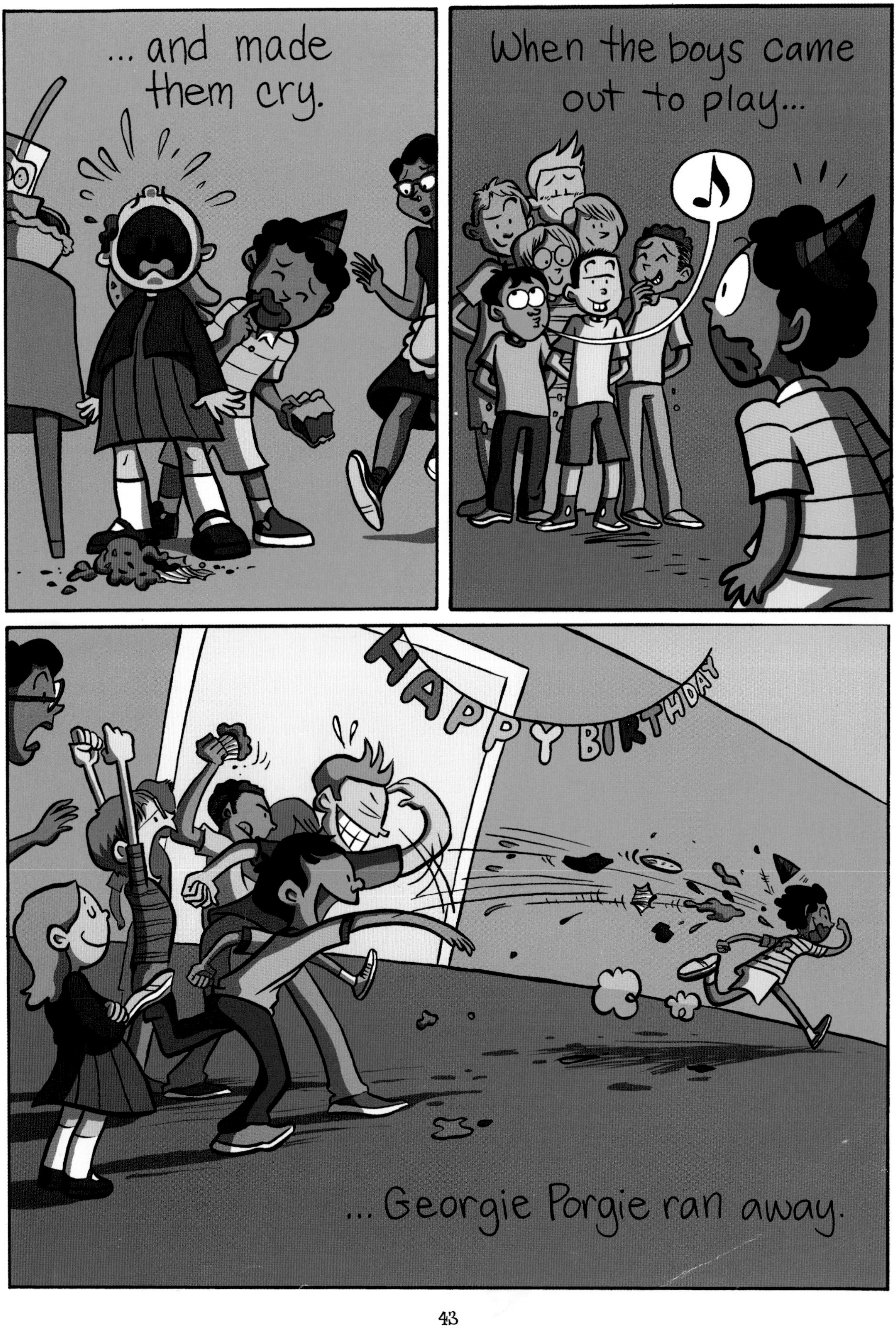
...and made them cry.
When the boys came out to play...
HAPPY BIRTHDAY
...Georgie Porgie ran away.

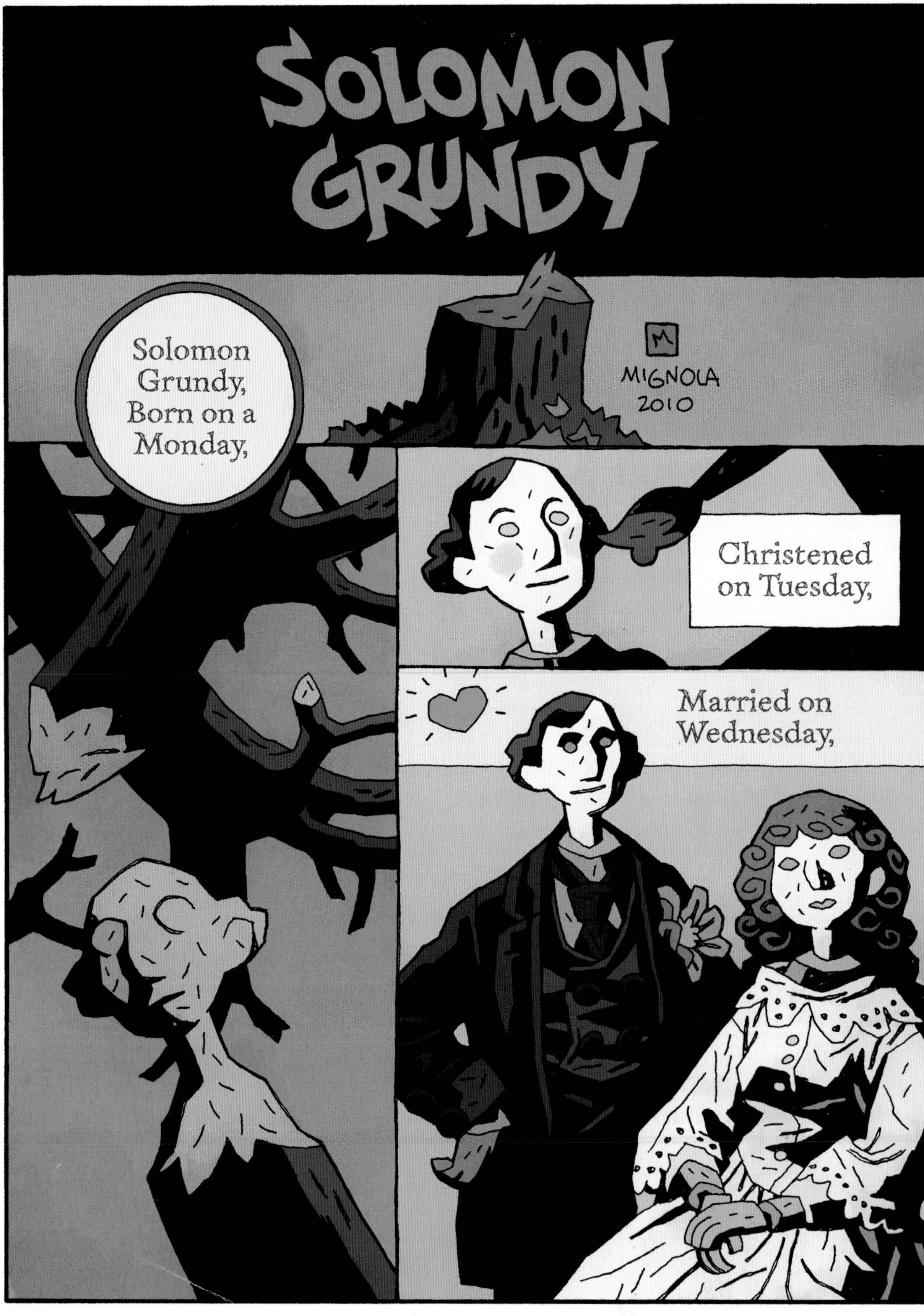
SOLOMON GRUNDY
Solomon Grundy, Born on a Monday,
MIGNOLA 2010
Christened on Tuesday,
Married on Wednesday,

Color by Dave Stewart

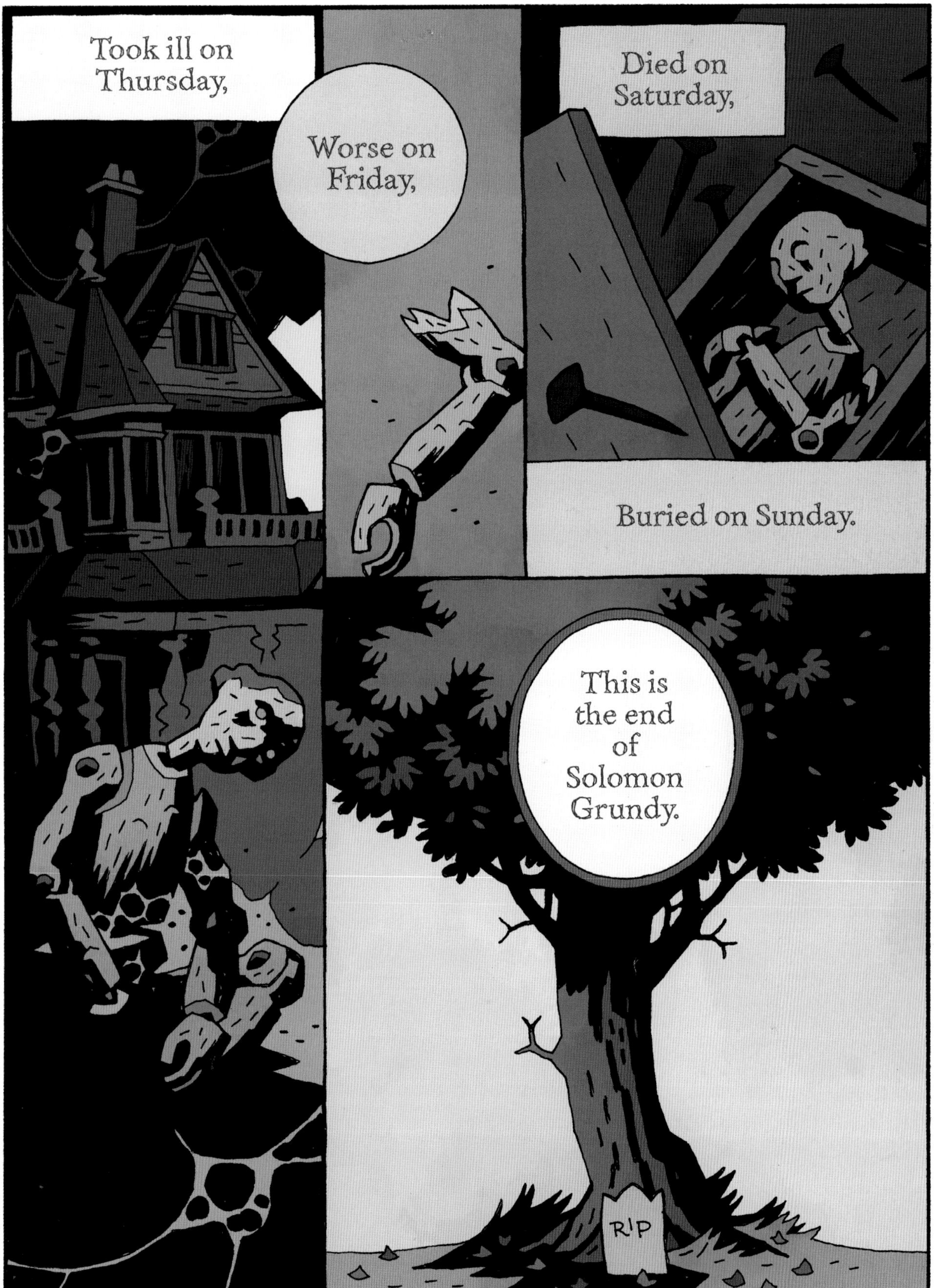
Took ill on Thursday,
Worse on Friday,
Died on Saturday,
Buried on Sunday.
This is the end of Solomon Grundy.
R.I.P

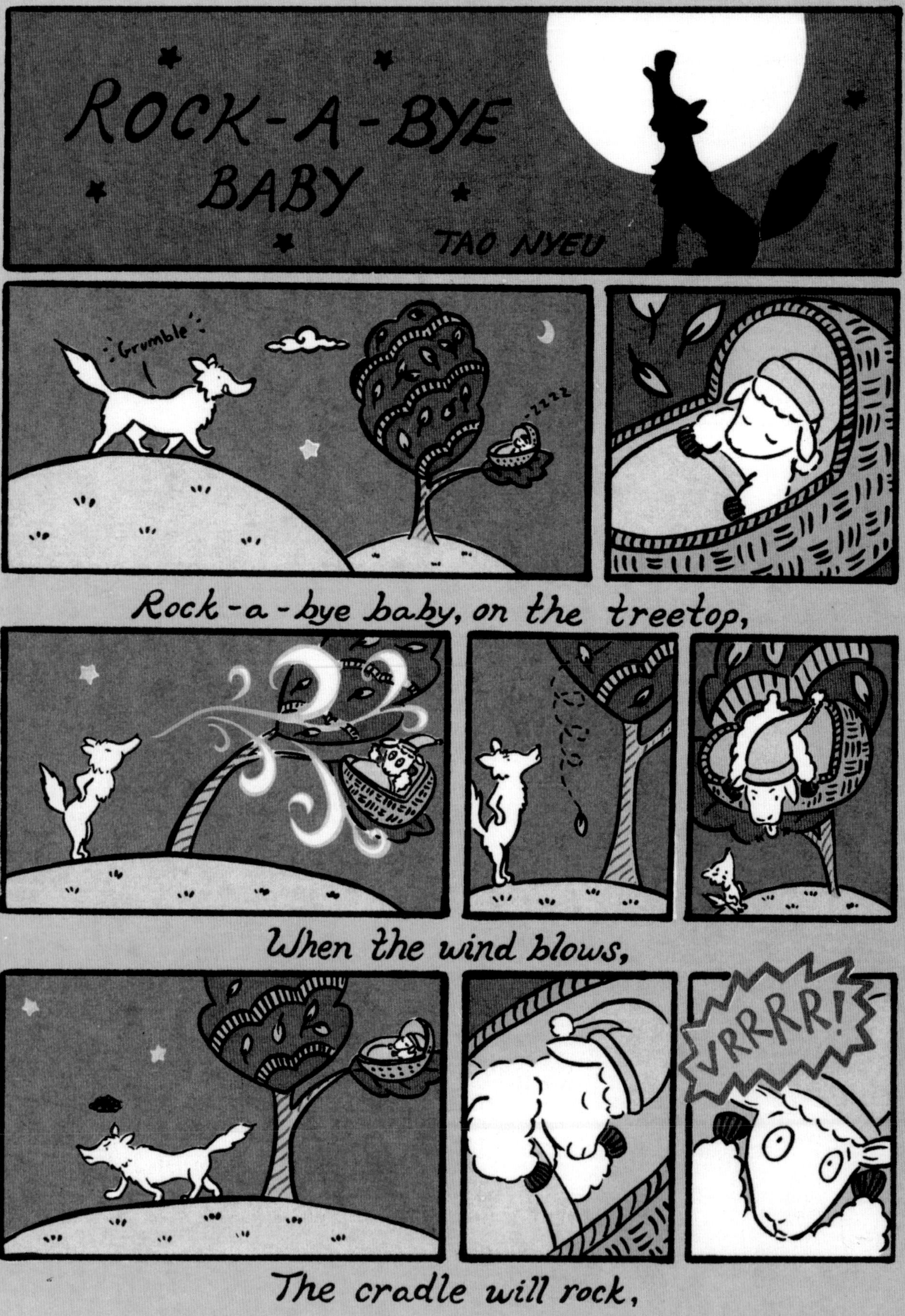
ROCK-A-BYE BABY
TAO NYEU
Grumble
-zzzz
Rock-a-bye baby, on the treetop,
When the wind blows,
VRRRR!
The cradle will rock,

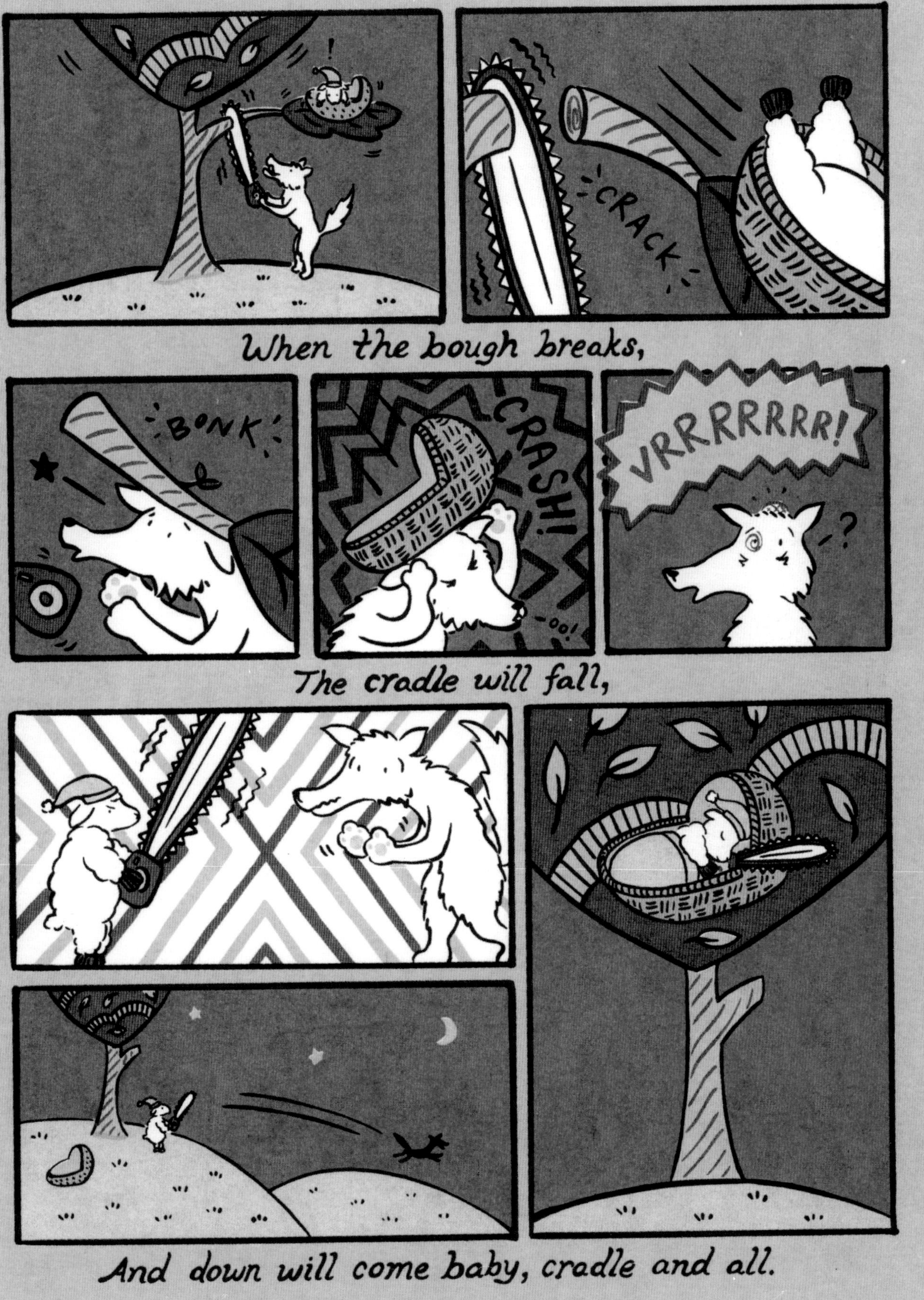

!
CRACK
When the bough breaks,
BONK
CRASH!
-oo!
VRRRRRRR!
?
The cradle will fall,
And down will come baby, cradle and all.

Tweedledum & Tweedledee

matthew forsythe

Tweedledum and Tweedledee
Agreed to have a battle.

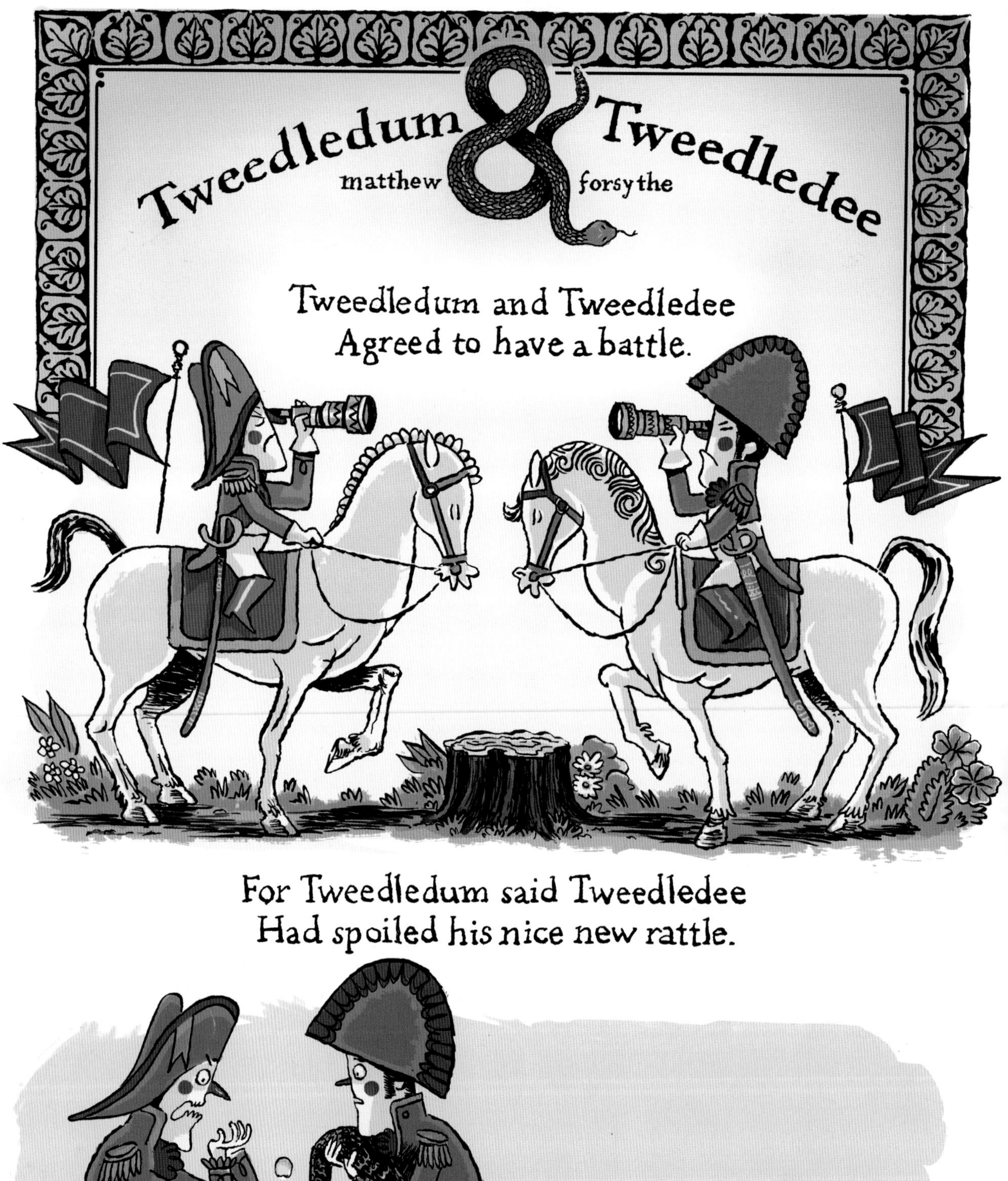

For Tweedledum said Tweedledee
Had spoiled his nice new rattle.

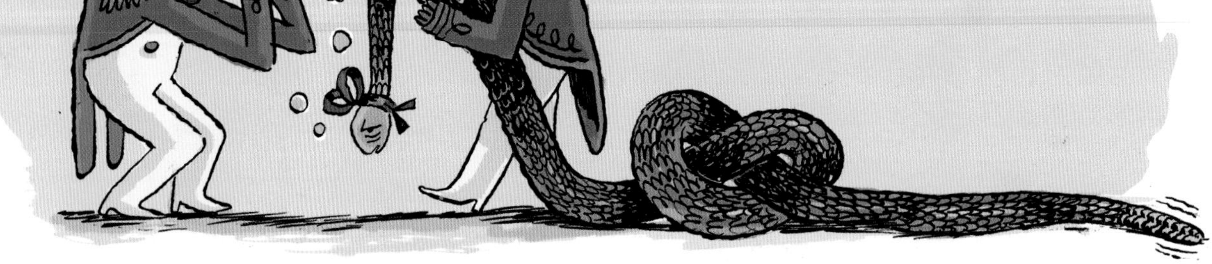

Just then flew by a monstrous crow,
As big as a tar barrel.

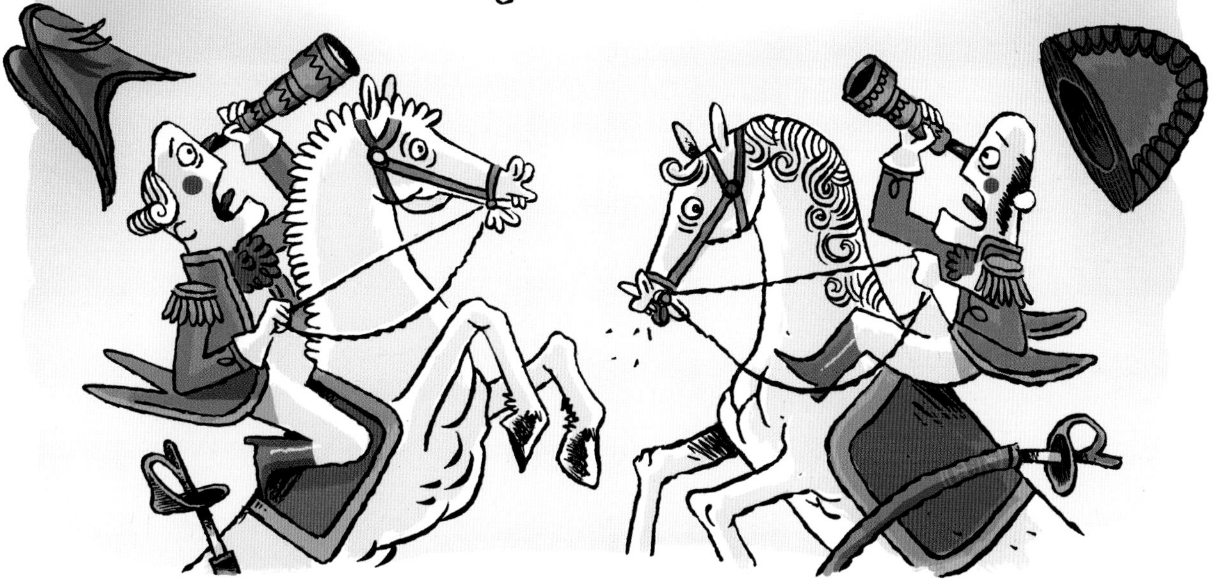

Which frightened both the heroes so,
They quite forgot their quarrel.

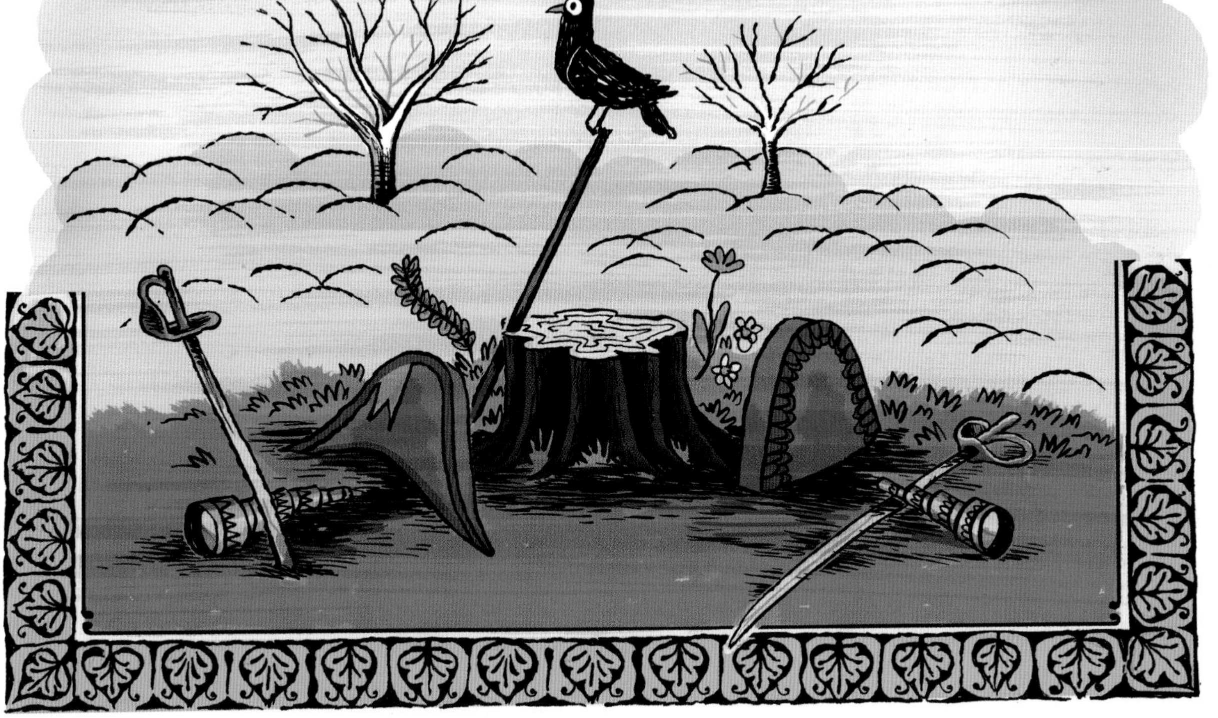

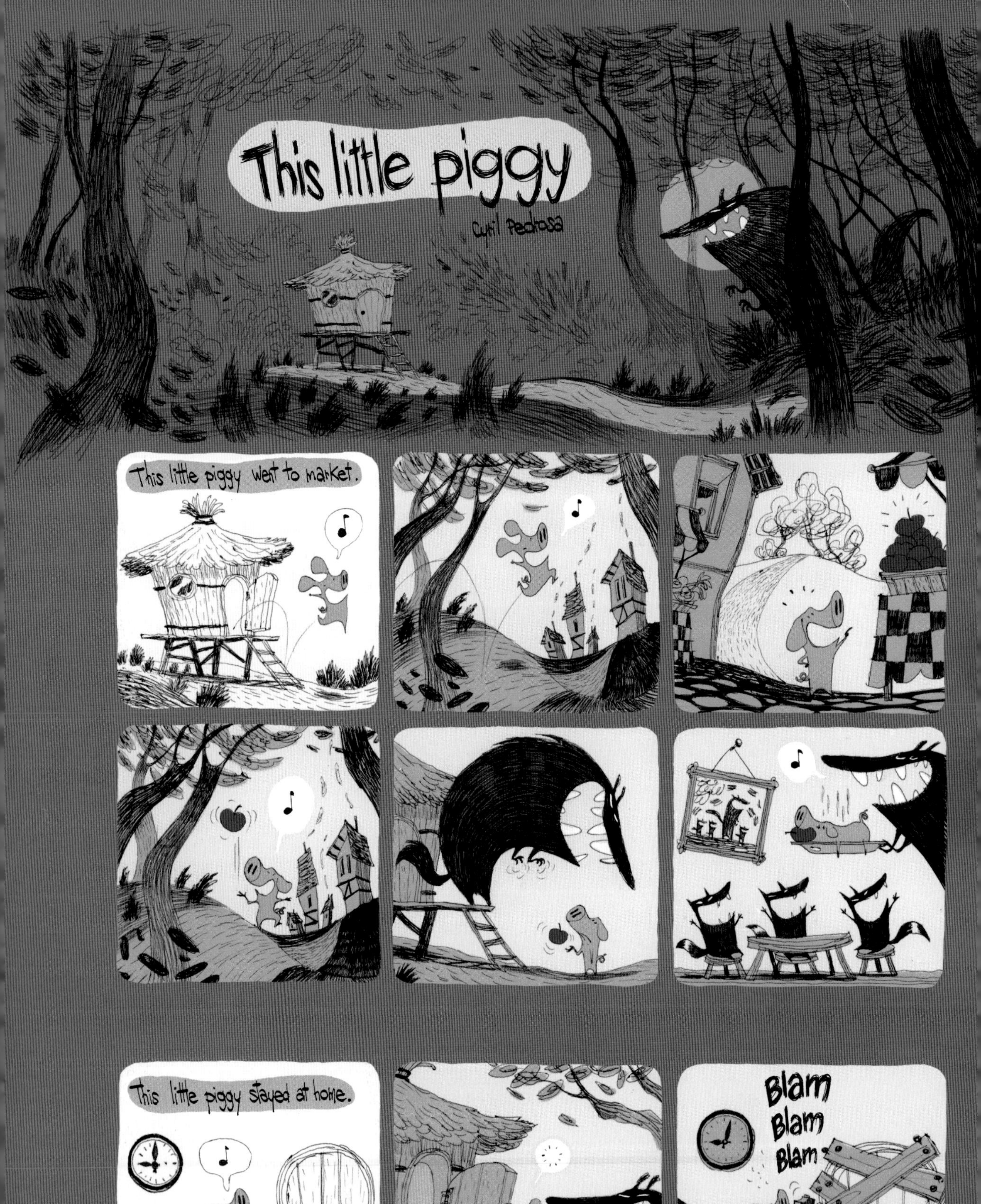
This little piggy
Cyril Pedrosa
This little piggy went to market.
This little piggy stayed at home.
Blam
Blam
Blam

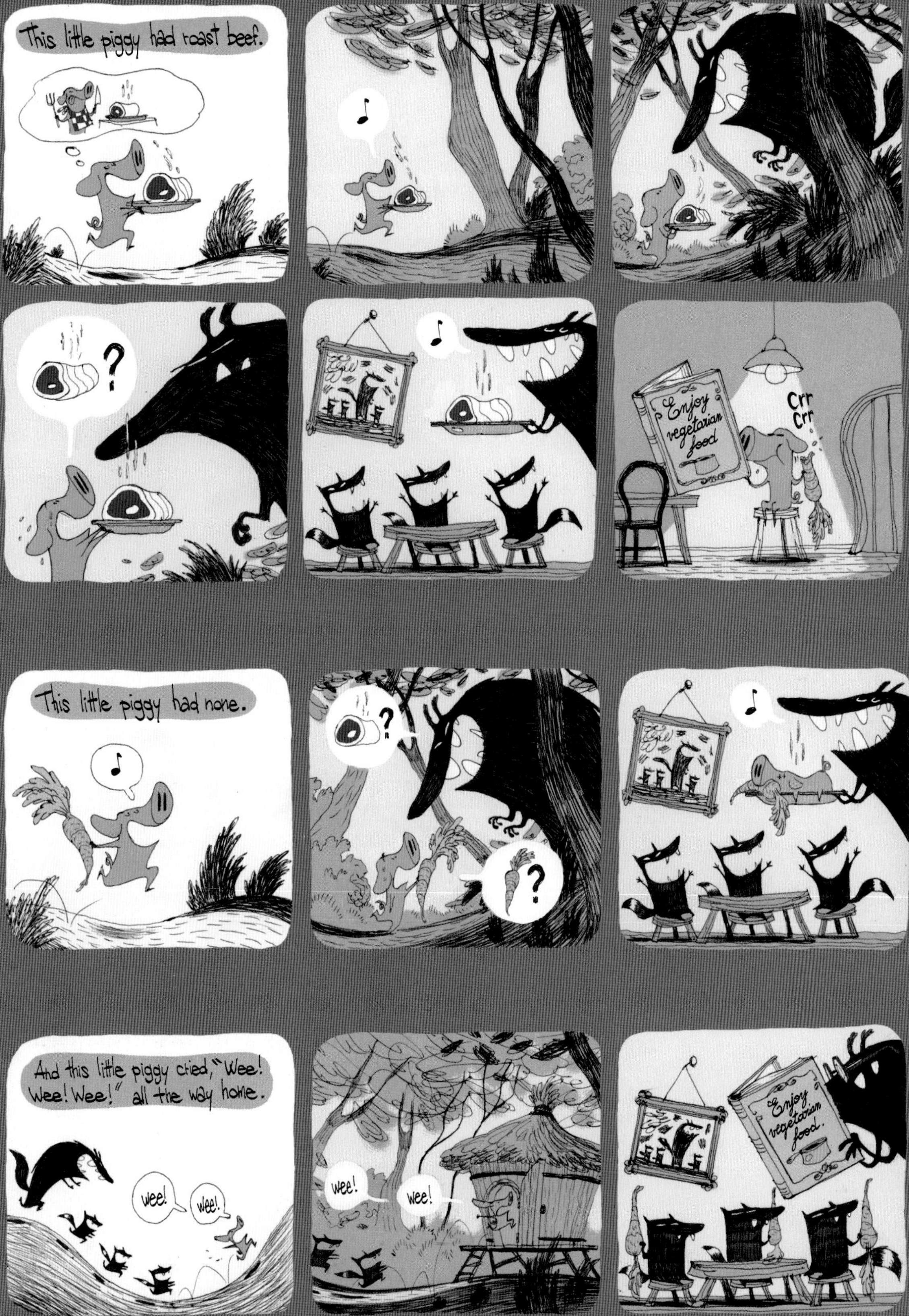

This little piggy had roast beef.
?
Enjoy vegetarian food
Crr
Crr
This little piggy had none.
?
?
And this little piggy cried, "Wee! Wee! Wee!" all the way home.
Wee!
Wee!
Wee!
Wee!
Enjoy vegetarian food.

Mary had a little lamb

by Sara Varon

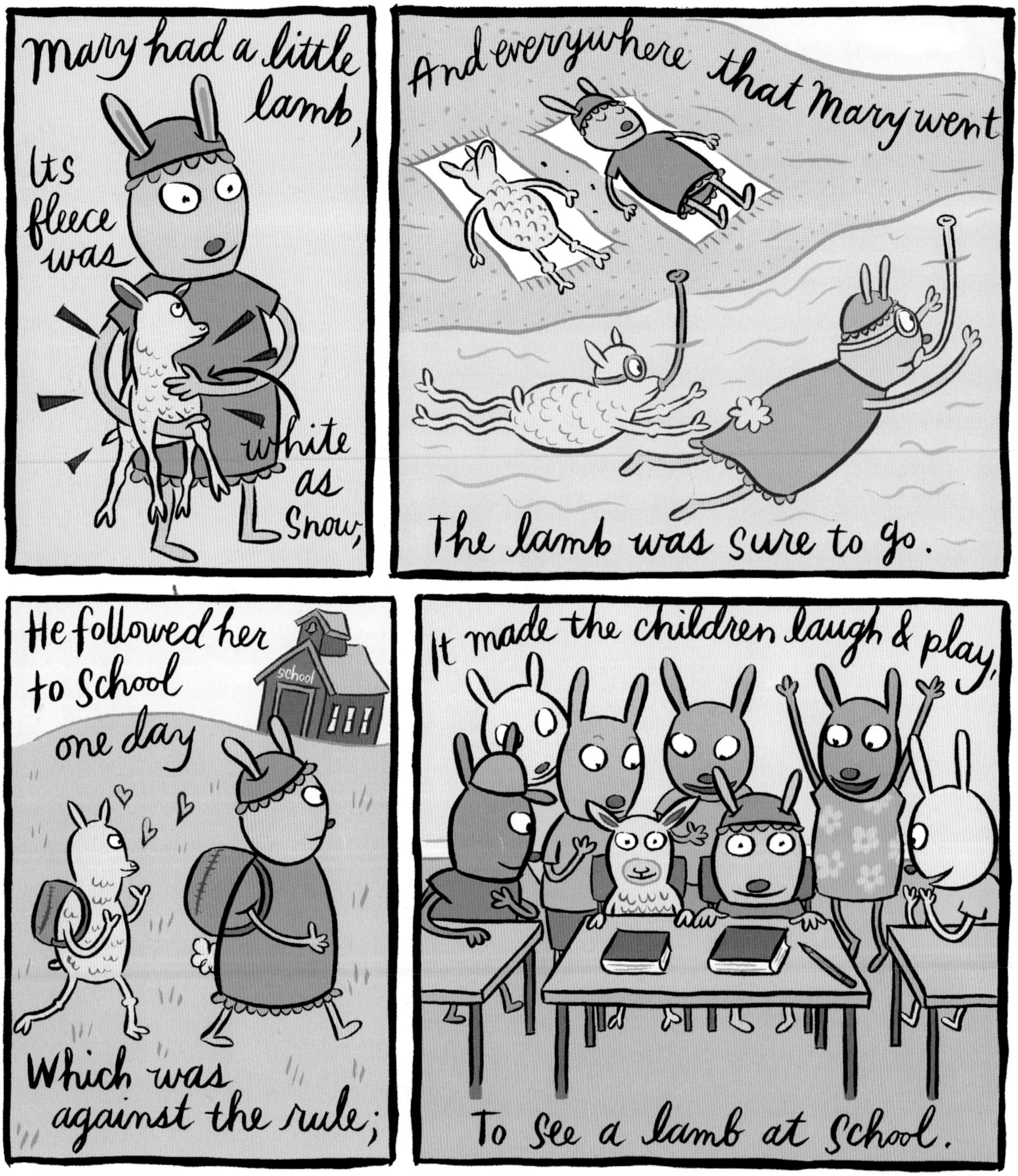
Mary had a little lamb,
Its fleece was white as snow;
And everywhere that Mary went
The lamb was sure to go.
He followed her to school one day
school
Which was against the rule;
It made the children laugh & play,
To see a lamb at school.

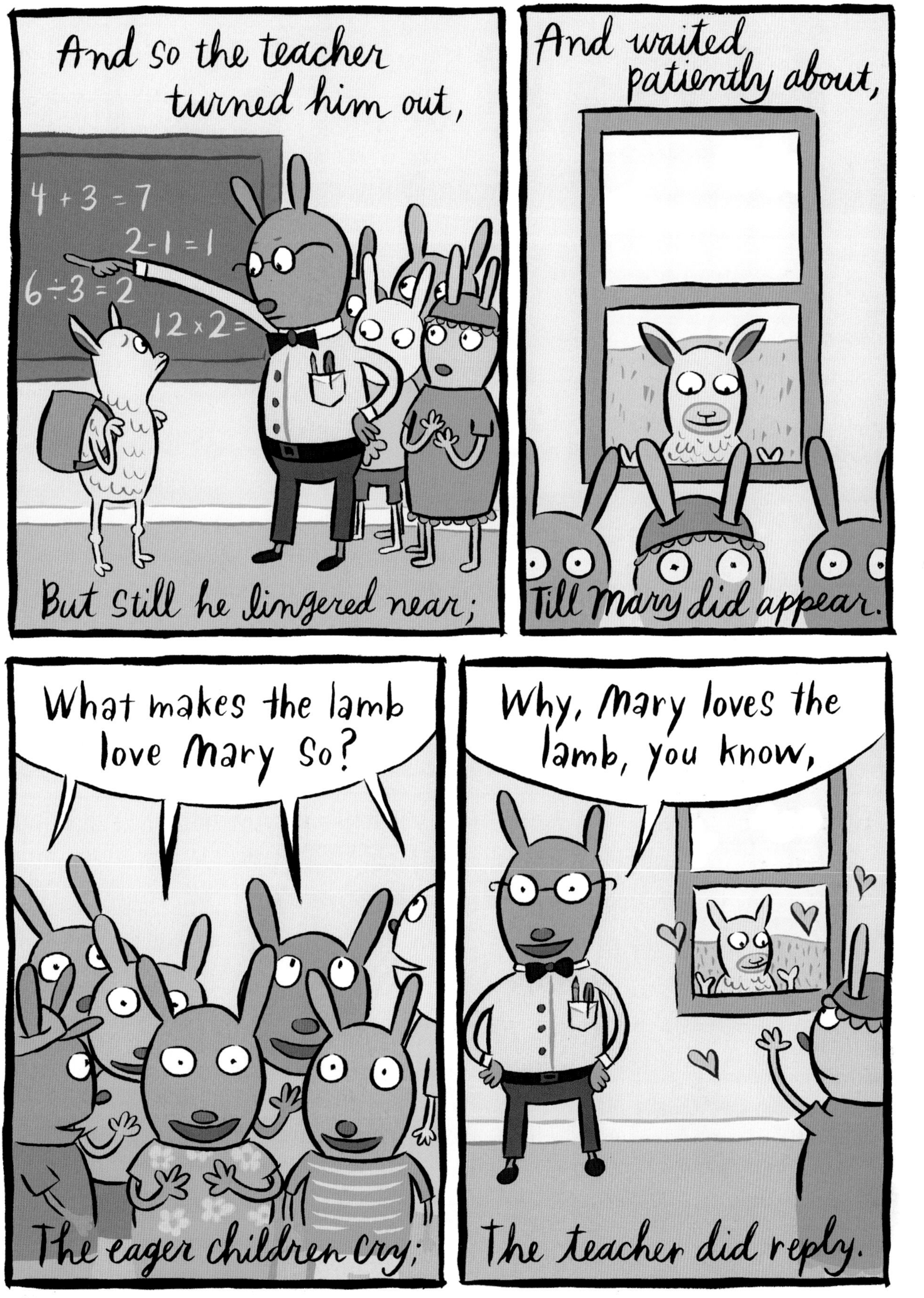
And so the teacher turned him out,
4 + 3 = 7
2-1 = 1
6 ÷ 3 = 2
12 × 2 =
But still he lingered near;
And waited patiently about,
Till Mary did appear.
What makes the lamb love Mary so?
The eager children cry;
Why, Mary loves the lamb, you know,
The teacher did reply.

"Croak," said the Toad

LAURA PARK

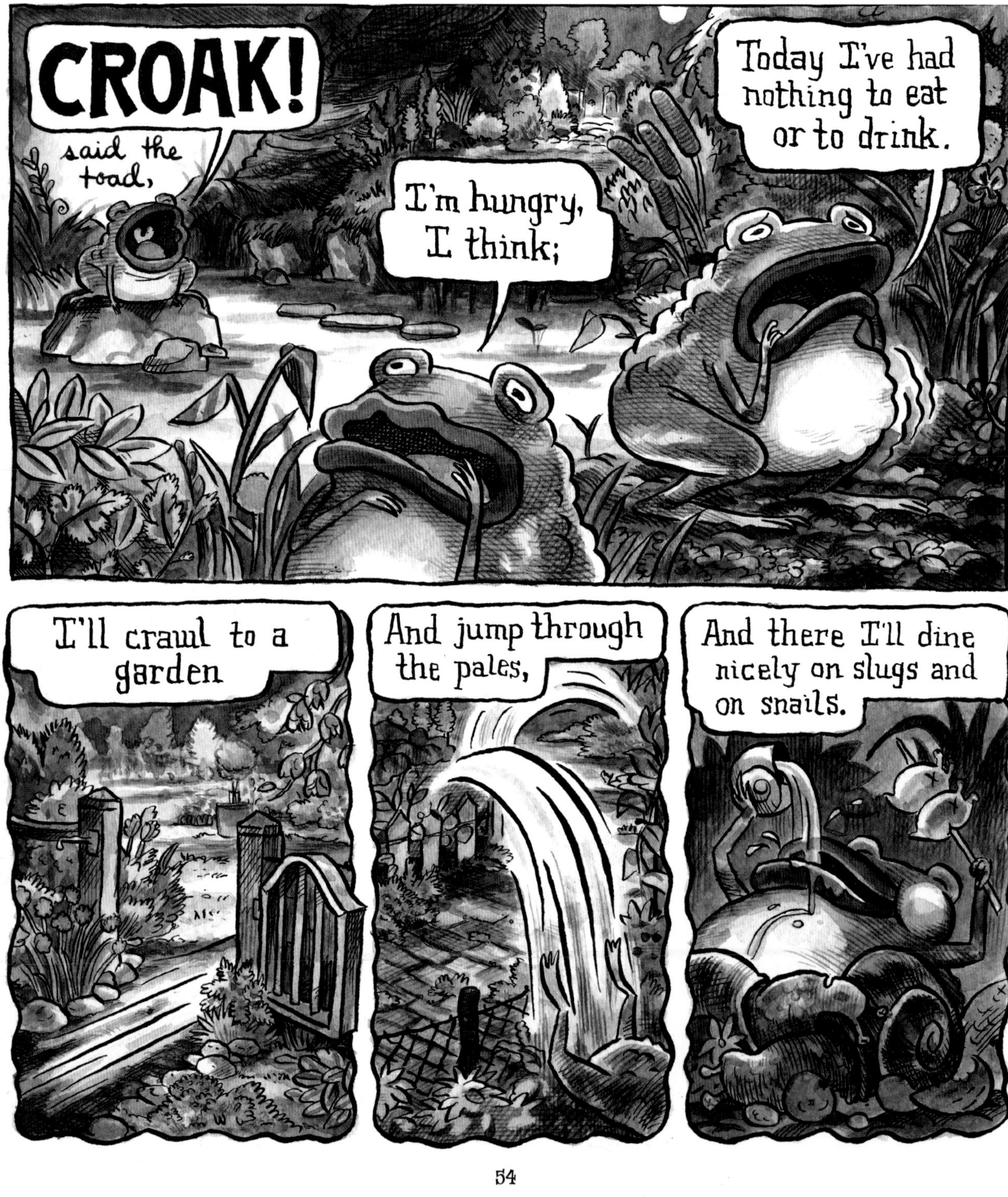
CROAK!
said the toad,
I'm hungry, I think;
Today I've had nothing to eat or to drink.
I'll crawl to a garden
And jump through the pales,
And there I'll dine nicely on slugs and on snails.

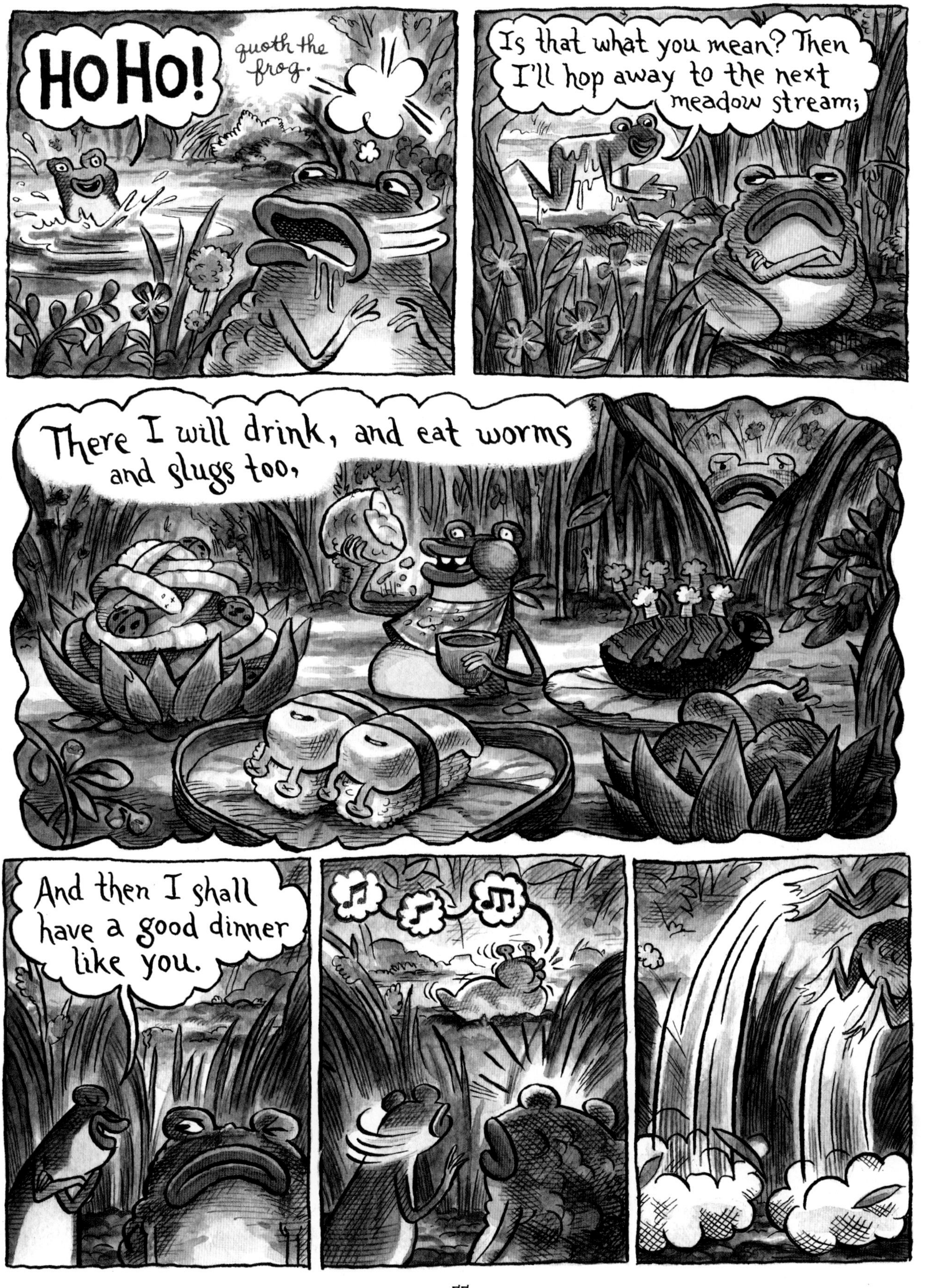
HO HO!
quoth the frog.
Is that what you mean? Then I'll hop away to the next meadow stream;
There I will drink, and eat worms and slugs too,
And then I shall have a good dinner like you.

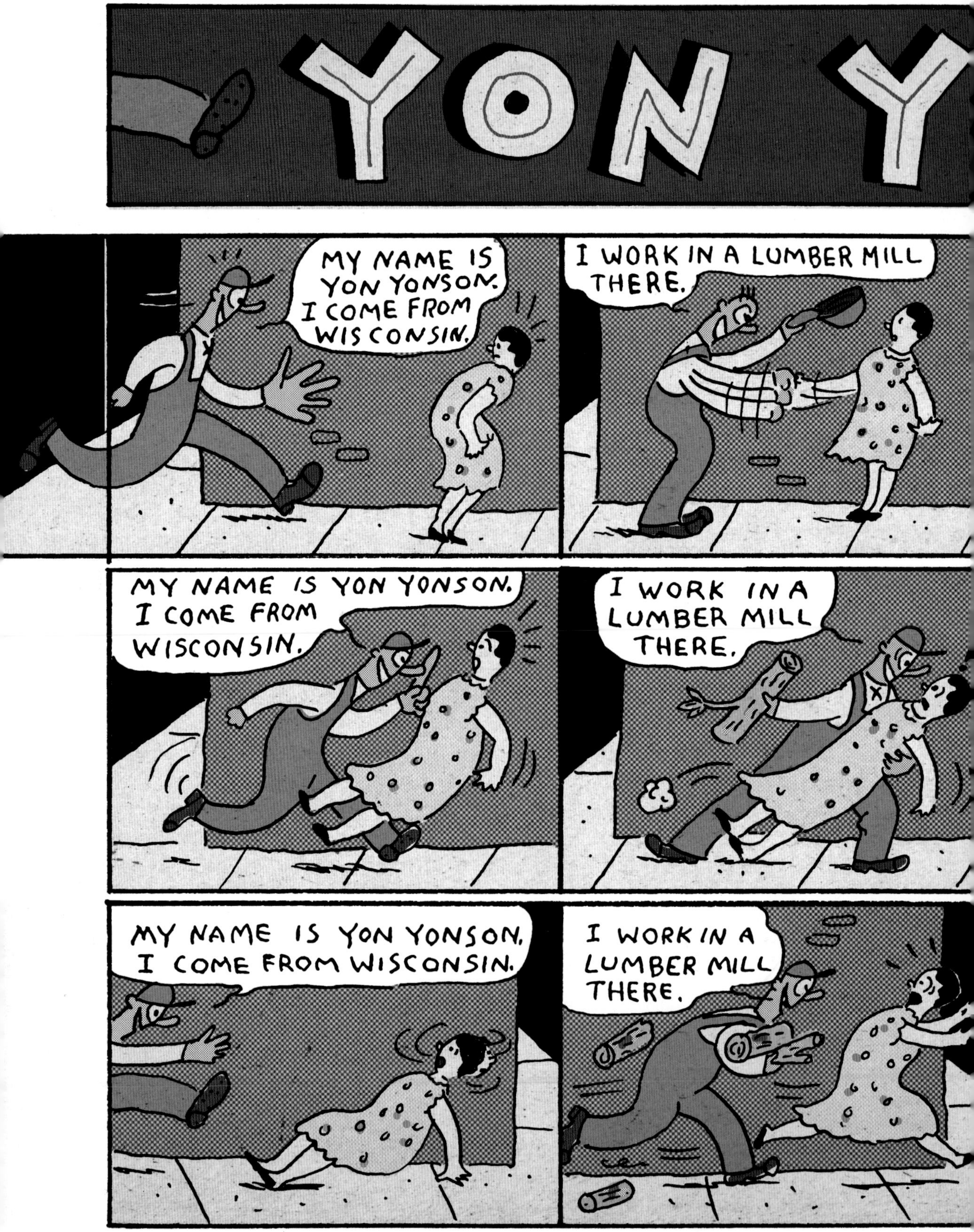
YON Y
MY NAME IS YON YONSON. I COME FROM WISCONSIN.
I WORK IN A LUMBER MILL THERE.
MY NAME IS YON YONSON. I COME FROM WISCONSIN.
I WORK IN A LUMBER MILL THERE.
MY NAME IS YON YONSON. I COME FROM WISCONSIN.
I WORK IN A LUMBER MILL THERE.

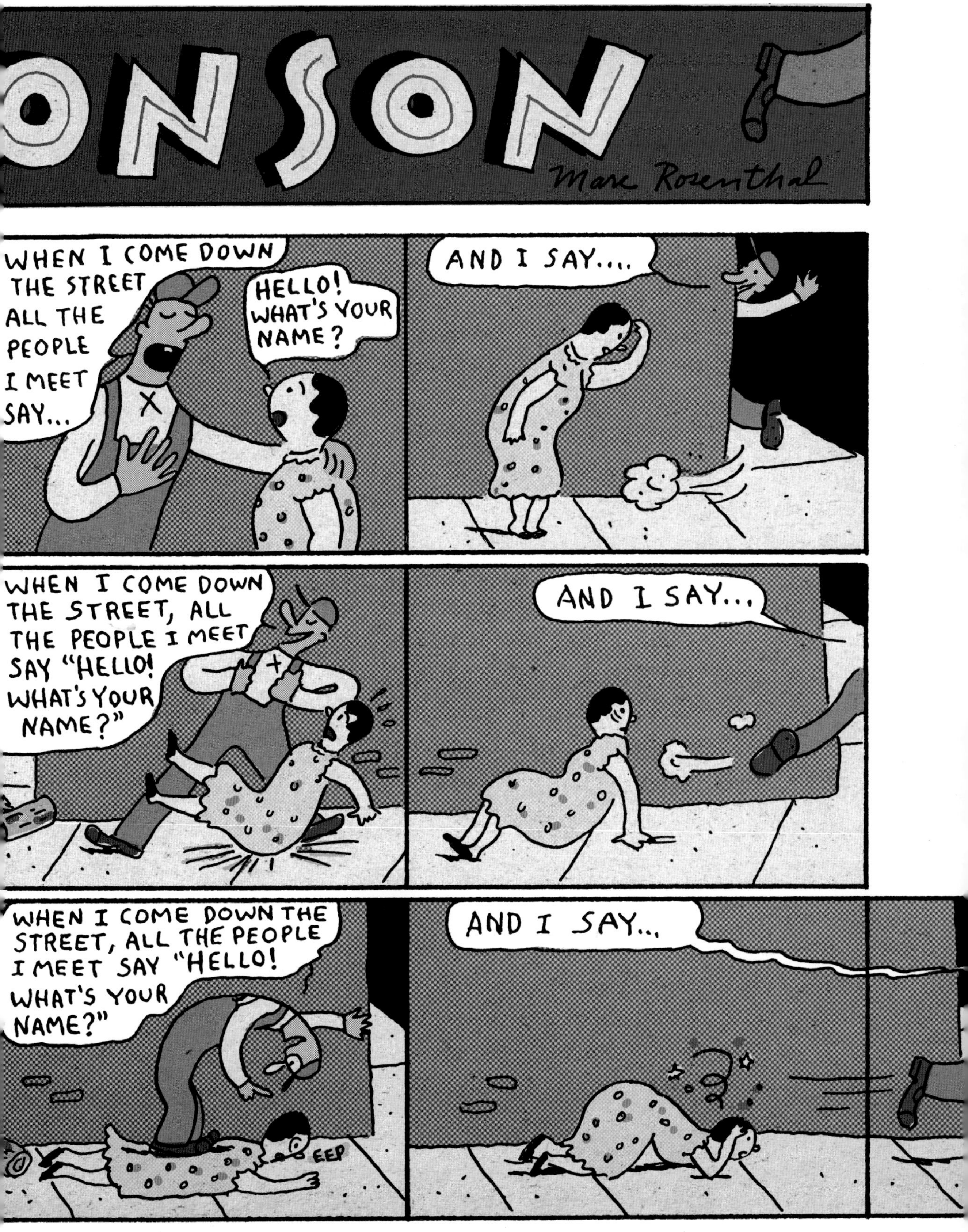
ONSON
Marc Rosenthal
WHEN I COME DOWN THE STREET ALL THE PEOPLE I MEET SAY...
HELLO! WHAT'S YOUR NAME?
AND I SAY....
WHEN I COME DOWN THE STREET, ALL THE PEOPLE I MEET SAY "HELLO! WHAT'S YOUR NAME?"
AND I SAY...
WHEN I COME DOWN THE STREET, ALL THE PEOPLE I MEET SAY "HELLO! WHAT'S YOUR NAME?"
EEP
AND I SAY...

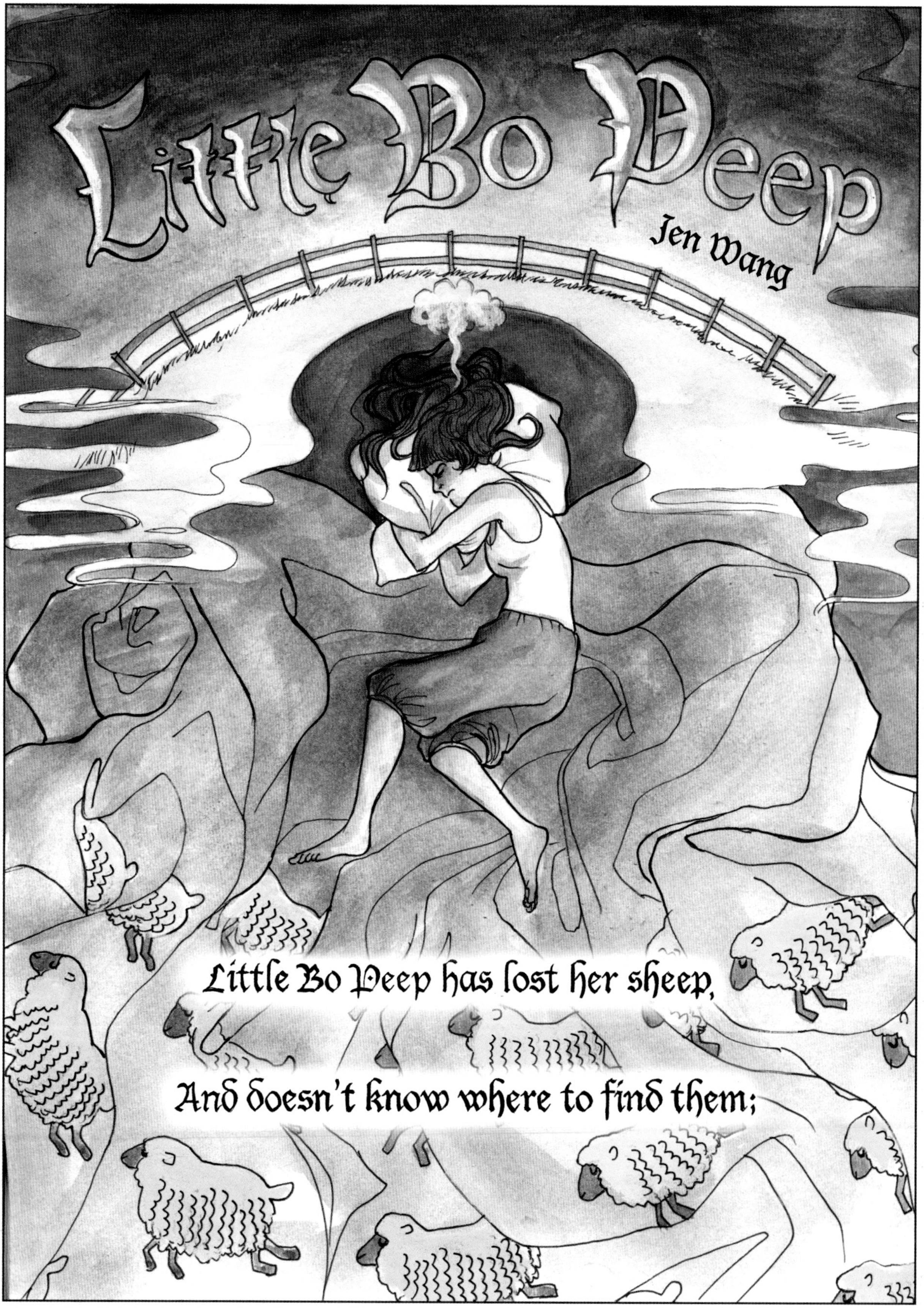
Little Bo Peep
Jen Wang
Little Bo Peep has lost her sheep,
And doesn't know where to find them;

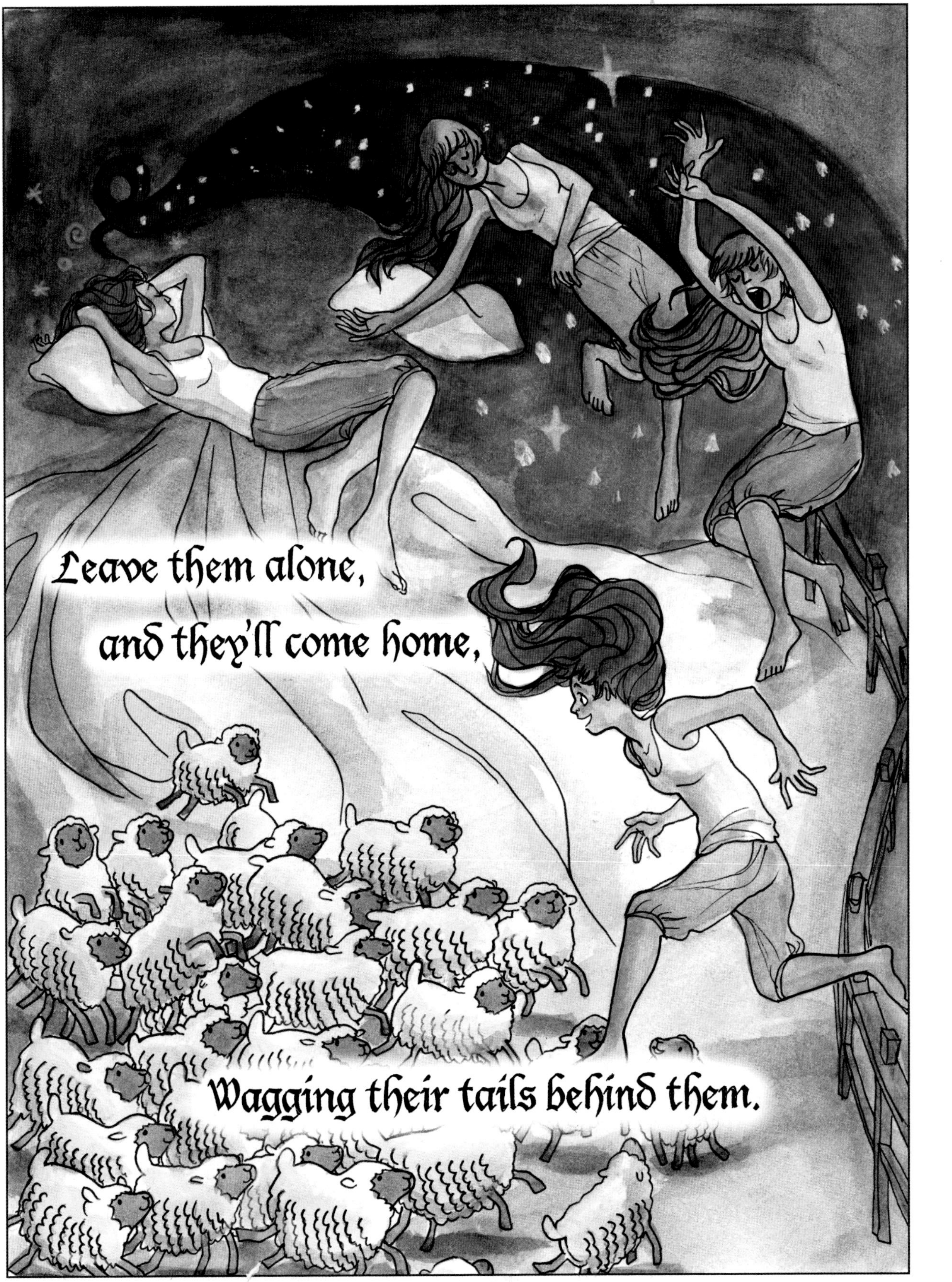
Leave them alone,
and they'll come home,
Wagging their tails behind them.

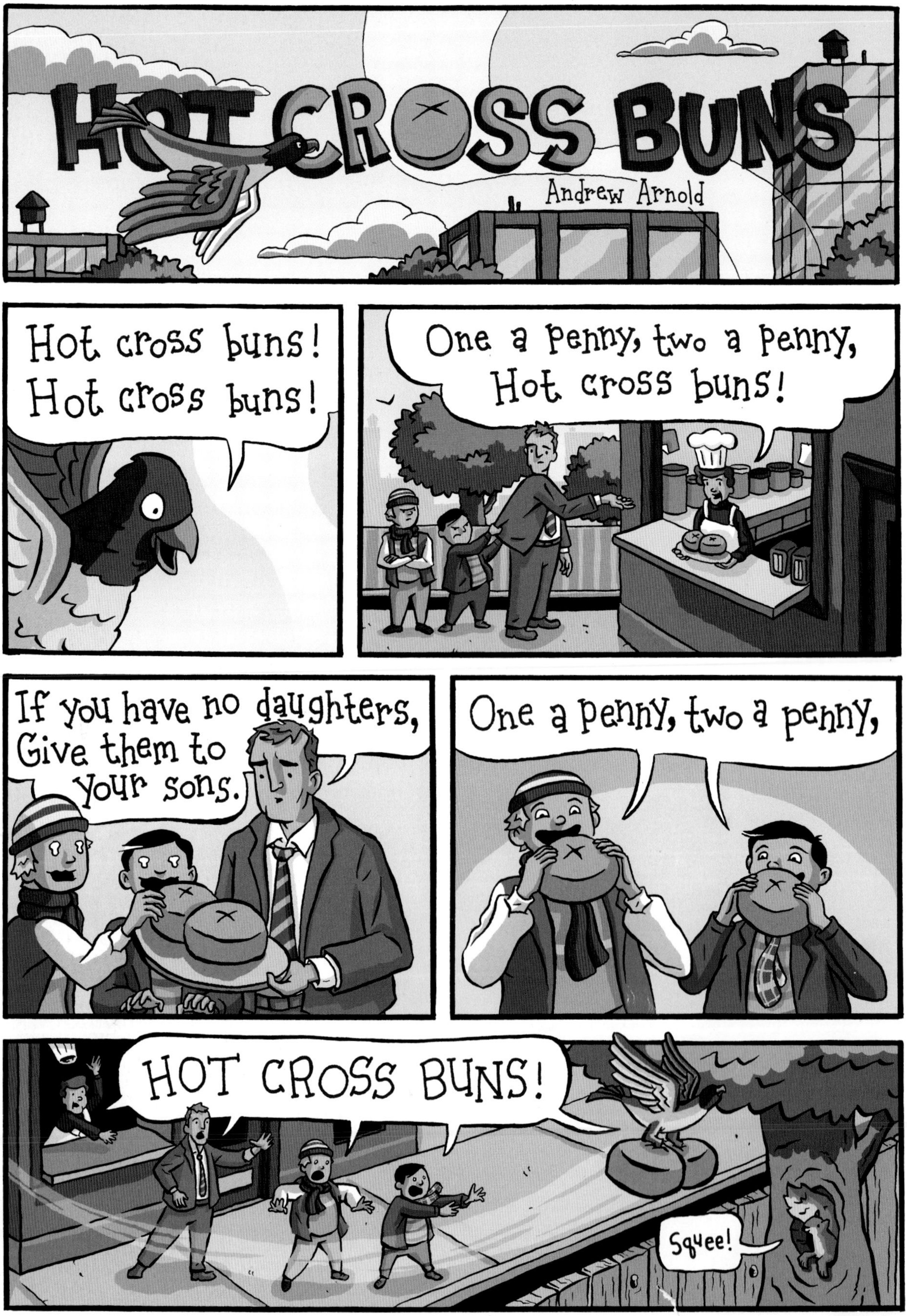
HOT CROSS BUNS
Andrew Arnold
Hot cross buns! Hot cross buns!
One a penny, two a penny, Hot cross buns!
If you have no daughters, Give them to your sons.
One a penny, two a penny,
HOT CROSS BUNS!
Squee!

OLD MOTHER HUBBARD

J Crane

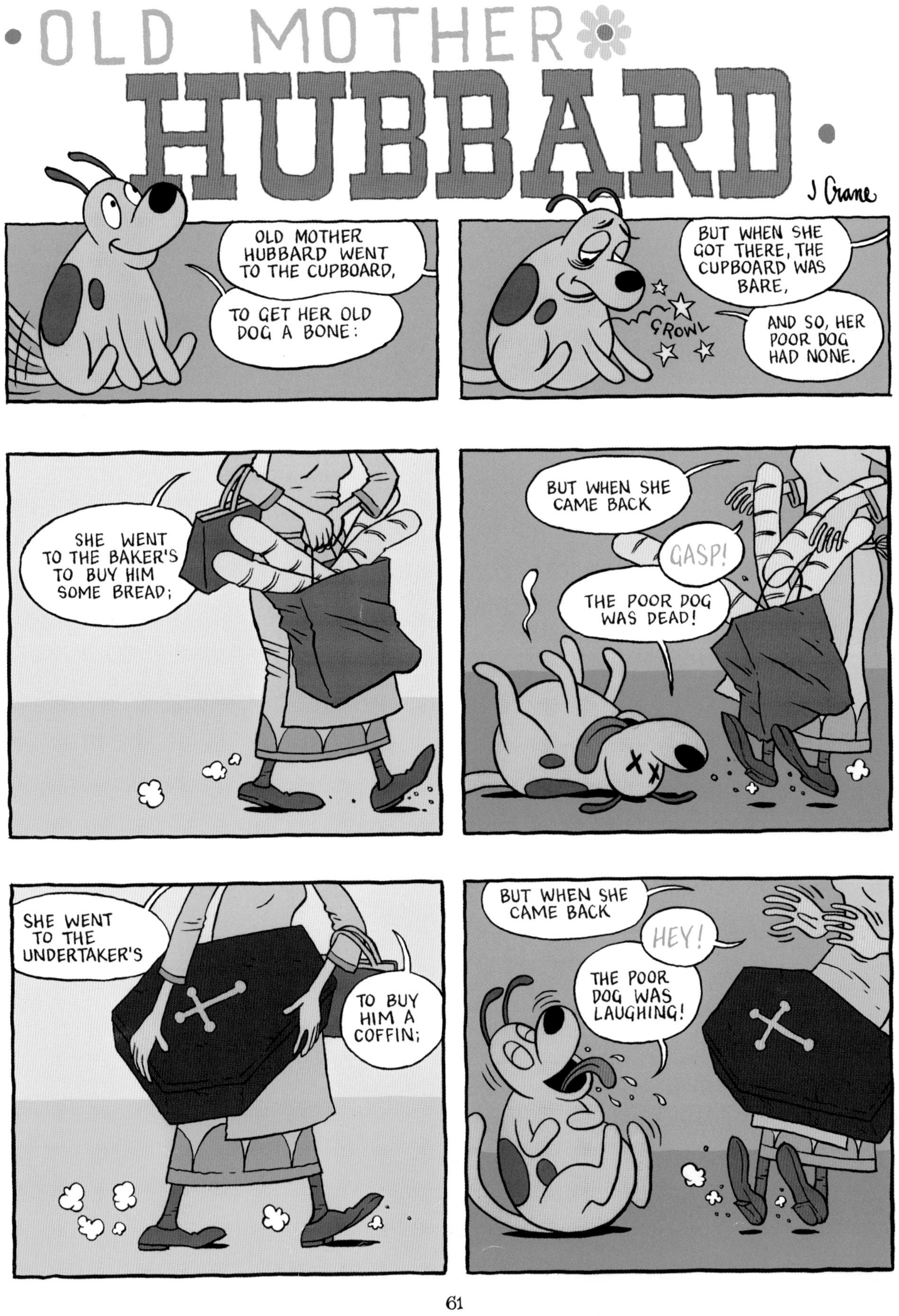
OLD MOTHER HUBBARD WENT TO THE CUPBOARD,
TO GET HER OLD DOG A BONE:
BUT WHEN SHE GOT THERE, THE CUPBOARD WAS BARE,
GROWL
AND SO, HER POOR DOG HAD NONE.
SHE WENT TO THE BAKER'S TO BUY HIM SOME BREAD;
BUT WHEN SHE CAME BACK
GASP!
THE POOR DOG WAS DEAD!
SHE WENT TO THE UNDERTAKER'S
TO BUY HIM A COFFIN;
BUT WHEN SHE CAME BACK
HEY!
THE POOR DOG WAS LAUGHING!

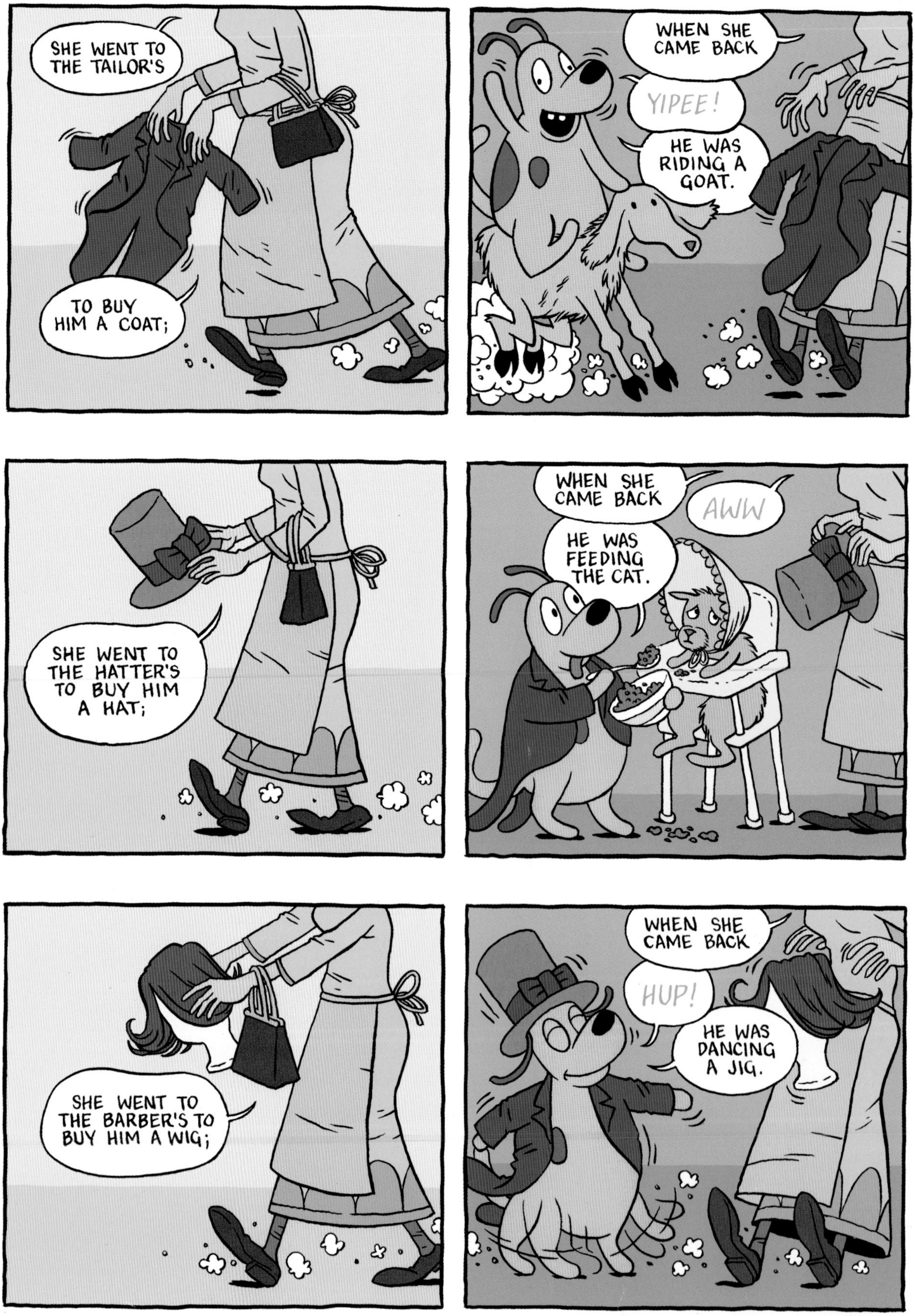
SHE WENT TO THE TAILOR'S
TO BUY HIM A COAT;
WHEN SHE CAME BACK
YIPEE!
HE WAS RIDING A GOAT.
SHE WENT TO THE HATTER'S TO BUY HIM A HAT;
WHEN SHE CAME BACK
AWW
HE WAS FEEDING THE CAT.
SHE WENT TO THE BARBER'S TO BUY HIM A WIG;
WHEN SHE CAME BACK
HUP!
HE WAS DANCING A JIG.

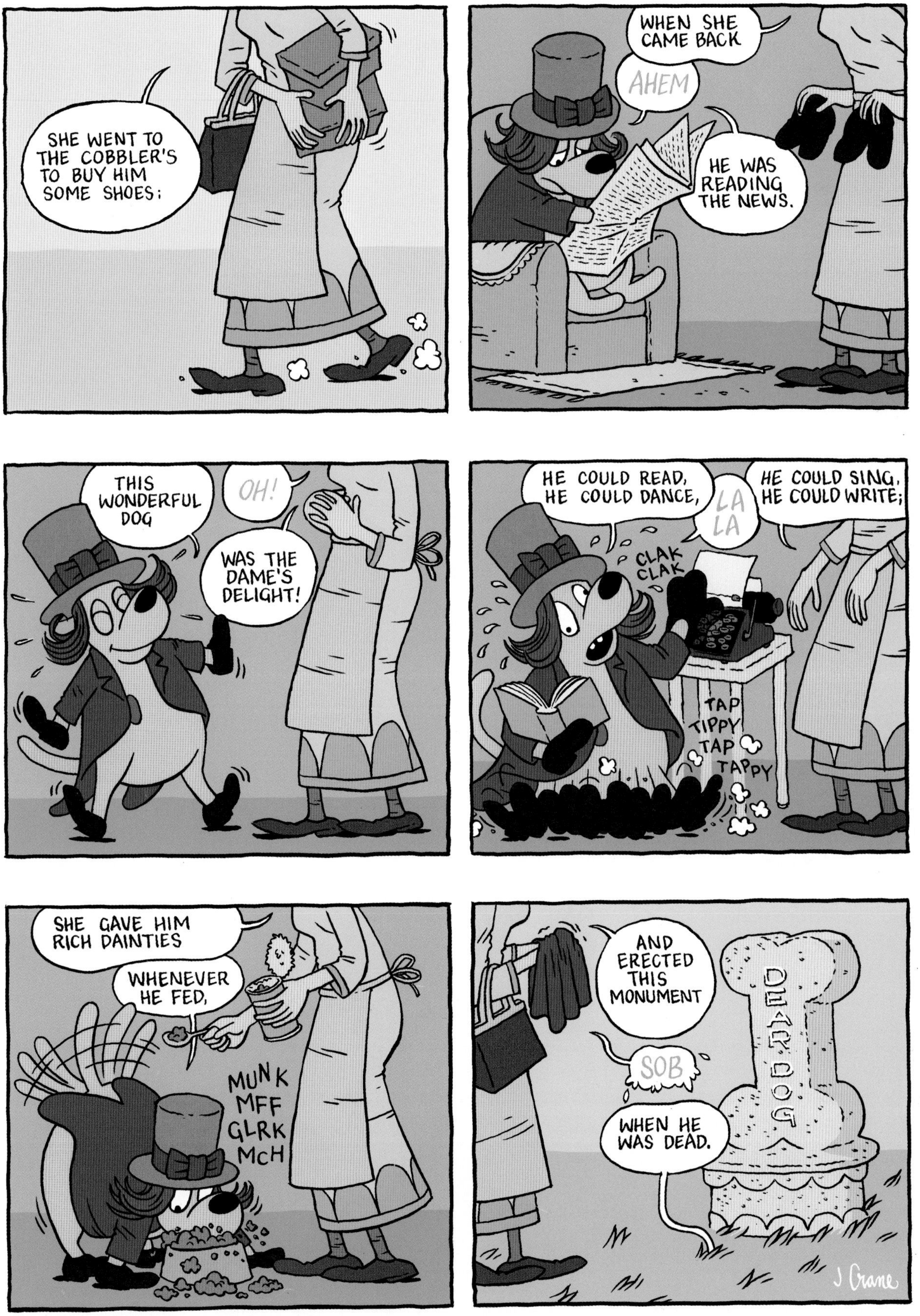
SHE WENT TO THE COBBLER'S TO BUY HIM SOME SHOES;
WHEN SHE CAME BACK
AHEM
HE WAS READING THE NEWS.
THIS WONDERFUL DOG
OH!
WAS THE DAME'S DELIGHT!
HE COULD READ, HE COULD DANCE,
LA LA
HE COULD SING, HE COULD WRITE;
CLAK CLAK
TAP TIPPY TAP TAPPY
SHE GAVE HIM RICH DAINTIES
WHENEVER HE FED,
MUNK MFF GLRK MCH
AND ERECTED THIS MONUMENT
SOB
WHEN HE WAS DEAD.
DEAR DOG
J Crane

Jack and Jill

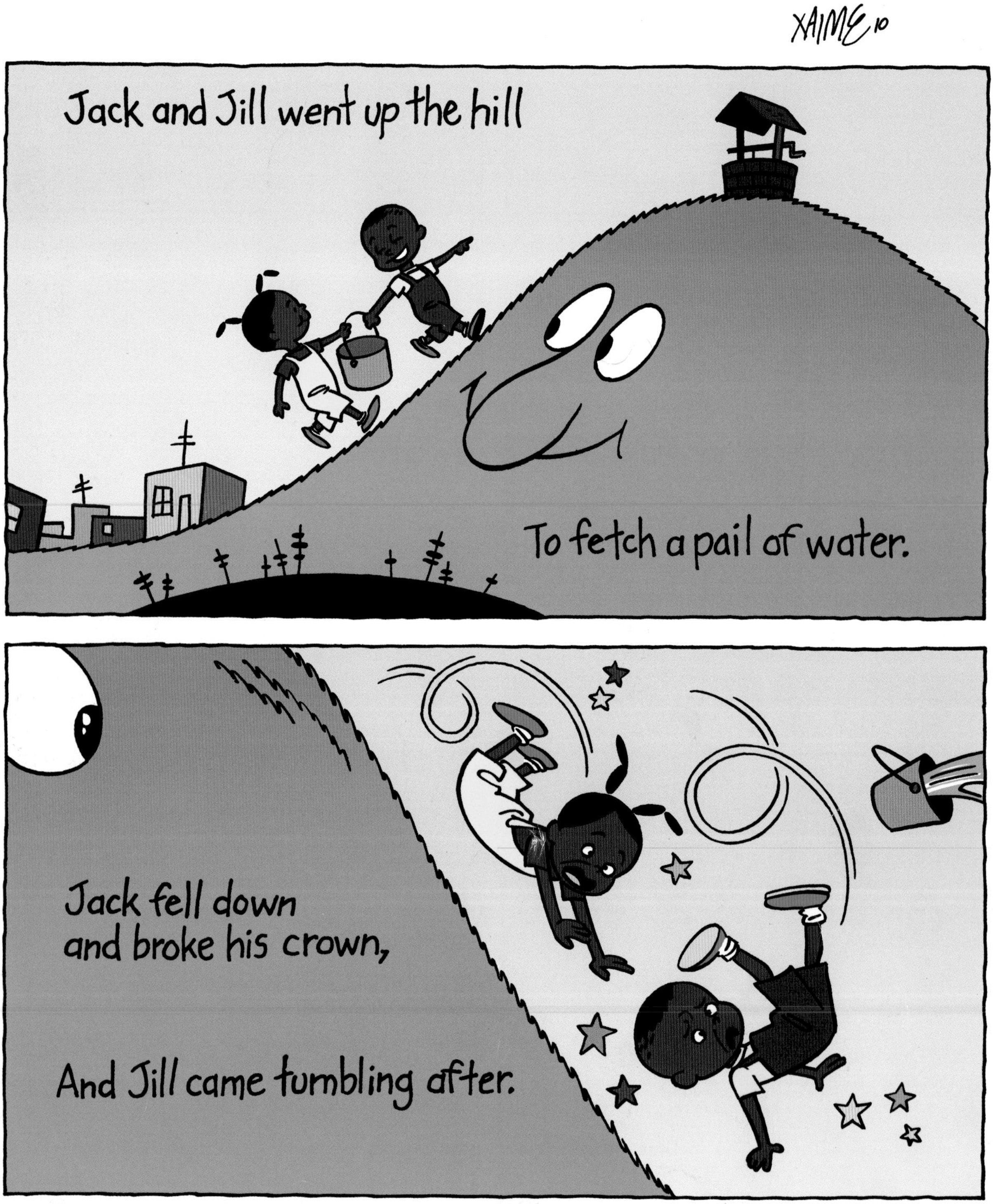
XAIME 10
Jack and Jill went up the hill
To fetch a pail of water.
Jack fell down
and broke his crown,
And Jill came tumbling after.

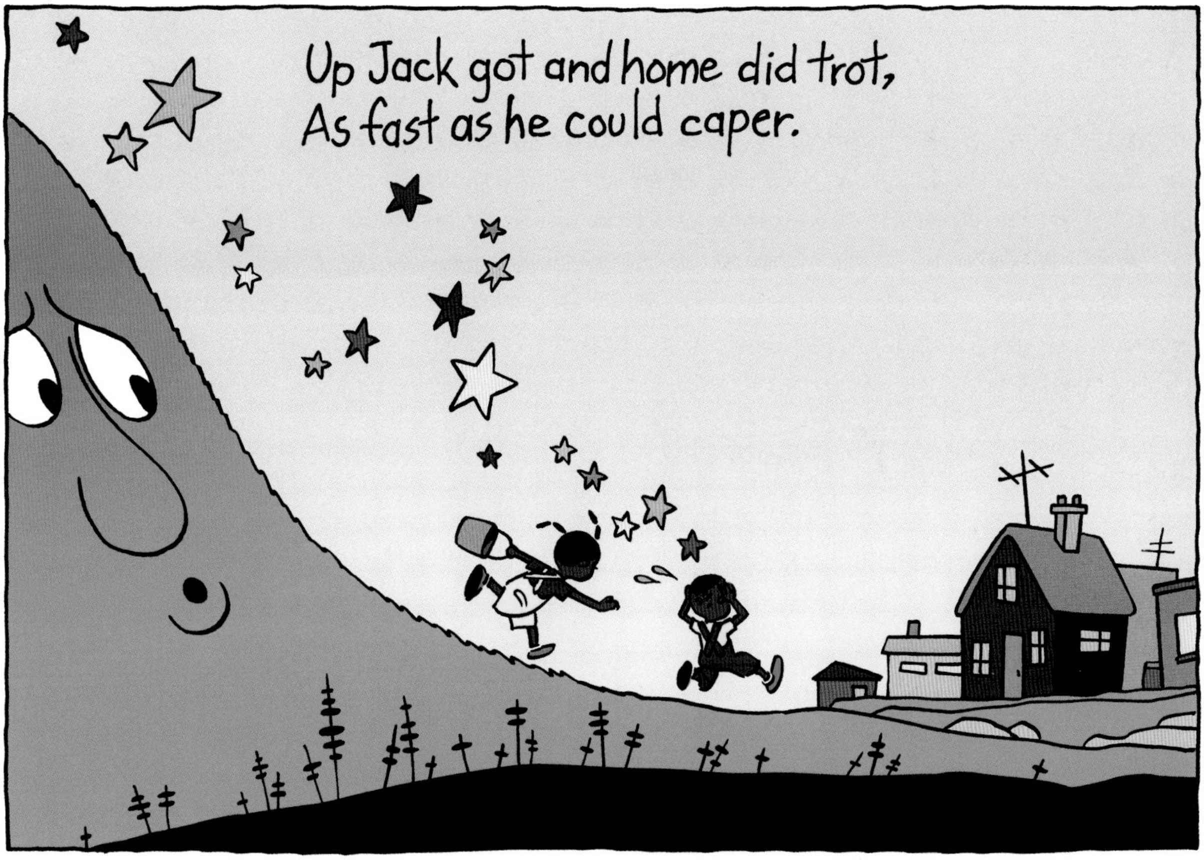
Up Jack got and home did trot,
As fast as he could caper.

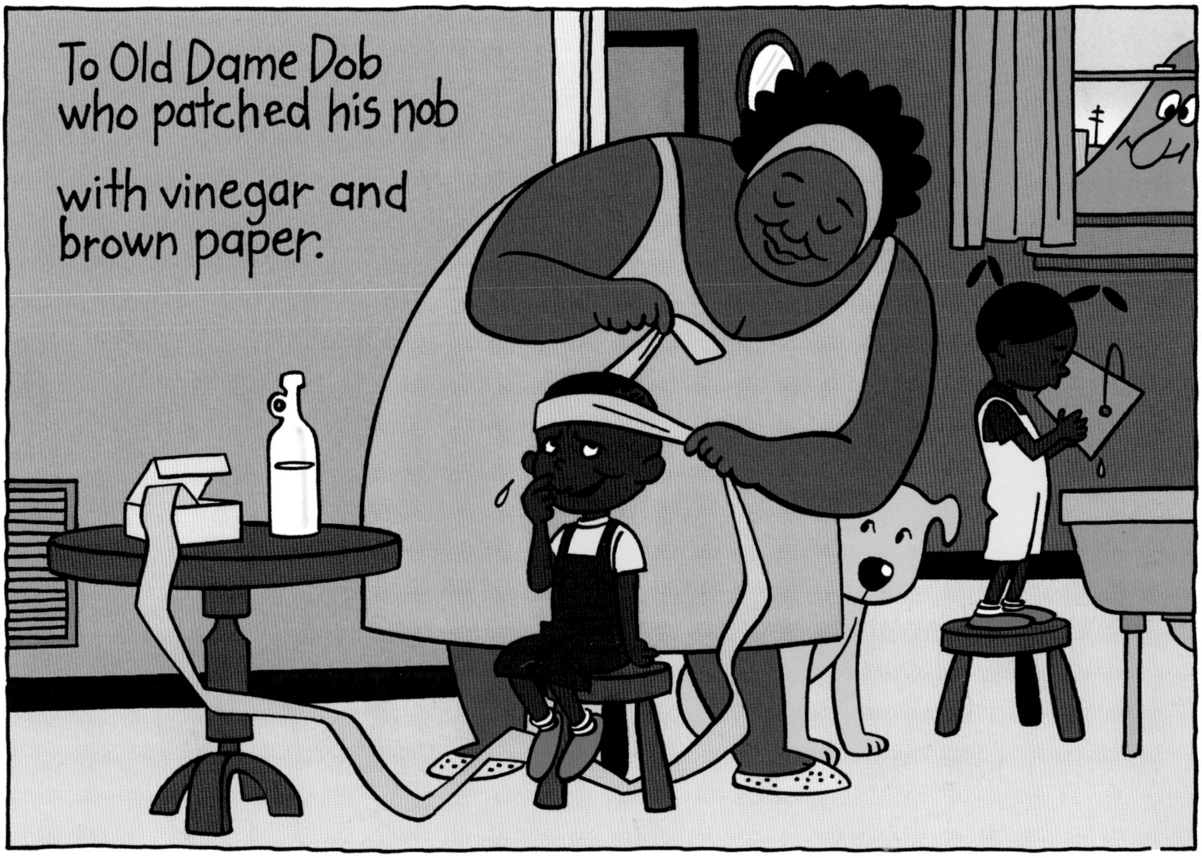
To Old Dame Dob
who patched his nob
with vinegar and
brown paper.

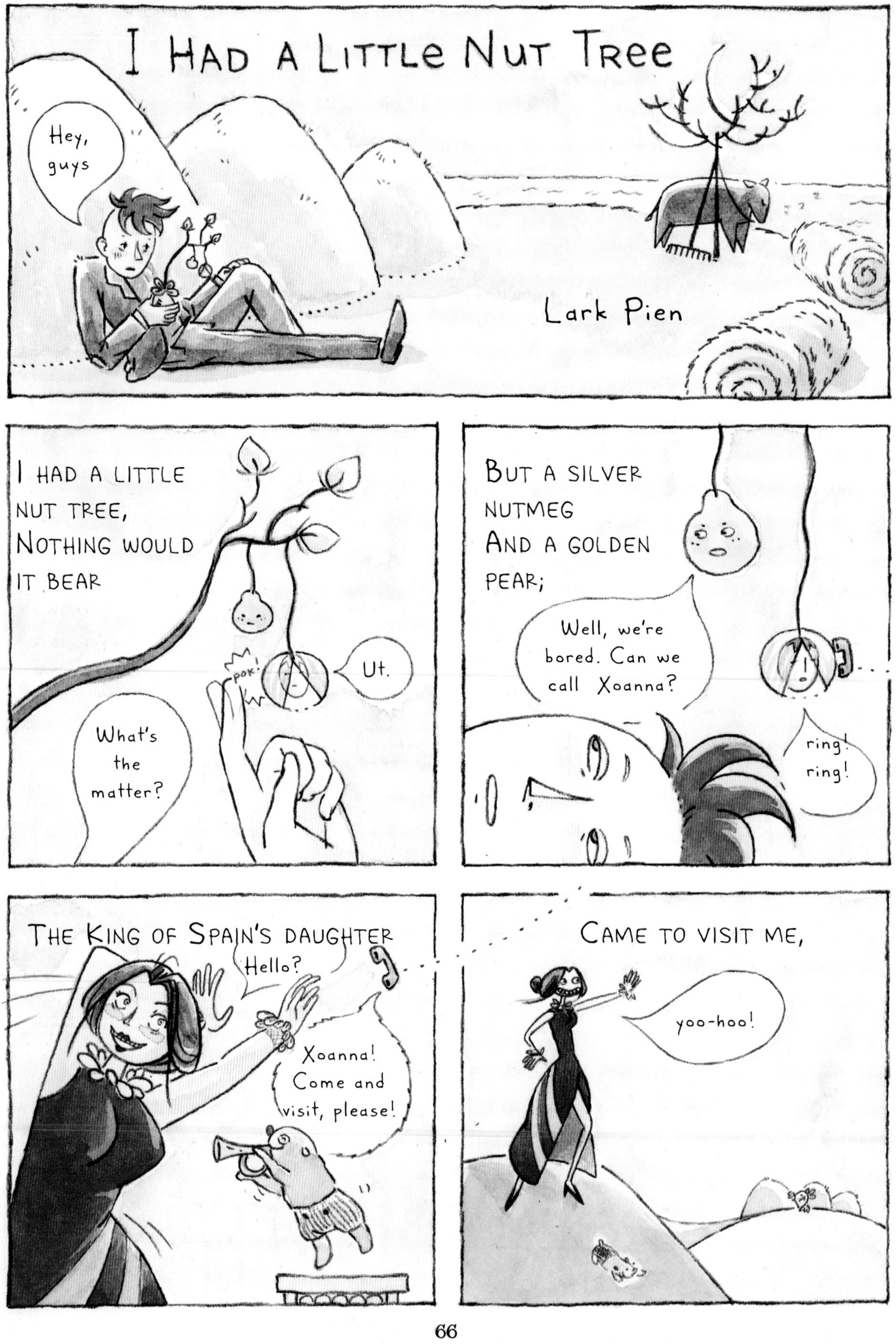
I Had a Little Nut Tree
Hey, guys
Lark Pien
I had a little nut tree, Nothing would it bear
pok!
Ut.
What's the matter?
But a silver nutmeg And a golden pear;
Well, we're bored. Can we call Xoanna?
ring! ring!
The King of Spain's daughter
Hello?
Xoanna! Come and visit, please!
Came to visit me,
yoo-hoo!

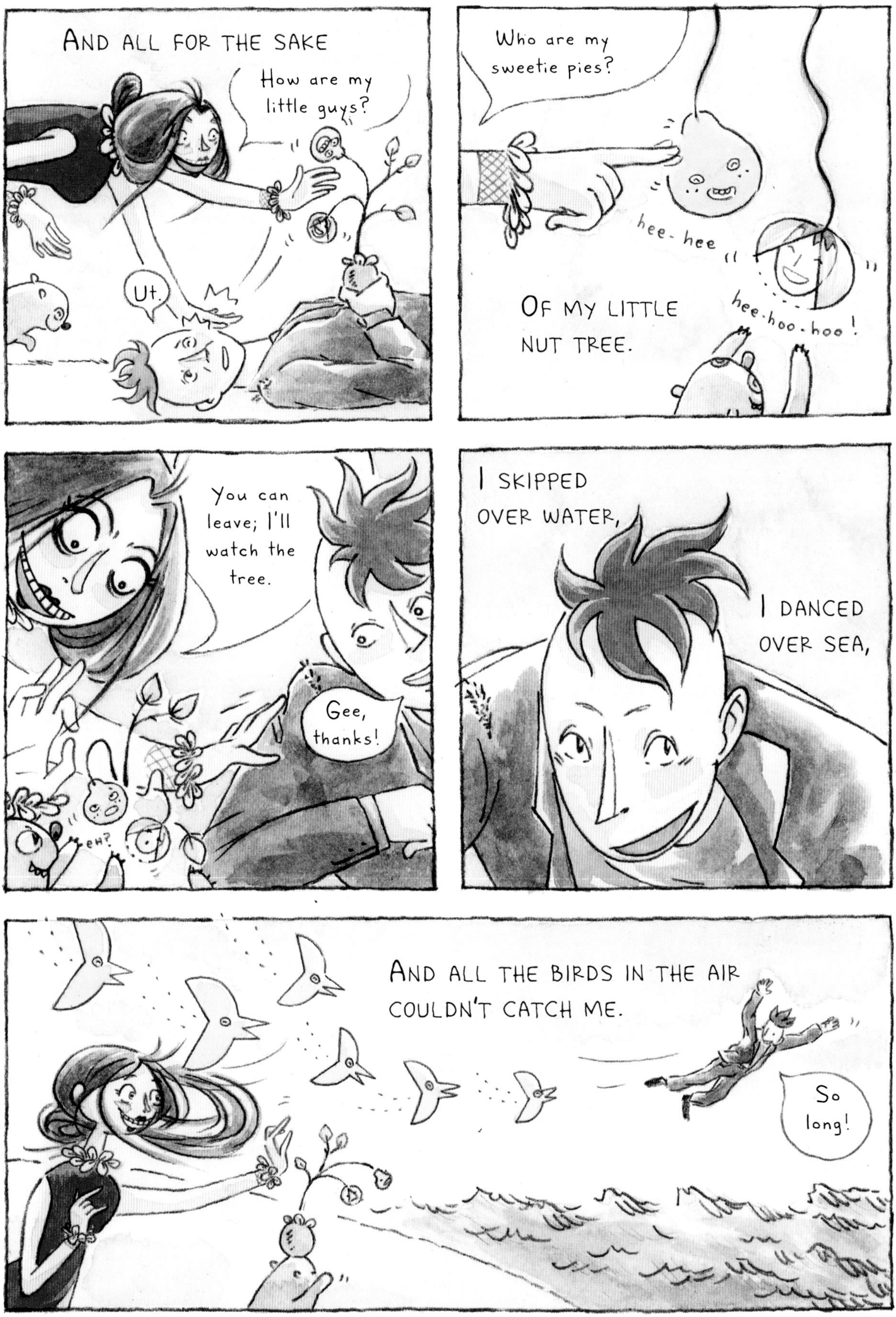
AND ALL FOR THE SAKE
How are my little guys?
Ut.
Who are my sweetie pies?
hee- hee
hee-hoo-hoo!
OF MY LITTLE NUT TREE.
You can leave; I'll watch the tree.
Gee, thanks!
EH?
I SKIPPED OVER WATER,
I DANCED OVER SEA,
AND ALL THE BIRDS IN THE AIR COULDN'T CATCH ME.
So long!

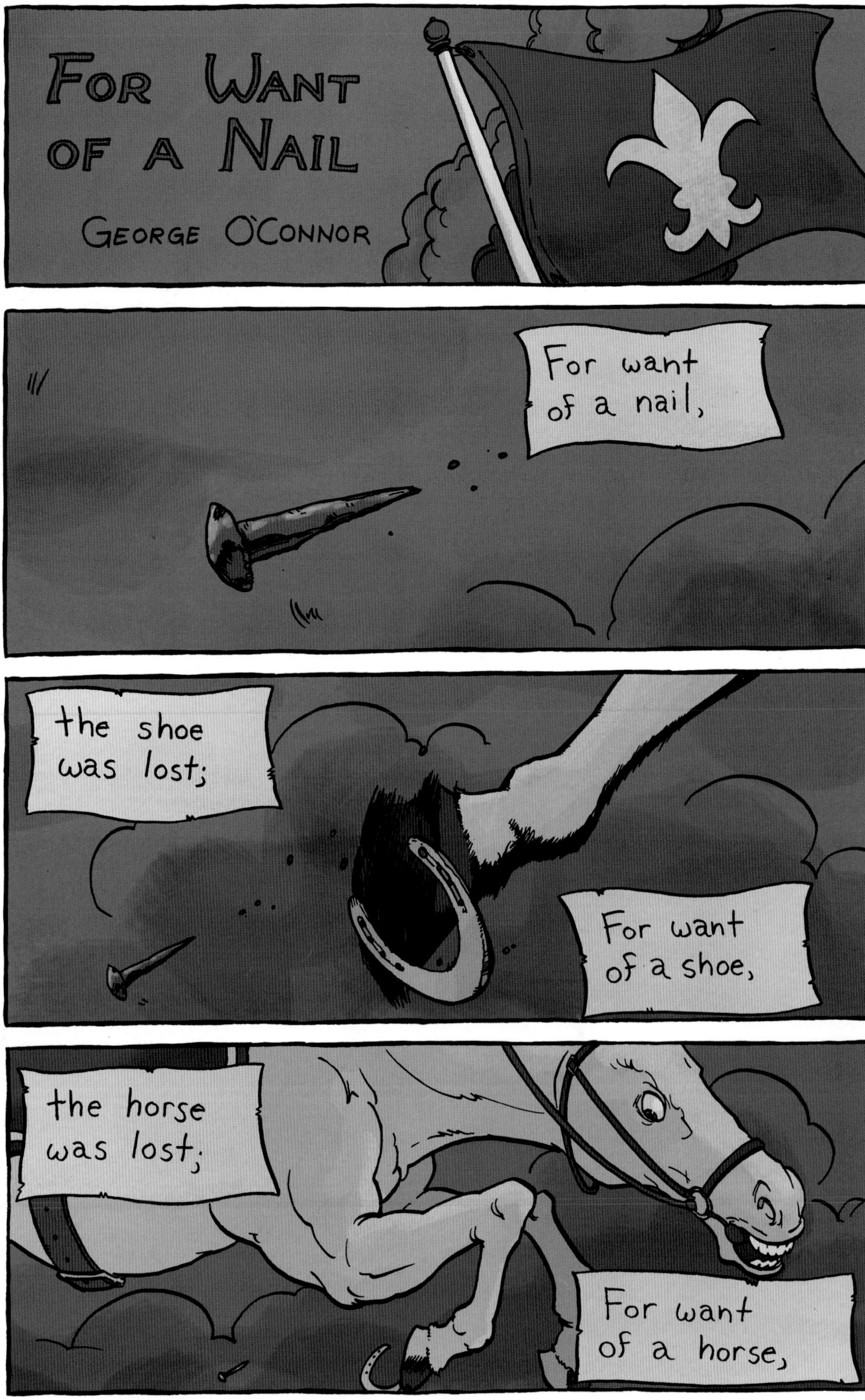

FOR WANT OF A NAIL
GEORGE O'CONNOR
For want of a nail,
the shoe was lost;
For want of a shoe,
the horse was lost;
For want of a horse,

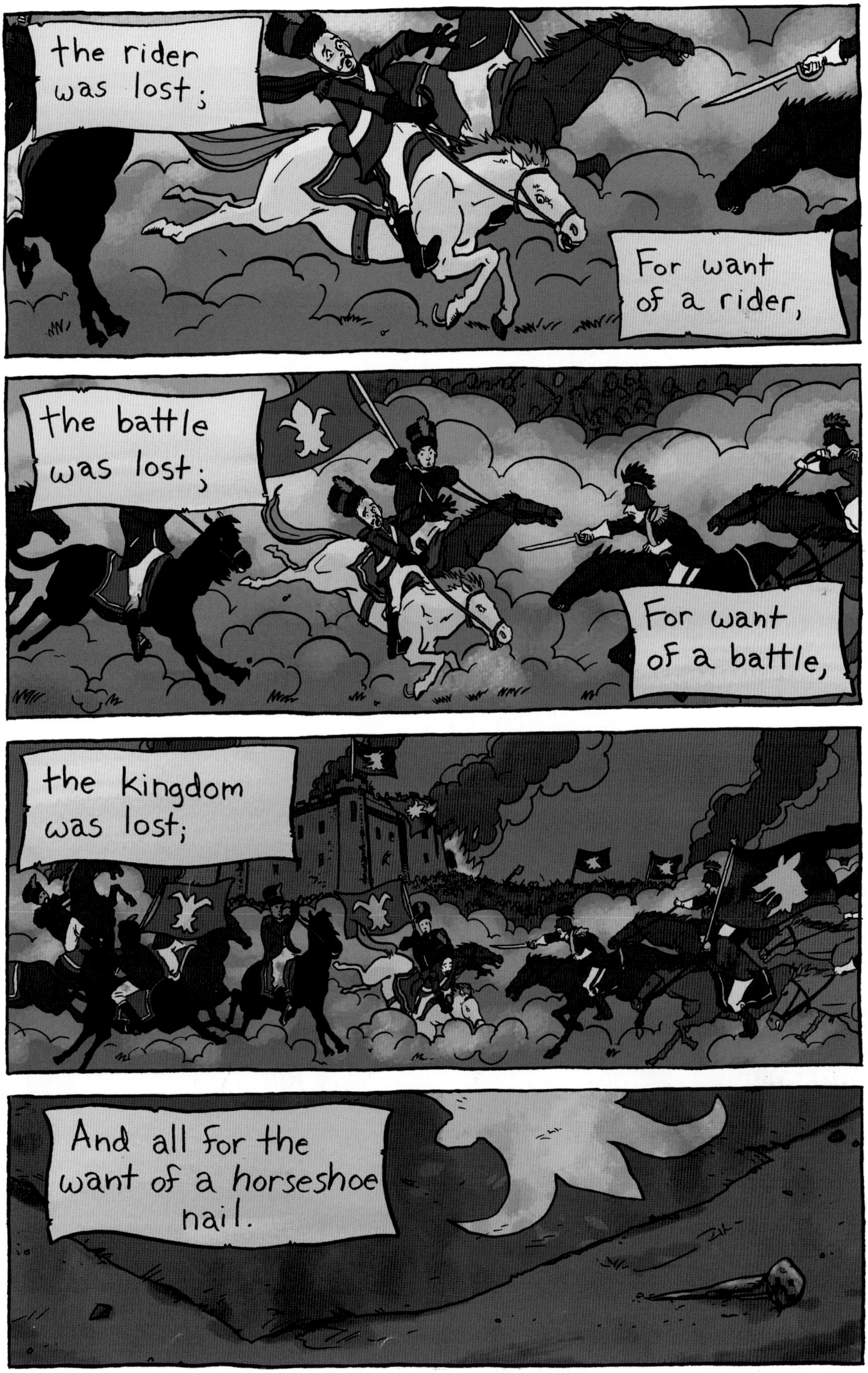
the rider was lost;
For want of a rider,
the battle was lost;
For want of a battle,
the kingdom was lost;
And all for the want of a horseshoe nail.

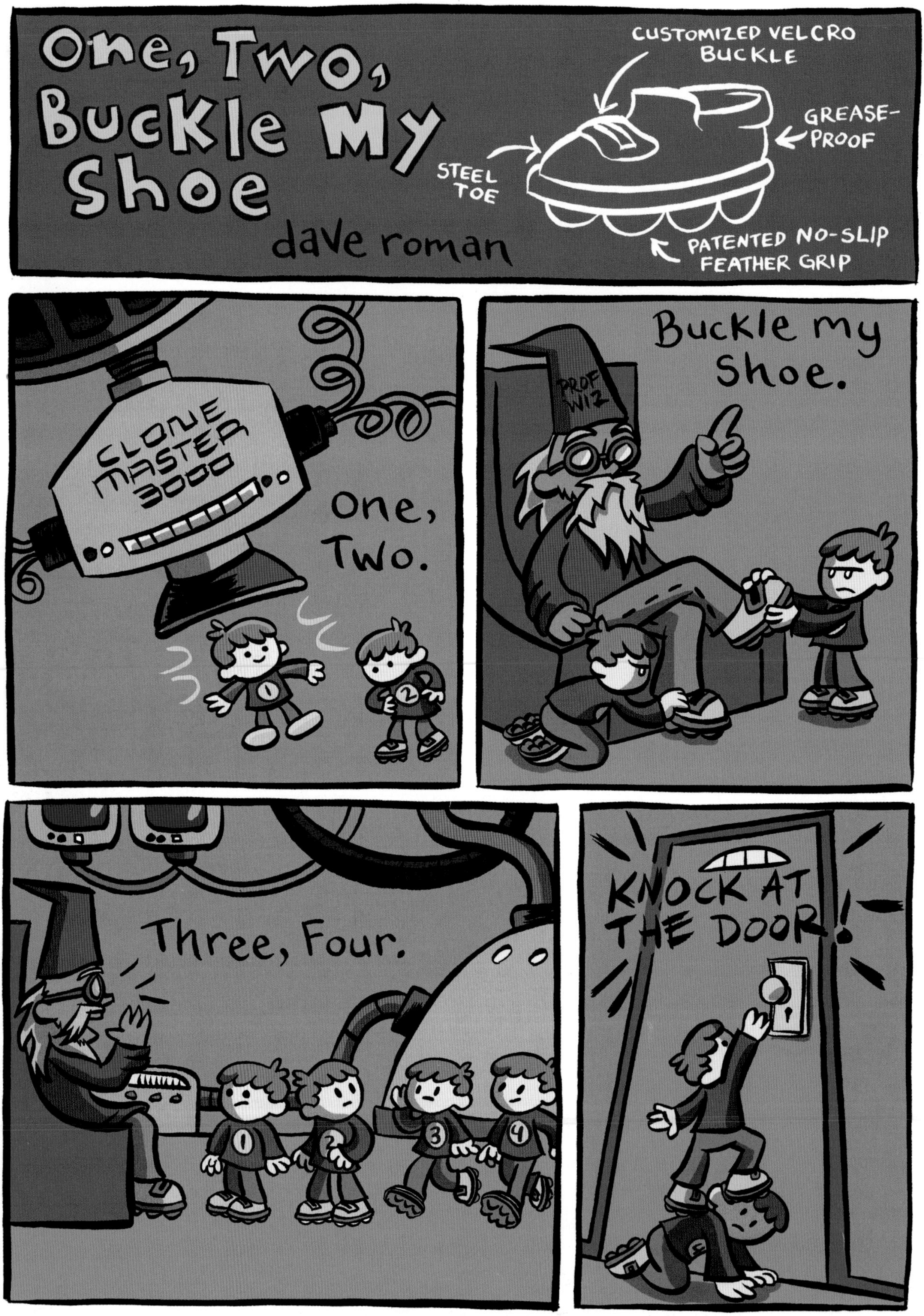
One, Two, Buckle My Shoe
dave roman
CUSTOMIZED VELCRO BUCKLE
GREASE-PROOF
STEEL TOE
PATENTED NO-SLIP FEATHER GRIP
CLONE MASTER 3000
One, Two.
Buckle my Shoe.
PROF WIZ
Three, Four.
KNOCK AT THE DOOR!

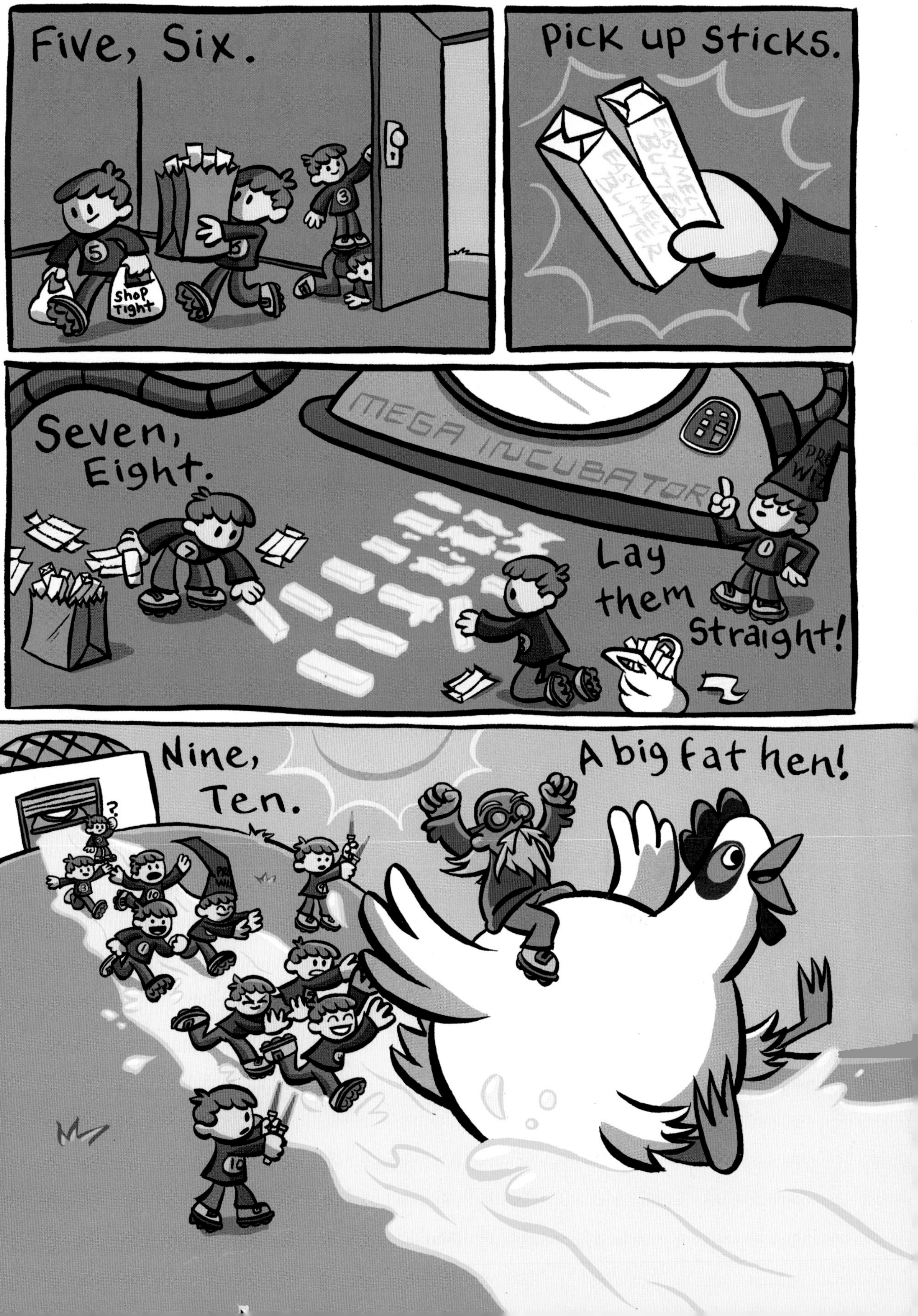
Five, Six.
Shop Tight
Pick up Sticks.
EASY MELT BUTTER
EASY MELT BUTTER
Seven, Eight.
MEGA INCUBATOR
Lay them Straight!
Nine, Ten.
A big fat hen!

PUSSYCAT, PUSSYCAT, WHERE HAVE YOU BEEN?

Hatke '10

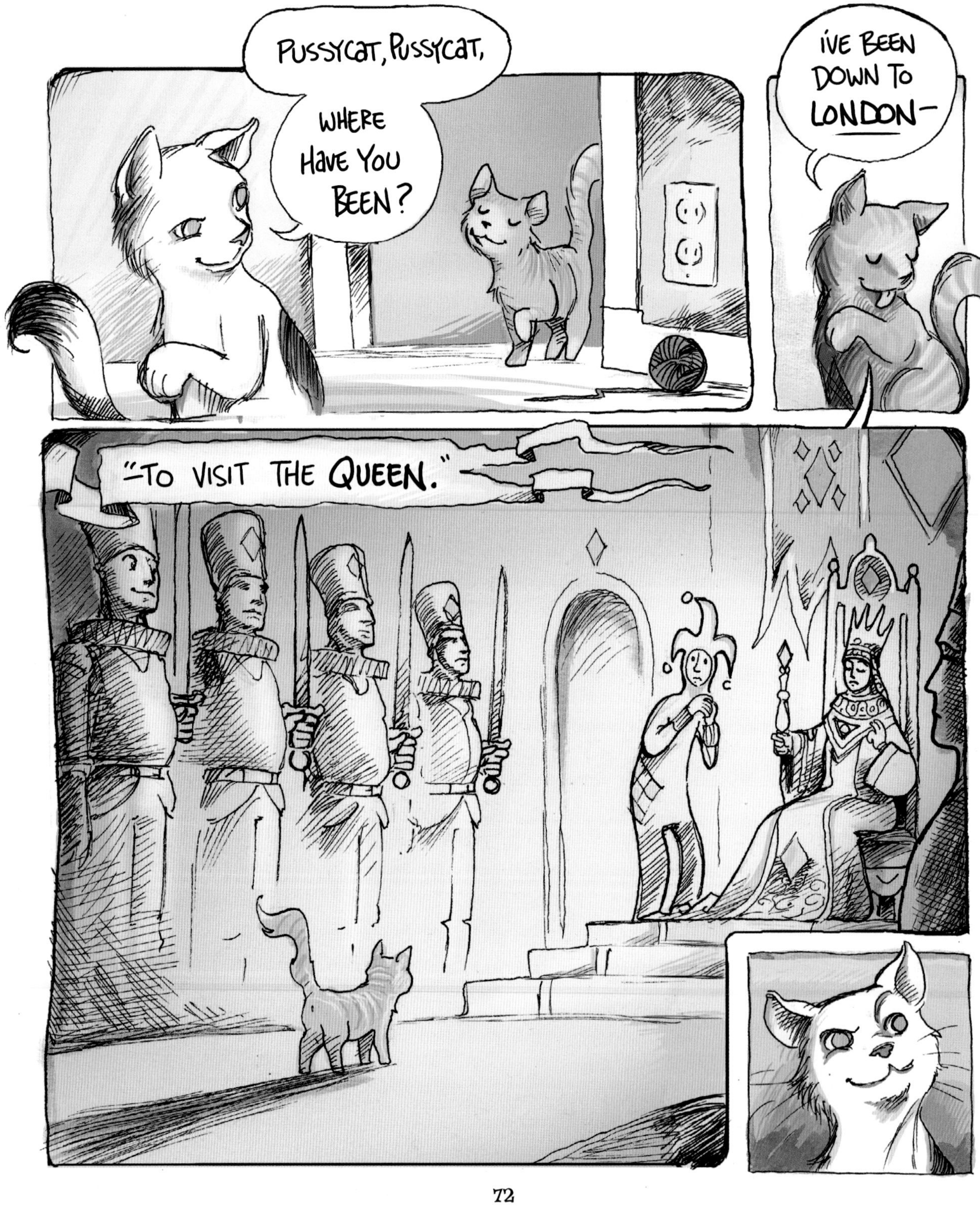

PUSSYCAT, PUSSYCAT,
WHERE HAVE YOU BEEN?
I'VE BEEN DOWN TO LONDON—
"—TO VISIT THE QUEEN."

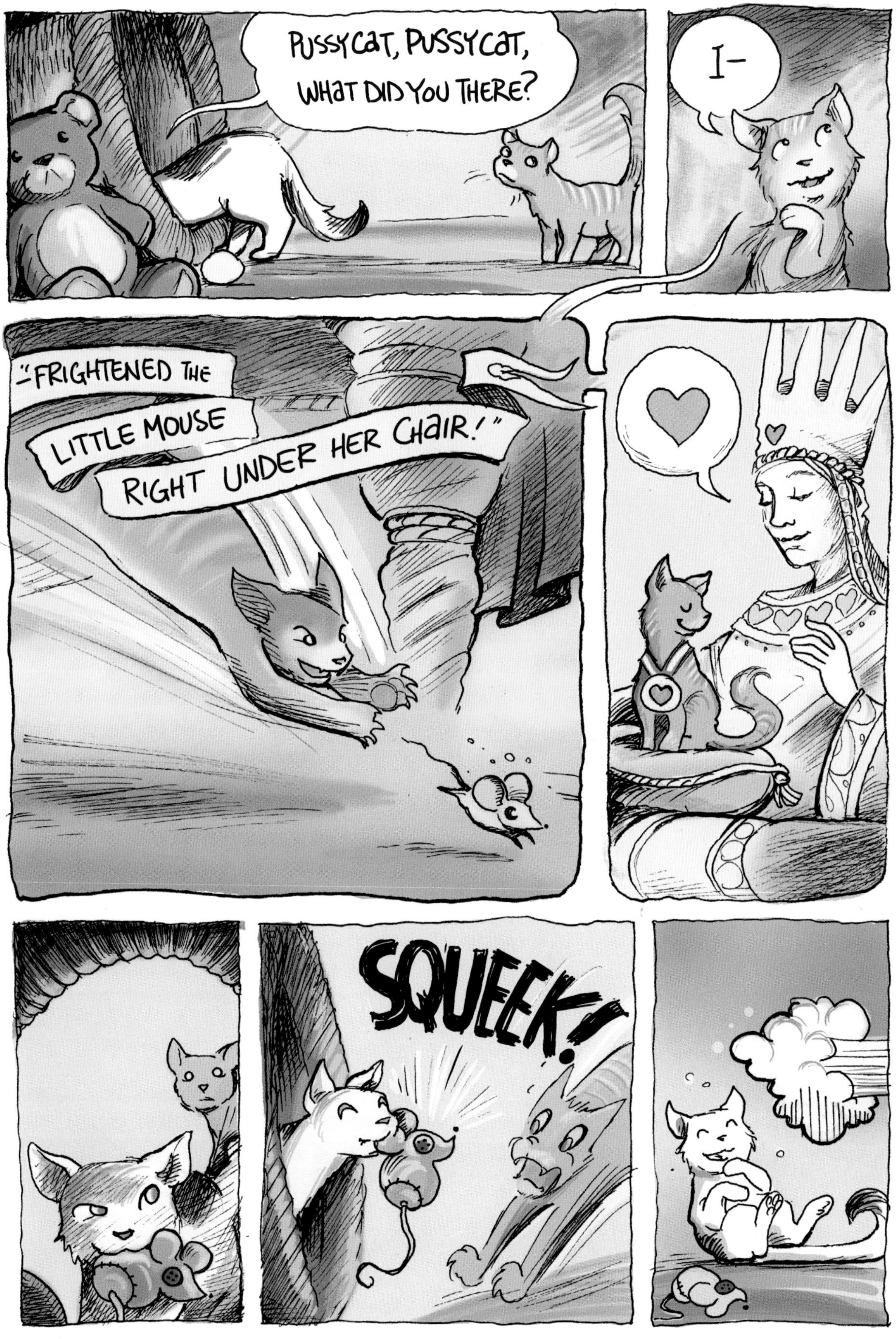
PUSSYCAT, PUSSYCAT, WHAT DID YOU THERE?
I-
"-FRIGHTENED THE LITTLE MOUSE RIGHT UNDER HER CHAIR!"
SQUEEK!

THE GRAND OLD DUKE OF YORK

K. Beaton

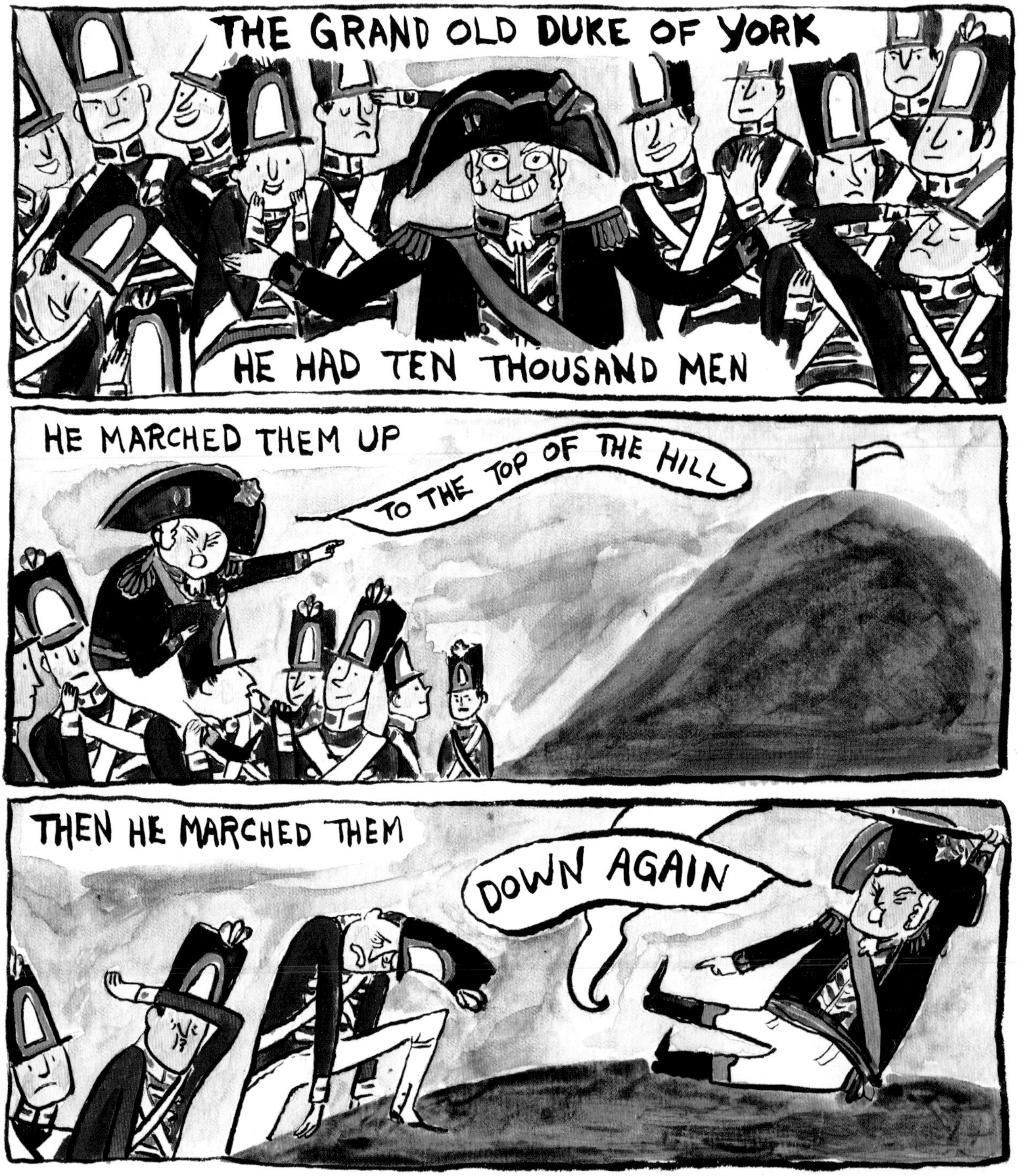
THE GRAND OLD DUKE OF YORK
HE HAD TEN THOUSAND MEN
HE MARCHED THEM UP
TO THE TOP OF THE HILL
THEN HE MARCHED THEM
DOWN AGAIN

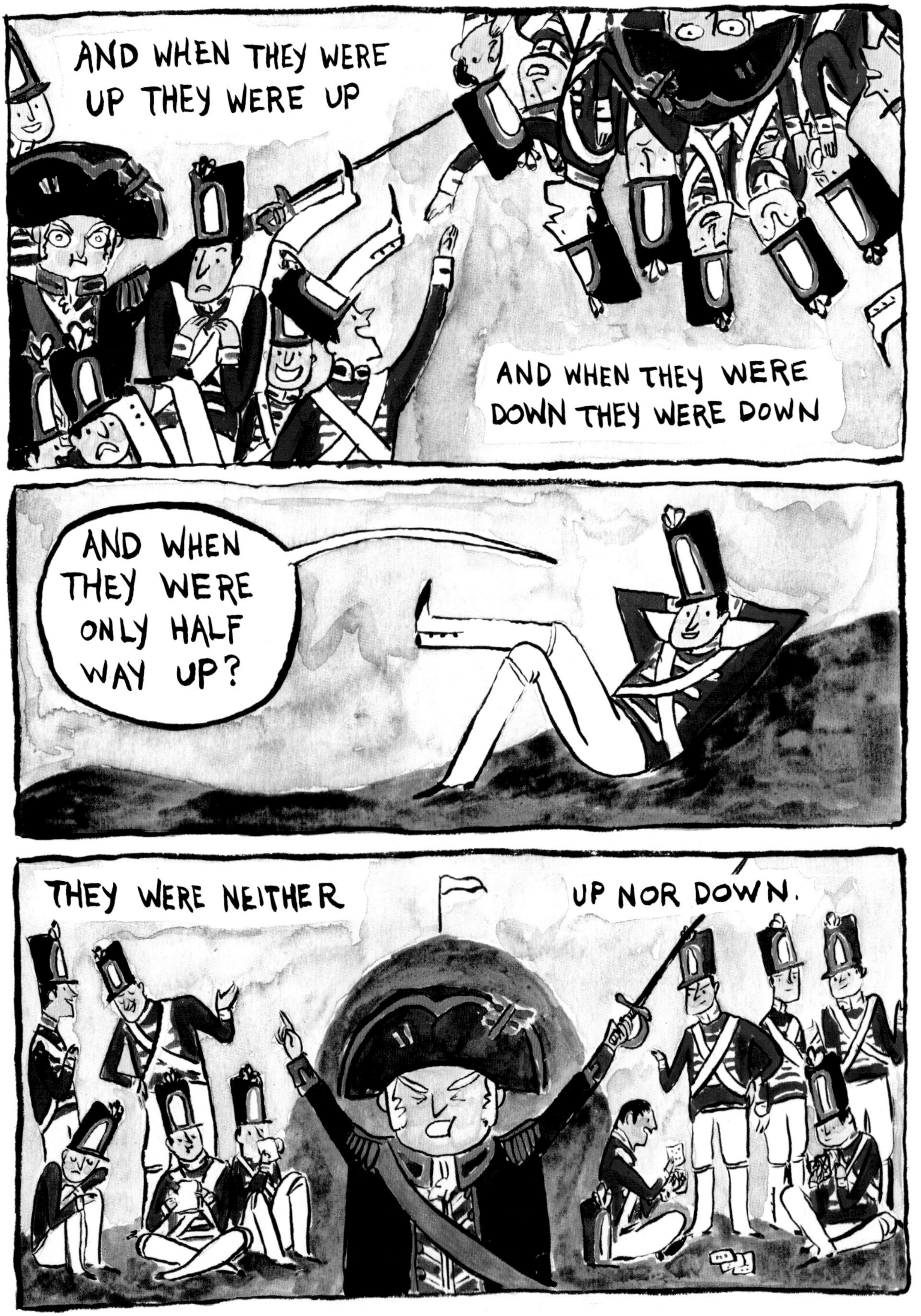
AND WHEN THEY WERE UP THEY WERE UP
AND WHEN THEY WERE DOWN THEY WERE DOWN
AND WHEN THEY WERE ONLY HALF WAY UP?
THEY WERE NEITHER
UP NOR DOWN.

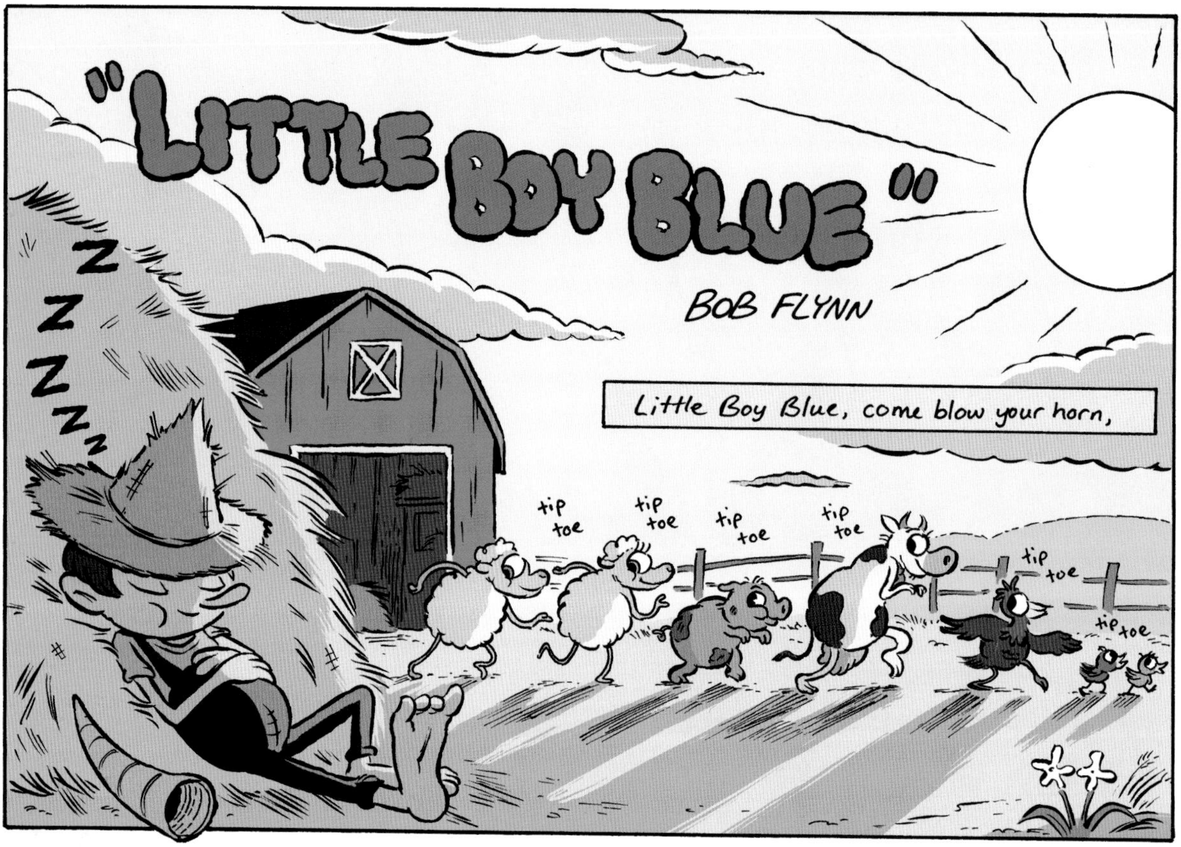
"LITTLE BOY BLUE"
BOB FLYNN
Little Boy Blue, come blow your horn,
Z Z Z Z Z Z
tip toe
tip toe
tip toe
tip toe
tip toe
tip toe

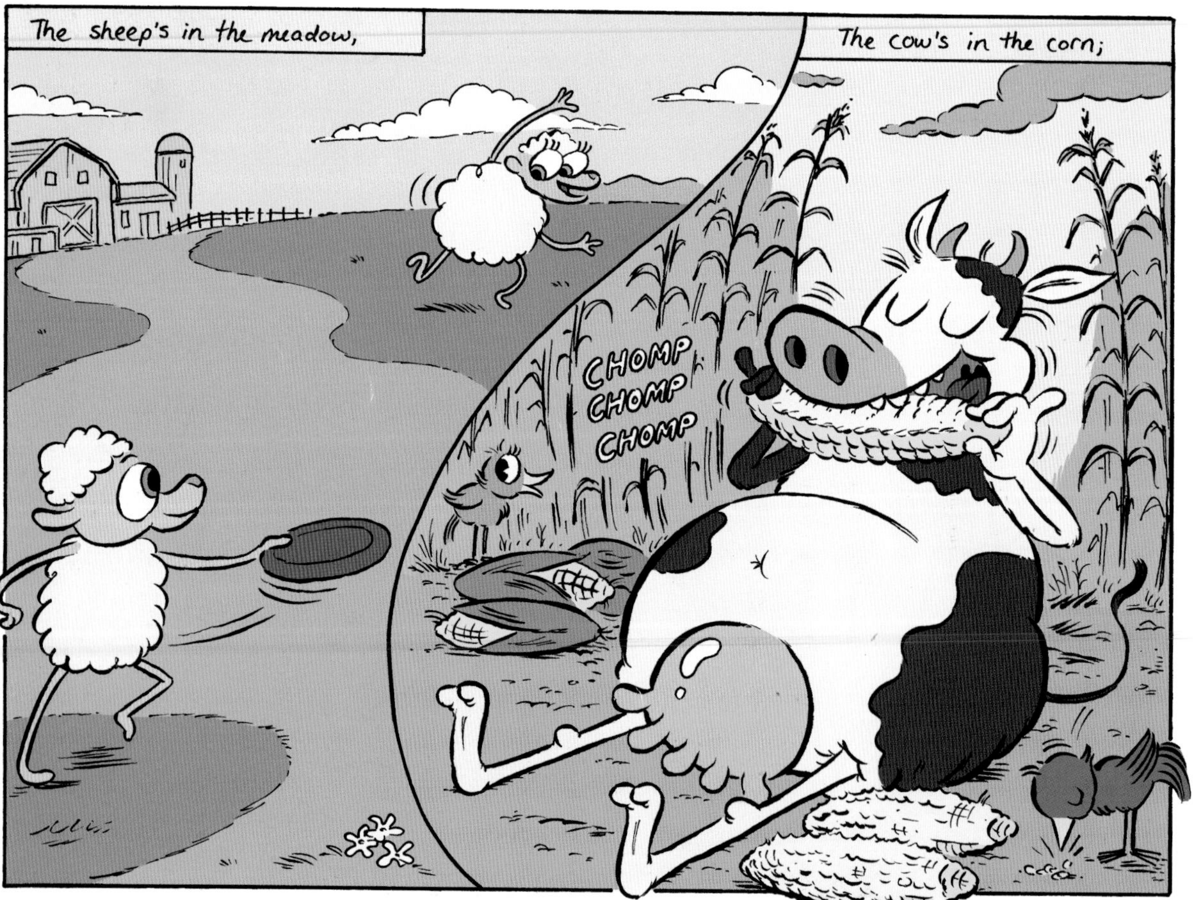
The sheep's in the meadow,
The cow's in the corn;
CHOMP
CHOMP
CHOMP

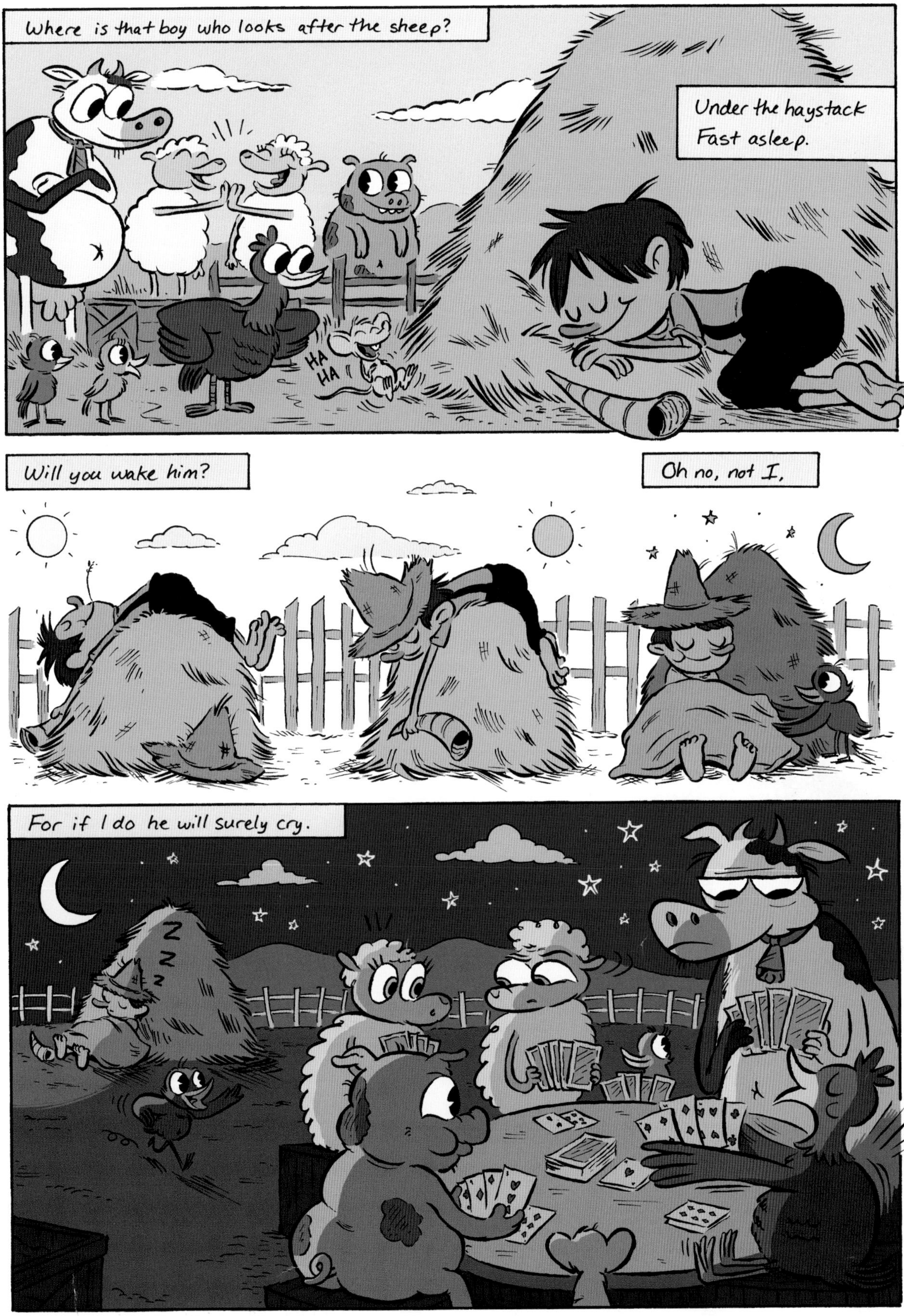
Where is that boy who looks after the sheep?
Under the haystack
Fast asleep.
HA
HA
Will you wake him?
Oh no, not I,
For if I do he will surely cry.
Z
Z
Z

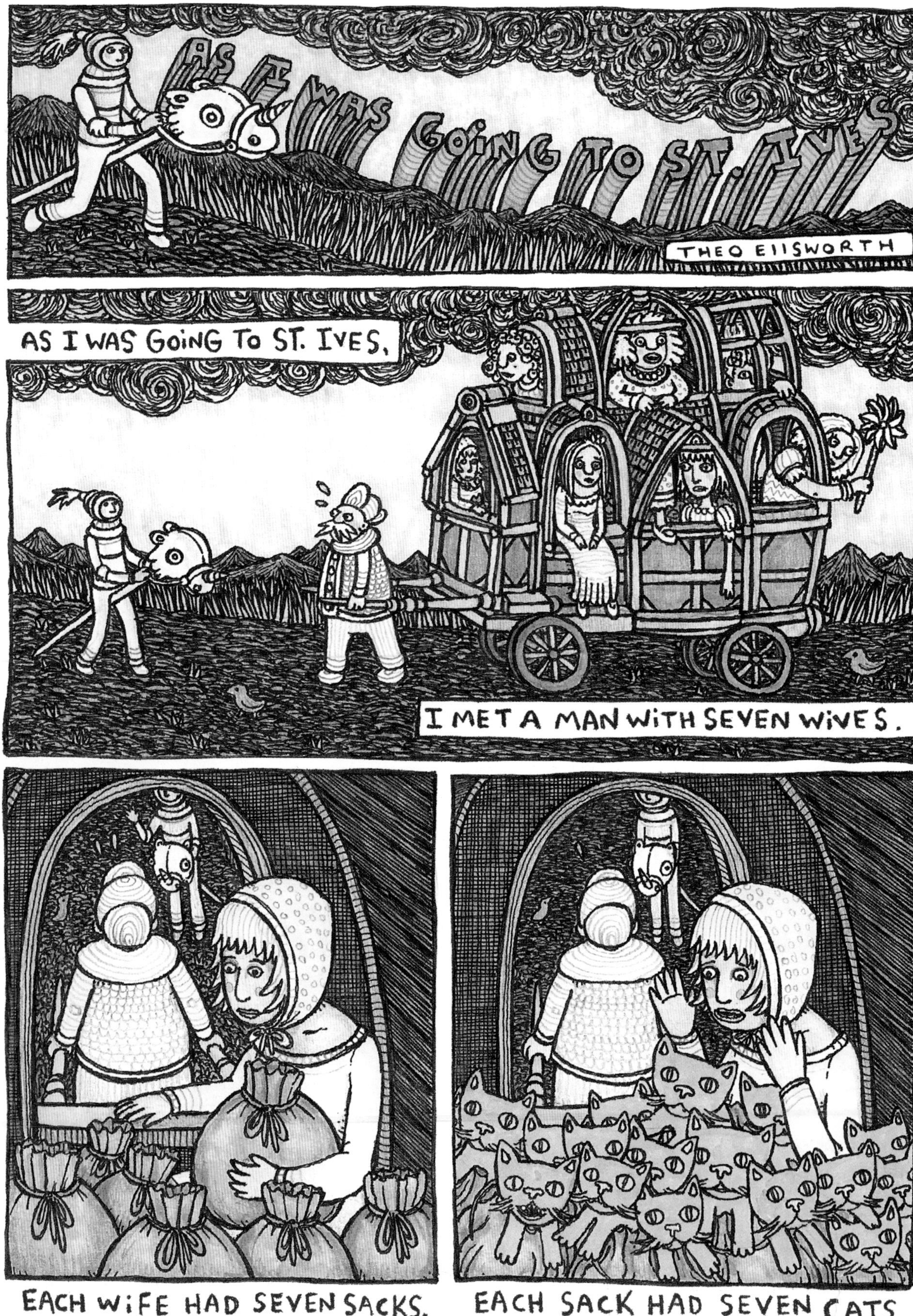
AS I WAS GOING TO ST. IVES
THEO ELLSWORTH
AS I WAS GOING TO ST. IVES,
I MET A MAN WITH SEVEN WIVES.
EACH WIFE HAD SEVEN SACKS,
EACH SACK HAD SEVEN CATS,

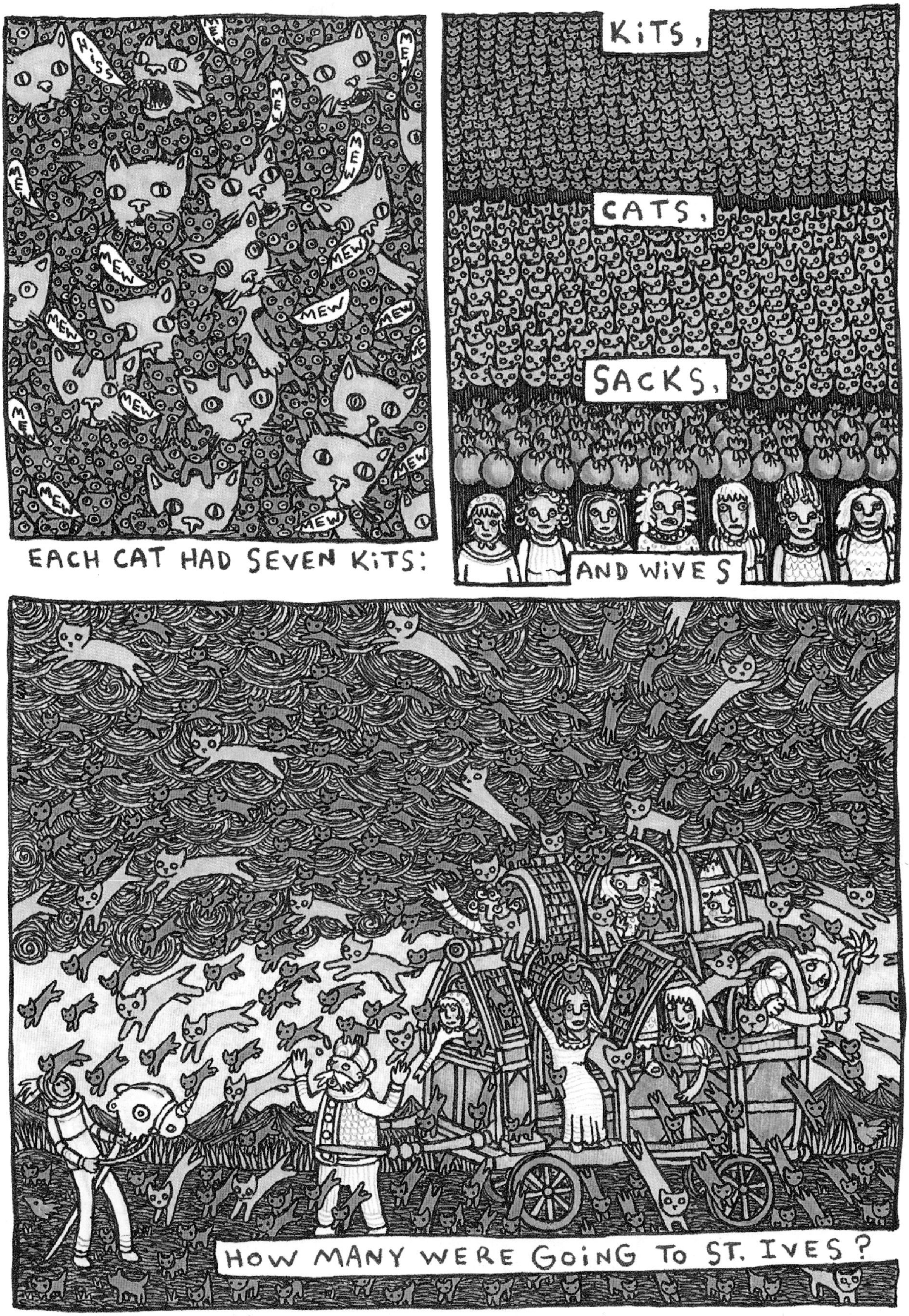
HISS
MEW
MEW
MEW
MEW
MEW
MEW
MEW
MEW
MEW
MEW
MEW
MEW
MEW
MEW
MEW
EACH CAT HAD SEVEN KITS:
KITS,
CATS,
SACKS,
AND WIVES
HOW MANY WERE GOING TO ST. IVES?

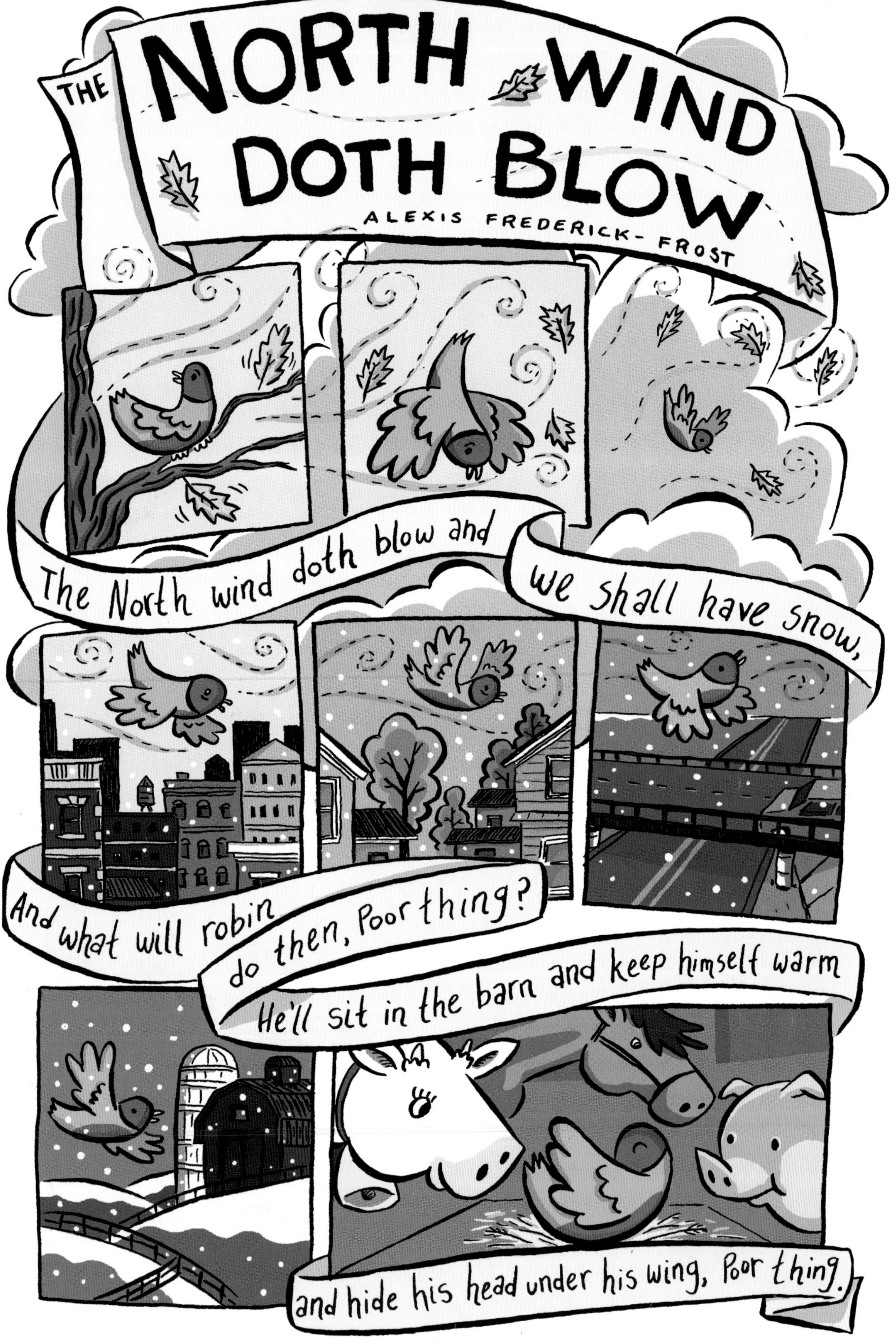
THE NORTH WIND DOTH BLOW
ALEXIS FREDERICK-FROST
The North wind doth blow and
we shall have snow,
And what will robin
do then, Poor thing?
He'll sit in the barn and keep himself warm
and hide his head under his wing, Poor thing.

LONDON BRIDGE
IS FALLING DOWN

David MacCaulay

London Bridge is
   falling down,
Falling down,
   falling down.
London Bridge is
   falling down,
My fair lady.

Build it up with
   wood and clay,
Wood and clay,
   wood and clay,
Build it up with
   wood and clay,
My fair lady.

Wood and clay
   will wash away,
Wash away,
   wash away,
Wood and clay
   will wash away,
My fair lady.

Build it up with
bricks and mortar,
Bricks and mortar,
bricks and mortar,
Build it up with
bricks and mortar,
My fair lady.

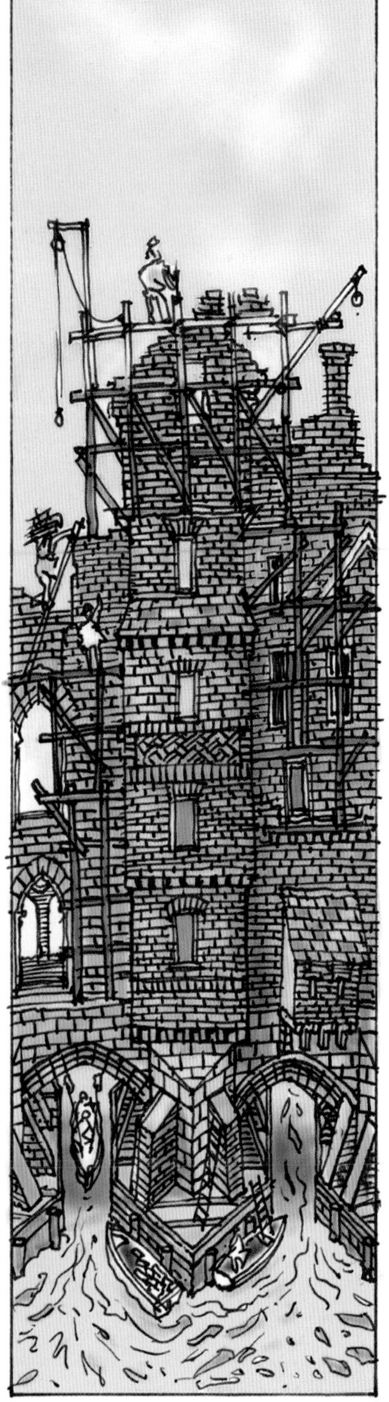

Bricks and mortar
will not stay,
Will not stay,
will not stay,
Bricks and mortar
will not stay,
My fair lady.

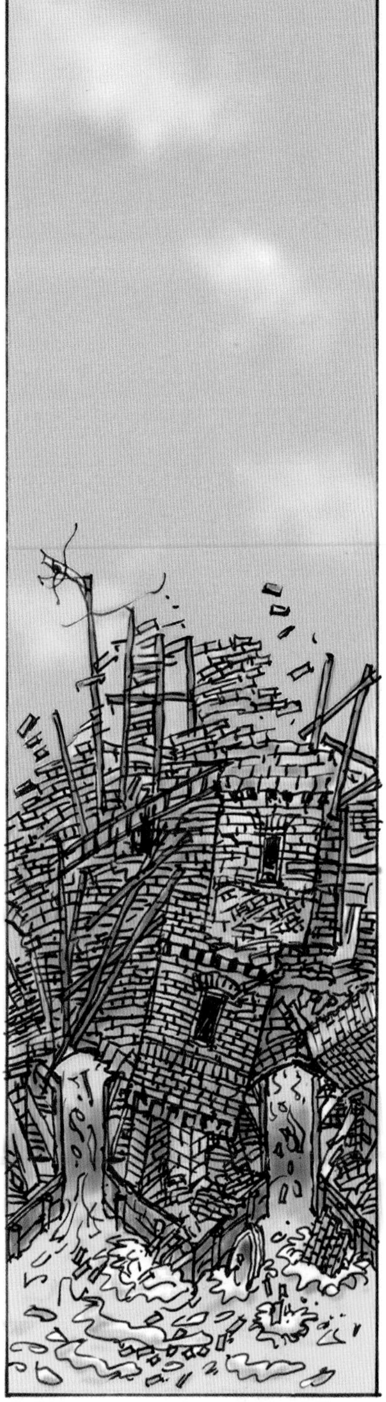

Build it up with
iron and steel,
Iron and steel,
iron and steel,
Build it up with
iron and steel,
My fair lady.

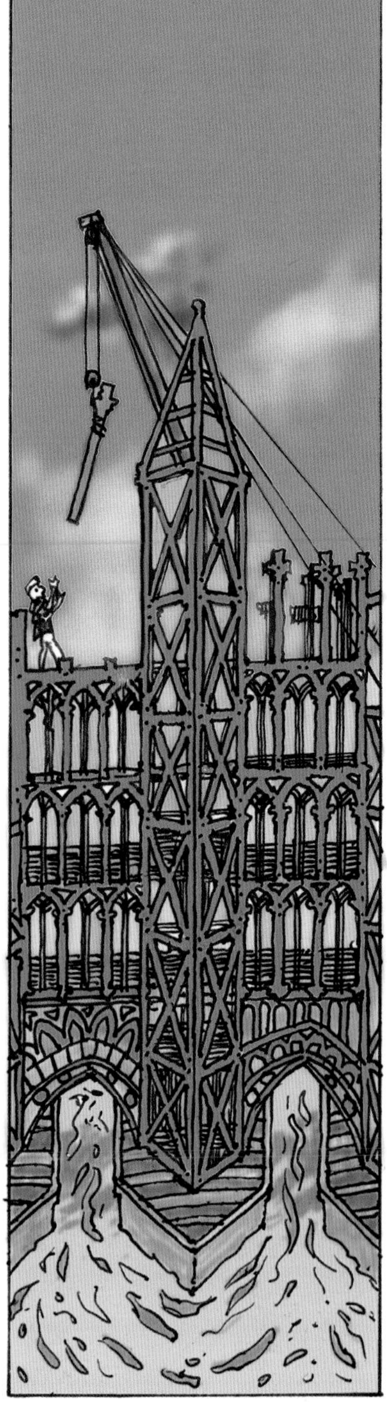

Iron and steel will
bend and bow,
Bend and bow,
bend and bow,
Iron and steel will
bend and bow,
My fair lady.

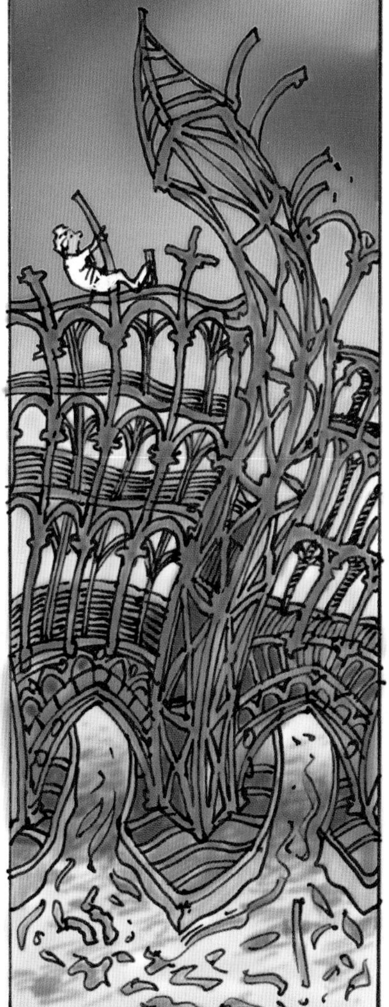

Build it up with
silver and gold,
Silver and gold,
silver and gold,
Build it up with
silver and gold,
My fair lady.

Silver and gold will
be stolen away,
Stolen away,
stolen away,
Silver and gold will
be stolen away,
My fair lady.

Set a man to
watch all night,
Watch all night,
watch all night,
Set a man to
watch all night,
My fair lady.

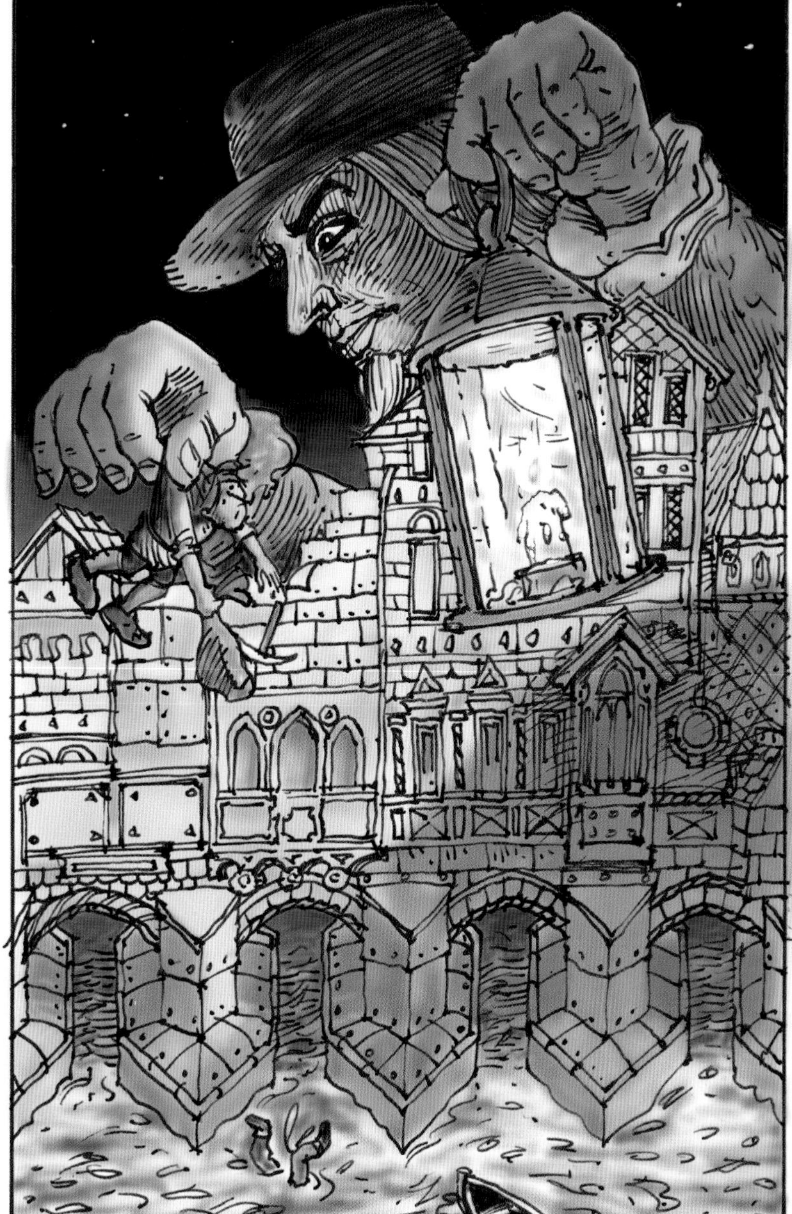

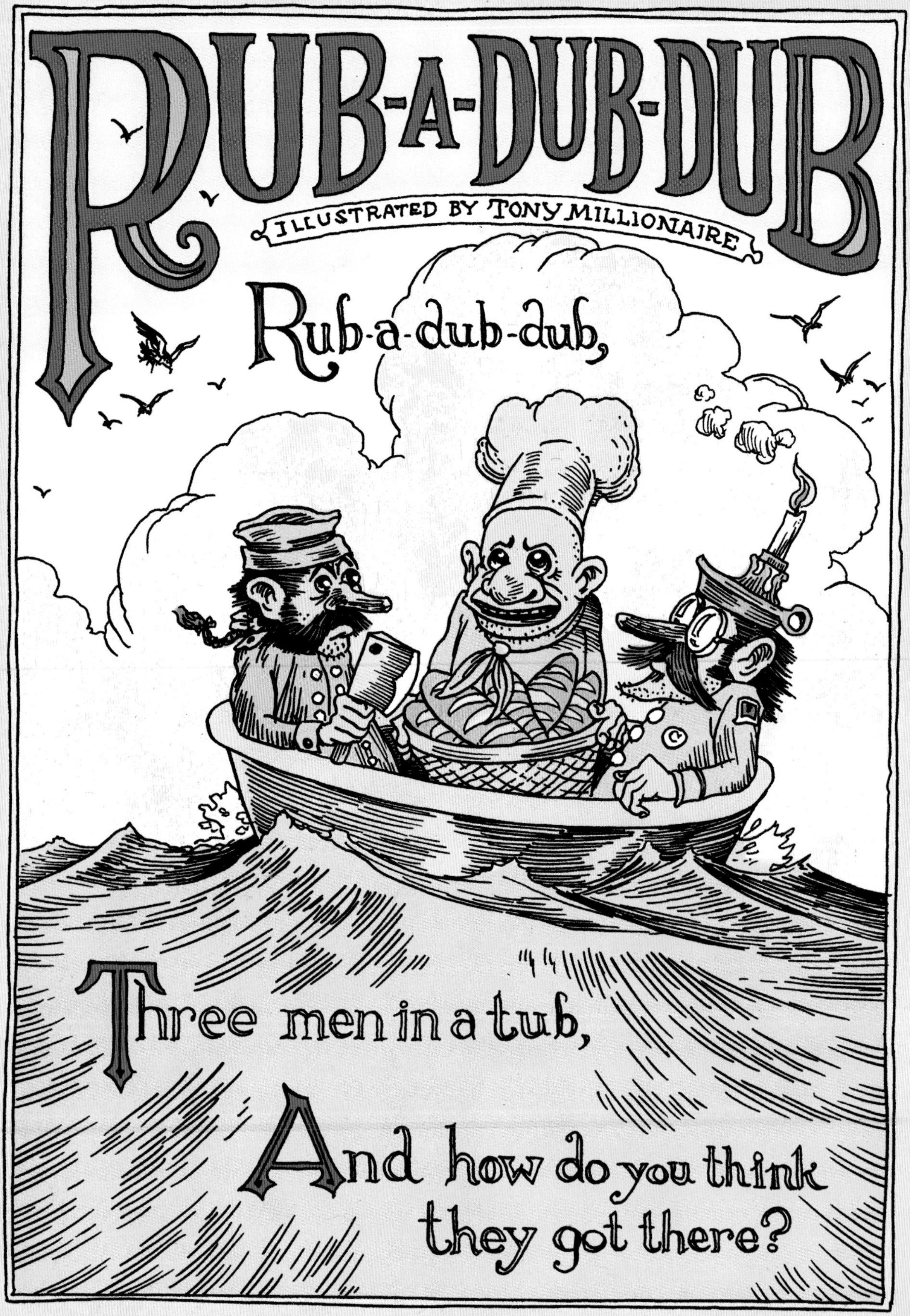
RUB-A-DUB-DUB
ILLUSTRATED BY TONY MILLIONAIRE
Rub-a-dub-dub,
Three men in a tub,
And how do you think they got there?

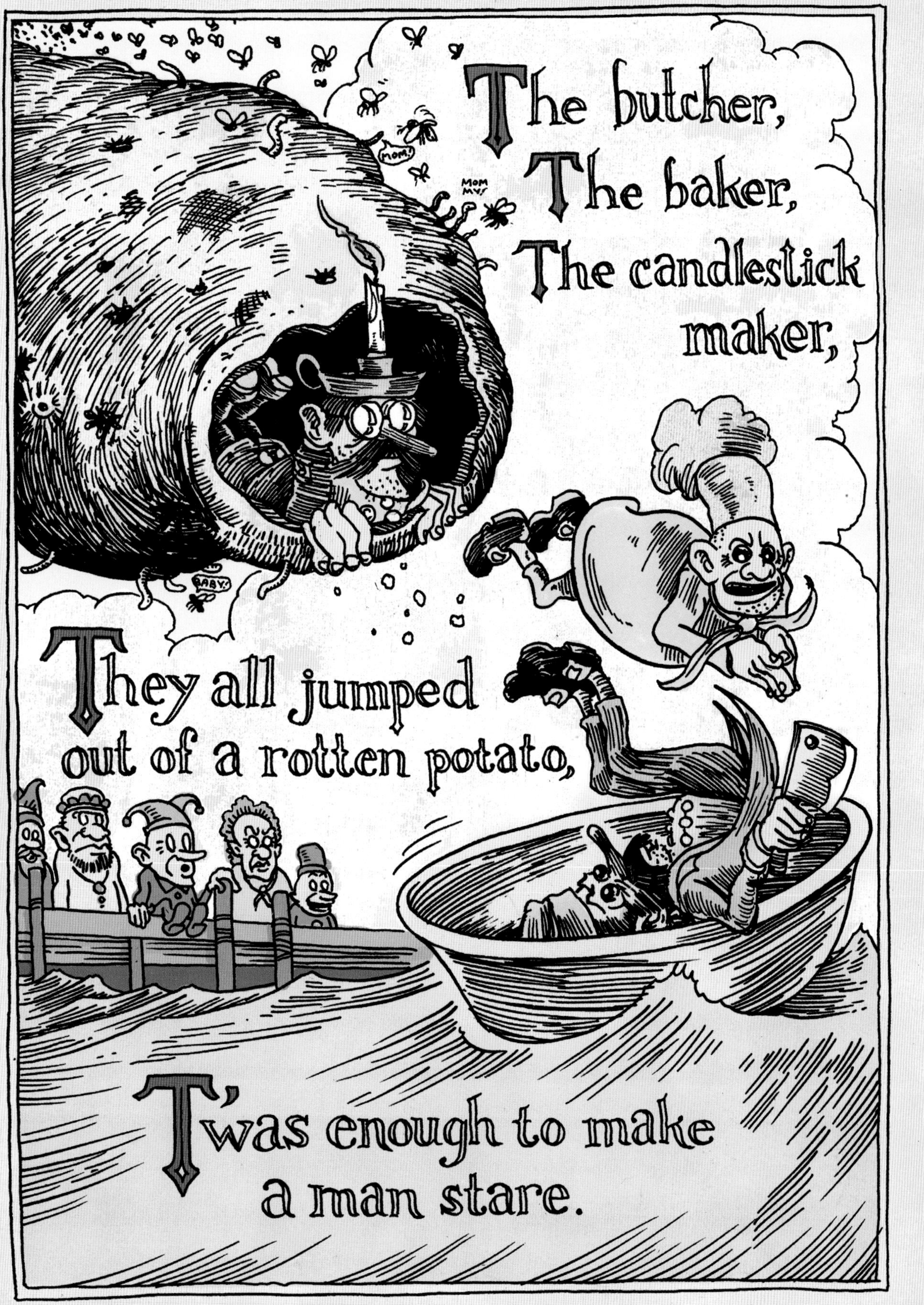
The butcher,
The baker,
The candlestick maker,
MOM!
BABY!
They all jumped out of a rotten potato,
'Twas enough to make a man stare.

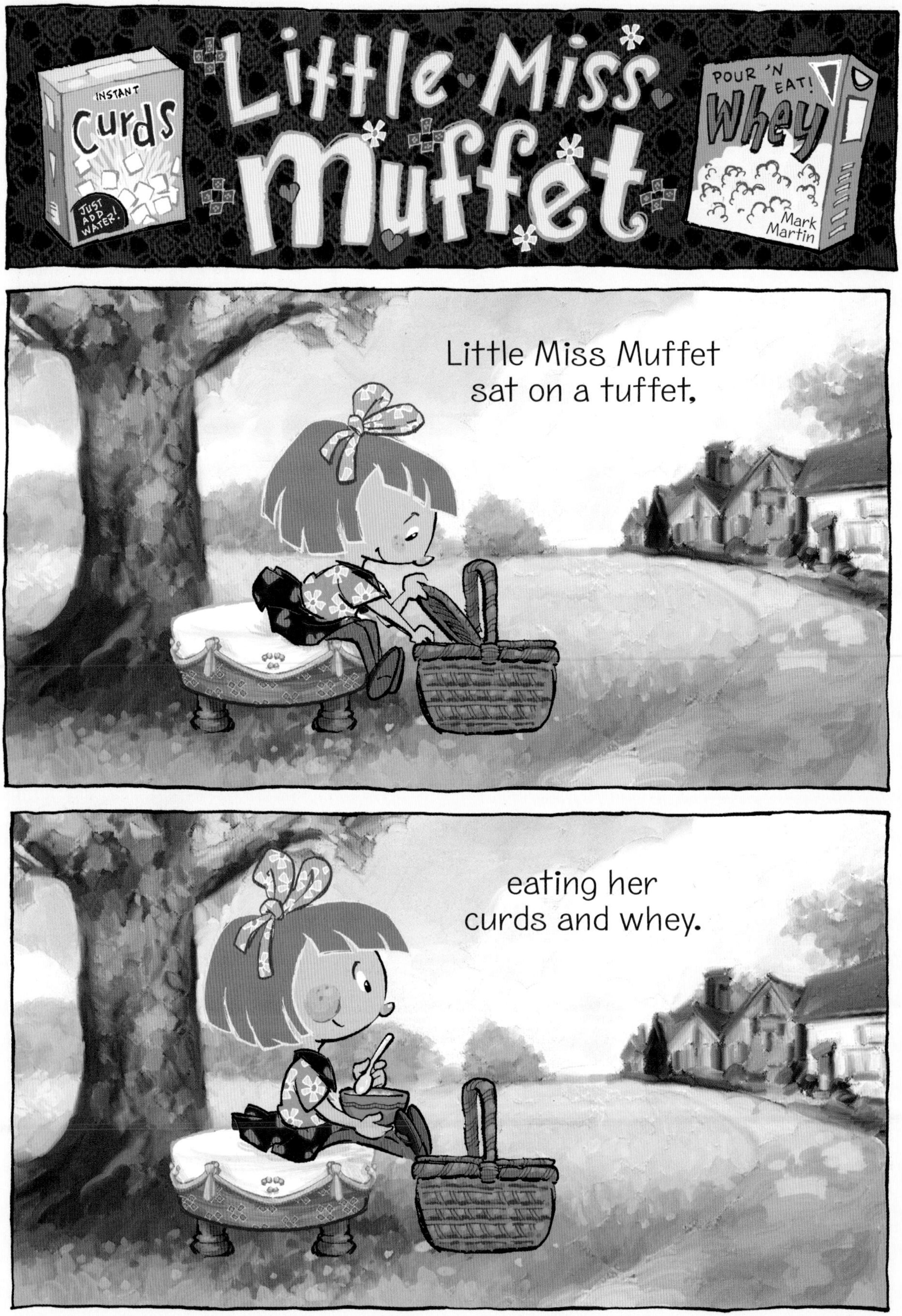
INSTANT
Curds
JUST ADD WATER!
Little Miss Muffet
POUR 'N EAT!
Whey
Mark Martin
Little Miss Muffet sat on a tuffet,
eating her curds and whey.

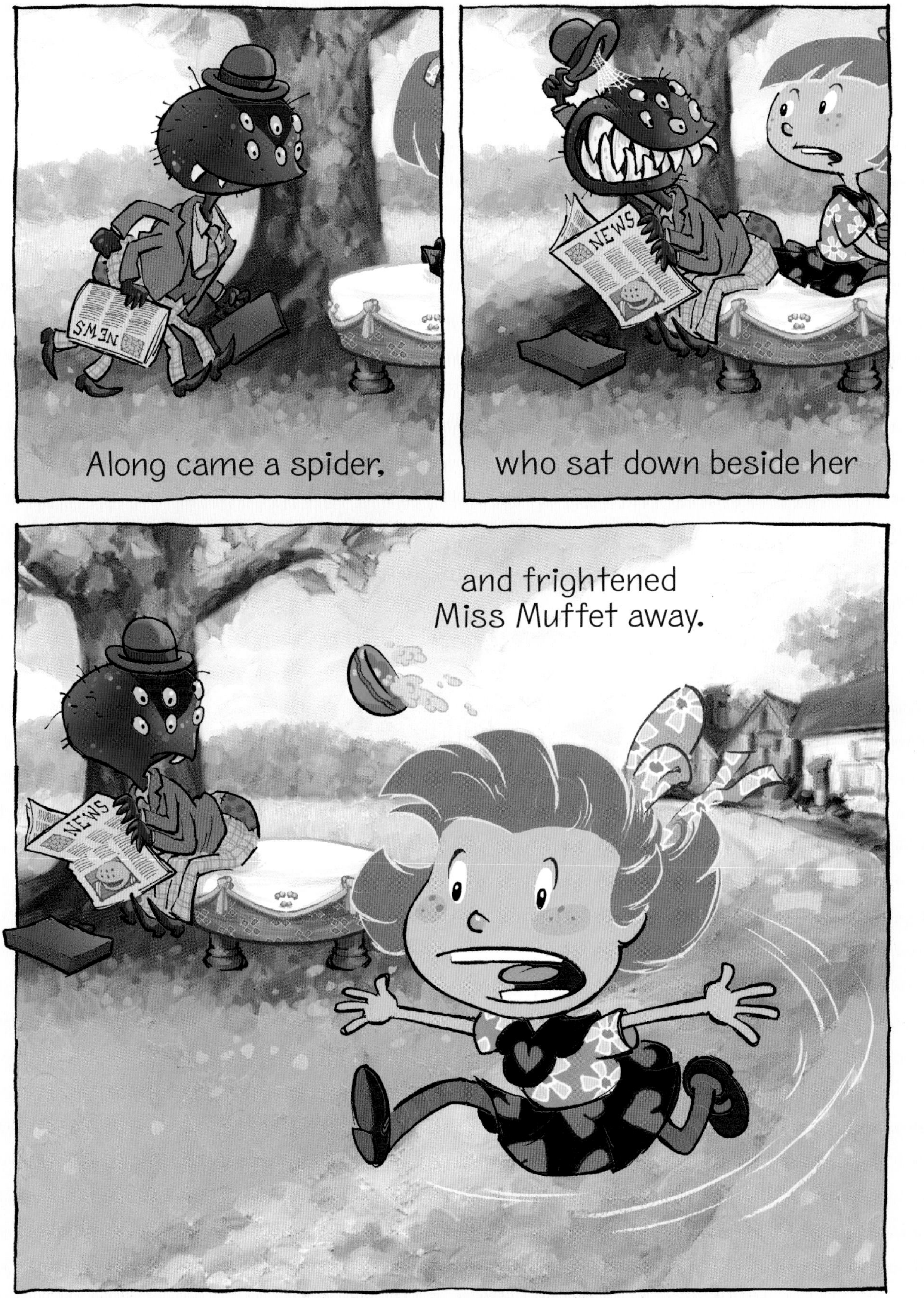
Along came a spider,
NEWS
who sat down beside her
and frightened
Miss Muffet away.
NEWS

Peter, Peter, Pumpkin Eater

Eric Orchard

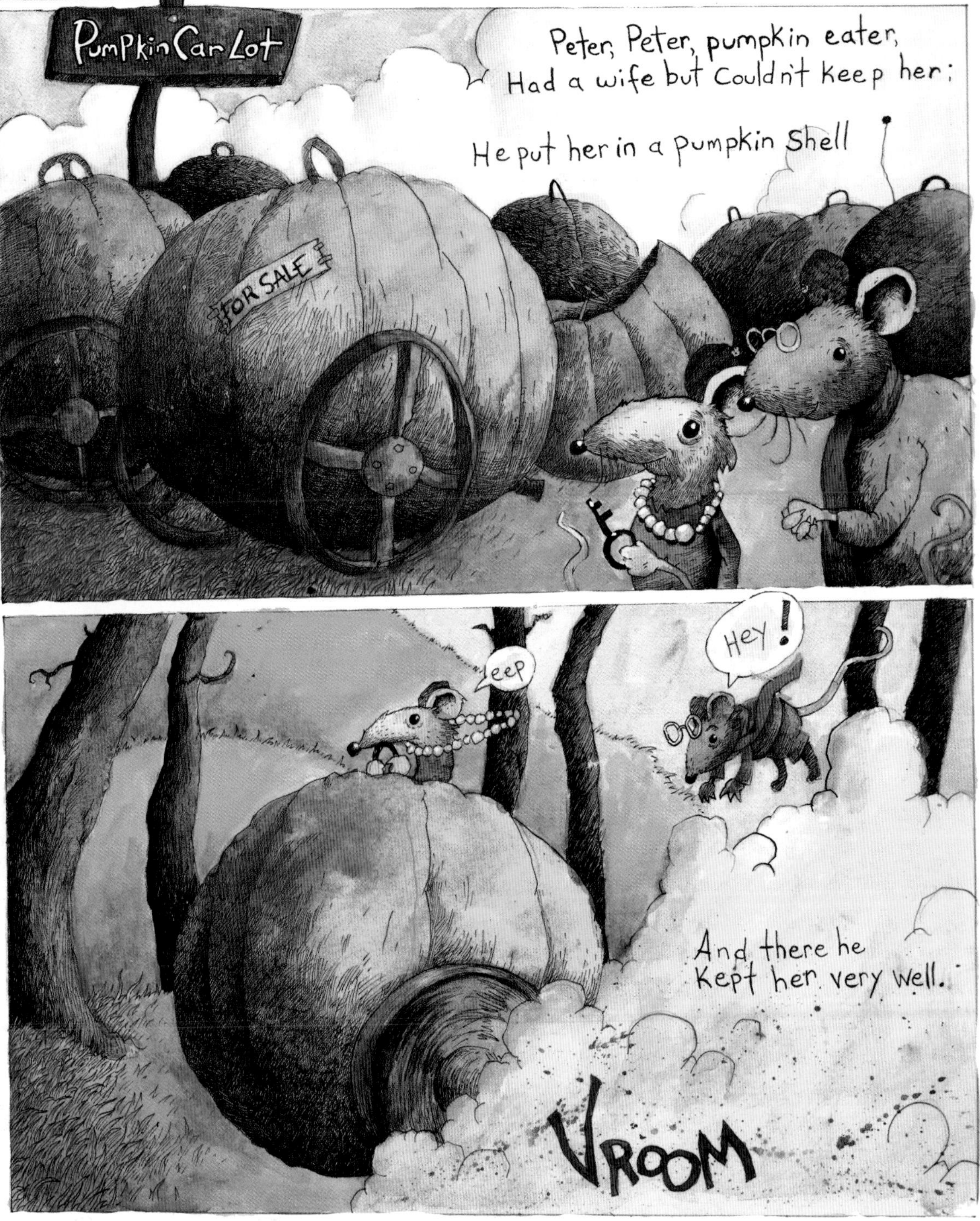
PumpKin Car Lot
Peter, Peter, pumpkin eater,
Had a wife but couldn't keep her:
He put her in a pumpkin shell
FOR SALE
eep
Hey!
And there he kept her very well.
VROOM

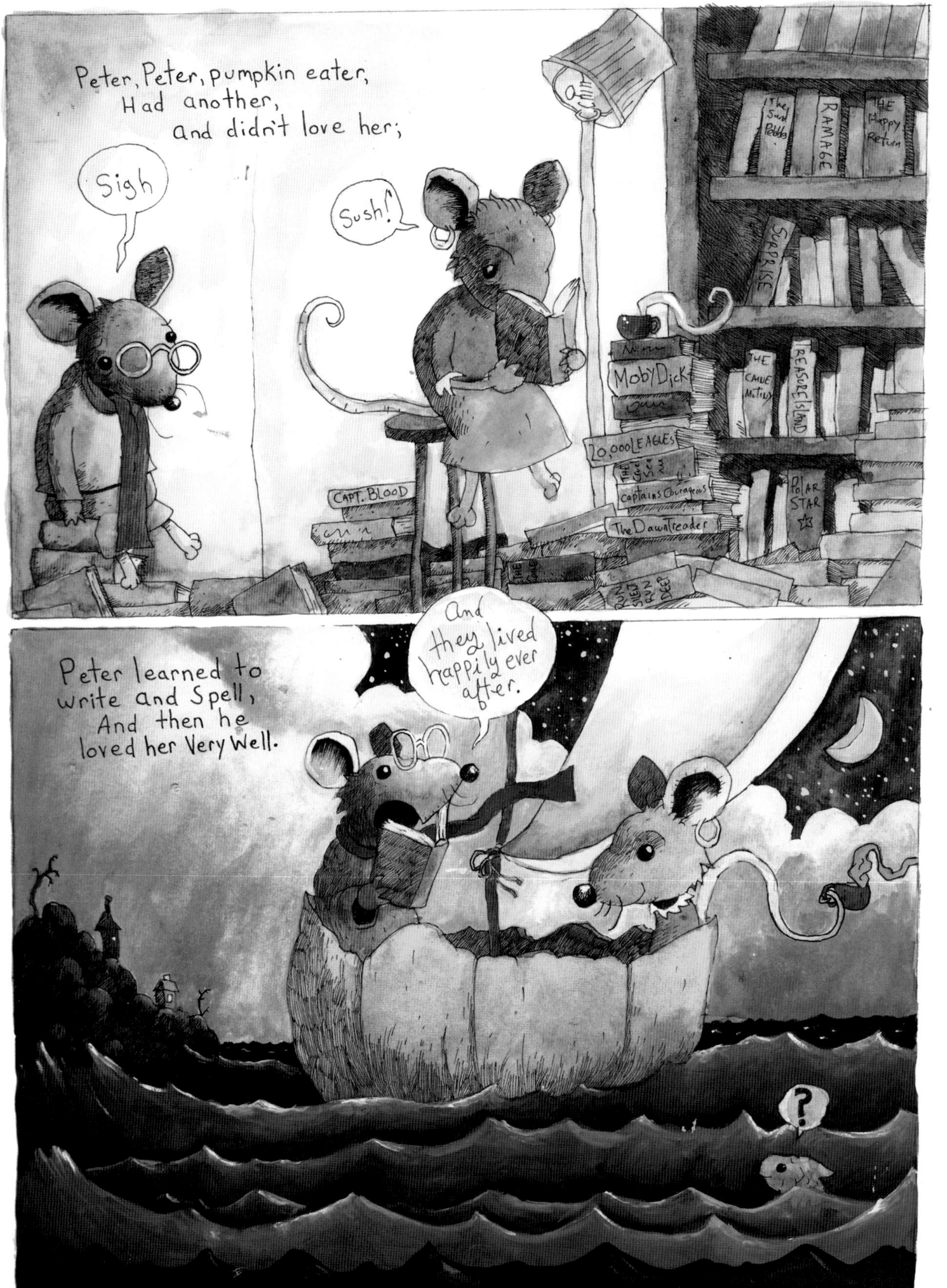
Peter, Peter, pumpkin eater,
Had another,
and didn't love her;
Sigh
Sush!
RAMAGE
THE Happy Return
SURPRISE
MobyDick
20,000 LEAGUES
CAPT. BLOOD
Captains Courageous
The Dawn Treader
POLAR STAR
Peter learned to
write and Spell,
And then he
loved her Very Well.
And they lived happily ever after.
?

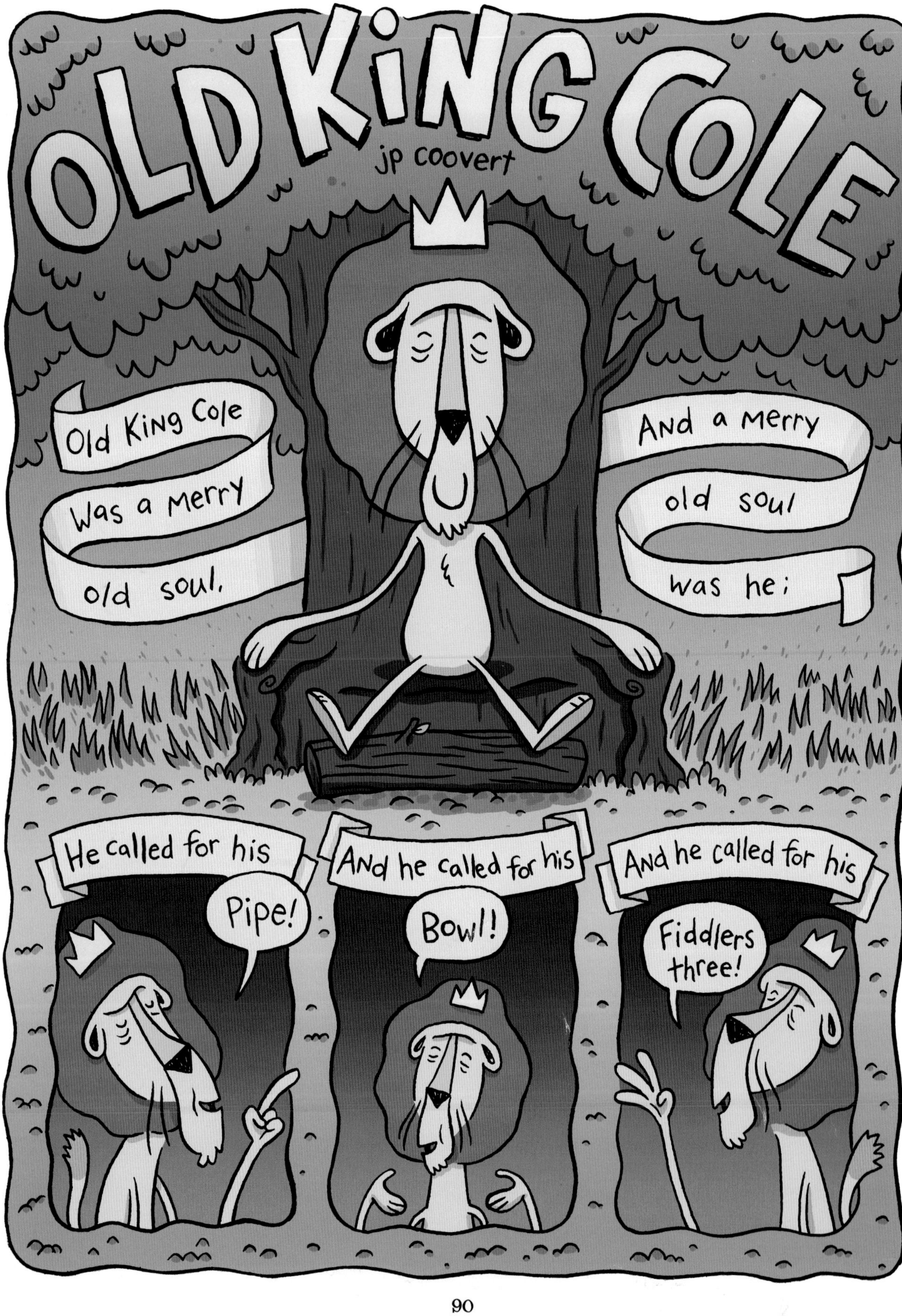

OLD KiNG COLE
jp coovert
Old King Cole
Was a merry
old soul,
And a merry
old soul
was he;
He called for his
Pipe!
And he called for his
Bowl!
And he called for his
Fiddlers three!

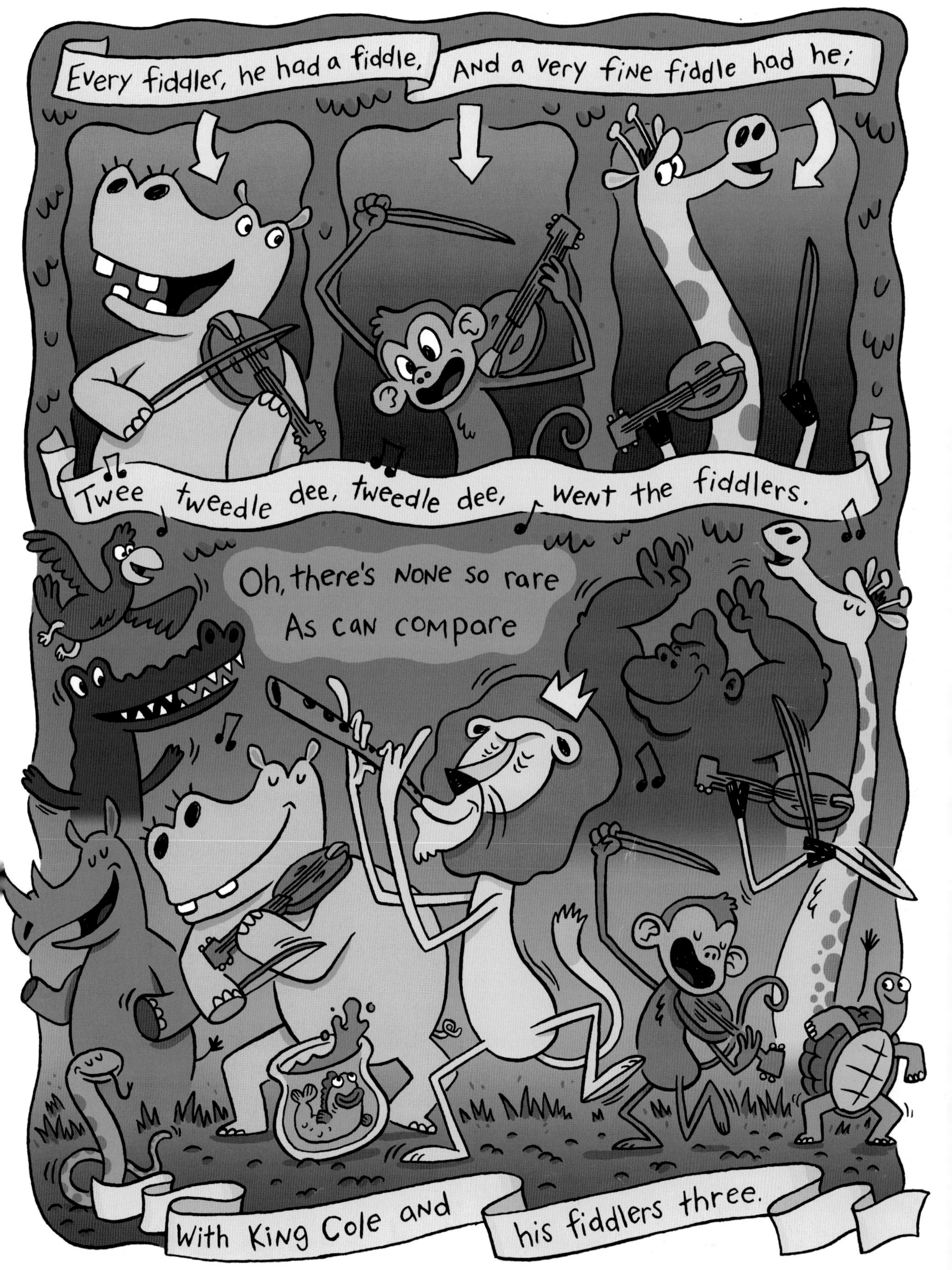
Every fiddler, he had a fiddle,
And a very fine fiddle had he;
Twee tweedle dee, tweedle dee, went the fiddlers.
Oh, there's none so rare
As can compare
With King Cole and
his fiddlers three.

The Lion and the Unicorn

Aaron Renier

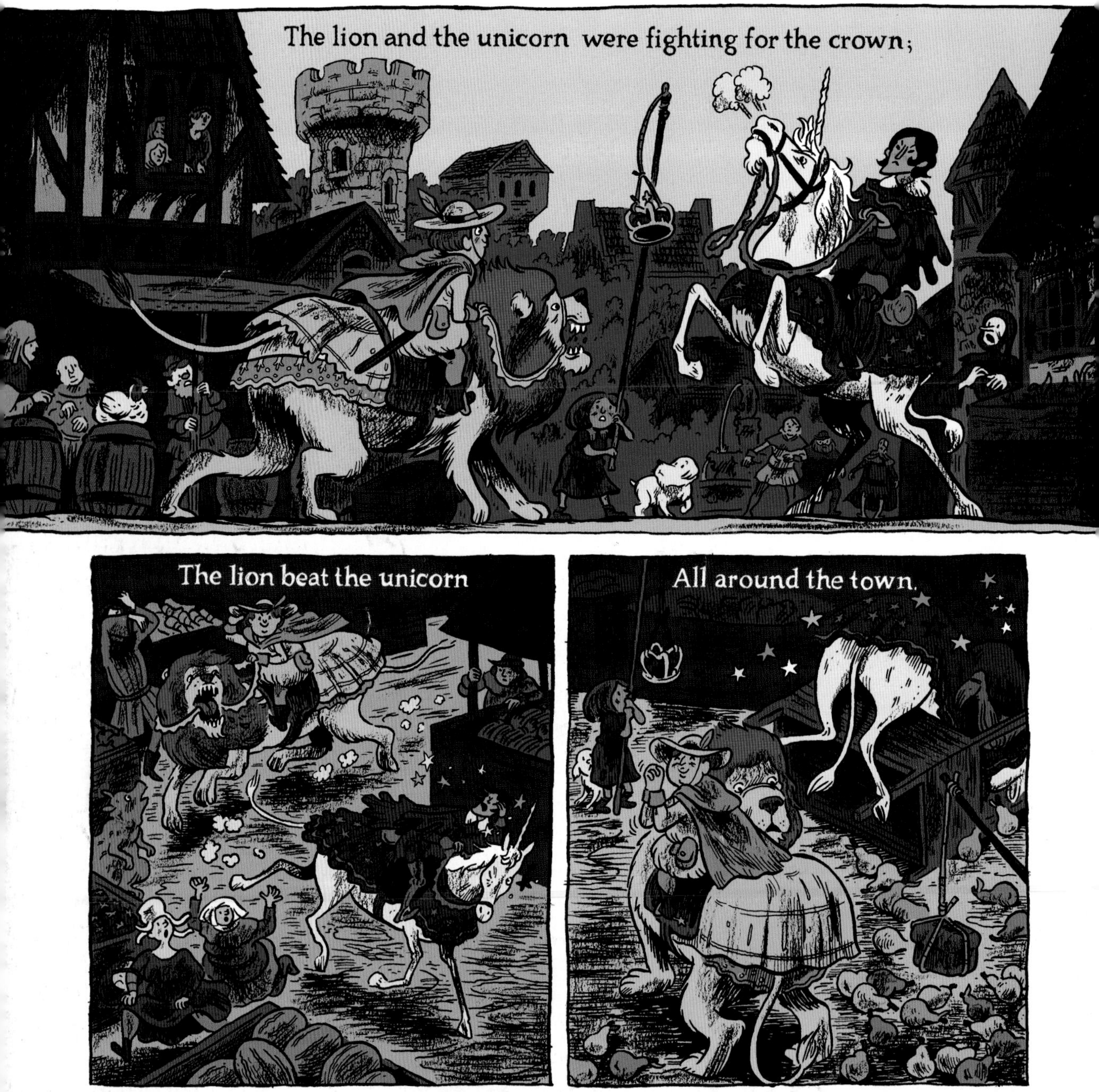
The lion and the unicorn were fighting for the crown;
The lion beat the unicorn
All around the town.

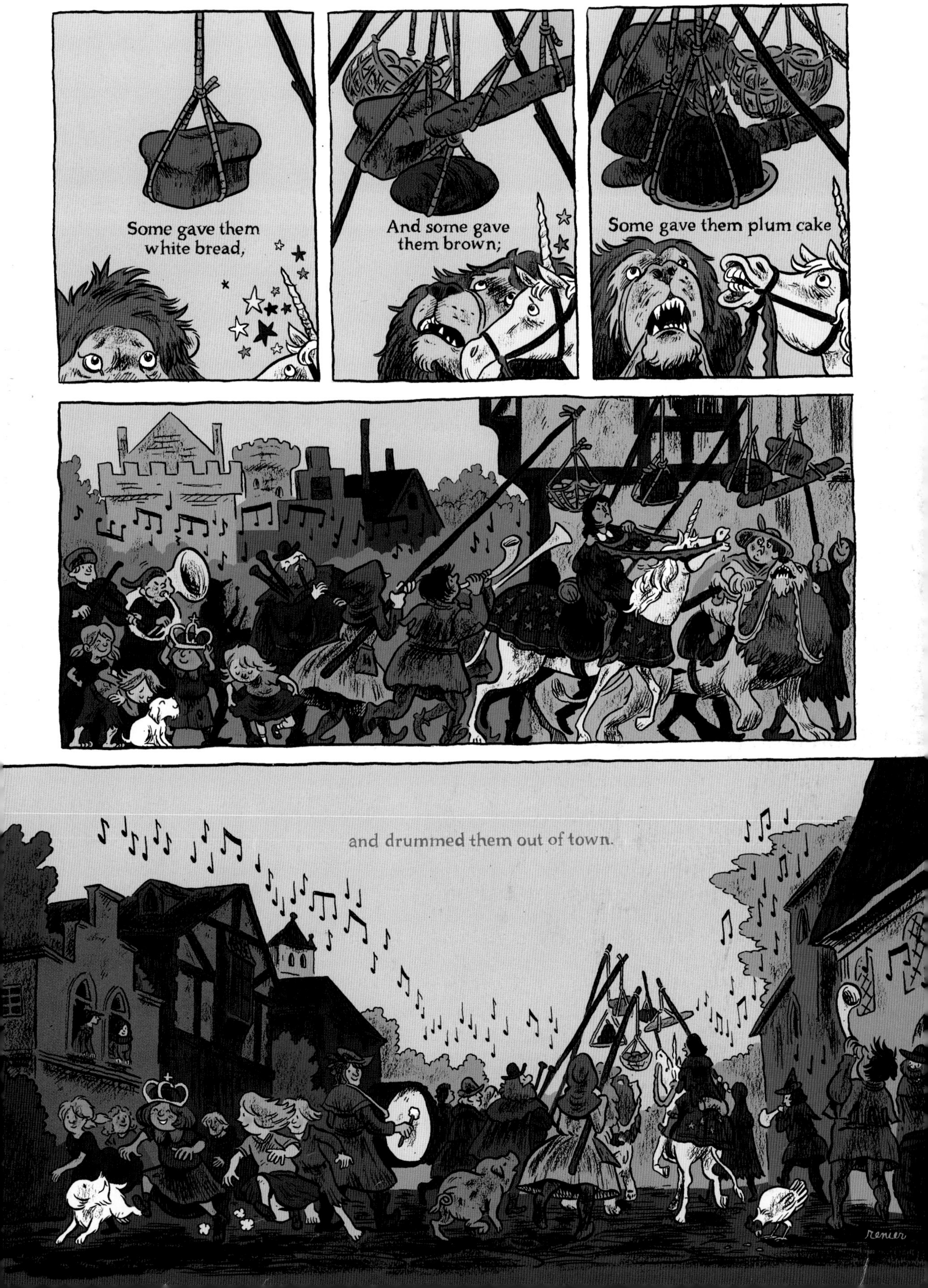
Some gave them white bread,
And some gave them brown;
Some gave them plum cake
and drummed them out of town.
renier

There was a little girl

by vera brosgol

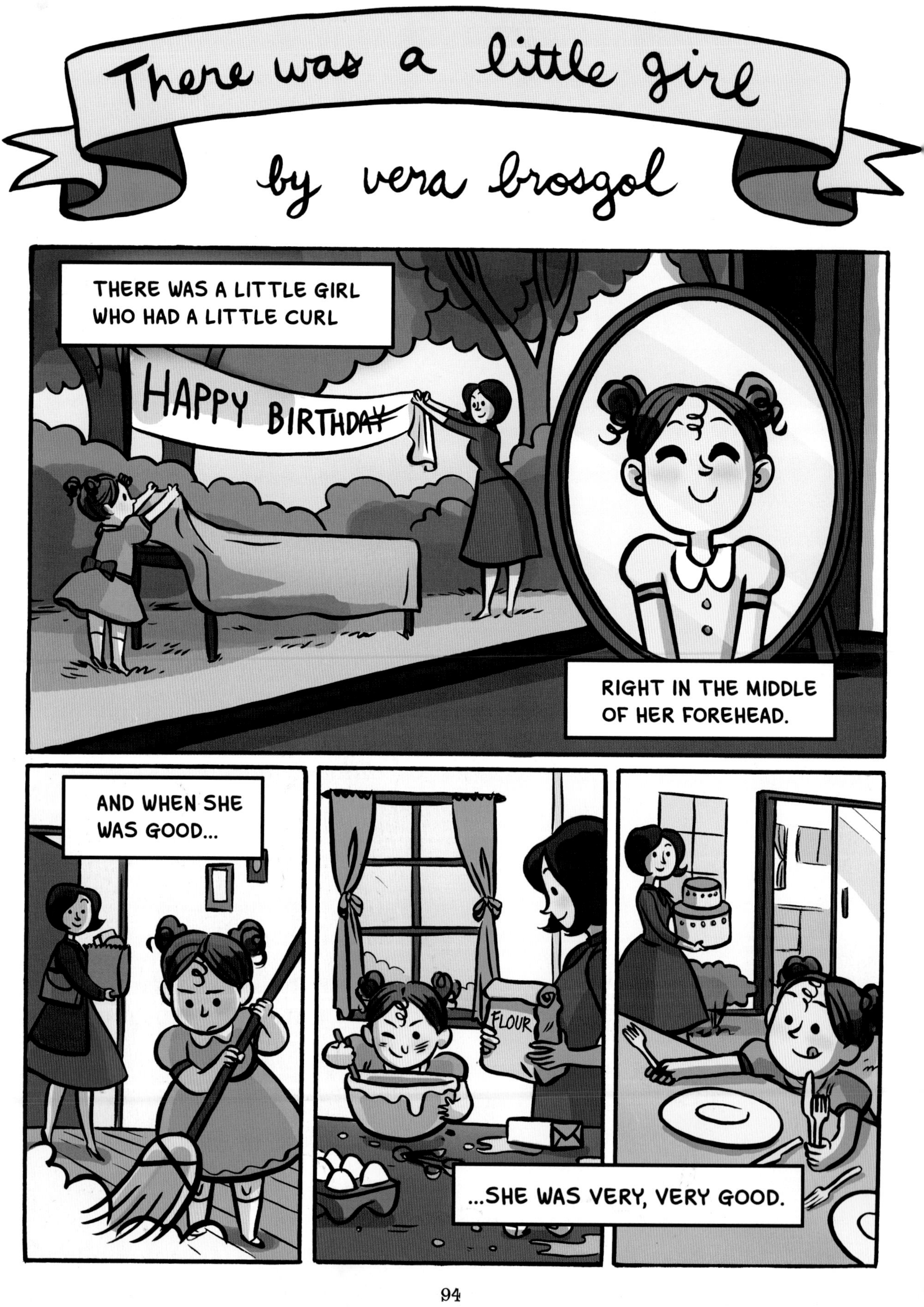

THERE WAS A LITTLE GIRL WHO HAD A LITTLE CURL
HAPPY BIRTHDAY
RIGHT IN THE MIDDLE OF HER FOREHEAD.
AND WHEN SHE WAS GOOD...
FLOUR
...SHE WAS VERY, VERY GOOD.

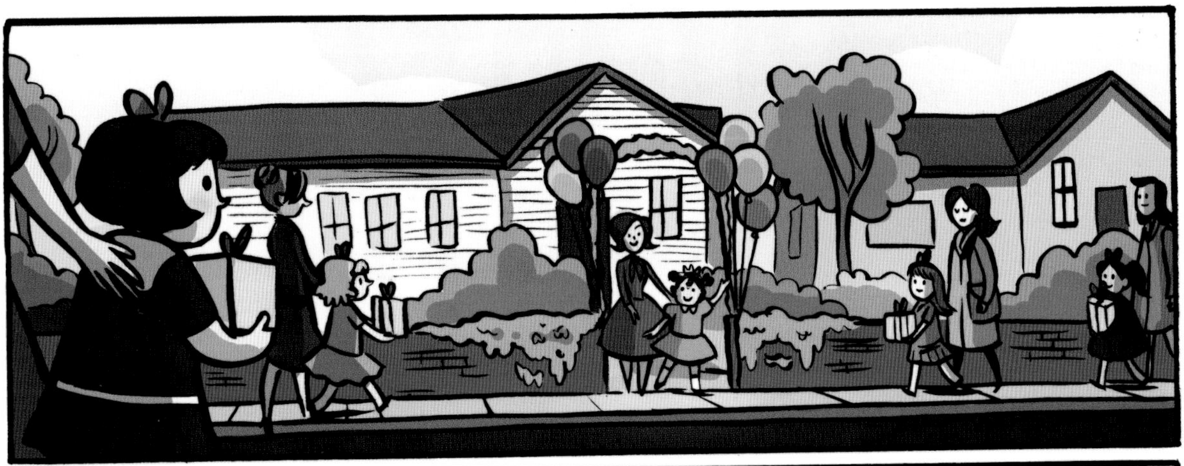

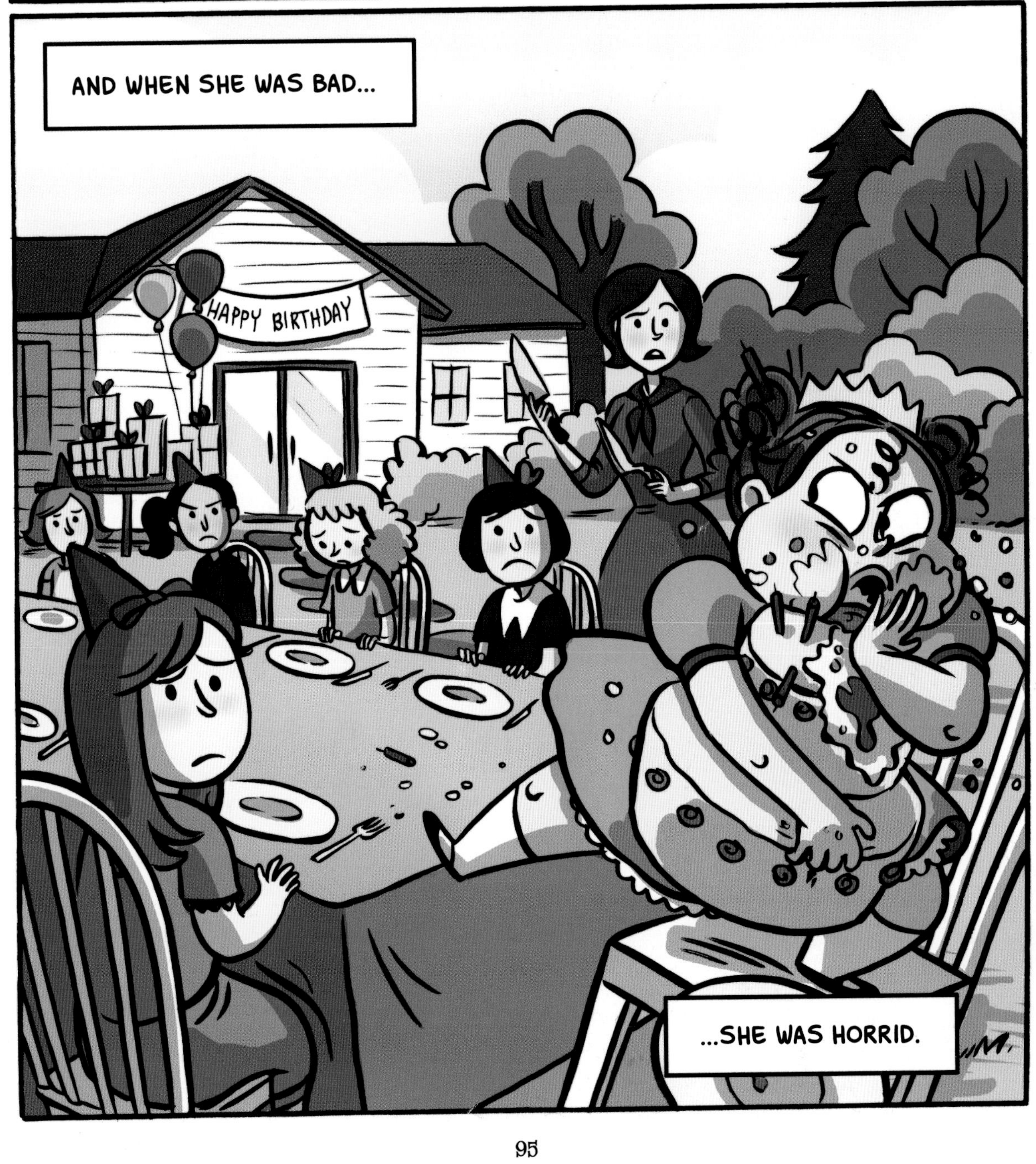
AND WHEN SHE WAS BAD...
HAPPY BIRTHDAY
...SHE WAS HORRID.

HUMPTY DUMPTY

by
GILBERT
"BETO"
HERNANDEZ
2010

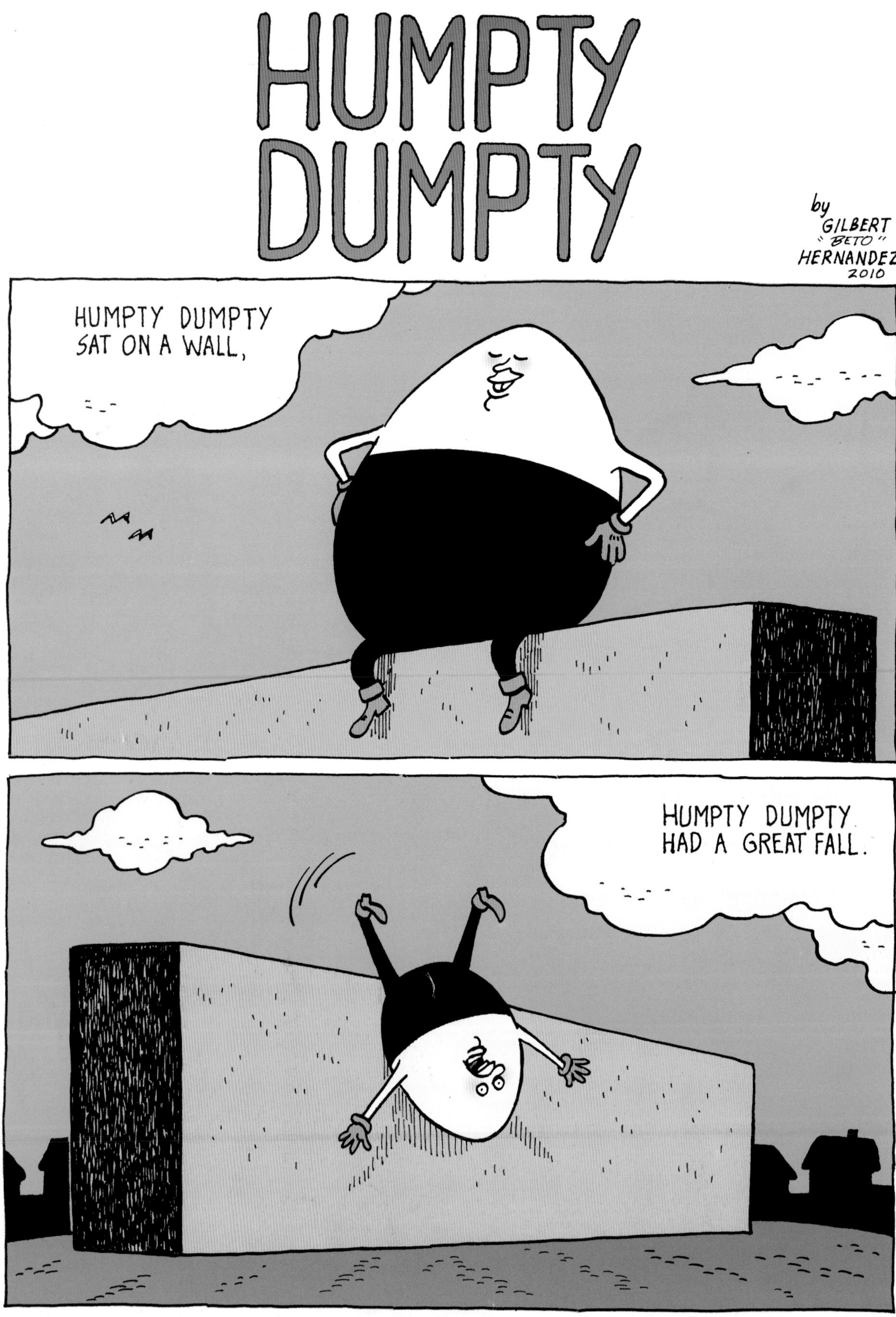
HUMPTY DUMPTY
SAT ON A WALL,
HUMPTY DUMPTY
HAD A GREAT FALL.

Color by Steve Weissman

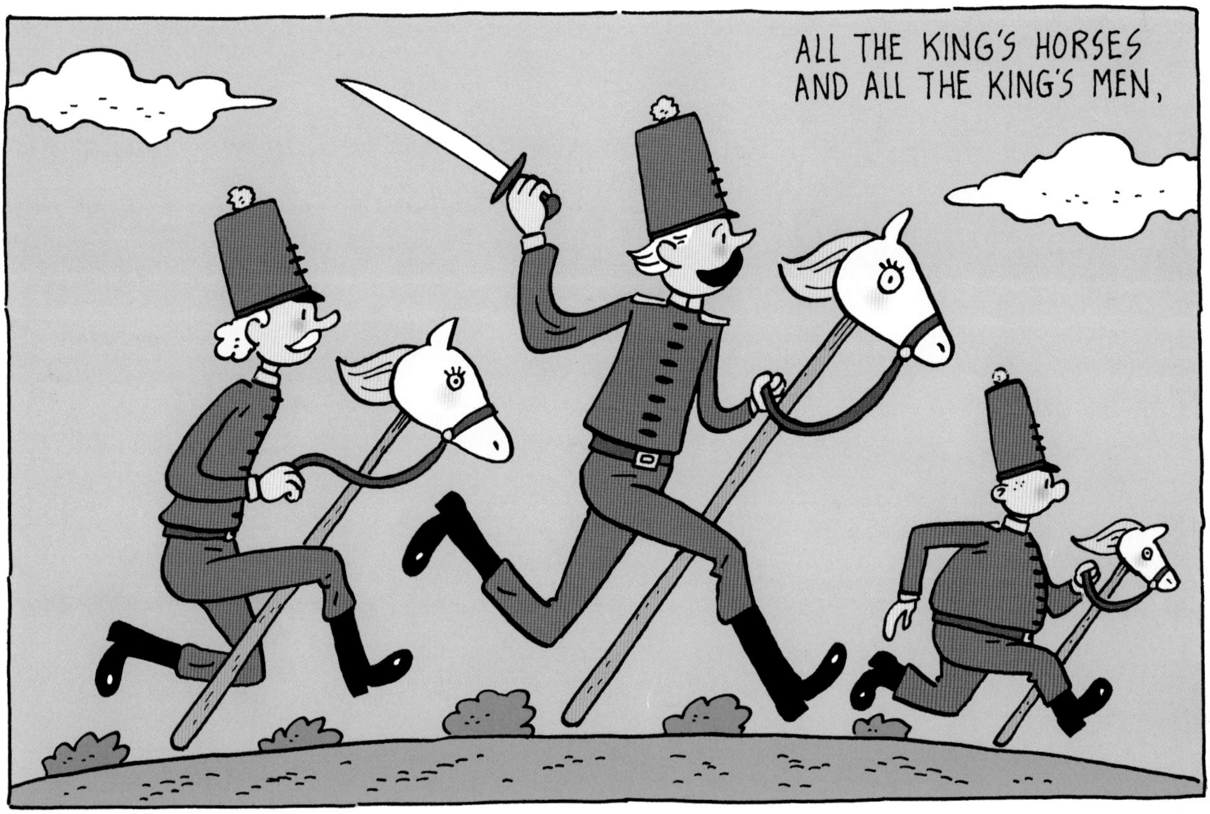
ALL THE KING'S HORSES
AND ALL THE KING'S MEN,

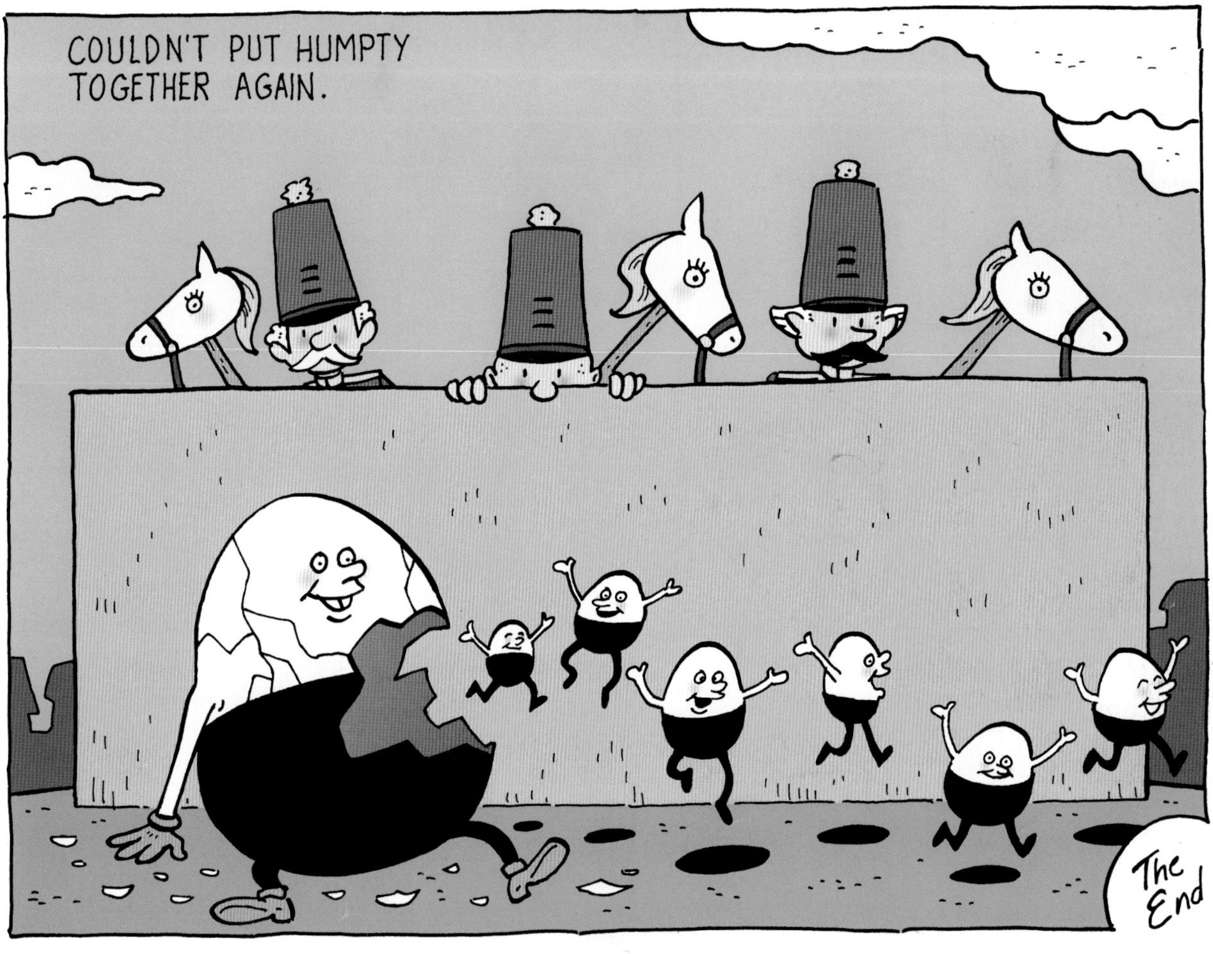
COULDN'T PUT HUMPTY
TOGETHER AGAIN.
The End

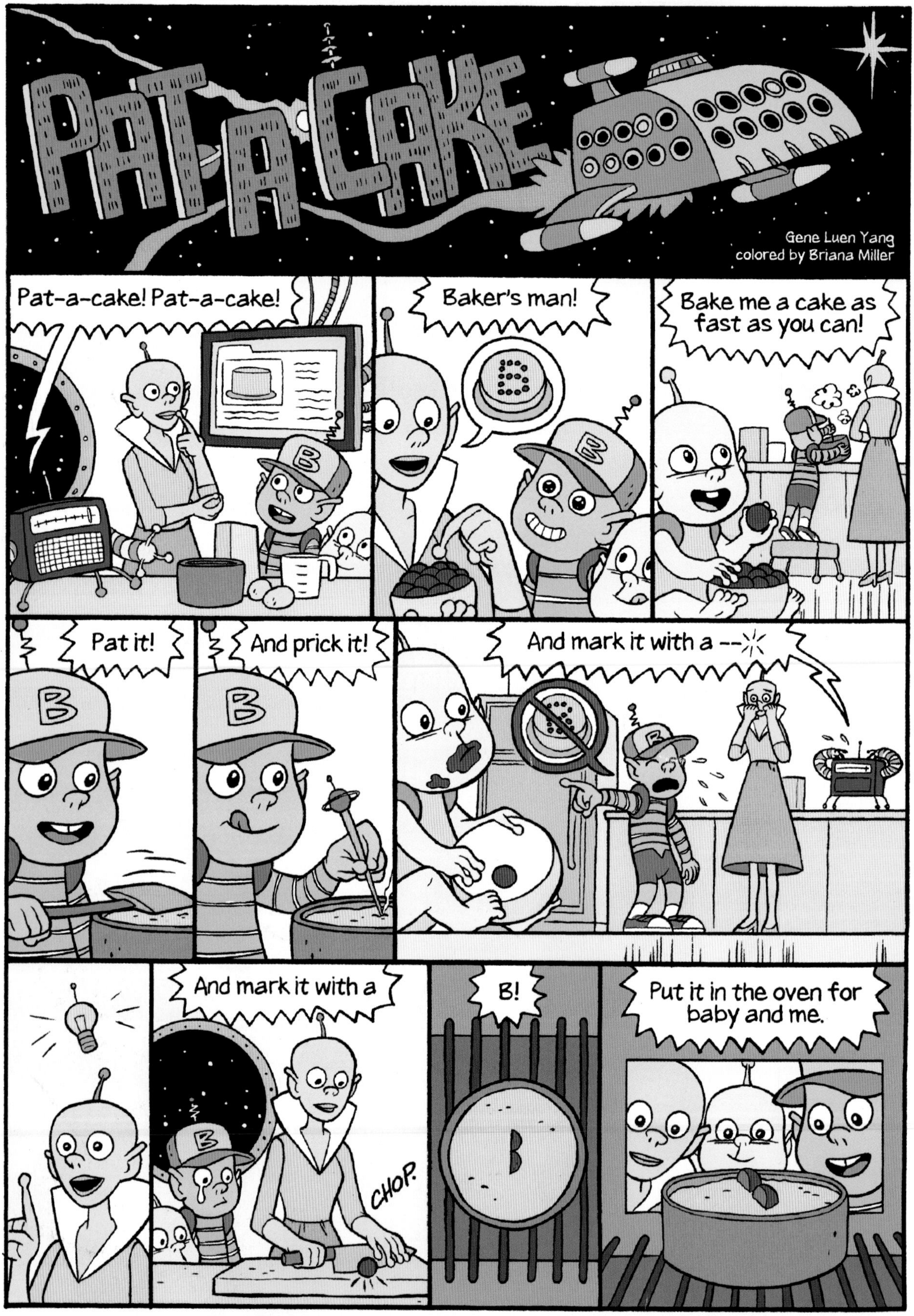
PAT-A-CAKE
Gene Luen Yang
colored by Briana Miller
Pat-a-cake! Pat-a-cake!
Baker's man!
Bake me a cake as fast as you can!
Pat it!
And prick it!
And mark it with a --
And mark it with a
CHOP.
B!
Put it in the oven for baby and me.

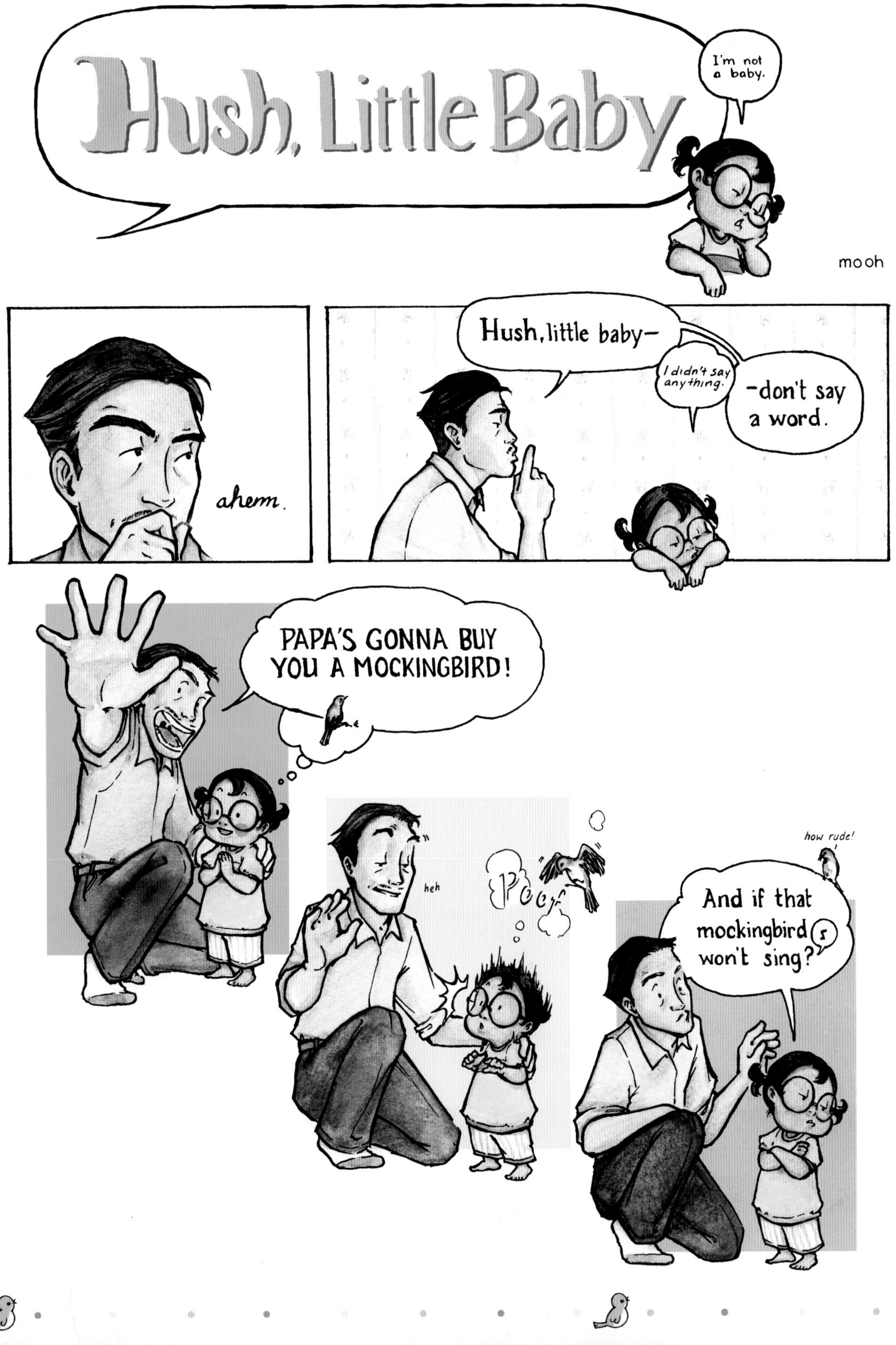
Hush, Little Baby
I'm not a baby.
mooh
ahem.
Hush, little baby-
I didn't say anything.
-don't say a word.
PAPA'S GONNA BUY YOU A MOCKINGBIRD!
heh
Poof
how rude!
And if that mockingbird won't sing?

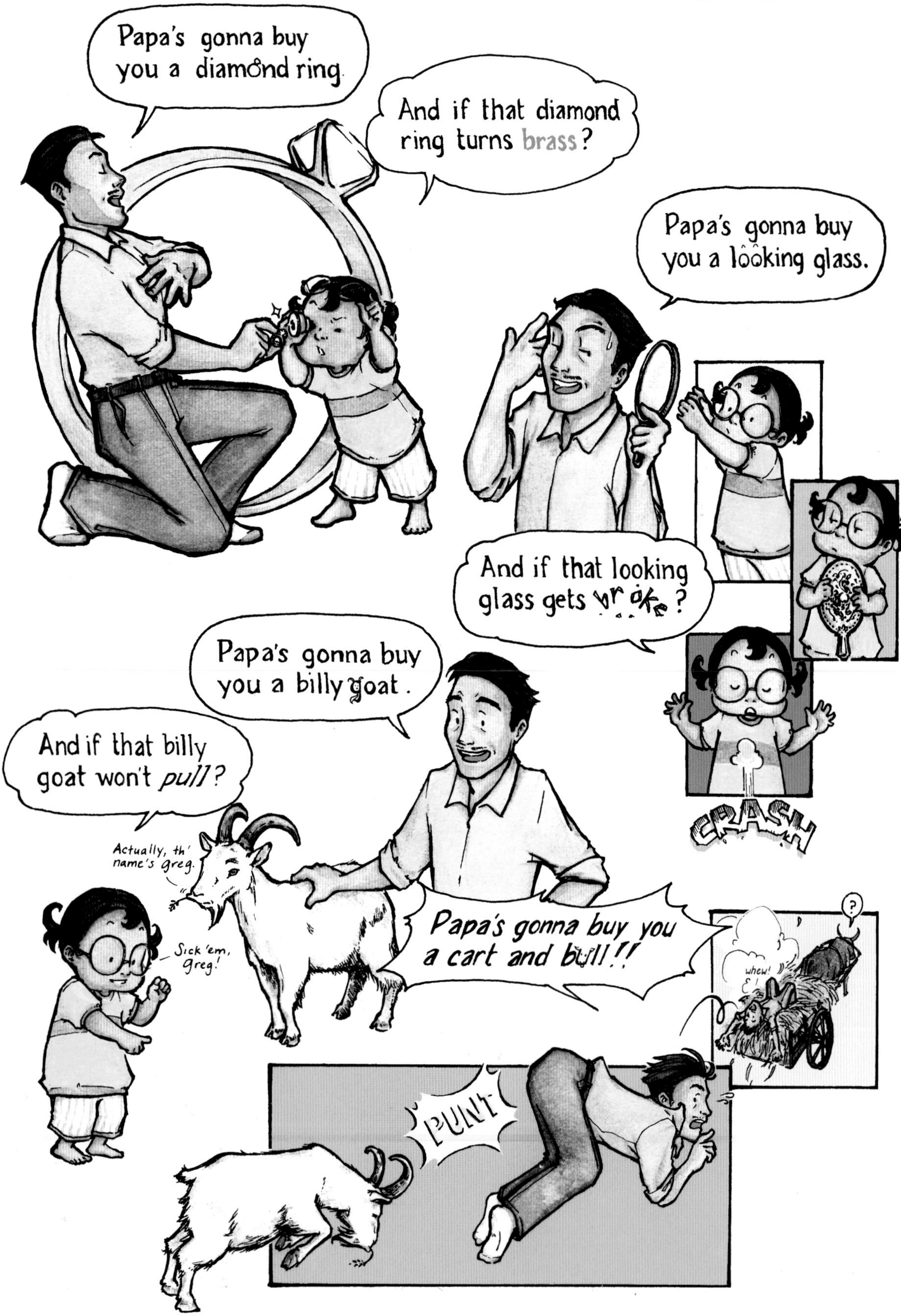
Papa's gonna buy you a diamond ring.
And if that diamond ring turns brass?
Papa's gonna buy you a looking glass.
And if that looking glass gets broke?
CRASH
Papa's gonna buy you a billy goat.
And if that billy goat won't pull?
Actually, th' name's greg.
Sick 'em, greg!
Papa's gonna buy you a cart and bull!!
PUNT
whew!
?

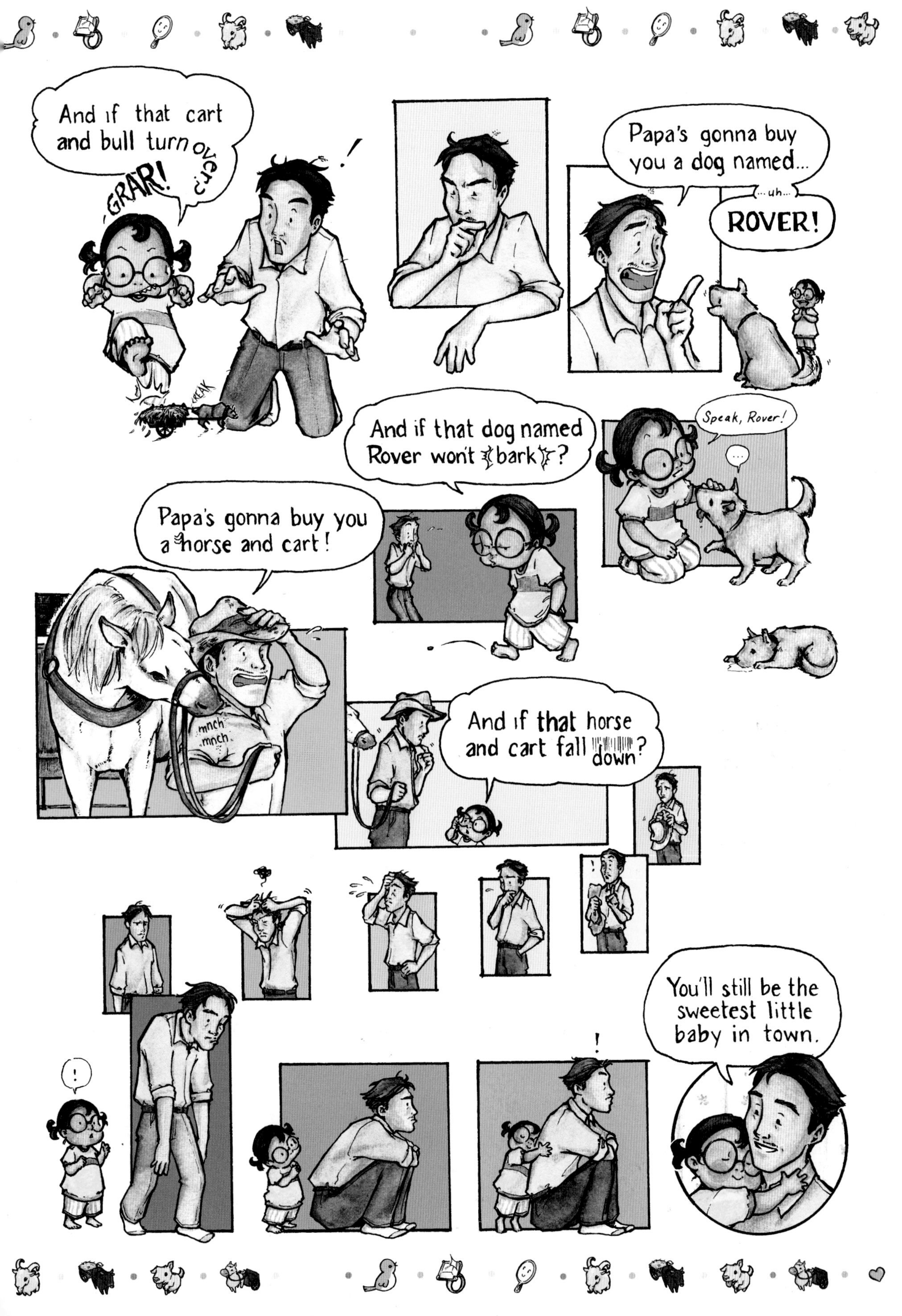
And if that cart and bull turn over?
GRAR!
!
CREAK
Papa's gonna buy you a dog named...
...uh...
ROVER!
And if that dog named Rover won't bark?
Speak, Rover!
...
Papa's gonna buy you a horse and cart!
mnch mnch
And if that horse and cart fall down?
!
!
!
You'll still be the sweetest little baby in town.

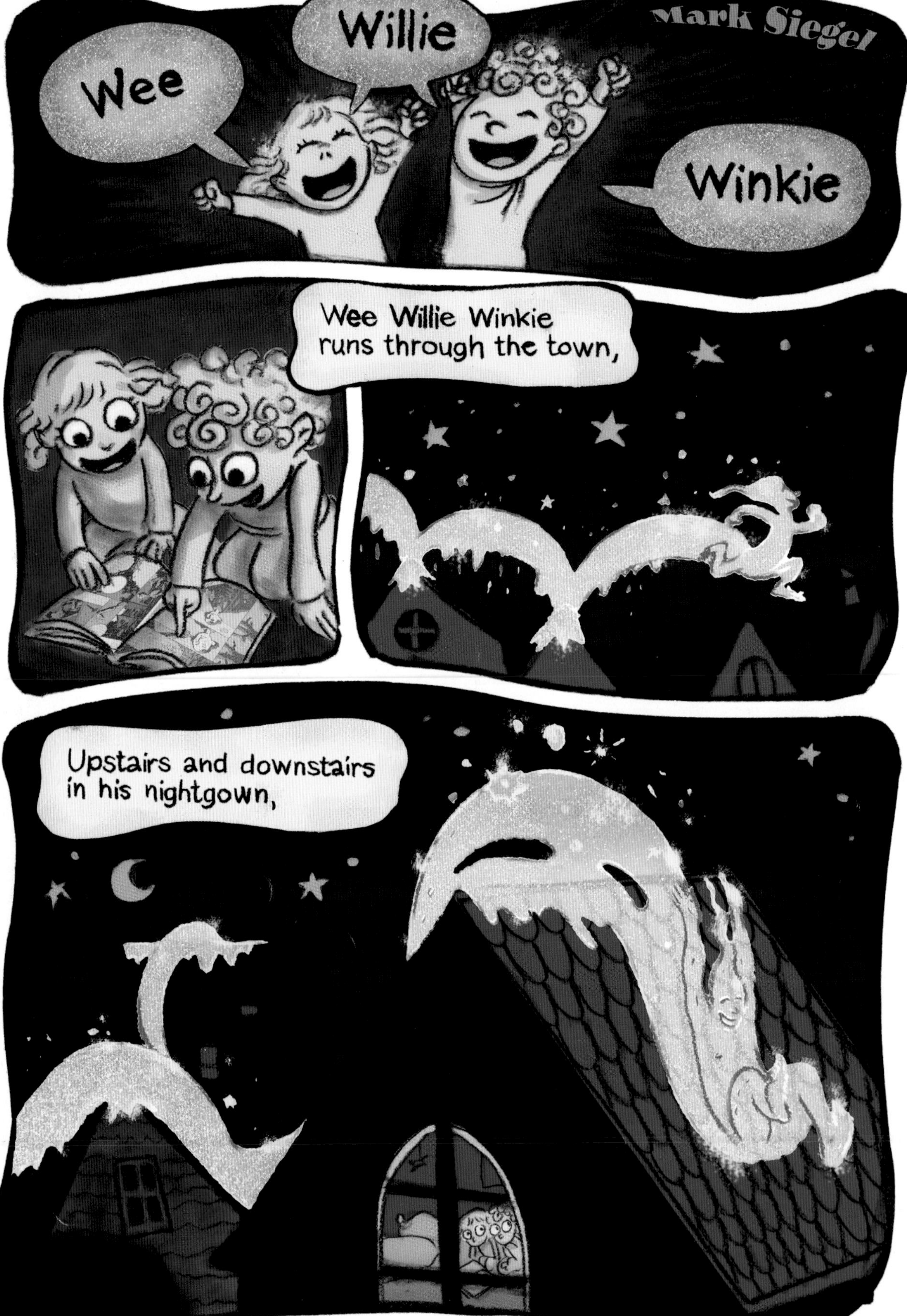
Mark Siegel
Wee
Willie
Winkie
Wee Willie Winkie runs through the town,
Upstairs and downstairs in his nightgown,

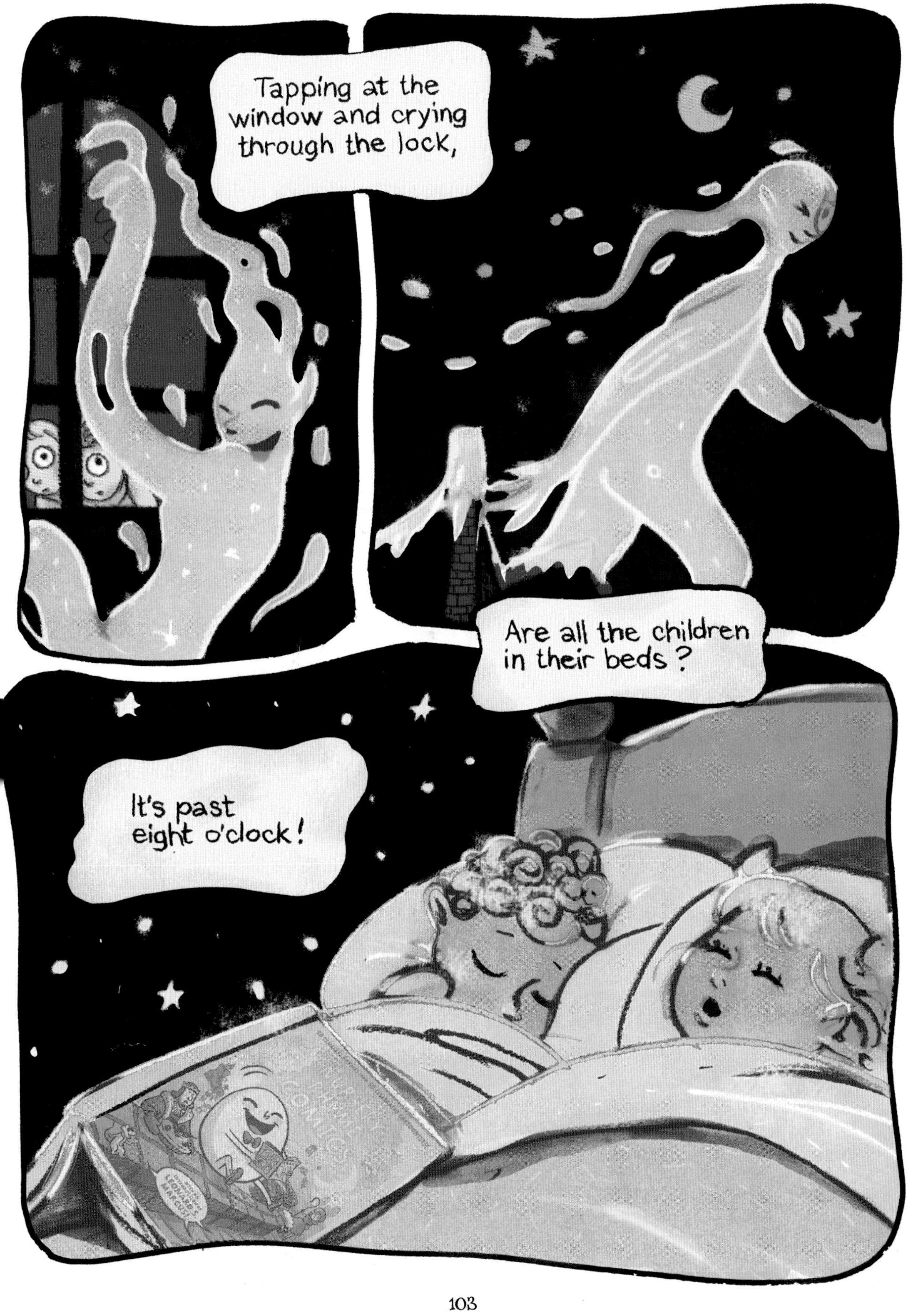
Tapping at the window and crying through the lock,
Are all the children in their beds?
It's past eight o'clock!
NURSERY RHYME COMICS

EDITOR'S NOTE

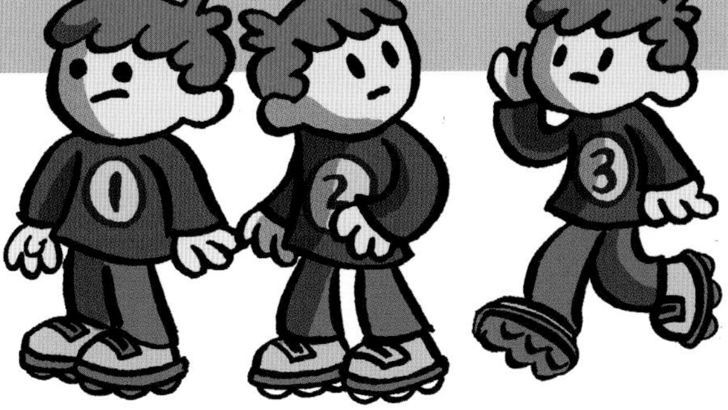

Why has First Second allowed a rowdy gang of twenty-first century cartoonists to run rampant through a volume of traditional nursery rhymes?

From an editor's point of view, the answer is easy: Why bother hiring fifty of the best cartoonists in the world if you aren't going to let them do their thing?

From a historical perspective, there are few sacred cows (moon-jumping or otherwise) when it comes to nursery rhymes. First let's take care of the notion that the rhymes have some firm historical meaning. You often hear that a rhyme is really about some real person or event. "Hey, Diddle, Diddle" is about Egyptians fleeing rising floodwaters; "Georgie Porgie" refers to Charles II; "Mary, Mary, Quite Contrary" is about the extravagance of Mary, Queen of Scots. Nearly always, these assertions of special significance are speculation or provably false. (Most of my confidence on this topic is owed to the classic *Oxford Dictionary of Nursery Rhymes*, by Iona and Peter Opie, who are great at tearing down accepted wisdom about nursery rhymes.)

Not only are rhymes' true meanings a fruitless quest; their sources are all over the place. Rhymes derive from published songs, folk songs, bawdy songs, plays, children's games, chapbooks, poems with known authors, anonymous poems, riddles, and from that most elusive of canons, the oral tradition. Very few were even originally created to entertain children. On the way to becoming a nursery rhyme, lines are sometimes cut and lines are sometimes added. Words are changed. Names of characters are changed. Bits and pieces of other rhymes are cobbled on. There are usually many variations of the same rhyme being spoken and read to children at any given time. Some rhymes were old in Shakespeare's time; some come from songs recorded in the twentieth

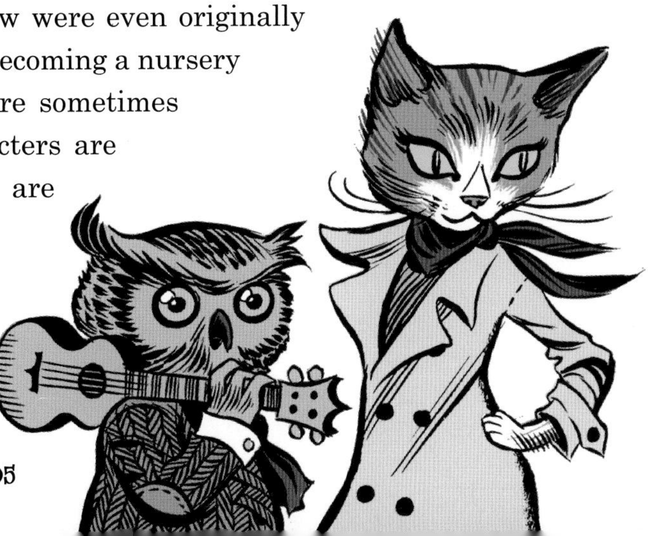

century. It's a tradition of appropriation and change—or, to put in a way that appeals to the teenage comic book reader in me: It's a tradition of mutation.[1]

Nursery rhymes have a mysterious hold over children and adults (and publishers). The power they have is partly due to their catch-as-catch-can origins and their continuing fluidity. If they never changed, then "Wee Willie Winkie" would have stayed in Scottish dialect and would never have made it into English and American rhyme books. If rhymes couldn't be shortened, then sleepy parents would have to recite fourteen verses of "Mother Hubbard" to somewhat less-sleepy children. If they couldn't be added to, then "I Had a Little Nut Tree" wouldn't end with its beautiful, but non sequitur, final couplet. And here, furthering this tradition of mutation, fifty cartoonists transform fifty rhymes. We're just letting history take its course.

—CHRIS DUFFY

[1] A good illustration of the haphazard nature of nursery rhyme origins comes from the Opies' dictionary. In 1846, Boston publisher and author Samuel Griswold Goodrich—who hated nursery rhymes and strove to banish them from children's literature—wrote this parody:

Higglety, pigglety, pop!
The dog has eat the mop;
The pig's in a hurry,
The cat's in a flurry—
Higglety, pigglety—pop!

The Opies report that, in 1945, Goodrich's verse was heard spoken as a real nursery rhyme in England.

CONTRIBUTORS

 **NICK ABADZIS** (Hey, Diddle Diddle) is the author of books for both adults and children that have been published on several continents, and he has been honored with various international storytelling awards, including the prestigious Eisner for *Laika* in 2008. He's a big fan of nursery rhymes.

 **ANDREW ARNOLD** (Hot Cross Buns) is the co-author of *Adventures in Cartooning* and the *Adventures in Cartooning Activity Book*. He lives in New York and designs books for a children's book publisher.

 **KATE BEATON** (The Grand Old Duke of York) is a Canadian cartoonist best known for her historical humor and energetic style. Her cartoons are more fun than educational, but you may learn something on the side all the same.

 **VERA BROSGOL** (There Was a Little Girl) lives in Portland, Oregon, and draws storyboards for animation. Sometimes she makes comics and knits mittens.

 **NICK BRUEL** (Three Little Kittens) is an author and illustrator of several children's books including the highly popular Bad Kitty series of picture books and chapter books. Nick lives in Tarrytown, New York, where disaster struck after he coaxed his own cat Esmerelda to wear mittens and model for his contribution to this book. He has since made a full recovery and all of the bandages have been removed.

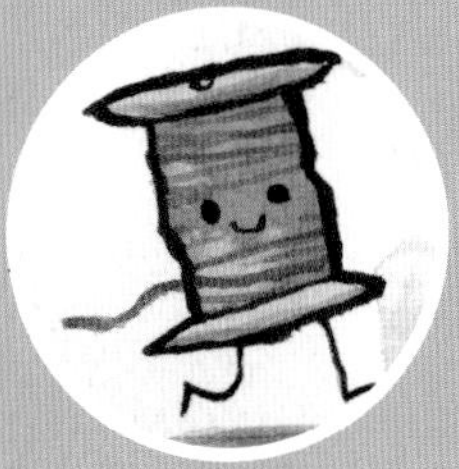

SCOTT CAMPBELL (Pop! Goes the Weasel) has created award-winning comics such as *Igloo Head and Tree Head*, which appeared in the *Flight* anthology, the webcomic *Double Fine Action Comics,* and the Great Showdowns series. He has art directed video games such as *Psychonauts* and *Brütal Legend*.

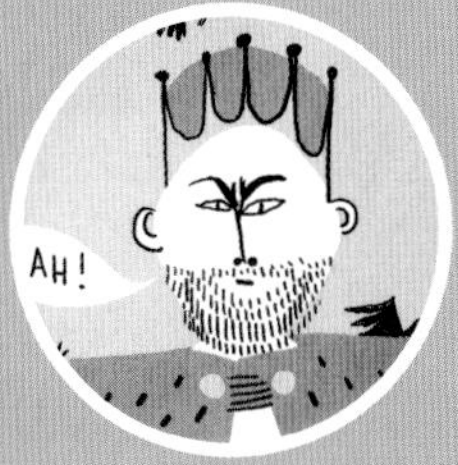
AH!

LILLI CARRÉ (Sing a Song of Sixpence) is an animator and cartoonist living in Chicago. Her books of comics are *Tales of Woodsman Pete*, *The Lagoon*, and *Nine Ways to Disappear*.

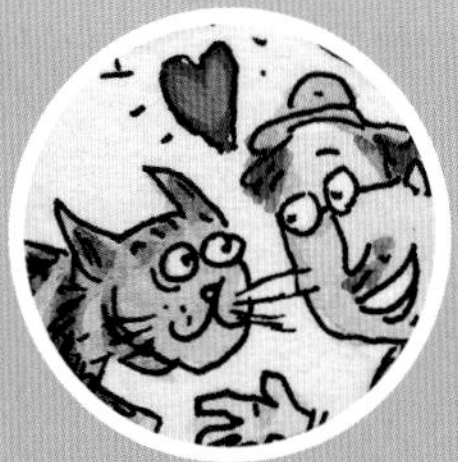

ROZ CHAST (There Was a Crooked Man) is a staff cartoonist for *The New Yorker*.

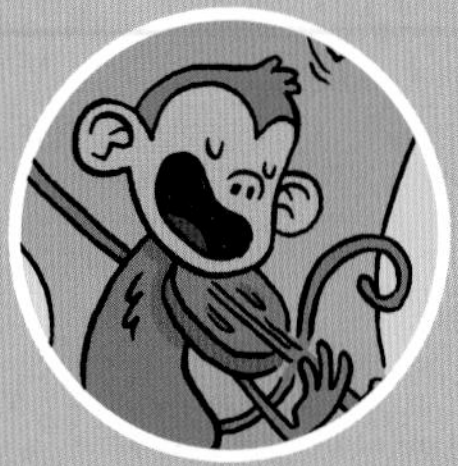

JP COOVERT (Old King Cole) lives in Minneapolis, Minnesota, where he designs T-shirt graphics, watches movies with his wife, plays fetch with his puppies, and draws comics about his fun, imaginary adventures.

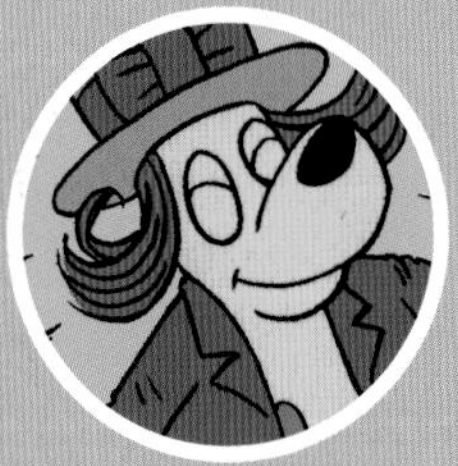

After losing his used car business to the vicissitudes of the economy and then losing the little remaining money to a Ponzi scheme, **JORDAN CRANE** (Old Mother Hubbard) spent his last dollar on a pencil and a tablet of paper. He is now a cartoonist.

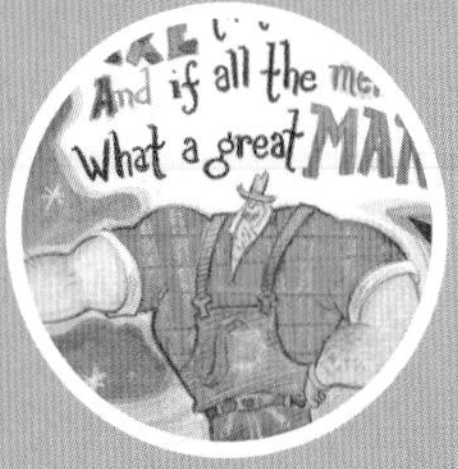
And if all the
What a great

REBECCA DART (If All the Seas Were One Sea) is an animator and comic book artist living in Vancouver, British Columbia, with her husband and a fat, black, asthmatic cat. Rebecca has shaped her life philosophy from the teachings of a Megaforce poster: "Deeds Not Words."

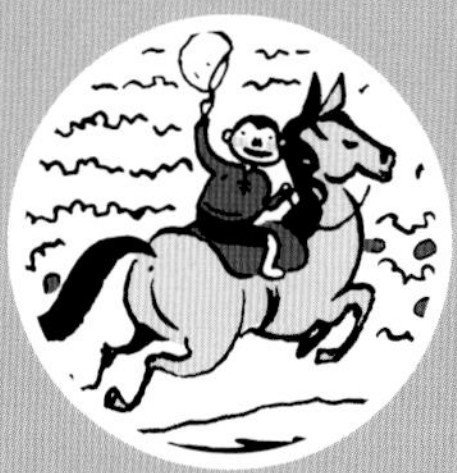

ELEANOR DAVIS (The Queen of Hearts) has been making comics all her life, most recently the nerdcore kid's adventure comic *The Secret Science Alliance and the Copycat Crook* from Bloomsbury books. She lives in beautiful Athens, Georgia, with her husband and three cats.

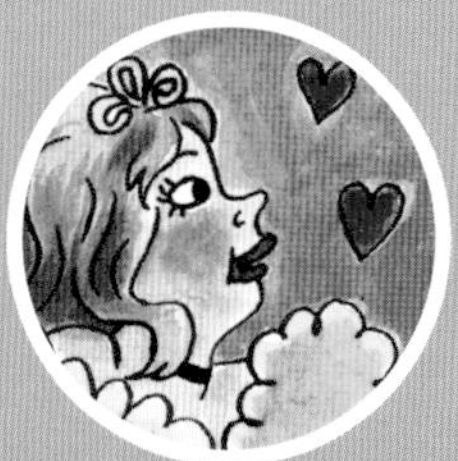

VANESSA DAVIS (Cindereller) is a cartoonist and illustrator originally from West Palm Beach, Florida. Her most recent book, *Make Me a Woman*, was published in October 2010 by Drawn & Quarterly.

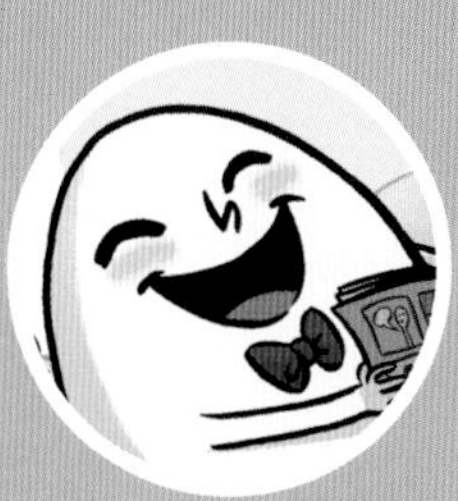

CHRIS DUFFY (editor) is a freelance cartoonist, editor, and writer living in Cold Spring, New York, with his wife and son. He edited *Nickelodeon Magazine*'s legendary comics section for thirteen years and is now editing *SpongeBob Comics* for United Plankton Pictures.

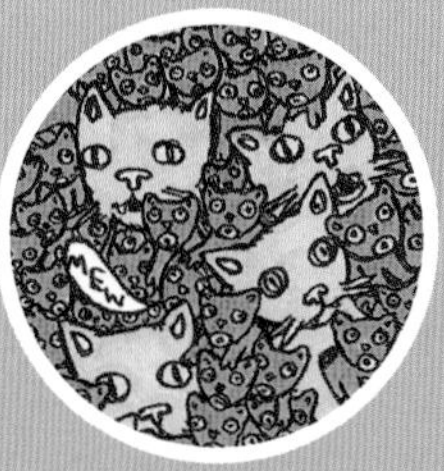
MEW

THEO ELLSWORTH (As I Was Going to St. Ives) is the author of *Capacity* and *Sleeper Car*, both published by Secret Acres. He lives in Portland, Oregon, with one wife, one cat, and no kittens.

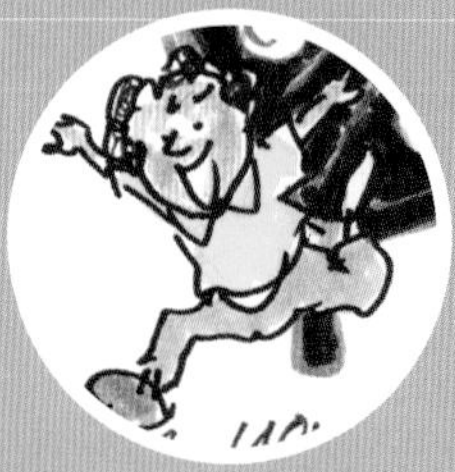

JULES FEIFFER (Girls and Boys, Come Out to Play) has won a number of prizes for his cartoons, plays, and screenplays, including the Pulitzer Prize for editorial cartooning. His books for children include *The Man in the Ceiling*; *Meanwhile*; *A Barrel of Laughs, A Vale of Tears*; and *Bark, George*.

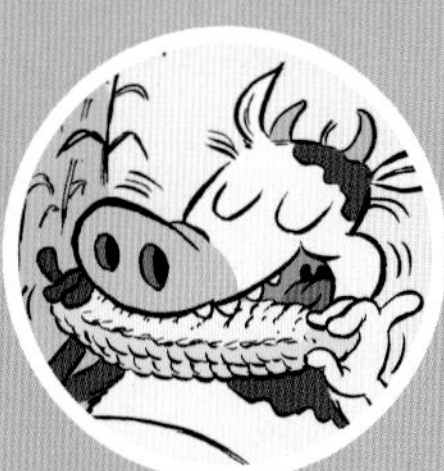

BOB FLYNN (Little Boy Blue) currently resides in Boston, where he is the director of animation at FableVision Studios. His comics and illustrations have appeared in publications including *Nickelodeon Magazine*, and he is the co-creator of Heeby Jeeby Comix.

MATT FORSYTHE (Tweedledum and Tweedledee) is an illustrator and comic book artist. He lives in Montreal.

ALEXIS FREDERICK-FROST (The North Wind Doth Blow) is an award-winning cartoonist who lives with his lovely wife in a tiny house near the New Hampshire coast. He is a co-author and illustrator of the popular Adventures in Cartooning series of comic books.

BEN HATKE (Pussycat, Pussycat, Where Have You Been?) is the creator of the *Zita the Spacegirl* graphic novels and a longtime lover of fairy tales and folk literature. He has a boisterous pack of daughters and loves a good adventure.

GILBERT HERNANDEZ (Humpty Dumpty) has been the co-creator of *Love and Rockets* for almost thirty years. He's been into comic books since he can remember, and the first comic book that he drew, when he was five years old, was called *Spaceman*.

JAIME HERNANDEZ (Jack and Jill) has been making comic books for thirty years and hopes to make them for thirty more. Most of his work has been in *Love and Rockets*.

LUCY KNISLEY (There Was an Old Woman Who Lived in a Shoe) is a comic artist and author who lives in Chicago. She wrote and drew the acclaimed travelogue *French Milk* and is presently working on a graphic novel about food and growing up with a chef mom.

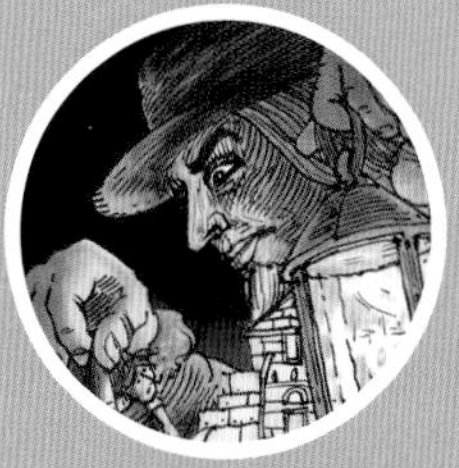

DAVID MACAULAY (London Bridge Is Falling Down) is the award-winning author and illustrator of *Cathedral*, *The Way Things Work*, and *Baaa*, among many other books. He lives with his family in Vermont.

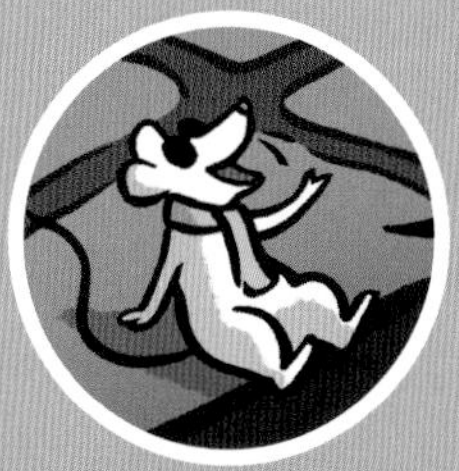

LEONARD S. MARCUS (Introduction) is one of the children's-book world's leading historians and critics. His many books include *Minders of Make-Believe*, *Golden Legacy*, and *The Wand in the Word: Conversations with Writers of Fantasy*.

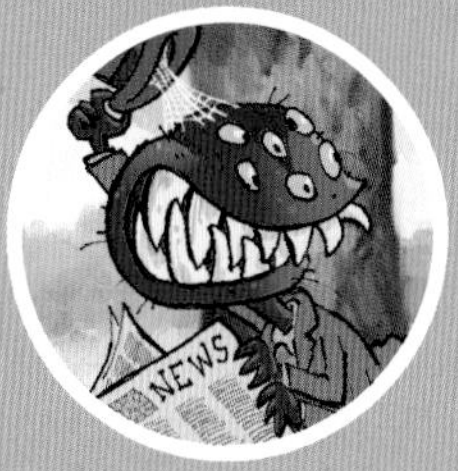
NEWS

MARK MARTIN (Little Miss Muffet) is an award-shunning writer and artist of comics, games, puzzles, and stories for kids of all ages. He has an enormous collection of vintage children's books.

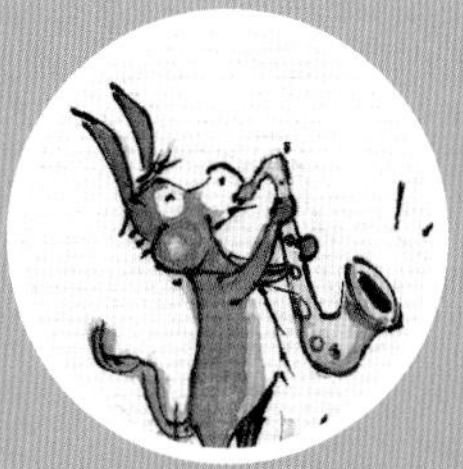

Cartoonist, illustrator, and children's book author **PATRICK MCDONNELL** (The Donkey) is the creator of the award-winning *Mutts* comic strip, which is syndicated in over 700 newspapers worldwide. With more than twenty books in print, he has received numerous awards for his art and international recognition for his promotion of animal protection.

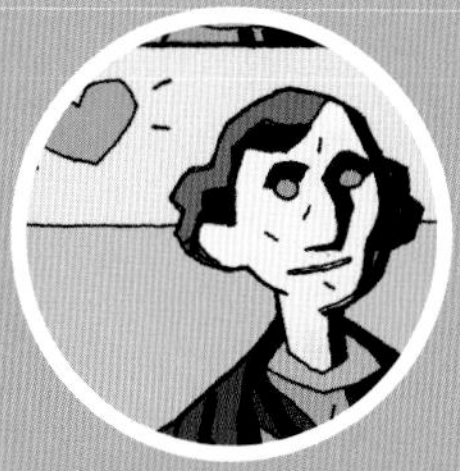

MIKE MIGNOLA (Solomon Grundy) is the creator of Hellboy.

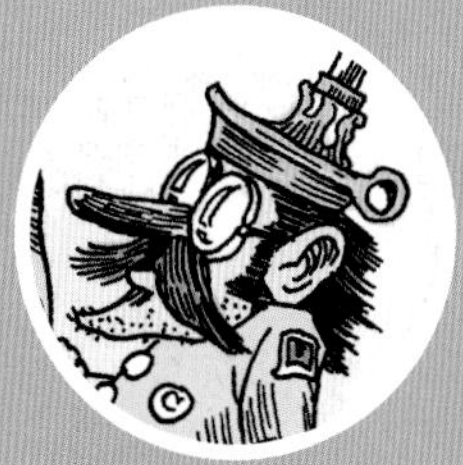

TONY MILLIONAIRE (Rub-a-Dub-Dub) was born in Boston and grew up in Gloucester, Massachusetts. He writes and draws the ongoing adventures of Sock Monkey, published by Dark Horse Comics since 1998. He is the creator of the syndicated comic strip, *MAAKIES*, which has been collected by Fantagraphics, who also published his graphic novel *Billy Hazelnuts*.

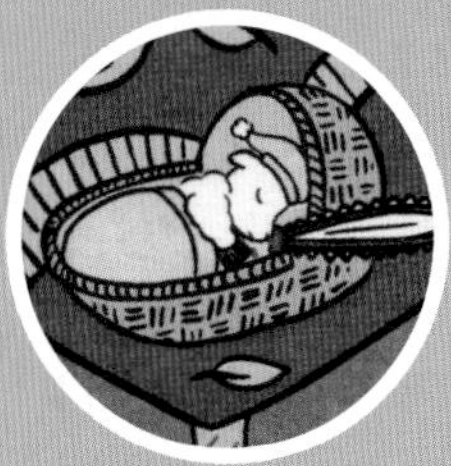

TAO NYEU (Rock-a-Bye Baby) is an illustrator and author known for her silkscreen artwork. Her books include *Wonder Bear* and *Bunny Days*.

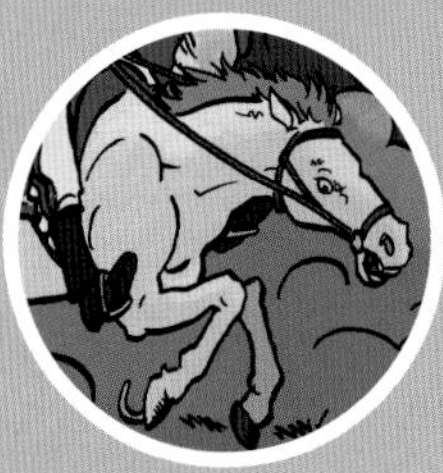

GEORGE O'CONNOR (For Want of a Nail) is the author of several picture books and graphic novels, including the *New York Times* bestseller *Kapow!*, *Sally and the Some-Thing*, and *Journey into Mohawk Country*. His current project is Olympians, an ongoing series of graphic novels for young readers retelling the classic Greek myths.

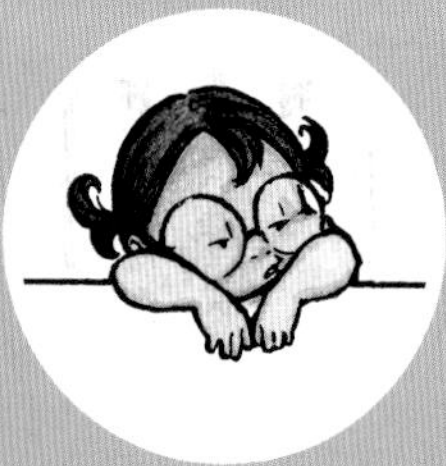

MO OH (Hush, Little Baby) is a recent grauduate of the Center for Cartoon Studies. She likes to draw. She also likes to read, bake, and eat (mostly eat), grow plants (mainly for eating), and sit in the sun.

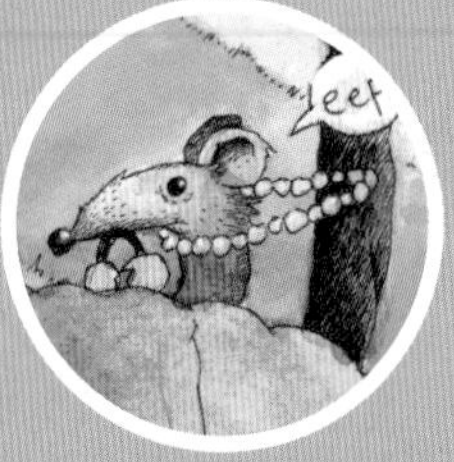
eet

ERIC ORCHARD (Peter, Peter, Pumpkin Eater) is an award-winning cartoonist and illustrator based in Toronto. His first graphic novel, *Maddy Kettle*, will be published in late 2011 by Top Shelf Productions.

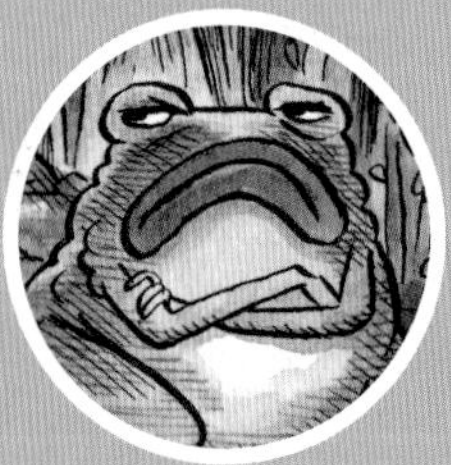

LAURA PARK ("Croak," Said the Toad) is a cartoonist and illustrator. She is the author of the minicomics series *Do Not Disturb My Waking Dream,* and her work has appeared in *Mome*, *Superior Showcase*, *The Best American Comics*, *Vice*, and *Nickelodeon* magazines. She lives in Chicago with her pet pigeon Nixon and is working on her first collection of autobiographical comics.

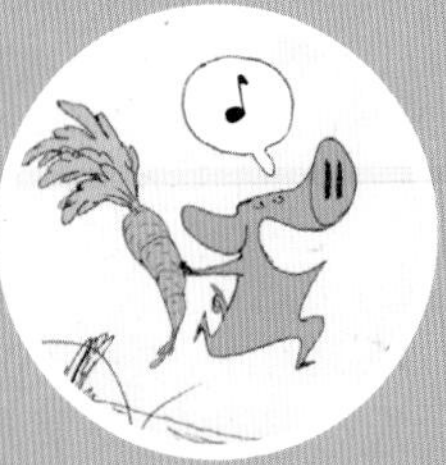

CYRIL PEDROSA (This Little Piggy) began his career in animation, working on the Disney films *Hunchback of Notre Dame* and *Hercules*. He has since authored the graphic novel *Three Shadows* and become a rising star in a new kind of graphic storytelling, combining the influences of animation and the literary traditions of Borges, García Márquez, and Tolkien to create a unique visual handwriting.

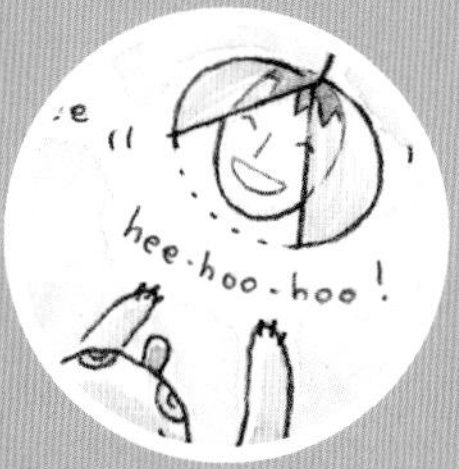
hee-hoo-hoo!

LARK PIEN (I Had a Little Nut Tree) began cartooning in 1997. She received a Harvey Award for her coloring work on *American Born Chinese*. Recent works include *Long Tail Kitty* (Blue Apple Books) and *Mr. Elephanter* (Candlewick Press). Both are children's books based on her handmade minicomics.

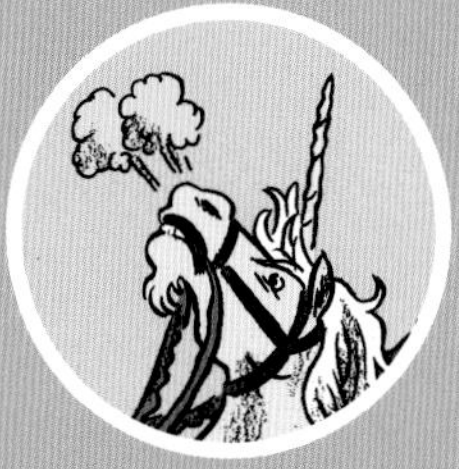

AARON RENIER (The Lion and the Unicorn) is the author of *Spiral-Bound* and *The Unsinkable Walker Bean*. He won the Eisner comic industry award in 2006 for talent deserving wider recognition and was an inaugural fellow of the 2010 Sendak Fellowship. He lives in Chicago, Illinois, with his trusty hound, Beluga.

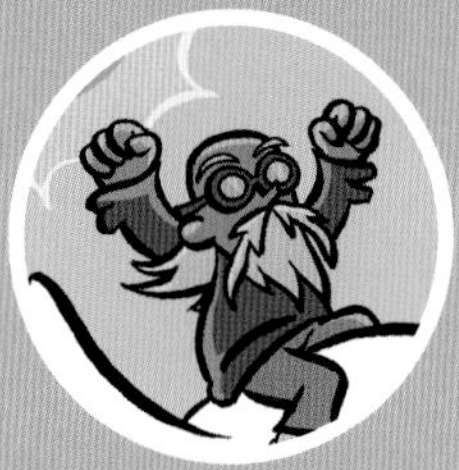

DAVE ROMAN (One, Two, Buckle My Shoe) is the creator of *Astronaut Academy: Zero Gravity* and *Agnes Quill: An Anthology of Mystery*. He has collaborated on several books including *Teen Boat*, *Jax Epoch*, *X-Men: Misfits*, and contributed to several volumes of *Flight*.

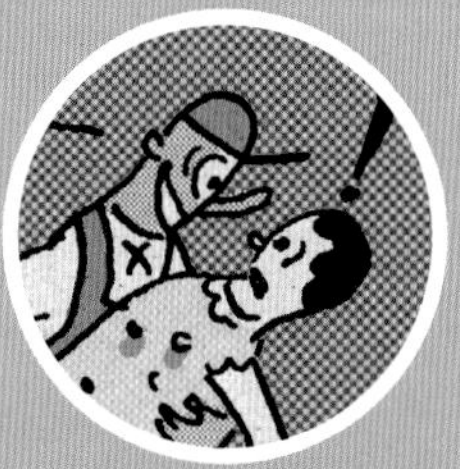

After receiving a B.A. in Architecture from Princeton, **MARC ROSENTHAL** (Yon Yonson) was a painter for about eight years before turning to illustration, working for five years for Milton Glaser, and then on his own. He has illustrated many books for children. His latest is *I Must Have Bobo*, in collaboration with his wife, Eileen.

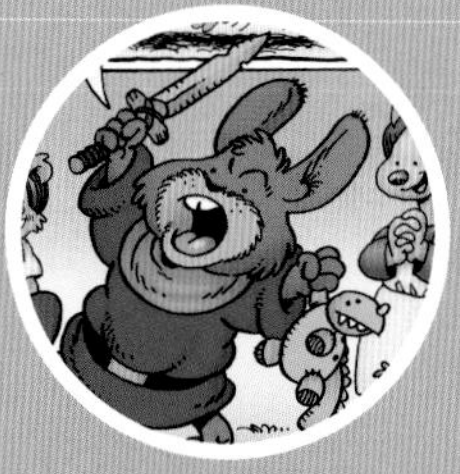

STAN SAKAI (Hector Protector) is the creator of the award-winning Usagi Yojimbo series of graphic novels. He is published in the U.S. by Dark Horse Comics and Fantagraphics Books.

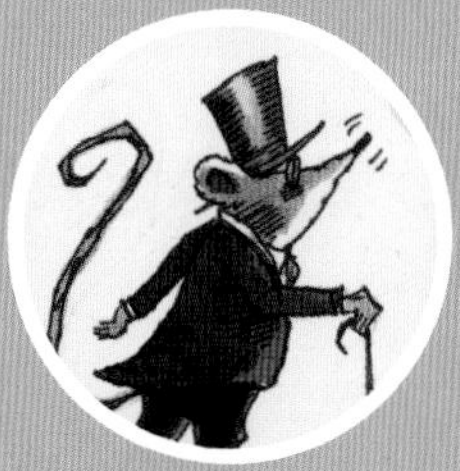

RICHARD SALA (Three Blind Mice) has written and drawn a number of unusual (some may say "spooky") graphic novels, including *Cat Burglar Black* and *Peculia*. He has also provided illustrations for a variety of clients all over the world.

MARK SIEGEL (Wee Willie Winkie) was born in Ann Arbor, Michigan, and grew up in France. He is the illustrator of *To Dance: A Ballerina's Graphic Novel*, written by his wife, Siena Cherson Siegel; *Seadogs: An Epic Ocean Operetta*, written by Lisa Wheeler; and several other graphic novels and children's picture books. He lives in Tarrytown, New York.

Cartoonist and Center For Cartoon Studies cofounder **JAMES STURM** (Jack Be Nimble) has burnt his bottom more times than he can count. He needs to be more nimble.

RAINA TELGEMEIER (Georgie Porgie) is the creator of the graphic novel memoir *Smile*, a *Boston Globe-Horn Book* Honor title, as well as the adapter and illustrator of the Baby-sitters Club graphic novel series. She co-authored the *New York Times* Graphic Books Bestseller *X-Men: Misfits* with her husband, Dave Roman.

CRAIG THOMPSON's (The Owl and the Pussy-Cat) graphic novels include *Good-bye, Chunky Rice*; *Blankets*; and *Habibi*. He lives in Portland, Oregon, where he has many exciting personal details.

RICHARD THOMPSON's (There Was an Old Woman Tossed Up in a Basket) drawings have appeared in lots of places, and his weekly cartoon *Richard's Poor Almanac* appeared in the *Washington Post* for twelve years. Nowadays he draws the comic strip *Cul de Sac* every day and naps when he can.

SARA VARON (Mary Had a Little Lamb) is an illustrator, comics artist, and printmaker who lives in Brooklyn. Her books include *Bake Sale*, *Robot Dreams*, and *Chicken and Cat*.

JEN WANG's (Little Bo Peep) first graphic novel *Koko Be Good* is available from First Second. She lives in Los Angeles.

DREW WEING (Baa-Baa, Black Sheep) lives and works in a small house with three cats and his wife, the cartoonist Eleanor Davis. When he occasionally leaves the house, he finds himself in beautiful Athens, Georgia. His most recent book is the nautical adventure *Set to Sea*.

GAHAN WILSON (The Itsy Bitsy Spider) has been fond of nursery rhymes ever since he came across them as a small child. He is now a cartoonist for grown-up magazines but is delighted to have the chance to illustrate one of his very favorite poems from way back then!

GENE YANG (Pat-a-Cake) began making comics in the fifth grade. His 2006 graphic novel *American Born Chinese* was the first to be nominated for the National Book Award.

In her developing years, **STEPHANIE YUE** (Hickory, Dickory, Dock) played in construction sites and electrocuted herself with her science project. In adulthood, she draws pictures of cute small animals for a living, including illustrating the Guinea Pig, Pet Shop Private Eye series, *Mousenet*, and publishing her own comics.

ACKNOWLEDGEMENTS

The publisher would like to thank the following people
for their help with *Nursery Rhyme Comics*:
Peggy Clements, Susan Hood, Karen O'Connell,
Eric Reynolds, Diana Schutz, and Julie Winterbottom.

And special thanks and appreciation to Lauren L. Wohl,
who first proposed this book.

ILLUSTRATION CREDITS

Illustrations for "The Donkey" copyright © 2011 by Patrick McDonnell

Illustrations for "Three Little Kittens" copyright © 2011 by Nick Bruel

Illustrations for "Hickory, Dickory, Dock" copyright © 2011 by Stephanie Yue

Illustrations for "Sing a Song of Sixpence" copyright © 2011 by Lilli Carré

Illustrations for "If All The Seas Were One Sea" copyright © 2011 by Rebecca Dart

Illustrations for "Girls and Boys Come Out to Play" copyright © 2011 by Jules Feiffer

Illustrations for "There Was an Old Woman Who Lived in a Shoe" copyright © 2011
    by Lucy Knisley

Illustrations for "Cindereller" copyright © 2011 by Vanessa Davis

Illustrations for "The Queen of Hearts" copyright © 2011 by Eleanor Davis

Illustrations for "Hey, Diddle Diddle" copyright © 2011 by Nick Abadzis

Illustrations for "There Was an Old Woman Tossed Up in a Basket" copyright © 2011
    by Richard Thompson

Illustrations for "Jack Be Nimble" copyright © 2011 by James Sturm

Illustrations for "The Owl and the Pussy-Cat" copyright © 2011 by Craig Thompson

Illustrations for "The Itsy Bitsy Spider" copyright © 2011 by Gahan Wilson

Illustrations for "Baa-Baa, Black Sheep" copyright © 2011 by Drew Weing

Illustrations for "Hector Protector" copyright © 2011 by Stan Sakai

Illustrations for "Pop! Goes The Weasel" copyright © 2011 by Scott Campbell

Illustrations for "Three Blind Mice" copyright © 2011 by Richard Sala

Illustrations for "There Was a Crooked Man" copyright © 2011 by Roz Chast

Illustrations for "Georgie Porgie" copyright © 2011 by Raina Telgemeier

Illustrations for "Solomon Grundy" copyright © 2011 by Mike Mignola

Illustrations for "Rock-A-Bye, Baby" copyright © 2011 by Tao Nyeu

Illustrations for "Tweedledum and Tweedledee" copyright © 2011
    by Matthew Forsythe

Illustrations for "This Little Piggy" copyright © 2011 by Cyril Pedrosa